OTHERWORLDLY

ALSO BY DWAIN WORRELL

Androne

Alliance

PRAISE FOR DWAIN WORRELL

"Taut intrigue reels readers into a thrilling yet thoughtful narrative about the futility of war and the cost of doing the right thing, and a clever, quantum twist will please sci-fi fans. Worrell should make a splash with this."

—*Publishers Weekly*

"Dwain Worrell's *Androne* straps you into the cockpit at page one and doesn't let go; it's a truly cinematic, character-centered Möbius strip of war, loyalty, and love, with action so good you might forget how to breathe."

—Karen Osborne, author of *Architects of Memory*

"A crazy-cool ride into the unknown. Paxton is a multilayered, futuristic hero, and [*Androne*] reads like a high-end video game on steroids with a destiny of Shakespearean magnitude."

—Niels Arden Oplev, director of *The Girl with the Dragon Tattoo*

"Original, clever, and a fun read from first page to last . . ."

—*Midwest Book Review*

OTHERWORLDLY

DWAIN WORRELL

This is a work of fiction. Names, characters, organizations, places, events, and incidents are either products of the author's imagination or are used fictitiously. Otherwise, any resemblance to actual persons, living or dead, is purely coincidental.

Published by 47North, Seattle
www.apub.com

EU product safety contact:
Amazon Media EU S. à r.l.
38, avenue John F. Kennedy, L-1855 Luxembourg
amazonpublishing-gpsr@amazon.com

ISBN-13: 9781662528248 (paperback)
ISBN-13: 9781662528255 (digital)

Cover design by Shasti O'Leary Soudant
Cover image: © David Paire / ArcAngel Images; © Rauf_Karimov, © Sergey Nivens / Shutterstock

Printed in the United States of America

For Ma

In 2091, NASA discovers that every globe, star, and galaxy beyond Earth is devoid of any sentient life. Thus the human race is alone in the universe.

PROLOGUE

The trick to beating sensory deprivation tanks is to cling on to a sense of loneliness, the feeling of inner amputation—that isolation, hold on to that. Hold tight. Because in the dark and monstrous quiet, a voice might emerge. It may cuddle up next to you because you're warm and it is molting. It's then that you'll wish you were alone.

It's test 11, session 3, in the dep tank when she hears it. *Listen* . . . They tell her that we evolved to sleep through the night and the dark. They tell her that a nocturnal mind is a mind hung backward, and unfolding the brain makes her dream inside out. Because in the same way shapes emerge in white clouds, things are forming out of the black. *Look* . . . They move closer, but not on limbs—they spin. They roll their sullen bodies toward her, nasty little mollusks, making their seashells out of her ears.

The end-of-session bell rings right there, right at the stray fringes of madness. *And just in time*, she thinks. Her fingernails are still caked in the umbra, or was that the black of scratched-up skin? Her heart beats bioluminescent; she can almost see it flapping wildly in the dark. But sanity is returning fast enough. The deprivation tank door opens, and light cuts rectangular into the shadows. The madness scatters, and she inhales light like oxygen.

The water, barely a foot high, drains fast through small ducts in the room's corners. High heels clap into the chamber; the woman is backlit and speaking to someone—speaking to her, and by her family name.

"Xavier?" the woman says, wreathing a towel over Cleo's wet shoulders. "It's Dr. Noah." Olivia, head physician for the space program. She squats in front of her. "You with me, Cleo?"

Cleo nods. *With you*, she thinks, but barely. A fog hangs heavy over the bridges between their eyes.

"How are you feeling?" Olivia aims the edges of her teeth at Cleo as she smiles.

Cleo nods again, to avoid the lie.

"Little tired, maybe?" Olivia asks.

"Maybe," Cleo says finally, still with that lying nod. "Little."

"Some sunlight will do you." Olivia's teeth fall away fast enough that the forgery of her smile is obvious. She lifts a tablet with pie charts and graphs and aims that at Cleo instead. "First the good news, 'kay? Then the better news." Good news, just bait at the end of Olivia's tongue, goading Cleo to ask: What good news? Or is she attempting to get Cleo to engage?

Fine, Cleo thinks. "What is it?" she says, faking her engagement. "The good news."

Olivia lights up. "You broke your own record, Xavier. No one's ever tested near this level. Nineteen conscious hours under full sensory deprivation. Next closest is half that time."

That long? "Wow." And yet it felt longer.

"There was barely a spike in your heart rate, except at the end there. A little shake at the end. But who knows how much longer you could've stayed in. Look, I'll say it. It's what everyone in the lab is saying: You're immune to loneliness."

"Immune," Cleo repeats with a smile. This is their attempt at flattery. Cleo's one shortcoming is now a blessing; her previous colleagues were artificial, literally—intelligence units with programmed personalities—and Finn was the only ever love interest, so . . . "Immune to loneliness?" she says in faux surprise, like it's the first time she has ever heard it.

"It's a compliment," Olivia counters. "Or what was it the med examiner said?" Her eyes roll upward as she tries to remember. "Right: 'She's solitude resistant.'" And Olivia chuckles.

"The better news . . ." Cleo squeezes the words through a forced smile.

"Yes," she says and pauses, building another mount of anticipation. "You're going to space, Xavier."

Now Cleo's jaw hangs. *Oh God* . . . she wants to say but can't wrap her lips around the words. It's impossible, but that thought doesn't shape into sound either. There is just awe. All these tests and training, and Cleo had been the least experienced: The mathematics, medical exercises, and physical training—she lacked in everything besides this tank of isolation.

"I'm going to space," Cleo manages to say finally.

Cleo doesn't even try to fight the tears. She will be one of the few traveling to the farthest known planet in the solar system. That's seven years in space, round trip. Seven years in darkness that drips like ink.

"It's real," Olivia rejoices. "You will be one of the first to set foot on Planet Nine. You're going to Orbis Alius."

PART ONE

ORBIS ALIUS

1

"We are alone in the universe." The antique audio player drifted in a gravity-less module. "There's nothing else out there." And the ancient words drifted with it. "The universe is vacant. And we searched. We searched like mad." The words were hoarse with static decay. "We scoured every planet and moon, every asteroid and their nebulae, but all the worlds on all the stars are empty—as empty as the blackest knots of space. We're all there is. Humanity. We are alone . . ."

Terraforming Engineer Cleo Patricia Xavier drifted in her modest module—the white walls, red lights, and a round window holding back the vacuum of space. And all her possessions floated with her. It was untidiness in motion, a trafficking of socks, pens, lotions, Dad's turtleneck sweater, empty MRE wrappers, and the audio player running on a loop. But she was oblivious to the disarray. Cleo was, at that moment, on the zenith of a narcotic high.

As she drifted in her module, an IV bag drifted with her. It flexed, then released, flex-release, pulsing like a plastic heartbeat, squeezing the drug down the tube to the cannula in her ear. But it was less of a drip and more a spray of narcotics across her eardrum. And Cleo auditivated without the pull of gravity.

Auditives were an old drug, some eighty years and counting. Now all the kids that had grown up and experimented with "the listening drugs" were either picking up pensions or outlasting each other on the Supreme Court. So they had legalized the old outlaws. Old drugs, but now with new genres. From K-Pop Ketamine to Opera Ecstasy, the drugs were commercialized, publicly traded stocks and ETFs. They were advertised on the sides of skyscrapers and sold at airport dispensaries, from Methyl-Metal to Classical Cannabis, Jazz Opium, and Gospel LSD. But Cleo's preference, as an island girl, was always Calypso Cocaine. The drugs sparked on her nerve endings, but to a certain pattern—to a rhythm. They were drugs that danced harmonic on the mind. Strangely, even the red light in her cabin pulsed to that biochemical strum.

Nearly forty months in space takes its toll on the mind. During these yearslong voyages, most space programs not only allowed for the use of nonaddictive drug therapy but also encouraged it. The grand future of suspended animation technology hadn't quite arrived just yet. However, meditative drug states were supervised by flight surgeons and limited strictly to microdoses. Not her. Cleo floated unmonitored and far above any microdose. *Is* macrodose *a word?* she wondered.

The *Antilles* spacecraft had voyaged through the desert vacuum for three years, with stars like sand and each grain a trillion miles apart. They were the first to come this far out, past the orbit of Neptune. The mission was a survey to test the viability of full-on terraforming and the finances and manpower that it required. All the great worlds and lesser moons had already been terraformed—everything, and all that was left was this: Orbis Alius, Planet Nine, the gravitational buckle of the Kuiper Belt.

She floated upside down. Even though there was no up or down in this place. But maybe that disorientation was the drugs in her system and all that desert vacuum nonsense too. It was just hallucinogenic hyperbole.

She drifted past the cabin window, and right there, she saw it. Undressed of every lens and telescope and infrared image, the planet floated naked in front of her eyes: Orbis Alius. So large now it appeared swollen against the glass. The red light flashing in her cabin miraged the planet into a Christmas tree decoration—or was that the drugs again, making strange abstractions in her mind? In truth, Orbis's tortured atmosphere was noosed in storm spirals; lightning stabbed deep and bright into ashen gray clouds of dust and ice. It was as terrifying as it was beautiful—a medusa, its spiral storms like snakes and venomous lightning. Their mission for the next three months was to run preliminary bio-terraforming processes and test whether that poisonous, unlivable rock was a suitable candidate for further Terra-Farm Inc. investment.

Officially, Orbis Alius had a radius of 5,800 kilometers, smaller than Earth or Venus but much larger than Mars. It had a higher atmospheric density than either Earth or Venus and a larger magnetosphere than Earth as well. The breadth of the atmosphere masked the deeper features of the planet, but the soup of argon and methane hinted at temperate surface pressures. The Earthlike gravity and high possibility of ice at its poles were unbalanced by its distance from Earth. The world was just too far out. Too many hours of light away from home.

The Atlantic Space Trade was the youngest space agency on Earth, and somehow its first terraforming mission was the most ambitious in human history, journeying into the Kuiper Belt. The farthest out any terraformer had traveled before was Saturn, the astronaut nerds dubbing themselves Lord of the Rings, working the moons Titan and Enceladus. But they were now surpassed by this crew of four, three terraformers and one pilot, venturing many billions of miles farther than any individual before them. There was just very little else to terraform in the solar system. Mars and Venus were both Earthlike right down to the seasons, the moon was a Goldilocks satellite, and even Uranus's Triton had conflicting claims by both NASA and ISRO in New Delhi.

Cleo was raised on a terraformed Venus, but her grandfather was Caribbean-born—Barbadian, and a bit of a national hero in the field of astronomy. The two other terraformers, Austin and Boston, hailed from Cuba and the Dominican Republic, respectively. The pilot, Daniel Walker, was from a mix of Caribbean backgrounds: Trini, Bajan, Jamaican, Haitian, and who knew what else. They were the best the

Atlantic Space Trade had to offer. And in about thirty-six hours, they'd prove themselves worthy of that distinction, or not.

She was thinking straight now, at least. Cleo felt her hours-long rhythmic trance coming to an end. She could hear the high slipping off her earlobes; medicated music was a moist sound, and the feeling was like water unclogging from the ears. The auditives were fading, and that was good because now she noticed something—that red light bouncing up and down on her pupils wasn't part of the high. No, that was the goddamn integrity alarm.

Son of a bitch!

Cleo jerked mid-drift. Her arms swatted at nothing, legs pedaling on an invisible cycle. She tried to swim to the surface of her subconscious, but there was a web in between, like a lucid dream for drugs. The quarter note and G-sharp distorted as she pulled at the IV—the cannula in her ear. She pulled and kept pulling—*Keep pulling*, she told herself—until it popped. The IV floated to the "ceiling," if there was such a thing, and Cleo floated back to the floor.

She could hear the noise now: alarms barking at her, Austin's voice screaming over the PA system. That meant sobriety was sinking back in. But coming off the serenity of auditives into this maelstrom was like sunlight beating dilated pupils with a belt. It burned at her ears, and the migraine kicked in her temple. There was a four-hour gap between the *Antilles* spacecraft and the hundred engineers, mechanics, and doctors at mission control. Whatever this alarm was, they would be dealing with it themselves.

"Just one second . . ." Cleo whispered to no one.

Space-atrophied tensors, glutes, and flexors kicked off the aluminum walls, and she aimed her anatomy at the module's gate. Cleo glided across an invisible line in her mind's eye, but she missed, and badly. She was a cat caught in a ball of rhythm string, fumbling in zero-g.

God, she was a mess, but chaos had always been like a rash underneath Cleo's skin, an allergy for her to scratch at. Just look at the untidiness in the module. And back on Venus, she had missed flights and appointments and even her own engagement party. She'd lost things too. Cleo had had three passports issued to her in the span of a year. She'd lost people, so many friends, a fiancé.

But Cleo never cared too much for people. *Introvert* was the first of many tags pinned on her, then *loner*, *recluse*, and most recently, *that float chick*. Cleo had overheard a fellow crewmate call her that, on account of the many hours she just floated in "meditation." But that loneliness was part of the reasoning behind her selection for this mission. Isolation was as dangerous as the radiation out here, and Cleo could withstand it. She was immune, they had told her—solitude resistant.

She regained her orientation, still a bit upside down, but managed to unlock the spiral door nonetheless. Neon reds hemorrhaged into the long, cylindrical corridor. Alarms screamed into her dilated ears. The beat of the engine palpitated and the *Antilles* shuddered. Everything that had been magnetized whirled loose—a spinning flashlight juggled its light, a fire extinguisher lashed against the walls. Forks, brushes, duct tape, even Cleo herself rattled along the *Antilles*'s slender throat.

What the hell was going on?

She climbed into the rotational arm of the vessel. The deeper into the arm she drifted, the heavier she felt. Her feet bounced off the floor. Hints of gravity pulled greedily at her soles, but it wasn't gravity, that was centrifugal force. The rotating arm of the spacecraft swung at just over 2 rpms—revolutions per minute. And with just enough of that fictional gravity, Cleo climbed the ladder down toward the command module hatch.

She popped the hatch open and dropped into the module. She ignored the pointless ladder and felt the full brunt of one-third G as she hit the floor. The command module had been designed by a Venezuelan architectural firm that had opted for a rotunda architectural interior. Everything was rounded or domed, from the hatch and window to the miniature greenhouse built into the wall. It was there on that rounded and slightly sloping floor that Cleo saw the impossible. Were they donning their space suits?

Captain Austin Zachariah was tall, fibrous, and bronze, like a weightless statue as he moved buoyantly in the low gravity and armored himself in his EMU, extravehicular mobility unit, the fancy term for their space suit. First Officer Yasmin Boston, from her cheekbones to her hips, was all cold edges except for the dance of nappy curls in her hair; she bent her seemingly elastic limbs into the breastplates and boots of her space suit. The dynamic duo were so caught up in the dressing and undressing of things that they hadn't even noticed little Cleo.

"What's going on?" Cleo shouted over the alarms, but her words couldn't quite penetrate. She added volume. "Austin?"

Austin's hulking six-foot-four frame spun around, mid-step into the leg of his EMU. His face told her everything. His ocean-blue eyes appeared dislocated from the rest of his face. His lips were rubbery and drooped over his chin like they might fall off. It wasn't a look of fear, or the worry that some bad thing might happen. Whatever the bad thing was, it had already happened. It was done. His look was dread.

"Where were you?" Austin asked, fitting his second foot into the EMU. "We made, what . . ." He glanced at Specialist Boston. "Three calls?"

"Four," Boston said. "Four calls."

"What were you doing?" Austin asked again.

And again, Boston answered. "Floating," she goaded.

That float chick. Cleo remembered those words in that same Dominican accent. Specialist Yasmin Boston had devised Cleo's spaceflight moniker. Boston was a prenatal bioengineered masterpiece. They blueprinted the DNA for profound beauty, height, artistry, athleticism, and pure genius in mathematics. Boston shone in her outer space armor, emerald-blue footwear, scarlet-red gloves, and Pepsi, FedEx, Nestlé, and Adidas logos embossed from her shoulders to her boots. She clutched a million-dollar helmet underneath her arm. By far, she was the most famous person on board and one of the most well-known people on any planet.

"Float?" Cleo said it with such absurdity, as if it weren't a real word. "I wasn't . . ." She started the lie but shook her head and shrugged, lying in the language of the body instead.

A hundred million individuals stared out from Boston's eyes. At least, that was her average congregation. Her body was their church. Because Yasmin Boston was an Idol—or Eye-Doll, as that generation had christened them. Idols had every sense available for plug-in. Boston's followers saw through telephoto contact lenses; they smelled through nasal implants and tasted through dentured molars. Boston had well over a billion followers, her most devout patrons offering millions in tithes daily. She was a goddess of social media. And right now, those hundred million souls scrutinized Cleo's drug-intoxicated posture through Boston's sharp eyes.

"Your fingers are still twitching to the tempo," Boston said.

She was right. Cleo could feel the echoes of Calypso Cocaine tickling at the back of her ears. But instead of admitting it, Cleo fought back. She made a fist like she was squeezing the melody out of her fingers. She had done it before at school, once with Dad, even during a callback interview for this very mission. Squeeze. Fingernails dug into her palms, and the shaking stopped.

"What twitch?" Cleo asked. "They're sanctioned, by the way—auditives." Which was true too. The AST had authorized auditives as a form of nonaddictive drug therapy, following NASA's and other space agencies' precedents. "So, what's going on?"

"We're launching," Boston said.

"What?" Cleo snapped back. "No, it's . . ."

Cleo glanced at the watch on her wrist. She had set it to match the official countdown to launch toward the planet's surface: still L-minus thirty-eight hours. That was over a day and a half from now.

"Forget the watch," Austin said. "It's irrelevant now. Get into gear. We're launching."

"Now?" Cleo said, but she shook her head, denying it.

"Now." Austin gestured her toward the EMU lockers by the air lock.

But Cleo didn't move. She stood there, stuck in herself. This wasn't the plan. This wasn't what they had trained for. Since their launch from Havana Air Force Harbor in Cuba, they had stuck to the plan, down to the very millimeters and seconds. So why the hell were they launching a day and a half early?

"MCs said it was a mis-cal." A voice spoke up from behind her as if he had heard Cleo's own inner monologue.

Daniel sat on the floor, his head resting against the mini-greenhouse glass and his eyes fixed on the dandelion's starburst gold petals. Like he was avoiding her eyes? His lanky frame wrapped around itself, long arms tied around his knees, and he smiled at her, but a dull smile, without the sharpness of teeth. The sort of smile you make to reassure others when you're not sure yourself. He was their lone pilot now, and he alone would be the one to guide them down.

"Hey," Cleo said, reflecting that same dull, toothless smirk. "What did we miscalculate?"

"We?" Boston twisted her voice into a knot. "Eli. He screwed up the numbers in his little spiral."

"Eli," Cleo said for the first time in a month, and the name felt stale, the pronunciation of it sounding wrong now.

Eli had been their head pilot. Smart, well experienced, and witty, he was sharp as a tack, and attractive . . . in a grizzly sort of way. But Eli's most important feature was his personable affect. He was great with people, even with the reclusive Cleo. Eli had intentionally overdosed two months ago. His suicide came just days after the medics in Havana had declared him unfit for duty. Vacuum madness, space dementia—their diagnoses ran the entire spectrum of space-age medical jargon. Maybe if they had just used softer words, without perhaps those technical sharp edges, Eli would still be there. Maybe, but probably not. Eli had been hearing voices out in the dark, an "isolating smog," he called it.

Madness had played a major part in his suicide, for sure, but the other factor was this place. Light-years of loneliness and without the compassion of stars. Eli never stood a chance, did he? He wasn't like

Cleo. Poor Eli, he was a people person, garrulous, even a little gossipy. He wasn't made of those same solitary threads that she was.

"What did Eli miscalculate?" Cleo asked.

"Can't blame Eli completely," Austin said. "Even Mission Control didn't see it."

"See what?" Cleo asked.

"It's the gravity," Austin said. "We miscalculated the planet's gravity."

The word *gravity* stuck in her ear like it was high-altitude ear pressure, and everything else Austin said was muffled. The severity of it hit her now; miscalculating the gravity of a planet wasn't a mistake, it was murder. Eli's breakdown was now an infectious thing, and it might take them all.

"Gravity?" Cleo snapped. "So we haven't adjusted our approach or what—what's going on?"

"We're in tow," Austin said, holding his hand up as if to say, *Relax*. "We're in its orbit now. That's why the *Antilles* is shaking. We either boost out of orbit and that's all the fuel we have left, and so we go back home without ever landing. Or we launch our capsules now and we save the mission."

"Go home or launch?" Cleo asked, making sure she heard it right.

"And we have to decide now," Boston said.

"Looks like you already decided," Cleo whispered to herself.

"Speak up, Xavier," Boston shot back.

"You're all suited up. The decision's been made."

"MCs gave the go-ahead to launch the capsules so . . ."

Mission Control—or the MCs, as Daniel called them—were four hours away in Havana. That was how long signals took to bounce from Earth to Orbis Alius.

"Did Mission Control advise we launch?" Boston said to Daniel, but her gaze fixed on Cleo. "That's what Xavier's asking, yes?"

She dipped her head in a curious nod of agreement. *How'd she know that?* Cleo mused.

"They just gave us the option," Daniel said, voice aimed at Cleo but his look turned toward Austin. "They didn't try to sway us in either direction. The decision was on us."

All their glances maneuvered like a game of chess, steering their vision across a board of black-on-white eyes. There was some obvious friction here, and Cleo could guess at what—there wasn't a consensus on launching. But who supported it, and who was against it?

"Those weren't Mission Control's exact words—" Boston interjected, but Austin cut her off, then Daniel again. So many words were exchanged, but none of them were answers.

Cleo's eyes steered away from that chessboard, noticing movement between the dandelion leaves. That tiny greenhouse was a living memory of a world she was starting to forget. Over this past year, Cleo had spent full-on hours just gawking at the dirty bronzes, floral yellows, and earthy greens; it was color therapy from the *Antilles*'s white interiors and the infinite black outside. *Look*, she told herself, *they're swaying again*. This tiny spot of dirt and weed, with its incandescent suns, pulsed at her. And it wasn't just the UV lights glinting—the dandelion petals pulsed yellow, the grains of dirt maracaed brown, and veins of root strummed. She could hear an entire grainy carnival under there.

"Xavier," Boston barked sternly. "Are you with us?"

Not really. She couldn't quite shake this goddamn high, but . . . "Yes. I'm listening," Cleo lied, squeezing her twitching fingers into a fist again.

"Bottom line is, we voted," Austin said. "Results of that vote were to launch. Two to one."

"Who voted against?" Cleo asked.

Boston raised her hand, smiling all the way back to her molars. "Guilty."

"Why?" Cleo said, a note too quiet.

"Say again?" Boston asked, annoyed and leaning in ear first. "Speak up."

"She asked why," Daniel answered for her.

"Doesn't feel right," Boston replied and shook her head. "Something . . . I don't know. It's not right . . ."

She had been saying it since Eli's suicide, and she hadn't been the only one. Eli's own last words to Cleo were the same—*something's not right.* But the haunting part of that wasn't the words, since Eli was undeniably deranged; it was the idea that maybe Cleo could have consoled him. Could she have? That hadn't sat well with her, still didn't. Cleo had never been the savior type—for that, you first needed to be good with people. But what was not right, she knew, was that the limits of long-range space travel were being tested with this mission, and only Cleo seemed naturally equipped to handle it.

"We made up our collective minds," Austin said, looking to Daniel for support. That support came in slow, tepid nods of the pilot's head and didn't appear to suffice. "We have scrutinized the data. And we must trust that data. Not a gut feeling."

"She didn't vote," Boston said, gesturing in Cleo's direction. "Xavier should have a vote."

Austin turned to Cleo, his mind made up but his body open to ideas. *Check out his posture*—shoulders thrust back and his chest unfolding as he stepped closer. Faux intimacy. Meanwhile, his expression hardened, he smiled with incisors, and the splash of Caribbean blue in his eyes was a darker, icy teal.

"Of course," Austin said, standing over her with his six-foot-four-inch frame. "She should vote. She shall. Xavier, what is your vote? Launch or . . ." He folded his arms. "Do we withdraw back to Earth?"

Austin was an Apostle—or as he called it, a *transhumanist.* That religion or cult or belief system—his words—gave him an extra sense of purpose. He represented more than himself up here. He wanted this vote official and in his favor. The designated captain of the mission, he was all about appearances. Even now his posture was upright, chin raised with noble bearing. Austin wanted no debate from Mission Control on his decisions. And so, he looked to her, hoping she'd say yes, she assumed. Hoping it could be that easy.

"I don't know . . ." Cleo said. "We didn't plan for this."

"But we did," Austin said. "We ran trial and tribulation for worst-case scenarios, didn't we?"

They had. "Yes," Cleo said, recalling their time in the simulators: program #13 or program #67, the shallow reentry, the gimbal lock, orbital decay. Those programs weren't that dissimilar to this.

"You remember?" Austin asked, and she nodded. "Good. Remember the people too. Mission Control. Your father. Family. The pride of the Caribbean and their diaspora." He gestured to her. "The Venusians. Bajans. Dominicans. We were the cheap labor sent out to build worlds. 'Out of Poverty and On to the Stars.'" He repeated the AST's slogan better than the voice actors in the ads back home. "Our failure would be the top story for every media outlet around the world. 'The Atlantic Space Trade fails on their first attempt at flight.'"

"No," Boston said. "Nobody cares, Cleo. What was it, eighty years ago? Ninety? The world discovered that we are alone in the universe. Twelve billion people found out that there's no life anywhere beyond Earth. Like, nothing. We're talking about the biggest discovery in the history of astronomy: We are alone in the universe, and that was only the second-biggest news story on that day. Between a basketball trophy and some royal family scandal. Our failed spaceflight won't trend or go viral. You make your vote for you, nobody else."

Boston was right. The worlds were obsessed with transhumanism or Idols or their war games and virtual Valhallas. On Earth, its moon, or the terraformed Venus, there was an epidemic of social apathy. No one would care about some third-world nations attempting to terraform their way to second place.

It was quiet then as glances flicked from Boston to Austin and back, but eventually, every dot on every eye rolled back to her. *I hate this*, Cleo thought, this maneuvering of social dynamics. That was why she kept herself isolated—goddamn people.

Cleo averted her eyes, turning to the greenhouse. The dandelions still pulsed, trying to show her something, maybe. So many individual dandelion stalks blossomed individual flowers, but underneath, they were all entangled in one root system. *It rhymes*, she thought, *the concepts rhyme*. The dandelions, with their communist roots, all spun into one another, rhymed with the idea of four individual votes finding a single consensus.

"It rhymes," she mouthed, or was she still high?

"She say something?" Austin asked.

"Jeez," Boston sighed. "Speak up, Xavier."

"I vote yes," Cleo said, turning to Austin. "Launch," she affirmed. "Let's do it."

Austin grinned, but he tried not to show his teeth. "Copy that."

Cleo didn't know how much of her vote was for the actual landing and how much of it was a vote against the Idol, Yasmin Boston, and the hundred million voyeurs behind her eyes. Cleo didn't hate her younger, smarter, wealthier crewmate, but the transcendent media that Boston represented irked her in all the wrong ways.

Still, if Cleo had said no to launching, Austin might have simply pointed to the effect of Calypso Cocaine hitchhiking through her bloodstream. He spoke like that, you know, full of oversophistication, imagery, metaphor, full of himself. Look at him, feathery hair dyed a perfect brown, a golden tan without sunlight, and naturally thick eyelashes that gave him masculine mascara.

"Let's run a systems check," Austin said, turning to Daniel. "We either launch now or abort. And let's relay to Mission Control."

"Copy," Daniel agreed but nodded uneasily. Daniel was the youngest among them and had the most to prove. A great wingman, in both senses of the word, but deep down, Daniel was a political animal, that subspecies that flocked with the flow of murmuration, never against it.

"Cleo," Daniel called. "Let's get you in your EMU?"

She agreed. Cleo tucked her shoulders in, and the suit slid down her torso. Daniel assisted, attaching the top half of the suit to the bottom by a belt on the waist. The beta cloth and its Teflon skin suctioned in on her body, form-fitting to Cleo's figure. They were really doing this. She was about to drop onto an uncharted planet. Suddenly, her heart grabbed hold of her chest. Her saliva went bitter. The auditives, still in her system, made a melody of the alarms outside. Cleo wasn't coming down off her high—she was crashing, burning up in its atmosphere.

Austin's capsule launched first at 0320 hours and landed on the outskirts of the northern pole some minutes later. Boston launched at 0410 hours. Daniel lost her signal for four minutes, but she remerged safely on the surface.

Cleo launched into the western equatorial ranges at 0455 hours. Her descent was steeper than anything in the sims. The storm's spiral arms throttled the tiny capsule, shaking it until Cleo's eyes rolled up into a violent sleep. But she dreamed of retaliation, that she was a shooting star, screaming light and a tail of fire. She dreamed of thrusters burning underneath her, braking against gravity, then a jellyfish chute guiding her to the dirt.

2

Condensation smeared the visor, but Cleo could still see the systems display flashing yellow, and there was some red in there too. Lights blinked on the display, and she blinked too, and somehow she wasn't conscious yet. It felt like she was dreaming with her eyes wide open; maybe she was stunned or something. Her limbs wouldn't move, but that was probably the restraints, right? Cleo lay in a kind of lucid, waking dream. And she heard Dad out there. He was saying something, but the words were too low. "Dad?" she called out, and that echo of her own voice finally woke her up.

The capsule was claustrophobic. Eight feet long, a little less than that wide, and every drawer and floor and ceiling panel was filled to the brim with rations, medicines, repair equipment, and a billion-dollar rover. This capsule was a bedroom, research lab, kitchen, communications hub, and toilet, and it was home for the next three months.

Cleo unbuckled her harnesses and fell out of her seating. She stripped off the gloves first, then the helmet, even the boots, and limped toward the systems display. "But why?" she mouthed. *Why am I limping?* There were no sensations of pain anywhere. Then, right on the subsequent step, it dawned on her—*oh*, she realized, *gravity*. There was an authenticity to Orbis's downward pull; it lacked the bilious side effects of the swinging centrifugal placebo she had on the *Antilles*.

The read on the system display was 98 percent integrity. Good news, depending on what that remaining 2 percent was. Hopefully, just the superfluous systems, right? Secondary comms and satellite. "Please," she hoped out loud.

"*Antilles*. Systems check," Cleo said to the AST's intelligence unit—or the IU, as they were more commonly referred to.

"Systems check," the IU replied in posh British high notes. "Running comprehensive systems analysis . . . Abington Unit shield: two percent damaged. Aft skirt: one percent damage. Alpha Transistor systems data: unavailable. AMS: one percent damage. Auxiliary systems data: unavailable . . ."

The IU continued its alphabetical rant, but Cleo listened with only vague concern. The capsule was a self-repairing system and would "heal" itself if the individual systems weren't too far damaged. So she stored her EMU, then changed into warmer thermals that evened out the low temperatures and socks that suctioned into the spaces between her toes.

"Where's the *Antilles* spacecraft? Is it in transmission range?" she asked.

"The *Antilles* spacecraft is not currently in your line of sight," the IU replied. "It is approximately eight hours out of synchronicity."

"Copy." Cleo nodded. Eight hours.

Daniel's orbit was not geosynchronous; the *Antilles* was in low planetary orbit and currently on the other side of the planet. It would be at least another eight hours until he swung back around to her side of the world. Until that time, there would be no communication—not just with Daniel but also with Austin and Boston, who were beyond the bend of the planet's curvature and needed the *Antilles*'s satellite to relay their signals. There would be enough time for rest until then. But there was no way she'd sleep here or now, standing on another world. So instead of pretending to wrap herself in sheets and blankets, Cleo would spend the anxious hours in speech recital and booting up her two-ton rover. And food, she remembered. Cleo couldn't feel the hunger with her stomach in knots, so she had to remind herself—eat.

The meals ready-to-eat, MREs, came in a variety of flavors: cou-cou and flying fish, shepherd's pie, dandan noodles, and chicken roti, among others. The calcium, iron, and all the vitamin ABCs were hidden between their spices. The crew was also allotted a small compartment for "comfort foods." Cleo had loaded her space with desserts: sweetbread, sugar cakes, and turnovers.

That first mouthful of sugarcane-enriched coconut rewound her body back to Venus: Venusian skies and its cotton candy clouds, pink in the daytime and neon at night, and the greenhouse skyscrapers lining the Neo Oistins horizon. That penthouse view from Dad's hospital window was a reminder of why he was sulfur-sick. Nothing grew in that dirt, leading to imported soil and high-rise farms. Apples hung from branches two thousand feet up. These were terraforming's imperfections, and Dad had fragile lungs—"like glass," the surgeons claimed. Was that what had inspired her to be a terraformer? Partly. *And was it the very reason why I ended up stranded here?* Cleo wondered as the tape in her mind unwound to the present.

It was minus two hours until the *Antilles* circuited into broadcast range, and that was when the first signs of drowsiness hit. *Of course*, she thought sarcastically, *now it hits me*. But she couldn't nap now, with just a couple of hours to prep and all the worlds watching. "No," she scolded herself with the same temper her stepmother would. Ava, the stepmother—she'd be watching too as the *Antilles* broadcasted Cleo's first footsteps on Orbis back to Earth, Mars, Venus, and all the lesser moons.

For the collective, that was the winning campaign slogan for the AST. That mantra was printed on every notebook and EMU on the *Antilles*. Maybe it was her penchant for solitude that revved Cleo's skepticism, but she didn't buy into it. For what collective? She knew there was more behind this mission than the hope for the Caribbean space ambition. The funding arose from too many dubious corners of the private sector. Prime Minister Rowe didn't care, of course; he had netted his percentages for the coming reelection campaign.

There were institutions that wanted to know what was happening on this anomalous rock, where all their probes went to die. But no one wanted their own programs crashing and burning this far out. There was too much money involved. The European Space Agency lost just one lander in the Giovanni Plantation crash and their stock bottomed out. The Japanese happily received Mars's subsequent ten-term contract.

So this mission was a win-win, not only for backers wanting to explore the strange world, but for the Caribbean countries receiving the funding to fling five of their own into space. But the anomalous Planet Nine had its amateur paparazzi behind backyard telescopes. They scripted tabloid-style gossip columns about the planet's strange orbit and its impenetrable atmosphere. Some even believed that Orbis Alius wasn't a planet at all but an alien vessel. It was obvious now that Orbis wasn't any sort of vessel—the alien part, though, Cleo wasn't sure.

Her specific mission, aside from testing the terraforming viability of the world, was to interpret the strange signals emanating from deeper within the planet. Originally radiative noise, the emissions were now termed *radioactive music*, because that accelerated half-life had a pattern to it—a *rhythm*, as the more pioneering astro-journalists scripted it. And Cleo needed to find its tune.

She unlocked the largest storage space on the capsule. Her reinforced titanium rover was folded gymnastically into the space. It was a mass of big-budgeted alloys and novel 2D protective polymers. Inside the bleeding-edge battery technology was the heartbeat of the machine, powering two hundred pounds of hardware alone.

Cleo pressed her palm against its cold metal anatomy. "IU System. Shakes," she whispered, almost unsure whether the billion-dollar behemoth would even work.

Four legs built on metallic muscle lifted the machine out from storage. Apart from a tail, the quadrupedal had a doglike shape, though it was closer in size to a small horse—standing on all fours, the rover came past her elbows. Its single unlit eye stared out into the shadows. But as it lifted itself to a more formal, steed-like posture, that lens lit up.

"Hello? Shakes?" she said, leaning her ear toward the machine as if the rover might be whispering. "Are you on, Shakes?" Still nothing.

"*Antilles*, can you run diagnostics on . . ." She paused then as the rover's lenses whirred. It was focusing on her.

"Copy that," the IU said in a gentleman's tone. "Unit 196. Your copycat."

Shakes was not part of the *Antilles* IU. It was a unique personality type, one that was honed to support Cleo's solo work on the planet. Personality-based intelligence units were the vogue on Earth. Venus was late to the craze but catching up quickly.

Companies like TCC (The Companion Company) and Cambridge Capital were the leaders in the "companionship" industry. They created IU companions for the elderly, babysitters for children, partners for singles or divorcées, and friends for loners like Cleo. The new marketing gimmick in the companion industry was personality cloning. Marilyn Monroe, for example, was an industry favorite. Her personality was "cloned" via large data sets of information. Monroe's biographies, old interviews, even bank statements and court documents—it was all compiled and aggregated. Gaps were filled in with an IU's psychological training, creating an approximation—a best guess of what the legendary actress was like.

Her IU didn't have Marilyn Monroe's personality. Instead, Cleo had opted for a combination of legends from her favorite eras of music. Busta Rhymes, Lauryn Hill, Big Pun, Rihanna, and Red Plastic Bag, to name a few. Therefore, there was a natural cadence of rhyme in Shakes's dialogue. But for the first personality tests in Havana, even with the presence of Hill and Rihanna, the IU spoke with tones of misogyny, so Cleo added the likes of Missy Elliott and Nicki Minaj for balance, and somehow, that personality was even more sexist. Over the last few months before launching, the programmers helped mold the personality, filling the necessary holes with Maya Angelou and Emily Dickinson, finally sprinkling in William Shakespeare to round out the rhyme scheme in its speech, and therein was its namesake.

"Shakes," she said. "I need you to run weather patterns and diagnostics on the surrounding region. Best spot for planting the flag, best lighting setup for cinematics."

"It's my birthday, let my thoughts *corral*. I'm barely out of this processor's birth *canal*."

Shakes's cocktail of toxic personality types resulted in an irreverent, quipping, rhyming intelligence. But there was something in that mixture that she liked. Deep down in Shakes's makeup, there was an element that connected it to her.

"It is your birth date, huh?" she said and smirked. "Happy birthday, Shakes. You're the first Orbis Alien."

Shakes's diagnostics appeared via holoscreen pie charts and bar charts that hovered in thin air. She twisted her wrist toward the gesture controls, flipping past the arithmetic and other data-related tabs to search the capsule's exterior cameras. Images from outside appeared around her. The camera's "owl-oculars" wiped away the darkness of Orbis's 0.06 percent sunlight in comparison to Earth. She saw small rocks, sand, and little of anything else. Jagged ice particles were caught in the poisonous air, and the atmospheric pressure stood at a psi that would squeeze her eyes right out of her skull.

Orbis Alius would never be the Venusian miracle or even the disappointments of a terraformed Mars. Just from the glance through those images, she knew this world was barren beyond repair. No venture capitalist would take on the financial burden of terraforming this cold, ancient rock. They should have just spun into its orbit and returned home; the mission had already failed. But she had to go through the motions anyway: space suit, rover, plant a flag, then run atmospheric testing equipment for Orbis's viability as a terraformed world. She was a Xavier.

Cleo donned the space suit in slow motion. Her movements were so deliberate, almost ceremonial, like the EMU was her Catholic vestments. She tiptoed into the boots; the Nike swoosh was embossed into the soles so as to spread its marketing in the form of footprints across the alien dirt. The gloves tightened around her palms; the *G* printed on them stood for Google, not *glove*. There were countless brand affiliations tattooed across the million-dollar suit that helped recoup its costs. Except for the helmet.

She crowned herself in that glass goblet, fashioned by a young haute couture designer. A yellow platinum base magnetized to the collar. Beyond that, it was all glass, and so invisibly clear that it barely appeared to be there at all. It also acted as a display with temperature and terrain readouts, and it immediately tinted to changes in sunlight. But she was superfluously overdressed with no sunlight to tint the lenses, a near-constant cold, and little variation in the temperature. It was all for show, but she would flaunt it as best she could.

The oxygen breathed into her. The breastplate suctioned around her torso, and Cleo allowed it. She allowed the gear to absorb her, a symbiosis that had to be perfect because right now Cleo was being televised, and all the worlds would be watching.

She hoped they'd all be watching.

The AST's space suits were sleek technological marvels. Smaller and tighter than anything that had come before. They were as formfitting as a space suit could be. "In vogue," one trendsetter outlet had called them. "A New Frontier of Fashion," *ELLE* magazine had praised. GQ Media, as well as its Venusian affiliates, praised the suits as game-changing. But those puff pieces didn't carry that flattery over genres. *World Science* magazine called the AST's space program "overzealous." Another called the space suit "the overpriced inferiority complex of the fledgling space agency."

Pricks, but they were half right. The AST was made up mostly of Caribbean islands, a few Central American neighbors, and charitable funding from USMCA. That was why they had to come this far out, farther than any others before them. That was why so much of the budget was contributed to things like space suit design, PR, and hiring renowned architects for the interior of the *Antilles*. That was why they chose an Idol, Yasmin Boston, and rushed her through the astronaut program. It was part of that second-world feeling of inadequacy. They couldn't even call it the Caribbean Space Trade. *Caribbean* felt too small. The Atlantic, though, that vast ocean between the continents, like the space between stars—that would work.

"Xavier!" Daniel's voice tumbled clumsily into her earpiece, stuttering in his corporate panic. His huffing breathing was its own sort of static.

"Slow down," she pleaded. "What're you saying?"

But it was nothing life-threatening, just Daniel overexplaining how his MCs wanted the broadcast "*now*, now," his words for the immediacy of it. He was on comms early, by at least thirty minutes, and he almost made it sound like this was her fault. *Calm down*, she thought, but let him run his mouth through a marathon of classy adjectives anyway, only to respond with a single word.

"'Kay," she remarked, and was ready as ever. *Let's get it over with.*

The air lock hissed open, inviting her and Shakes into the pressure corridor. That first chamber depressurized, another venomous hiss, and she unlocked the outer door. Orbis's cold, barren corpse stood shadowy on the other side. Her Frankenstein, and she would bring it back to life.

"Wow . . ." she said, both intimidated and awestruck. "All right, Shakes. Time to point those pretty lenses of yours toward me."

"So you're ready to record, Clee?"

"I guess . . ." She shook her bottled head, the sleek helmet feeling cumbersome now as the rover took position in front of her and aimed the muzzle of its lenses. "Just in a little bit of disbelief. Can't believe I'm actually here. I'm actually doing this."

"Better believe, cuz you're about to be live, Clee. Starting recording in five—three . . . two . . . And I'm on you."

Shakes zoomed in just as Cleo breathed deep. She sashayed down the capsule's ramp. The rover walked backward, with its spotlights washing over her suit's synthetic polymers. The Boeing planetary logo shone, as did LEGO, Starbucks, McDonald's, Google, and Coca-Cola, all the trademarks embossed along the sleeves, chest plate, legs, and sideways along the spine of her EMU. Those were the literal money shots.

Cleo peered up toward the cloud-twisted sky; that way, her helmet caught the lens flares from the rover's lights. She stared out at the wind-whipped landscape and squinted with a valor that resembled all the old Western film actors. The grit in her teeth was her feigning determination against these wild elements. Cleo had practiced that look and the posture in every mirror since Havana. She knew Shakes was transmitting her image up to the *Antilles* spacecraft, which would then relay the signal to Earth, the lunar surface, Venus, and all the lesser territories.

"Our solar system," Cleo said, gesturing to the landscape around her. "A black ocean full of its spinning islands . . ." She paused dramatically, both in voice and motion. This was her "one small step for a man" speech; she had to draw it out. "This is our last undiscovered country. The new world, Orbis Alius. And as a Xavier, as a Bajan, and the first of the Orbis Aliens, I plant our flags, and what germinates will be a unified humanity. We all are responsible for the collective and for all humankind."

She lifted a pole from the storage on her rover's back and stabbed it into the dead soil. A trio of flags flapped in the alien breeze: one Barbadian (representing Cleo's ancestry), another for the Caribbean Union, and a third with the JP Morgan Bank logo, one of AST's top financial backers.

Cleo heard applause in her head. "Xavier," someone cheered, and her name was a big part of the reason she stood there on that planet. Her great-grandfather had been a chief member of the team that made the greatest discovery in astronomy. Maybe the biggest discovery in science. The hollow universe principle—it stated that the human race was alone in the universe. No other life was out there, anywhere. The only intelligence, human or otherwise, was on Earth, Venus, Mars, and the moons. Old man Xavier's use of gravitational waves to map every moon, planet, and star was infinitely complex. Nobel, Turing, Webber—he won every science award for the next decade, from astronomy to the utilization of artificial intelligence. He was the pride of a nation, the pride of his species, and having the Xavier name represented here was a good investment.

Why, in all that vastness, was there nothing else? It had been debated for the past ninety years. But Cleo could see the answer in this place, in the cold, the dark, the crumbling sand underneath her feet. The universe was too dead for life.

She stumbled there on the unstable soil. It sloshed like a grainy liquid. She fell back clumsily and, in the slow motion of weakened gravity, at half speed, landed on her back for all the worlds to see.

"Cut the feed," Cleo said quickly as she crawled upward, hands on knees, then hips. "Shakes, cams off."

"Embarrassed?" Shakes asked. "You shouldn't *be*. I wouldn't, *Clee*."

"You would understand if you were a Xavier with dirt on your million-dollar helmet, or however much this thing is worth."

"Still four hours 'til that feed gets to Earth."

"Sure, but . . ." Cleo shrugged. "Is a four-hour delay supposed to make it any better?"

"That's time *debt*. And I *sure bet*—after that time you'll *for-get*. No need to feel insecure . . . *yet*."

She smirked. "Four hours embarrassment-free," Cleo agreed, eyeing the landscape ahead. "Let's try that even ground over there. Unload the geo-sampler."

The IU followed her command without a quip, bending and twisting its quadrupedal body, and wagged its tailless backside to insert the half-ton mini monolith into the dry, glassy soil. An eruption of gas-station-like hoses slithered out of the geo-sampler, worming their way into the ground. When they stopped, a green light at the top of the geo-sampler lit up.

"Complete. Geo-sampler in position. Topsoil suffers from tremendous detrition."

"I noticed," Cleo said, her eyes now on the horizon and nothing else. And there was nothing else to see on that rusted rim of a world. It was like an ashtray of geological decay. Her Hummingbird, the drone, flapped its polymeric wings overhead. Wings, but halfway like rotors, a half rotation, bobbing up and down at 9.9 flaps per second. Though the "hummingbird" more resembled a dragonfly with a long and narrow body design and a four-wing flutter created specifically for Orbis's gravity.

The Hummingbird's high lumens shone over the rolling landscape. Cleo understood just then how her ancestors might have seen gods made out of the topography. Valleys that bent like legs and hills like hips—the terrain ahead resembled a body. Upon a second glance, though, she reconsidered. This landscape was a corpse. The detrition revealed itself under the drone's high light: The sand itself was like rust, flaking away and exposing the bedrock underneath.

Cleo stooped and dug her fingers into the soil, if it could be called that. This shrapnel-sharp dust would never bear fruit or even a weed. Nothing could live here. The clouds were in a mood, darker than the dark grays on Earth or the pinks on Venus. They were the deepest black she had ever seen, like they would rain volcanic ash. This was not a world that terraforming could save. But she knew that already. This world was dead.

And it was her fault somehow. Somehow, because failure was Cleo's genetic defect. Even deeper than her DNA, maybe, Cleo's atomic state had this luckless quantum probability, like her mother and mothers before her. And now she had infected this expedition. Her inauspicious germs moved across the *Antilles* walls, and they were airborne now in this planet's atmosphere.

"It's my fault," she whispered to herself. "It's my damn—"

"Talking to that pent-up self. Is not great for our mental health."

"No, I'm just . . ." Just what? She needed to answer fast. The psyches didn't like her talking to herself. Psychiatry was a crucial part of Shakes's programming. Maybe the most important. *Get her talking*. That was the code running through the rover's head right that second. "Just . . . thinking out loud," she said. "But thanks, Shakes."

Cleo got down to her pre-terraforming tasks, analyzing the miserable atmospheric numbers and mineral figures on the visor's display. Reading between the lines and decimal places, she saw the subtext—radiation, hints of half-lives deeper in the soil. Cleo lowered her head as she set expectations lower too, considering now whether Orbis might become a refueling outpost. That would be the best they could hope for. Like terraformed Mars, the great disappointment, no one would ever settle here. Not with mineral-rich moons Ganymede and Titan out there, or the true miracle of terraforming: Venus. Even with its residual poisons, Venus was an interplanetary Eden. A fairy-tale world with pink skies painted over an epic sun. Even beyond the terraforming, the planet had 92 percent of Earth's gravity, an active core, and abundant sunlight. Things grew bigger, grew faster, life itself was frenetic. The air seemed charged, its own sort of high-oxygen stimulant, and all that delirious sunlight.

I'm gonna be like you, she remembered telling Dad. *I'm gonna make everywhere like Venus.*

But Orbis Alius would never be Venus—*I mean, look at these numbers.* Strontium-90 was off the charts, as was cesium-137, among other isotopes. It was as if this rock had just emerged from the big bang. The only real questions remaining were these patterns flashing across her readouts. What were those rising and falling radiant lines? They were like volumetrics on a musician's computer. It was as if something was speaking out there, or singing with radiation, and all at once, singing over each other. But muffled by something.

Was there something out there? How the hell was she supposed to know? Cleo wasn't an interpreter of strange signals or radiant lines. She was a terraformer; she studied the work of Michael Müller. The German microbiologist had engineered bacteria that ate the "bad" compounds in a planet's atmosphere, then pooped out the good ones: oxygen, nitrogen, and the trace gases of breathable air. On Venus it took just a few years for that same bacteria to change the chemical makeup of the planet. It then took decades, not centuries, to upend Venus's runaway greenhouse effect and separate the carbon from the oxygen. In just over thirty years, the first colonist set foot onto their miracle world. The goddess of beauty, pink skies and lavender oceans, Earthlike gravity. Hundreds of millions migrated, her grandparents among them.

"Cleo," Daniel's voice came through her helmet. "This is the *Antilles*. Over."

"Hey," she said and suddenly found her proper posture: head upright, shoulders back, even though she knew Daniel couldn't see her. "I mean . . . copy, *Antilles*."

"We got a category one rolling in your direction. Not sure if you picked that up."

Cleo twisted back and saw it. A spool of twisting clouds with glints of lightning. How'd she miss that? She'd read her comms before stepping out, and it was all clear skies.

"*Antilles*, I saw that," she lied. "I just thought I'd do a few minutes of reconnaissance before I hunkered down. Over."

"Solid copy. Got about forty-five minutes before it's on top of you. How are things looking?"

"Readings aren't up yet but . . ." She took another glance out at the wasteland. "I don't know. Not great."

"No . . . ?" he asked, and he sounded younger suddenly, smaller. He sounded like he was falling away from the microphone, shrinking in disappointments.

"An outpost," Cleo blurted. "Could make a great outpost. The Apostles want to head out past the Oort, right? This could be, uh . . . great refueling, pit stop–type thing." *Where did that come from?* she wondered. That sudden burst of, what? Was it empathy for a younger crewmate? It was. She was trying to spare him the disappointment.

"Right," Daniel said eventually, his voice a notch lighter. "The Apostles."

Apostles were believers in the post-humanist movement. Some stitched computer hardware into their cerebellums, others voluntarily amputated limbs to replace them with cutting-edge prosthetics. There was almost a spiritual nature to their science, some would even say religious fervor, and that helped them achieve the monikers Posties, among many other nicknames. Their captain, Austin, was an Apostle himself.

"That's right," he said, seeming to remember something. "Eli, um . . ." The name was like a sore on his tongue. "He, um, said that you didn't like them."

"Eli . . ." The name came out the same for her. She spoke softly, like it was reverent now that he was gone. "Why'd he say that? I don't hate . . ." Did she?

"Just the way you say it—Apostle. Like you kinda whisper it, you know?"

She didn't know. But her stepmother, Ava, was an Apostle. And Cleo hated her. She hated that woman like calluses on the skin, the type of hate that hardens over time. So was there some subconscious intertwining between Cleo's stepmother and the Apostles as a whole? But Ava wasn't truly an Apostle; she just hooked herself onto whatever was trending at that current moment. That was how Ava had met Dad, and like her name suggested, Ava was a bird. A wicked, graying crow that built her nest in Dad's ear. *She's not yours*, Ava had chirped, and kept on chirping. *That girl's not yours.* And those four words were the reason Cleo was standing on this rock.

"You there, Cleo?" Daniel asked. "Over?"

Shoot, she had gone quiet and hadn't even noticed. "Yeah, sorry. I'm here."

"Suggest you get inside. The wind's picking up fast. Gonna be a rocky night."

3

It was a hailstorm, and one that lasted a week. Ice pellets the size of pine cones scratched against the capsule's hull, each one screeching—clawing its way inside. The hull's tungsten skin kept the ice at bay, but an invasive cold would eventually crawl into the capsule; then it crawled into her, snaillike, as if she were its shell. Cleo tied herself into the blanket, her toes binding the bottom and her arms choking it around her neck, but the draft kept finding openings in the fabric.

The past few days consisted of rock sampling, subsoil tests, digging alien dirt out from under her fingernails, troposphere measurements. Orbis wasn't just dead, it turned out; it was deathly. Radioactive isotopes were living out their half-lives in some of those rocks. There was radiation deeper in the subsoil and bedrock several hundred meters down.

Her Hummingbird performed most of the daytime observations, but the dragonfly drone went dark by the end of the first week. Austin and Boston were experiencing similar conditions: all the hail and frost, a tempestuous world unsuitable for colonization. Outside of one pep talk from Austin and daily briefings from Daniel, it was just her and her rhyming rover.

The second week on Orbis was the coldest, the ninth day especially. She dressed herself in the space suit, relying on its internal heating, and somehow the cold was there too. The last deep sleep Cleo had was on that night of drug release in the *Antilles*—the auditives. And hidden between her sorrel and soursop drinks were a dozen IV bags containing the many genres of drug music. *Just one microdose,* she thought. Just enough to get her to sleep. Auditives weren't habit-forming, and the better she slept, the better her performance would be on Orbis, right?

Cleo grabbed the IV line from her medical supplies and plugged it into a cannula made for the ear. Opera Ecstasy was the genre tonight. It dripped deluges and her pupils dilated, then undilated, strobing in, then out. The folds of the ear opened, like rose petals in sunlight, she imagined, and the drug music was her photosynthesis. She dreamed of dopamine-soaked B-flats washing over her, or G-sharps doused in serotonin. Warmth squeezed in around her. She dreamed that night and most of the next day. For a while she was conscious of her own dreaming—and it was that glitch in sleep that woke her up. You can't know that you're dreaming and truly stay asleep. It's the knowing that breaks the reality of the dream.

She wondered if that was how it worked for sentience too. "Shakes?" Cleo grumbled sleepily, her eyes barely open. "Does being aware of your own subconscious mind wake you into being? Does it wake you to a self-aware state? That's the catch-22 for intelligence, isn't it?" And suddenly Cleo felt like she was onto something. Like she alone had figured out the meaning to life. "All the chimps, and wolves, and bowerbirds in the world were caught in that sleepy, subconscious state, locked in the waking dream just below sentience." *Sleepwalking,* she thought, *yeah, like that.* Millions of sleepwalking mammals on planet Earth, and only we are aware of our dreaming, and we woke up.

The bulb inside Shakes's lenses bloomed into a dull shine. The rover was in "sleep mode" itself. And now it stared at her with artificial judgment.

"Don't . . ." she grumbled. "Don't judge."

"Did you see me budge?"

"No," she admitted, but she still felt that disparaging angle to Shakes's lens, and so she kept explaining herself. "Auditives aren't even habit-forming, so . . ." She shrugged, still waiting for a response that wasn't coming. "They aren't. That's the truth. And I couldn't sleep."

"You try counting *sheep*?" the rover asked. "*Still, though* . . . go on and lie your head to *sleep*. That's a *pill-low*. And you're still high."

Auditives had started in a pill form, a spongy tablet that, when inserted into the ear, dissolved into a pharmaceutical symphony. *Pill low*. Cleo started to smile. "But I'm not high, Shakes." She stared at her palms as if that would reveal anything. "It was just a microdose. I'm good."

"Then why's your pupil's *dilation*—in rhythm with the comm's *vibration*?"

Comms? That was the ringing in her ears, but it rang in melody. Everything was music now, even as she sat up. The room spun backward, dancing with her. "Damn it." This was the wrong genre, not Opera X. Cleo held her neck, feeling for the pulse—boom, ba-ba-boom, ba-ba-boom. "K-Pop Ketamine. Shit."

Cleo staggered into her food storage and slapped a caffeine patch on her wrist. An immediate warmth burned as coffee beans slow-roasted directly into her bloodstream. She already had a vitamin D patch on her arm for this sunless world, calcium and iron patches on either leg for her bone density on the zero-g voyage to Orbis, fiber patches, and blood thinners, so what was one more?

But what could Daniel want this late in the day? He was only five minutes from spilling over the horizon and his signal with it. But as the holoscreen came into focus, it was YASMIN BOSTON that flashed green on the display. Boston? The two hadn't spoken since deploying to the planet's surface.

Cleo tapped in. "I'm receiving, Boston," she started. "How's my copy? Over?"

"Loud and clear," Boston said. "What took you so long to answer?"

"I was asleep," she lied, although *that float chick* came to mind. Cleo had been floating. "But I'm gonna lose signal in a couple minutes. Daniel's nearly out of range. Over."

"I know. I just . . . One question."

It was then that Cleo noticed the call was locked, a secure call. Not only could Daniel or Austin not join, they wouldn't even know there was a transmission. A call from Boston was peculiar enough, but to lock on an "invisible" feed . . .

"So . . ." Cleo paused, wondering, *Why call me?* "What's wrong?"

"Nothing's wrong," Boston said, almost in contempt. "I just need some . . . information." Boston breathed, seemingly unsure of what to say next. "So . . . there are a million conspiracy theories out there about every planet, right? Enceladus has diamond geysers or Ceres is haunted after the crash, whatever, sure. In one ear, out the other. But there's one about Orbis that an astronomy-oriented follower sent to me. He's a somebody at Tsinghua University, and honestly, it's not even a conspiracy theory. It's a math problem."

"Math problem?" Cleo asked into the gap of Boston's breathing. "This . . . somebody just sent this to you?"

"No. A while back," she said in quieter confidence. "About a month, I think."

A month ago, Cleo mused. That'd be just two weeks before they deployed onto Orbis's surface. And Boston had been high-strung that day, hadn't she? Cleo squinted into her memory. Boston making a show of voting against deploying. Even now there was a distant tremble in her voice. Was this why? A math problem?

"What's the problem with the math?" Cleo asked.

Boston cleared her throat. "Basically, an algorithm for a history of the planet's orbit. Following its trajectory backward to see where Orbis Alius was positioned a year ago or a hundred years ago. You get me?"

"I think . . ." But Cleo didn't understand a word. Somewhere between her barely passing AST math grade and the K-Pop still thrumming in her lungs, she was completely lost.

"It takes Orbis a hundred and seventy years to orbit the sun way out here," Boston said. "But where was the planet on its orbit a year ago? Well, we examine its gravitational effect on asteroids or other bodies in space. So even though Orbis wasn't only discovered a hundred years ago, the math will show where it was two hundred years ago, five hundred, a thousand."

"Right," Cleo said, nodding now. "Tracking the history of its orbit."

"Mm-hmm," Boston hummed. "But once you get past three hundred years ago or so, the math doesn't work anymore. There's no effect on asteroids or even when it's on its Neptunian flyby, no effect on the moons, nothing. It's almost like . . ."

"Like what?"

"Like Orbis Alius didn't exist until three hundred years ago. Like it came from somewhere else. I worked on this problem for weeks, and that's the answer. It's wrong, obviously. But . . . I ran it by other physicists back home; the best of them couldn't figure it out. I think that's why the gravity calculations were off. Why we had to launch early. There's something here that's . . ."

Wrong? Strange? "What?" Cleo asked.

"Never mind." And that was the quietest she had ever heard Boston speak.

Yasmin Boston's celebrity was, quite simply, because she was perfect. Among all the bioengineered generations, she was the archetype. Ferocious beauty, elite in dance, literature, and painting. She was a polyglot and songstress. Her physical architecture was brutalist. Her athleticism was Olympian. But her truest genius was in the field of mathematics. Two-time Witten Award winner, MacArthur Fellowship, Fields Medal. If Boston couldn't solve this thing, no one else could.

"Look," Cleo said with a forced chuckle. "If you can't figure out the math, then I definitely can't."

"I know," she said, and very matter-of-factly. "I'm not calling you for help on the math problem. The AST blocked my IU from any information on that. They locked me out from communicating with most of my followers, outside of close relatives, and I've only got about two of those. They don't want me mining into this, because I don't think they can figure it out either."

"Why'd they send us to this planet if they can't figure out the math of its orbit?"

"I don't know. I asked. Up and down that roster, I asked. And Prime Minister Rowe . . ." Every word after *Rowe* was swept up in coughs of static. The signal was sinking into snow death.

"Boston?"

"Here," she said quickly. "Your signal's low. I don't think they blocked your IU. Ask it what it knows about Prime Minister Rowe. Where he derived his funding for . . ."

Boston's voice gargled under another wave of static. Michael Rowe was the prime minister of the Caribbean Union and the main political backer of the Orbis Alius mission. "Out of poverty and into space" was one of his campaign slogans for years. But Cleo was Venusian and mostly illiterate to the politics on Earth.

She turned to Shakes. "You heard her, right? What's the deal with Prime Minister Rowe?"

"Rowe's greed is his soul's *cancer*. He's a poll *dancer*. A political Rowe-*mancer*."

"Wow." She smirked. "Didn't know you leaned politically left."

"Well, his policies are so *sinister*. I call him the crime *minister*."

"Cleo?" Boston's voice resurfaced in a frothy hiss. "Did I hear that right? Is that rover . . . rapping?"

"A little . . ." Cleo quickly tried to change the subject. "You got a lot of interference on your end."

"You're getting staticky too. Look, I'll catch you on the next round. So, *uh* . . . yeah, good talk."

"'Kay. Over and out."

"Wait," Boston said. "Do you believe in God?"

"God?" Cleo asked but didn't get a response. Nothing but static hissed back at her, so she continued, "I, *um* . . . My mom believed in God. Said if there are no aliens, if we're alone in the universe, then there needs to be a god. She said God is our sixth sense. Whatever that meant." Cleo waited for a response, but not long. Boston had lost her signal—she was long gone. Cleo knew it too, with all that static buzzing in her ear. And that was probably the reason there was so much honesty in her response.

4

Week three was the warmest on record, at least since they had touched down. The stratosphere was stark naked of any clouds, and the sun—her sun—was a glint the size of a marble on the skyline. It shone the equivalent of Earth's full moon. Barely there and yet beautiful in its four-hour-old light.

There was no wind or hail in the day's meteorology reports. The *Antilles* IU had predicted clear skies. The perfect time, then, to recover her drone, even if Cleo was still on the decline of another auditive high. Shakes had recommended the drone's recovery in the aftermath of Boston's impossible algorithm. The rover couldn't crack the history of Orbis's orbit either, and the drone's data readings for weather-pattern analysis and geological makeup weren't making sense. The data suggested that this world couldn't be placed in a state of terrestrial transformation because the planet itself had already begun terraforming.

Shakes led the way across the wasteland as Cleo trampolined on the spongy gravity, getting as high as two feet off the ground and then descending gradually. Nike-size footprints followed her every hop-step of the way. The landscape was a belly dance of rising mounds and sunken basins. The winds wound around the rolling terrain and sharpened, spattering dust particles against her helmet.

Almost on cue, Cleo's visor opaqued slightly as a half-transparent image flashed on the left side of the screen. It read ANTILLES—INCOMING. It was

Daniel. *But why?* She had logged this walk before heading out, and he had approved. So what was this all about?

Cleo tapped in.

"Xavier?" Daniel's voice echoed in her helmet. "You copy? I'm tracking you at ten o' northeast of the capsule. You're still en route to collect the drone?"

"I—" Cleo's throat and lips had dried, panting all that recycled air. She released the serpentine straw, a firm but flexible plastic utensil on the suit's collar that coiled up to her lips. She sipped and cleared her throat. "Sorry. Yeah, I'm collecting the drone. It's got the organics, the bacteria, and seeding and fertilization. I need to run chems."

She lied. But what surprised her moments later was that she hadn't even noticed. Yes, the drone had bacterial precursors and fertilization minerals, but that wasn't the goal. She was in Boston's conspiracy now, like she was one of her goddamn followers—a fanatic marching on this desert pilgrimage, sand clattering into her visor, and lying to the rest of the crew about why.

"Solid copy," Daniel said. "But I've got some nasty weather heading your way. Over."

"Weather?" Cleo shook her head. "No, there's not . . ."

She spun toward the girdling horizons. To the southwest, a monster of a cloud did its own spinning. It was a buzz saw of cumulus that tore at the air and snarled its white lightning jaws. A monster in every sense of the word.

"How . . ." Cleo mouthed, barely audible. Had she misread the forecast readouts? Was her auditive breakfast mixing things up in her head? "It said the weather would be . . ." Clear skies, she remembered. "It said clear this morning. Or am I crazy? Over."

"Not sure about your sanity overall," he said with a playful chuckle. "But you're right, the MET log was clear this morning. Weather's got a mind of its own out here."

"No kidding," she agreed. "Is it headed toward me?"

"Directly. Straight line. And it's sprinting. You need to head back."

"But I'm . . ." *I'm right there.* She could probably throw a rock and hit the drone now. Maybe five minutes at this bouncy pace, less if she really moved. "Five minutes."

"Xavier, once this thing's on top of you, I'm going to lose signal. Come on. Turn back. Get it tomorrow. You copy?"

"Copy."

Daniel disappeared from her visor. But standing there alone, Cleo knew she wasn't turning back. It was five minutes. Screw it.

Cleo made a mad dash toward the drone. *Five minutes,* she told herself. Or three if she gunned it. And with Daniel strangled in interference, he couldn't stop her. She leaned her body diagonally, and instead of leaping upward, she lunged forward, the momentum carrying her almost in a straight line ahead.

But it was like the wind noticed and pulled carpets of dirt from underneath her feet. She hit the ground, and the wind tugged her in one direction, then dragged her in another. She clung to Shakes's two-ton body, an anchor for the last hundred feet.

She and Shakes arrived at the pin on her radar in a little more than five minutes. The pin indicated her drone. But the drone wasn't there.

"No," she told her eyes. "It's here . . ." But it wasn't.

The sand spun around her in spirals. Cleo's helmet was like maracas made inside out as kicked-up dust particles clinked against the glass. She switched on the lights on the sides of her helmet to supplement the automatic low-light adjustment on her visor. Still nothing but glassy sand shone under the nine hundred lumens.

Sand, she realized. "Under the sand." Cleo dropped to her knees and dug up fistfuls at a time, counting as she did.

"We're getting ground like coffee, *decaffeinated.* And hang here any longer, we'll be *decapitated.*"

"One minute," she huffed into the echo of her helmet. "I got it here."

"Suggesting that we *retreat,* it's now or *never,* then *repeat* in calmer *weather,* before we *meet—*"

"I. Got. It."

And she should have. The drone should have been there, right there, but an arm's-length deep and Cleo couldn't get a grip on anything. She poured herself into the hole now, headfirst and limbs liquid, flowing down until her fingers tapped the drone's polycarbonates.

With Cleo's fists under the soil, she was eye level with the dirt, and that was where she saw it, a thing that couldn't be. A newborn sprout frisked in the wind, so tiny but so boisterously green amid all the gray dirt.

"You see?" she said to her rover.

But Shakes was two paces behind her, eyeing the storm and ready to flee. By the time Cleo turned back to the sprout, the wind had taken it, or the dirt had buried it. Or was it even there to begin with?

"Clee . . ."

"We're moving. I got it." Did she? The soil wasn't giving up the drone that easily. It was stuck there, and even in its mini-gravity hold, Cleo couldn't drag it out. "Shakes. Please."

And Shakes understood in just two panicked words. It released a cable that Cleo quickly attached to the drone. Shakes dragged it out gently enough, but the Hummingbird had lost a wing in the process of unearthing. But who gave a shit? What mattered was the CPU at the head of the machine. The memory. The imaging. Cleo fixed the thing onto Shakes's back faster than she thought humanly possible, and they were off.

But the way back was hard. She had lived without gravity for so long that now the pull of it felt dizzying. Erratic winds lashed both westward and easterly, and she tumbled over every few steps. The storm had beaten her to the capsule, but just by a mere minute. That close. And she would have made it too, but a stir of nausea in her belly broke Cleo, snapping her gut open, and she hunched over, vomiting into the glass bowl of her helmet. The liquid splashed, staining the inner surface.

Just a few hundred feet away from the capsule, gusts reached down and pelted stones and dust particles. Sheets of powder obscured the path ahead, and she panted fog onto the glass. She was blind, crawling beneath the wind, as if that could hide her. Even with Cleo's fingers clawing into the dirt and the toes of her boots dug in even deeper, there just wasn't enough gravity. Cleo was a lightweight sixty pounds on this world, and the winds were shearing at least forty miles per hour.

She anchored herself to Shakes's two-ton frame for the next hundred feet. She connected another cable between the rover's tail and latched it to her utility belt. Then all she could do was hang on for dear life.

"Good, Shakes . . ." She grimaced, her teeth sawed together. "Almost there."

Cleo could see the capsule on her radar and little else. She had made it. But the wind picked her up—ten feet, maybe—and slammed her, helmet first, into the ground. Cleo's visor cracked. Shit. It catapulted her backward, but Shakes's cable kept her tethered to the ground. The gusts spun her to the ground again, and another crack slithered across the helmet. She was flapping in the wind, a kite, slamming against the ground, impact after impact. Her helmet was like a transparent eggshell, breaking away until the glass opened up.

"No—"

Cleo's voice disappeared in the loss of pressure. Dust-rock-glass poured in, the cold with it. Instant frostbite glaciated her skin like white sunburn. She was breathing argon, carbon, yet Cleo was somehow conscious for another full minute. The levels of methane and carbon monoxide should have killed her much faster—so much faster. But when her eyes did eventually close, she was airborne, wrapped up in the winds and tethered by a cord. A human kite. Then everything, even the pit of her subconscious, went black.

5

"I predicted you," it preached—a noise rising in her sinuses. "Twin helix," it said. "We intermingle and that is the only escape." But none of it made sense. "The getaway gateway. But my pheromones are dead. Find me living. Live. This is a broadcast. To sim by oh sis." But its words started to break apart. "The gate way get a way. This is a broad cast." It was dissolving into her. "Find us a live."

"What?" The words drooled from Cleo's lips.

"I predicted you," it started again. "Twin helix." It repeated itself like a long-winded echo, word for word, all the way to its stuttering end. "This is a broad cast. Find us a live."

That inner voice wasn't hers, and it wasn't anyone else either. It almost sounded like God's voice, or at least how she imagined it when she had prayed long, long ago. There was something in her, steering her blood vessels as if God was encapsulated into a drug. But maybe this was what near death felt like. A last rush of random babble leading up to God's bright light.

Because she should be dead, *right*? Instead of lying in the center of the capsule with her thoughts bleeding out from her head. She had burst like the neck of a wine bottle—ruptured eardrums, bleeding nostrils, bloody lips, even her tear ducts leaked. Any hole the blood could escape from, it did. Her eyes were swollen and her lips too, into a false pucker. Her nostrils were inflamed, and her breathing was labored. Every contraction of her heartbeat strained.

"Shakes," she croaked. "What . . . happened?"

"You were ripped up from the earth—like the *blizzard had claws*. Dorothy in *The Wizard of Oz*. But I was Toto, I pushed against that *wind tide*. Until I got you *in-side* . . ."

Cleo could barely hear the rover and was already drifting, slipping into the unconscious black, then just as quickly getting her consciousness back. She couldn't distinguish between the two, wakefulness and brief naps or her own thoughts and Shakes's raps. Reality was in a blender right now.

She wanted to sleep but the pain rioted across her body, and it was difficult for her to fall asleep. But her body eventually gave in, falling unconscious, and Cleo thought at that moment she might not wake up. But she did, and the second day was just as painful. She urinated on herself, and that hurt too, but it was warm, at least for a while. And with her tongue swelling subsiding, she could beg Shakes for water. The rover dripped the water between her lips. And by the end of the day, she could command the voice controls to take over the temperature inside.

By the third day, Cleo could sit up, almost, though not without discomfort. She felt bold enough to kick off her left boot and rest herself against the curve of the wall. She even ventured to stand, but that failed fast. Still, she undressed herself from the defecation- and piss-stained space suit; it took two hours, but at least now she lay half naked, freed from her own excrement, finally able to call up to the *Antilles*.

"*Antilles*. Open channel. Is it in range?"

"Channel open," the IU said. "*Antilles* orbiter in range."

"*Antilles*. This is Specialist Cleo Patricia Xavier. I've sustained injury and . . ."

Mission abort. Say it. Cleo imagined herself warming the rockets and then launching the capsule against this faint gravity, back to the comforts of weightlessness. "*Antilles*, do you read? Over."

No one answered, and Cleo had half expected that. She was still in that dark space of her mind. *I'll die here*, she knew it, and that would be her last recorded word—*over*.

"This is *Antilles* . . ." Daniel's voice over the radio. "Cleo, I read you but no copy. Please, say again. Over."

Repeat? It was her voice, everything still half swollen or inflamed—lips, tongue, larynx. Cleo cleared her throat. She inhaled deeply, then exhaled her words. "This is Engineer Cleo Xavier." She took a breath. "I've incurred injury." Another breath. "I will begin prepping medical procedures."

"Injury?" Daniel said. "Cleo, what happened? Over."

"My visor broke, and it just . . ." She remembered now, not that she had forgotten, but saying it brought the images to mind. "I got caught in the, uh . . ." She imagined herself whipping in Orbis Alius's winds like a kite, crashing down as atmosphere and pressure poured into her helmet. "My helmet broke and . . ." Her eyes welled up, but she couldn't cry through the swelling. "Shakes—my rover pulled me in. I've been here three days, and none of you . . ."

Her voice went terminal, and Daniel didn't fill the empty space. Cleo's words were so jumbled and her throat so full of glass that she'd be surprised if he understood any of it.

"Three days?" Daniel eventually said, and in confusion. "Not three, Cleo. It's been six days, almost."

Six days. "But . . ." It didn't make sense. "Why?" No one thought to check on her?

"Sorry, I think you broke up. Why what? Over?"

"Nothing," she said, her despair now turning into anger. "Nothing—"

"What's your status?" Daniel asked. "How bad are your injuries."

Pretty goddamn bad, she wanted to scream. Instead, she whispered, "Six days? You're sure?"

"Eight hours short of six days," he confirmed. "Can you run me through your accident, Cleo? I need to log this. Over."

"I got caught in the storm, Daniel," she said, hostility in her tone. "My visor shattered. The dust and the air poured in . . ." Cleo breathed there to stop from crying. "I was choking and blacked out." She made a faux clearing of her throat, which helped to hold the breaking of her voice. "But my line was tied to my rover, and so . . . it brought me back in. I woke up here three days—no—six days later."

"Cleo?" He heard something in her voice, didn't he? "You okay? Over?"

"No." Jeez, was he listening? "No, Daniel, I'm not okay."

"What's your medical? I'm overriding your capsule controls."

"Don't," she said, but it was his choice. Pilots had discretion on whether to take control of the machinery within the capsule, including cameras. And she didn't want him to see her undressed, with diarrhea stains running down her inner thigh. "Don't. Please."

"I won't."

Another long pause then. It hurt, being an afterthought. She had always been the person no one ever noticed, the one who wasn't invited to the parties. And even when she was there, it was as if she wasn't. She was still that invisible girl, that narrow-bodied background noise. She thought about the days of bleeding and hallucinations, of that quiet God whispering for her to "find us." And none of her crew had the mind to notice that Cleo wasn't there.

"Why didn't you call down?" Cleo asked. "None of you. Six days? Six, Daniel? And no one thought to check on me?"

Why'd you say that? That wasn't her, that fragility, that unprofessional elocution. Where'd it come from? That neediness. Now Cleo had to stew in the static while he thought of something kind and false to say.

"We didn't . . . You returned to your capsule and . . . Because I can see that, your suit's signal. It was inside. So I knew that you were safe—I thought you were. And I did send messages. Last one was two days ago. Austin reached out too, but we just figured you were . . ."

"What?"

"We know about the auditives," he said, then quickly followed up as if apologizing: "But it's okay. It's all right. We all have our ways of coping."

But that apology made her more upset. And he kept going—kept on apologizing. Describing her usefulness to the team. Her importance. The mention of family members—Dad, Ava, and even Finn was on Cleo's emergency contact list. And he was just listing off names and corporate speech.

"Just . . ." She shook her head; it wasn't helping. "It's fine."

"On the *Antilles*," Daniel continued anyway, "you had that week where you didn't come out of your cabin once. I don't know if it was auditives or—"

"Stop bringing up auditives."

"Okay. But especially at the end, you would spend full-on weeks in the cabin. Cleo, you scored highest on the deprivation tank examinations back in Havana. MCs said you're immune to isolation."

And that was her superpower. Even before the rigors of spaceflight, Cleo would self-isolate for months. During the sulfur hurricanes over Neo Oistins. Three months of social chaos and she spent all of it in her apartment, following submersion artists or updating Dad every few days. She had maybe seen Finn twice.

"With everything that's going on," Daniel continued, "we should be more vigilant. I should be. It's on me—"

"I'm fine," Cleo interrupted, her voice put back together. She was whole again in an instant. "Wait . . . what's 'everything that's going on'?"

"Oh," he said. "Damn. You don't know. You don't—"

"Know what?" Cleo asked.

He paused. She heard him breathing. "You should get rest, Cleo. Run a body scan. I can take a look from up here."

"What?" Cleo insisted. "What is it?"

"Nothing." He said it fast, trying to move on.

"Gonna isolate me again?" Guilt him? That wasn't like her either, but he owed her at this point. "Tell me."

Daniel paused again, and it was longer, his breathing heavier. "There are a few things, uh . . . Specialist Yasmin Boston. She's been doing her own thing for a while. Not sure what, but it sure as hell isn't pre-terraform procedure. And she turned off her immersives too. More than a billion followers back on Earth can't immerse in Boston anymore."

Huh. But Cleo wasn't so surprised to hear that. Boston's obsession with the orbital origins of this planet had steered her to confide in Cleo. How many millions of followers would she lose, and how many more billions in advertising dollars: the Coke Zero-G endorsement, Ray-Ban helmet lenses?

"Has she said why?" Cleo asked. "Boston tell you her reasoning?"

"No. She's . . . not herself, I guess. But that's all irrelevant right now. There's been talk of real investment in this planet."

"What?" she said, nearly shouting, and it really did hurt. Cleo cleared her throat. "Posties—the Apostles?"

"Everyone," he said, tempering the animation in his voice. "Just . . . everyone." He had even stopped saying "over" after his transmissions. Daniel was genuinely excited. "NASA, India, CNSA. Everybody."

How? she thought. "How is that possible?" There was nothing here. Nothing but rocks and sulfur, radiation beneath the topsoil. And the cold. It would take a century to terraform. At least. "No," she said. "That doesn't make sense."

"There's an abundance of water bubbling up from underground. Austin found a way to distill it. And now with the planet rotating toward the sun, that ice is starting to melt. At least, that's his theory. But now he's experimenting with the soil, the deeper layers."

"It's radioactive."

"About a mile deeper, yes. But the soil is rich, Earthlike."

"The soil . . . Earthlike? How?"

"I'm not the geologist, but that's what the IUs are reading."

Then she remembered that mirage out in the desert, an infant weed bursting out from alien soil. But that had been drug-induced mania, hadn't it? Had to be, right? That dirt was glassy, dry, smut. There was no breathable air—not even a mouthful. Two rays of sunlight. That green was a myopic fantasy.

"But forget all of that. How bad are you down there? Do you think you need a mission abort? Relaunch back to the *Antilles*? Over."

There it was. Cleo knew the question was coming and still didn't have the answer. She considered relaunching, climbing the rungs of atmosphere to the comforts of zero gravity. Back to Daniel and the MCs' groupthink. She was not a team thinker like them, but she would play the role. Cuz screw this planet.

"Xavier . . . ?"

Xavier. The name echoed in her head. Because what would Dad think? Cleo Patricia Xavier, the first astronaut to retreat . . . It didn't sound right in her head, and she said it again with different words, a different tone. But still, it was wrong.

"No," she said, leaning forward, kneeling, trying to get her feet underneath her. "Negative on mission abort."

"You're sure? We could get you back on the *Antilles* with a direct line to everyone back home . . ." A tone interrupted Daniel's speech. Austin or Boston trying to get through. "And the MCs' medical staff looking after you."

"I'm good with Mission Control's med staff. But thank you."

He chuckled, and that audio gap came again. Someone was trying to connect with him up there. His MCs, maybe, Austin or Boston with their soil samples.

"Hey, I'm all right," Cleo said, lifting herself up, climbing to her feet, and standing finally. "You don't even need to log this. I'm fine, really. I hear you have another transmission."

"Copy," he said, and there was something in his tone, something like relief. "I just sent some painkiller dosage. But I'll check in again before I rotate over."

"Copy," she said.

"Good. Over and out, Cleo."

Over and out.

Daniel's painkiller dosage recommendations floated midair in front of her. But Cleo hobbled right through the projected image. She had true painkillers. Auditives wouldn't do anything to soothe the pain of internal swelling, frostbitten skin, and the endless ringing of ruptured eardrums. Every nerve ending rioted against her body.

Cleo excavated three "marble" stowaways she had hidden amid the hundreds of trial plant seeds in her organics drawers. These marbles were actually dimethyltryptamine-T, or a DMT Trigger, also known as a Kill Pill or KP and even Kristaps Porziņģis. It had a hundred names and a hundred laws against it. Unlike auditives, the Kill Pill was as dangerous a drug as its uninspired nickname implied. It killed you—dead, in the literal sense of the word. The user would be brain-dead for varying lengths of time, depending on the dosage, to see over the edge of mortality before the neuro-defibrillators within the pill snapped you back to resurrection. The actual high of it was the natural DMT released into the brain. A hallucinogen, the same type that may have killed her mother. Users would see their neurological nirvana and maybe their God too.

She remembered dreaming of Orbis's God this morning. The dream deity had told her to come find him.

Okay, she responded.

Three genres of death in those three marbles: head shot, drowning dream, or run over by octobus. She had a phobia of drowning and an even greater fear of octopuses, so she didn't even want to know what the hell an octobus was. *Head shot it is*, she thought, lying back and placing the marble into the pit of her navel.

These were Eli's pills. After he had passed away, she found his stash mixed in with the space-nausea medicines. She never mentioned that to anyone, hoping it might make him look better in his end. She truly hadn't planned on using them. Cleo had meddled with this level of drug only once, and that was with her ex-fiancé, Finn. This was his world: the drugs and tattoos, his whole retro-Rastafarian lifestyle. The marble dissolved into her navel, and like its name, the head shot was goddamn fast—bang. Painless, and thankfully she'd remain that way for the rest of the night.

6

Whatever it was that had Mission Control so excited remained a mystery to Cleo. She wasn't in the circle of secrecy looped around this planet. She was out of that loop, out of every loop, and it was better that way. *Silence is the quietest genre of music*, Dad used to say. He was never much into music.

She was on drugs again today—the prescribed kinds: indocin, ocufen, codeine, clot-busters like thrombolytic, and TPA. It was now a month on Orbis Alius and eight days since Cleo's misadventure outside, and the physicians at Mission Control had placed her in this medicated daze. She didn't just lurch when she walked; Cleo looked like a woman hanging over the cliff of her own torso, teetering over herself and ready to fall. The drug fugue made mazes out of her fingers, and picking up a bottle or even typing was a complex bending around the corners and curves of individual knuckles. Speaking was even more challenging, her tongue almost like a paintbrush. Cleo needed to dip her tongue in saliva to lap the words, to lick at vowels. Even now her mouth felt numb, like it wasn't there. Like she wasn't there. But God was. She still heard its voice, ungendered and quieter but still there. *Find us*.

A sudden bubbling of nausea rose in her chest and fell like waves inside her, but she would never actually throw up. And that was worse. Cleo wished she could just get it out, whatever was stuck inside.

Besides the twenty-some-odd physicians, only Austin had reached out to Cleo, sending well-wishes in the most eloquent of voices. He told her that she was a part of the mission's new successes and that her efforts would never be forgotten. Somehow that sounded more like a eulogy than anything else, but she appreciated it, especially since Boston hadn't contacted her or anyone else in days. And Daniel, shit—he had done something Cleo hadn't expected: He blamed the ordeal on her.

Mission Control had posted Daniel's report on Cleo's injuries, and he had proposed that the entire incident was due to her negligence. Daniel's MCs must have placed him under an official review or something. They must have used words like *evaluation*, *authorized inquiry*, or *legally binding*, because his backbone snapped backward and coiled up in a snakelike shape. He said that he had advised her to go back, flee the storm. Daniel had implored her—begged, he said—but it was Cleo who broke protocol. Then he used words like *reckless*, *negligent . . . drug abuse*. A desperate attempt to polish his career. He had shed his skin, and now she saw him, leather-faced and smiling through two poisonous fangs. He hadn't contacted her afterward either; Daniel had coiled up in his shame. His only contact had been to relay the medical staff's video messaging and a pair of written emails from her dad.

Cleo turned to her drone. It sat untouched in the corner of the capsule. The dragonfly head was all that had survived. The simple task of unscrewing the metal shell felt daunting in her medicated state. Then detaching the CPU, and syncing the I-input with the *Antilles* IU—that felt impossible.

But she'd go sober for the next few hours because she needed to eat and drink, because she'd need to piss one good time without wetting herself, but mostly to screw Olivia Noah. The head medical adviser at Mission Control. She'd previously served as Cleo's shrink, her mental health inquisitor in deep space. But now Olivia ran a hundred tests—pee, poop, and blood—and forwarded them to specialists from eleven different areas of expertise. Everyone in the world was examining her colon. If Olivia had to outsource all this information, then what was the point of her?

"Incoming transmission," the *Antilles* IU told her as the holoscreen appeared in front of her and YASMIN BOSTON flashed on the screen. A video-call request.

It had been two weeks since they'd last spoken, Cleo's accident the main cause of disconnection. But Daniel had mentioned that something was off about Boston recently. Cleo tapped in, and Boston's image appeared on the holoscreen. She was fully suited up, pressurized in her EMU and vaping within the helmet. Marlboro was a sponsor, and the gold, diamond-encrusted nostril-vape was also a jewelry accessory. The red-dye tobacco swirled through the helmet, obscuring her cinematic eyes. This would've been great advertising, but no one was watching.

"Good copy?" Cleo started formally, then cleared her throat just in case she sounded loopy from the drugs. "You reading me? Over."

"I read," Boston said. "We've only got a couple minutes."

"For . . ." Then Cleo noticed the time. The *Antilles* was about to fall over the edge of the world. Same twilight hours as the last time she'd called. *Why?*

"It's the hack," Boston said, as if she had read Cleo's mind. "Pass over is the best time to hack the signal because it all gets spooky anyway and they brush it off as white noise." Then she leaned in toward the screen. "Swollen up pretty good there. Did you miss the AST training for not taking off your helmet outside?"

Cleo smiled. "This . . ." She gestured to the swelling around her eyes and lips. "It's much improved. Two days ago . . ." She shook her head. "I was a balloon."

"Got to take care of yourself, Xavier. Who else am I going to conspire with?"

Cleo's smile widened. Boston's unfeigned concern surprised her. And not just surprise—there was something warm in the chestnut brown of Boston's eyes, like maybe she needed Cleo too.

"I solved it," Boston said, exhaling another forest-dye swirl of nicotine this time.

"The orbital-history problem?"

"Yup," Boston said. "You know what a Rubik's Cube is?"

Rube? Cleo shook her head. "No. What's a . . ." But she didn't want to muddle the pronunciation. *Why?* she wondered. *Oh, you want her to like you now? To think you're smart?* Ava's voice in her head. Years of therapy and there it was, loud as ever.

"A Rubik's Cube," Boston said. "A children's toy a couple centuries back. A cube with nine squares on each side. The goal was to have the same color on every side and—"

"Wait . . ." Cleo interrupted. "Yeah, I've seen those. Cube with the square colors. Yeah, yeah, yeah."

"Right. So imagine the universe as a Rubik's Cube. Orbis wasn't here two hundred and seventy-one years ago. But like one square on a Rubik's Cube, it was folded in . . ." There was a long pause of nothing.

"The planet folded in space?" Cleo said, and shaking her head, saying no, that was impossible.

"The math works," Boston snapped defensively. "I don't know what to tell you. I'd say check it yourself, but we don't have that type of time."

She could get like that—snappy. Boston was moody, and genius was the excuse. But Cleo didn't react. Dad had told her once, maybe twice, to try not to think like herself. *Try to think like others, bumblebee.* Cleo had never had many friends, and he tried to teach her to be a team player. Boston wasn't calling for any calculations. No, she didn't need help with the arithmetic. She just wanted to talk. That was the difference between Cleo and everyone else. She could carry her own burdens. She wasn't weak. But right now, she could hear the fragility in Boston's voice.

"If you say the math works out, then it works out," Cleo said. "You're the best mathematician on the planet. I'm only third best."

Boston nearly smiled, then burped out a blond nicotine haze.

"What fragrance are you smoking?" Cleo asked.

"Rainbow Rosé." Boston stuck out her rainbow-scarred tongue and smiled. "I've been tracking the gravitational waves along the path of that orbit. Orbis Alius's ripple pattern can be tracked backward about five billion miles, but before that . . . nothing."

"Numbers aren't my thing . . ." Cleo admitted, surprising herself into a sharp pause. Where had that come from? Maybe it was Boston and her badly hidden vulnerability. Yeah, maybe that had something to do with it.

"You don't understand?" Boston asked. "Any of it?"

Cleo breathed deep, then answered, "No." And that one word weighed more than an entire speech.

"That's fine," Boston said with finality, like the conversation was done.

"I mean . . ." Cleo blurted out, not wanting it to be done. "I get the whole history of the orbit doesn't make sense. And the math only works if Orbis was folded into our solar system like a Rubik's Cube. But what are you really saying, Boston?"

"There's something seriously fucking wrong with this planet, Xavier. Like . . . next, next level wrong. I showed them my math. The MCs . . . jeez, Mission Control, I mean. Sorry, he's got me saying it now. Spencer, the Trini with lung enhancers. He agrees. The math is right. The world manifested in our solar system from God knows where, and they don't care. They just shrug and keep it moving. All excited about current events. Nobody's looking into the history of this rock."

"Current events?" Cleo asked quickly, hearing the approach of oncoming static. "What's the excitement about?"

"You haven't been outside . . . ?" Boston said, then remembered. "Oh, right, the injury."

"What's outside?" Cleo asked.

"Better you take a look yourself," she said and shook her head like whatever it was scared her. "You won't miss it. I'm signing off. See you at the meeting tomorrow."

And before Cleo could respond, Boston was gone. Cleo glanced at the emails. There was a meeting tomorrow; they called it an assembly, and it was a big one. She scrolled down the list of attendees:

NASA? NOEL Industries. Cleo leaned into the screen now, scrolling slower: CNSA representatives and the ISRO. All these bigwigs just for some dirt?

Cleo checked the outdoor cameras and saw the same rocks and wind that had injured her days earlier. She ran radial scans and picked up nothing but fluxes in atmospherics. She asked the IU to run its own scan "and search for anomalies." It took only seconds. The cameras focused in on a spot of pale green growing out of the soil. The very seeds from her organics tests, meant to illustrate how quickly they would decay on this planet, were growing.

7

She overslept the day of the assembly. Her dreams ran long and unfinished, dreams of grassy roads and a path to God and a devil too. She dreamed it was all here, just beyond the air-lock doors. But twenty minutes before the assembly, Shakes whistled for Cleo to wake up, telling her the caffeine would be her makeup. It was in the gray cup, already prepared, and so she washed her mouth out with the java. Then she slapped on a caffeine patch for good measure as the call came to log in five minutes early.

Kinetic projectors sprayed images of a conference room into the space in front of her. Stale four-hour-old light lit Cleo's capsule to a grayed, overcast Havana afternoon. The projectors lit with such laser precision that they played tricks on the eyes. No visual contrast could be discerned between the projection and actually sitting among them, in person.

The lasers projected well-dressed minglers swapping laughter and the introverts quietly sipping glasses of water and wine. Prime Minister Rowe shuffled his way through the buffet of well-manicured handshakes, then posed for the photogs hanging in the wings and snapping photos. A quiet competition of designer suits and dresses was on display as well. Every aisle and row was a runway of flamboyant Caribbean hues and camo-coded fabrics that changed color in different lighting temperatures. And their wrist wealth bridged the four-hour time gap. They all represented some party of interest with trillion-dollar purses propping up their smiles.

But truthfully, there was something wrong with this world; she just hadn't been paying full attention. First, there were surface scans. For the past month, the *Antilles* laser scans and radio and X-ray imaging had attempted to penetrate the layers of cumulus and map the planet's surface. But after 257 separate attempts, nothing had been revealed. Only the few square miles surrounding their capsules were plotted. Ninety-nine percent of Orbis Alius's surface was still uncharted. That was absurd. Every probe launched into the planet's atmosphere disappeared, just like Austin's and Boston's Hummingbird drones, and just like hers.

Then there were the patches of weeds sprouting from alien soil. These organics were bioengineered to be tough, "resilient germs" made for non-Earthlike conditions. But Orbis was a feral world, rabid and snarling its glassy soil teeth. The extremes in temperature and atmos alone should have been a natural vasectomy to every seed.

But worst of all was the math, an algorithm so tall Cleo couldn't envisage its peak. The AST outwardly admitted that Boston's solution worked, and they didn't care. Every AST chair smelled capital investment. Michael Rowe's political gambit paid dividends, lending him a new term in office. They were already calling it a miracle world, the next Venus. Advertisers like Ford were proposing a new campaign for Orbis rugged transports. And Mount Gay rum imagined Austin pouring the liquor into the dirt and coconut trees rising skyward. But they weren't down here. They didn't hear the invitations whistling in the dark. There was no other life in the universe, or so they said, but what about a god?

The chatter quieted and pulled Cleo's attention back to the projection. Prime Minister Rowe stepped in front and center, smiling and waving, his nostrils flaring as the perfume of campaign contributions wafted in the air. "Out of poverty and into space," he gloated and they applauded, standing, then hollering, each competing with the others. "Yes . . . Yes. Thank you. Please." He gestured for them to sit like he was the conductor and they the orchestra. "And good morning to you, our brave explorers," he said directly to her, Austin, and Boston in their own capsules, and to Daniel in the *Antilles*. "As you may know, the initial reading on this world has changed in a significant way. We now realize that the planet has seasons, and what you experienced for the first four weeks was at the tail end of winter. The planet has warmed significantly in the past thirteen days, and as of today is only a few degrees below freezing."

"Seasons?" Cleo said and turned to her rover. "It's not seasons." But what did she know? Maybe the MCs were right.

"Now, we can make small talk with the age-old *How's the weather up there?*" A few soft chuckles came from the crowd. "I mean, what terraforms a more human environment than a conversation?" Fewer chuckles now, the joke having worn out its welcome. "We, uh . . ." He cleared his throat. "We believe these seasons are tied more to tidal heating. Between the planet and the sun. There appears to be more tidal flexing in its . . . apsis?" he asked someone outside the projector's range. "Apsis," Rowe confirmed. "It will go through a period now of two years in standard units, of spring and summer. That's at least what early estimates are revealing at this point."

Tidal friction, Cleo thought. "This is BS." She turned to Shakes again. "They just cooked something up for the investors. They don't know what's going on, and they're just—"

"But that is not the most interesting development." Rowe teased it out, that jaw and smile working together to reel them in. "The most interesting development is that this warmth has created lightning storms over the planet's surface. One of our brave terraformers found herself caught in one."

"He's going to say electrolysis," Boston said. She had opened her line of transmission.

"Clear the line," Austin said.

Cleo agreed with him for once. Quiet. She wanted to hear this.

"These storms," Rowe continued, "provided a nearly nonstop reign of lightning. This creates hydroxyls in the upper atmosphere and oxygen in the lower. Oxygen."

"This doesn't make sense," Boston said, clogging the line again, but none of them responded.

"So what does this all mean?" Rowe asked rhetorically. "The early estimates from the Atlantic Space Trade and our new partners—in NASA, the CNSA, and NOEL Industries to name a few—are that only nine standard terraforming expeditions would be needed to create planetary conditions habitable for colonization." They all gasped in unison—Rowe's orchestra. "We see this planet second only to Venus in both population and resources. Along with the support of twelve other national and private space agencies, we are declaring Orbis Alius as Earth-3."

Holy shit, and she wasn't the only one thinking it. The entire panel whispered their own curses and exchanged glances and conversation.

"Quiet, please," Rowe tried, raising his voice over the rumble of the crowd. But he didn't try hard enough or speak loud enough or . . . Was this on purpose? The more he hushed them, the more rambunctious the mob grew. Investors immediately tapped their earpieces, calling out stock prices. Reporters and bonds shifted in their direction.

Look at that mob, even though she tried not to. Like ants swarming along overripe plantains. They maneuvered with that sort of orderly chaos. A single line, but nearly crawling all over each other.

"This world is not Venus," Boston said. "It's not Earth-2."

"They called it Earth-3," Daniel responded. "They're upending Titan and Ganymede to provide for us. This is a good thing."

They were quiet after that. Daniel's comment had soured the conversation before it started. For Cleo, at least; maybe Austin and Boston were considering what he had said. Cleo just hated the sound of his voice. Monotone, an echo chamber for Mission Control. His precious MCs.

Rowe offered more details, adding legal terms as well as additional funding and an extension of their contracts. Illegal months were tacked on to the *Antilles* crew through contractual loopholes, and those unlawful months came with tax-exempt millions—$108 million per engineer. With the additional endorsements, none of them would have to work again.

And there was little time to consider any of this as news of a second, third, and fourth expedition to Orbis was announced, and they weren't coming from Earth. One was leaving from Saturn's moon Titan, and it would have the closest approach. Then a second from a survey mission orbiting the satellite Triton would allocate resources to Orbis, just a few tons of provisions and water. There was a ripple effect there. The Triton crew would then receive resources from a Uranus weather research mission. The Uranus crew would in turn receive resources from Saturn's ring mining mission. That ripple would go all the way back to Earth, where emergency launches would be sent up every other day to compensate. Their mission was sapping resources from every other moon and planet in the solar system.

Cleo tapped in. "Are we going to talk about this?" she asked.

"It's a lot," Austin said. "We'll discuss, but let's just get through this."

But now everyone was on the line and cutting each other off as the transmission hissed with static.

"They're sending more people," Boston said, finally getting through. "The Triton orbiter will be here in eight months."

"And their provisions will help the extra few months go by faster," Daniel said.

"They can't send more . . ." Boston said, then seemed to lose her voice.

"You'd rather we be out here solo, all lone-star and everything?" Daniel asked.

"Lone-star?" Boston shot back. "What does that mean? Look, we don't even have a map for ninety-nine percent of the planet. We don't know what's out there."

Austin cleared his throat. His deep and resonant tone seemed to clear the airwaves. "In a month or two, three thousand astronomers, navigators, terraformers, and their families are going to round their planet's orbit and slingshot this way. There is nothing we can do about that but work hard and pave a way. Please, we can discuss afterward. They're bringing out our families."

Cleo leaned forward, squinting, trying to make out the faces in the crowd. Dad stood next to Ava. Daniel's mother and his sister and so many nephews and nieces stood to their right. Boston's mother was accompanied by several fans, and Austin's adoptive parents stood hand in hand. They waved at the camera, saying their hellos as the microphone passed from person to person, eventually finding its way to Dad.

"Good evening," Dad started. "Wunna good?" *Wunna* was an old-country colloquialism meaning "you all" and even on Neo Oistins was rarely heard. That little part of Dad's speech was just for her. "I call Cleo my li'l bumblebee cuz of the yellow-and-black Bajan flag she wore when she was a girl." He held up a book, the smile swelling into his cheeks. "So, *The Porcupine Inside Out* was Cleo's favorite book as a little girl." It was. "Just need to embarrass her a little bit . . ."

"Not embarrassed," she whispered.

"My, uh . . ." A pause there, so brief that only she would notice. "My daughter has made me very proud. I am a true proud old man."

Dad reluctantly passed the microphone, hesitating as if there was just one more thing to say. And each subsequent family member did the same, voicing only a phrase or two as if there was limited time and structure to their discourse. The opening lines captured a smile or laughter, and the last sentences were sentimental, bringing tears to the audience's eyes. And even though she saw the simplicity of that wedding speech structure, Cleo smiled and teared up at her father's words.

Rowe made a closing statement, then handed off the microphone to AST leadership, who touched ever so gently on the idea that there were "unique features to the planet that we do not yet understand." But she asked for "patience" from the crew during these "early days of discovery." And that was it. The quiet hum of the kinetic projector went dead. The capsule went dark and the broadcast ended.

The four of them agreed to take an hour to digest things. "Let it marinate," Austin told them. "Read the transcripts. We'll record an official response together."

Official response? Cleo mused. And recorded? She glanced into the mirror, wondering what Dad might think seeing her swollen face. The transcripts, with details on the salary increases and term lengths, were in their inboxes. But Cleo didn't as so much as glance at any numbers. She spent the hour biting into a sugar cake and sipping on sorrel as she fixed her mess of hair. The swelling somehow seemed worse. But maybe that was from lack of sleep. She slapped another caffeine patch on her leg, hoping that somehow the synthetic coffee might bring down the swelling under her eyes.

"Swelling's mostly gone, right?" Cleo asked her rover, even though her cheeks and eyes were still a bit puffy. "Yesterday Boston said I looked okay, so . . ."

"Don't know what she *said but*—you look like a *headbutt*—"

"Fine," Cleo said, cutting the rover off before it could rhyme any further. Because she saw the butt-like roundness in her still-swollen cheeks. "Never mind."

"And when you speak, you're *twerking*. Wuk up and your four-head's *jerking*."

"Thank you, Shakes," she scolded. She turned to the rover with hands clasped like she was praying and bowed. "Thank you. Appreciate the honesty."

YASMIN BOSTON flashed in the air in front of her. Cleo tapped in fast—maybe she could get a second opinion before they recorded a message for the entire world to see. Yasmin appeared on the holoscreen with mascara-lit eyelashes and red-streaked lips to color her words. Her ethnicities intersected in circles. Her Afro-Indian and Latina features harmonized from the natural curl in her hair to the curves in her bone structure.

But as Cleo focused on the person in front of her, she noticed Boston's eyes appeared dislocated from the rest of her features. Her blinks flicked out of sync. Red, sleepless eyes, and dried crimson filled the cleft between her lips and nostrils. A nosebleed? Or just messy eating?

"Boston?" Cleo questioned, as if she might be talking to the wrong person.

"Cleo—" Boston said fast and leaned closer to the video receiver. "There's a vote. Whether to remain in an extension period."

"What? I don't . . ." Cleo stuttered. She couldn't get over Boston's look.

"They're going to ask us to vote on whether we extend our stay by a few months."

"How do you know?"

"I know," Boston said. She was sure, and trembled with that sureness. "You'll back me up?"

"Why . . ." Something was wrong. "What's wrong?"

"The planet, Cleo." Boston shook her head as if words alone couldn't convey it. "There's something wrong here, and it's not even the equation anymore or the weeds outside. It's . . ."

It's what? Cleo waited for an answer that never came. "What?"

"You won't believe me." She wiped a wet right eye. "You don't believe in . . ."

"I don't believe in what?"

"God."

Cleo's heart dropped to her gut. "What'd you say?"

"You see, you won't . . ." Then she started fixing her hair and wiping her eyes. "Just vote with me. Don't leave me alone on this. Please."

"No—*no*. Just tell me. What do you mean *God*?" Then Cleo realized why Boston was sweeping her hair and wiping her eyes.

Daniel's image flashed in midair in front of Cleo. He had just tapped in. His nap-red eyes and a saliva-stretched yawn told the story of how he'd spent his hour.

"Hey, guys," he said.

"You take a nap?" Boston asked, the weakness in her voice long, long gone.

"Power nap," he said, rubbing the red from his eyes.

A final holoscreen manifested in the air, and Austin sat with his space suit on, helmet off, as he loosened the straps around his neck. He had just come in from outside, and yet his hair was neatly combed. Lotions and lip gloss shone on his face.

"So . . ." Austin sighed the word. "Here we are. I should say congratulations, first. Very few believed in us, and we succeeded where no one else could. Now Mission Control has asked that we vote on whether to sign the contractual agreements to stay. And I, for one, believe that we dig in. Spend the extra few months and finish the mission. Not for us, but for everyone else."

"I agree," Daniel said, and so immediately it was almost as if it was choreographed.

Cleo could see the lines being drawn, one between the men and Boston. But Cleo wasn't floating right between them. She wasn't sure what side she was on. Not yet.

"I vote no," Boston said, quickly breaking into any momentum Austin was building.

"And what's the reasoning behind it?" Austin asked her.

"I thought we were just voting?" Boston said. "My reasons are my own. I vote no."

"Well, my reasoning," Austin countered very strategically, "is twofold. One, the financial incentive. We're talking over a hundred million in hand upon our return. And an eighth of one percent in the planet's net evaluation."

That was new.

"Wait . . ." Daniel seemed to hear but not believe. Or was this strategy again? The two of them trying to sway the vote? "Say it again."

Boston answered, "One-eighth of a percent of this planet, we would own."

"Fine print," Austin said. "Didn't you read the contractual obligations?"

No, evidently neither she nor Daniel had. Shares worth one-eighth of 1 percent, that was generational wealth—her great-grandchildren would be eating from the buffet of that bequest. Even if Orbis ended up being the lowest-valued planet in the system, each of them would hit eleven figures.

"I vote yes." Daniel raised his hand as he voiced his vote, like the good schoolboy at whatever institution he was attending.

"Good," Austin replied. "That's two vote yes to . . . still no, Boston?"

"Still no," she said.

Shit, Cleo thought as every eye turned to her. But Boston's look weighed especially heavy on her.

"Cleo?" Austin called to her. "What's your vote?"

"I vote n—"

"No." Boston spoke for her.

"That's not what she said," Austin interrupted. "Let her speak for herself."

"The MCs are all rooting for us back there," Daniel chimed in. "All of them."

"They are," Austin agreed.

Cleo felt sideways about her decision now. And it wasn't even the duo tag-teaming her; it was the mob. That swarm of influence, not just Daniel and Austin but the hundred-eyed monster at Mission Control, the physicians and sponsors and all their dollars, even Crime Minister Rowe, a proud Dad, and even an ex-fiancé in his basement tattoo parlor. Their numbers absorbed her. She wanted it so badly. That wasn't peer pressure, it was an aversion to isolation.

"I vote . . ." And Cleo gave in right there; right at that moment, the mob-mind consumed her. "Yes. But my reasoning—"

"Good," Austin said. "It's okay. It's settled."

Cleo wanted to explain to them and Boston, especially Boston, but there was no reasoning behind her decision. Not a single thought sparked in her head—that answer just slithered up from the lizard brain. Something primordial and cold-blooded had moved through her.

But Boston didn't appear to react. The Idol simply lifted her eyes, internalizing, then it was like a light bulb lit behind her irises. She was thinking up something.

"What's the other reason?" Boston aimed her question at Austin. "You said your reasoning was twofold."

"For all of us," Austin said. "We're doing this for the Caribbean. For all of humanity. The furthest planetary outpost. Gateway to the interstellar. We have a responsibility for the collective. For all humankind."

A responsibility for the collective, that was the AST's motto etched in fine print on the chest of the space suits, for all humankind. But weirdly that market-researched slogan appeared to strike a chord with Boston. She nodded her head in quiet contemplation, then smiled.

"Change my vote, then," she said. "I vote yes too."

"Excellent," Austin said, smiling without the sincerity of teeth. "Unanimous, then. I'll write a message for Daniel to relay to mission control—no need to record anything." He nodded, proud of them—proud of himself. "This is the right decision. And I'm glad we're all in agreement. You all have a good rest of your day. Thank you."

Daniel tapped out first. And that was good. Austin disappeared next. Then it was just the women, and Cleo didn't want to leave. Not yet. And she saw the same look in Boston's eyes.

"Sorry, I—" Cleo started.

"No," Boston interrupted. "I understand."

"You do?" Cleo said, because she didn't truly understand what had just happened herself.

"I understand," Boston said again.

"Understand what?"

"The collective," Boston said. "Responsibility for the collective. For all humankind. I need to figure this thing out."

"God . . ." Cleo probed. "You said, earlier."

But Boston stared at Cleo in the same way Dad did before, like there was one more thing to say that she didn't. Boston forced a flustered smile, then signed off.

8

Cleo didn't sleep that night, but somehow she managed to dream—dreaming of a wild god stalking the grasslands outside. *Wild*, she imagined, undomesticated of any institution or parish that might tame away the Greek rape and virgin sacrifice. In a universe empty of any alien life, could gods breed in this cosmic wilderness?

"No," Cleo said, stopping herself before her imagination went too far. "That doesn't make sense," she whispered, quiet enough that Shakes wouldn't scold her for talking to herself. "It's just a dream."

But she wanted to know whether Boston was having that same dream. Boston had brought up the idea of God twice already. Twice, and that meant something. Cleo's mind ran through the night, trying to fit the pieces together—was it just her, or Boston too? And what about Austin, because he was down here just like the rest of them?

The other reason she couldn't sleep, and maybe the real reason, was the absence of painkillers. The pain unwound every injury, like onions peeled back to the nerve. Cleo writhed with that unwinding, twisting leg over leg, arm into arm. She wondered if her own body was procrastinating recovery. How could it still hurt this much? But she wouldn't capitulate to the prescriptions—better the stinging in her lungs than the nausea, or that burning in her urine, or the dizziness that seemed to stretch one leg to uneven lengths and made her limp.

Cleo waited for Boston to make contact. She sat against the wall, anticipation building as she picked at the gauze around her neck until the whole thing unraveled. The swelling had receded, but rashes lingered. Unbalanced pigments of browns and purples zigzagged up her neck, zebrine along the mandible curve to the backside of her ears. And she was still waiting with nothing more to pick at.

Boston never made contact, not that day nor the next nor the day after that. In those three days, Cleo made up her own theories. It was something airborne. The dreams didn't start until she'd sucked down a mouthful of Orbis's toxic air. She tested her blood, and there were strange numbers in the hematology analysis. The *Antilles* IU suggested auditive residue—it was the drug music in her. But Shakes was a separate IU with separate opinions. Her rover said it resembled a tethered gene, a blood anomaly it had never seen.

Cleo messaged Boston by the end of that week. But she didn't answer. And whether she was upset or just asleep, deep down Cleo was glad Boston didn't pick up. There was still a heavy set of guilt in her.

But as static crackled in her earpiece, Cleo tensed up. Boston was calling back. Then, as Cleo reached to tap in, she found an unexpected name on the holoscreen: ANTILLES. It was Daniel. She tapped in with a bit of irritation and relief.

"Xavier," Daniel said, his voice choppy under a drizzle of static. "This is the *Antilles* overhead. I have Austin here for you. Over."

He sounded nervous, like a boy who'd just been scolded.

"Copy, *Antilles*. Austin—sure. Connect us . . ."

"I'm here, Xavier." Austin's voice boomed first over the speaker, then his image appeared on the holoscreen half a second after. He flickered like a flame in the interference. "How are your injuries? Over."

"Good," she said. "Ready to step back outside, I think."

"Of course," he said. "We need you back out there." His voice echoed deep and motivating. Austin didn't just have the mind for leadership, he had the anatomy for it. "We see you've been running blood samples and urine." She tensed, muscles and mind, and no response surfaced. "Over?"

"Yeah . . ." She nodded. "Just blood tests. To see how I'm healing."

That was a lie, and it felt like he saw it in the narrowing of his eyes.

"You know, Boston was running similar tests. That's the only reason we ask."

We ask? Who else was asking? Daniel, the MCs, or the whole AST?

"She find anything?" Cleo asked.

"There's nothing in our blood . . ." His voice slipped there, unlike him, but Austin recovered quick. "Your blood. Her blood. There's nothing to find. Over."

But what was that hesitation? *Our blood*, he had said at the start. There was something that wasn't being said. A question or comment Austin wasn't asking outright. Something he was trying to squeeze out of her.

"Boston . . ." Cleo realized and said at the same time. "Is this about her?"

"You two are getting close, it seems. Over."

Jealous? Austin and Boston had been the dynamic duo. Her physical prowess was outmatched only by his, and Austin's genius outwitted only by hers. They were the epitome of what the AST wanted to project. Boston stood at nearly six feet, and Austin was five inches taller. At the beginning, the pair were in sync—of one mind, finishing each other's sentences, and every decision was made as one, until Eli's death and the shape of Orbis Alius widened in their windows.

"Xavier?" Austin said. Cleo had gone quiet and back into the recesses of her own mind. "Did she say anything to you?"

I need to figure this thing out, that was Boston's last cryptic message to Cleo. For the collective—for all humankind. Boston was going to figure out what was happening on this planet.

"Or did you say something to her, Xavier . . . ?"

"What's wrong?" Cleo whispered, half to him but half to herself as she realized the destination of this vague, wayward conversation. "What happened to Boston?"

"Xavier, please, just tell me—"

"No!" she snapped. "I am a member of this crew, and if you and Daniel and the whole of the goddamn AST know something, then tell me. I was the last one to know about Eli. I'm the last to know about everything. Where is Lieutenant Boston?"

"Boston's missing, Cleo. She went off radar three nights ago. Somewhere beyond the mapped regions, where Daniel can't see. But she left a message for you specifically. And I don't know what to make of it. Over."

"Well, it was for me . . ." Cleo's voice riled in her throat. "What's the message?"

"She said: 'All I meant was the Nike Float.' That was it. Then her transmission cut out."

"Nike Float?" she said, shrugging at the sub-brand. "Was that all she . . ." Then it hit her. Nike Float BT was Cleo's sub-brand. Austin had Nike Drift, Daniel had Nike Orbit, and Cleo was Nike Float BT: Buoyancy Tech. Boston had taken Nike Float and turned it into a term of endearment—float chick.

"Does it mean something?" he insisted. "Over."

"You wouldn't get it."

The conversation went cold. Cleo had soured on Austin's bullshit, and he had probably felt the same about her. The steely edge in Austin's eyes had dulled. She should've ended the call right then, but there was another thread of information Cleo needed.

"One last thing," she said. "You believe in God?"

Austin's dull eyes lit up and his neck tightened veiny. It was as if she'd caught him in some woeful act. Austin was a staunch atheist, so that visceral reaction was something else. He had heard it too, the feral god out in the wild. His hesitancy to reply was uncharacteristic. The waver of lips and the shaking of his head. Her words frightened him. *Hell*, they frightened her.

"W-why did you say that?" Austin stuttered, and his breathing had picked up. "You know that I don't. I'm not . . . Why would you ask me that?"

"Never mind," Cleo said, and she tapped out.

The holoscreen disappeared. If they didn't have the decency to tell her anything, then why should she? Austin's callback rang immediately, but she was going to find out for herself what the hell was going on outside. She opened the locker for her reserve space suit.

This backup EMU had the same functionality as the original but without the yellow-black Barbadian (bumblebee) flair. This one was mostly white, with junctures of gray. The alternative helmet, though, that was quite different. The halo-shaped helmet was called a halogen, or *halo gen*erator. It was slightly smaller than a basketball rim and was magnetized to the collar of the suit when inside, but when outside, it demagnetized and spun like the rings of Saturn around the globe of her head. A halogen was safer than conventional glass helmets, unbreakable, and the spin generated atmosphere and pressure around her face. The glass helmets were vogue, retro, century-old style that caught the sun's glare—they were dramatic, flashy, and fashionable. Halogens, on the other hand, were not as photogenic. For cameras, they created a blur around the nose and ears. And the noise of that invisibly fast spin was mosquito-like and would nauseate her after just minutes of putting the helmet on.

Cleo pressurized her EMU and the halogen popped up from its collar, then began spinning around the equator of her head, just below the bridge of her nose and the center of her ears. It was like a helicopter rotor's blur, a black buzz just below her line of sight. And that was the other annoyance about a halogen, the energetic smear at the bottom edge of her peripheral vision. The atmosphere ballooned around her face immediately, Earthly atmospheric pressure and Mediterranean warmth, feeling as snug as a winter coat does around the body.

Shakes had rested itself into the downward dog pose by the air lock. It raised a judgmental eye to Cleo as she stepped toward the door. She knew what the IU was thinking and answered before it could speak.

"You're not coming," she said. "Just need a walk. Stretch my legs. Get my heart going."

"I have no heart, but I got that brave core *class*. I saved you once; you can call me *save your*—"

"Won't need a savior today," she cut the rover off. "Just ten minutes."

She paced herself, stepping slow through the air lock. *Breathe*, she said to the intimidation in her lungs. Then baby steps, soft and slow, into the shine of a flashlight sun, barely there and yet it felt like its spotlight was on her. Her white suit was a pale dot, bright white against all that black. The dirt beneath her was softer than she remembered. Not as glassy as days before. It didn't crack, but crumbled. The sharp edges in the soil had become strangely dulled down over just a few weeks.

Nike prints followed behind her, as all the same branding had been embossed into this suit as well. Google, Starbucks, Boeing, and Coke Zero-G on her back. Cleo splayed her palm to catch a sprinkle of rainwater. The atmosphere captured in her halogen's spin deflected the raindrops like meteors skipping off the Earth's ionosphere. But she wished they could penetrate the haloed atmosphere; she wanted to taste the water. Cleo wanted to drown herself in that rain. On Venus she listened to the rain play on her roof, the tap, patter, pat, or a heavier patter-pat-patter, and the moment when she found the rhythm, it would play her to sleep. There was no rhythm here, just a dead, hollow drizzle and the low hum of the halogen's spin buzzing in her ears, like a ring of mosquitos in synchronized song.

Green was everywhere out there, wild, boisterous greens, like something out of a painting. Even the dew seemed glossy, as if the weeds were still dripping ink. Some weeds rose past her ankles now, flexing their stems in athletic postures. And the taxonomy was diversifying—crabgrass stitched its webbed roots into the ground, chickweed and ground ivy invaded the Aliun dirt, even a pair of mushrooms umbrellaed the soil. Nearly half of Orbis's frozen landscape was melting into this green inferno.

She crouched to investigate, and the weeds twinkled in her light. Their roots crawled under the dirt. Every root species that touched and fondled, their green incest spread all around her. They were adapting at light speed, like a microwave evolution. It wasn't real. This was biological heresy. She stumbled back from the abomination but still stepped right into a larger patch of grass. The drum of her heartbeat accelerated, the maracas in her lungs rattled. This wasn't real. This was what Boston had needed to figure out, wasn't it? And her too now, Cleo needed to figure this shit out.

And she did have a mad idea far back on the rural side of her subconscious. It started as just an angry notion after the conversation with Austin, but now the auditives emboldened that thought. *This is why you didn't bring Shakes . . .* "Screw it."

Cleo pressed down on the emergency clamps on the neck of her space suit, and an alarm beeped in her earpiece as the halo lowered toward the collar. What was confusing the suit was that the atmosphere outside the halo was unsafe. The alarm kept ringing, preventing the halo from magnetizing to its collar.

"Override," she said.

"Confirm override," a feminine robotic voice said.

Cleo took a deep breath. "Confirm."

The halogen magnetized faster than she had expected. And suddenly, Cleo's lungs were naked in the Aliun air. The pressure squeezed in tight on either side of her ear. She stumbled. She fell. The pressure was bending her equilibrium.

"Dad . . ." she moaned, her vision blurring. Then she gasped and realized she had been holding her breath.

The complicated air burned her windpipe the entire way down and hit her gut with a punch. She retched. The air was like rusted copper as she inhaled; it scratched sandpaper down through her trachea. Cleo coughed, dripping saliva. Then she coughed everything up, vomit spewing out. Cleo felt lightheaded, but the sort of lightheaded that made her feel like she might float away, like her brain was a balloon and it would carry her back to Earth. It was intoxicating air. It was like a drug. And she breathed again and coughed again. And the air stank and smelled, but holy shit she was breathing it.

Cleo breathed hard, sucked in deep through the mouth. She was an infant nursing for the first time, understanding the taste of it and the sustenance. Then she stood and breathed in through vomit-white lips, out through bloodied nostrils, but she was breathing like the weeds all around her. There was just enough oxygen to prevent suicide—but this wasn't suicide.

For nearly two minutes she stood out there breathing poison, and it cured her. Each breath adapted to her as she adapted to it—it was as if the air was evolving to Cleo. She would wager her newly minted $100 million contract that within the coming weeks and months, the pressure outside would eventually reach 14.7 psi, same as Earth. The air's oxygen and nitrogen levels would rise and filter out everything harmful to her body.

Cleo stumbled back inside her capsule, one leg dragging the other. Her shoulder crutched against the wall, and as the air lock closed, she kneeled over in front of the old, cracked helmet. She spit into it, trying to vomit again. She thought there would be vomit. No. Just a nosebleed and some swelling in her lips and ears. She coughed for nearly a full half hour until her throat swelled shut and she couldn't respond to any of Shakes's medical concerns. But aside from the headache and the swelling, Cleo was fine. She'd stood outside on an alien planet for two minutes and she was absolutely fine.

That was why Boston's nose had bled—her hairstyle resembled Cleo's now . . . static mad. Boston had been out there without a helmet, and she survived too. *I'm gonna figure this out*, Cleo thought. *And I'm going to find you.* "And then we're going to get the hell off of this rock."

9

Cleo didn't sleep well that night, nor any night after. Something had clogged the arteries to her dreams. Nights stretched longer, and she lay awake as her brain spun in the dark. How much of that spinning was the antibiotic patches—the archipelago of them lining her back? Maybe she should have cut back on the dosage.

"Maybe you're right," she whispered back to herself.

That was what being alone did to her; she made circles of herself—a human loop. Cleo would converse with herself, jokes and laughter, debating her own opinions. She was her own best company in the quiet of those long nights. Some nights, she strained her eyes into screens—the maps of Boston's last known position. And it was like that for weeks, just her, Shakes, the meds, and a slow recovery. But by the end of their second full month on Orbis Alius, she had mostly recovered. The swelling in her limbs, toes, and thumbs had waned. And she could breathe now, each lung as strong as a fist, squeezing the nurture out of the oxygen and then exhaling what was left over. Soon she'd be back out there, running tests and analyses, and all would be back to normal, except that Boston might never return. Never, and it was her fault.

Guilt was the sort of parasite that burrowed deep in the subconscious; that was the thing that clogged the arteries to her dreams. "Wasn't it?" Cleo asked herself, monologuing a self-diagnosis. That was the feeling she didn't have words for. "It's my fault," she whispered under her breath, like a secret from herself. And it was her fault. Yasmin had come to Cleo. *Not Austin, not*

Daniel—to me. Cleo knew there was something wrong with this planet, so why didn't she vote with Boston? Why'd she allow herself to merge with the mob? In that way, she wasn't any better than Daniel, a worker bee listening to the buzz from the rambling crowd.

Gutless, she thought, then she said it. "You're gutless."

She felt a lump in her neck when she saw the AST's new promotional materials. Cleo's face lit the skyscrapers in London and Shanghai. That lump felt like a knot—a noose. And each time she swallowed, it choked a bit more. She wasn't just responsible for losing Yasmin; now she was replacing her. Every day the AST would send Earth's news feeds. She and Austin were the faces of the mission now. She would never be as beautiful as Yasmin, but now it was Cleo's round cheekbones and gummy smile that lit billboards from Times Square to New Washington on Venus. She was the feminist pioneer, the Venusian who ventured into the unknown. No longer was it Austin and Boston—that duo was fast forgotten. The new propaganda was Austin and Cleo, a pair of off-world prodigies lifting their islands out from the last-to-develop stigma.

Cleo's face flashed on the subway trains from Brisbane to Bangkok and was featured in advertising materials around the worlds. She lit up the cover page of the "lookbooks" and portfolios for investors. She had become the feminine face of the mission. Her body filled a space that Yasmin once did, and she didn't quite fit. Cleo had to square her posture now, straighten her jaw. She needed to smile more—more teeth, less gums. Shine, Cleo, like a star. Be a star for this dark planet.

But Earth-3 didn't need a star. The medium-density amorphous ice in the clouds had nearly the equivalent density of water but acted more like glass. The theory from Mission Control was that ice particles in those clouds acted almost like a magnifying glass, quadrupling the level of sunlight that hit the planet's surface. No one bought this made-up theory. The scientific method didn't work on Orbis. It was brighter outside during their daytime now, nearly as bright as on Earth—nearly, and warmer, just below freezing. Some nights there was even rain—drinkable, uncontaminated water.

Cleo had her own theories, simpler ones: There was something deeply wrong with this planet. Every bug, mammal, and banana on Earth took eons to adapt to their world. This planet . . . it was evolving to adapt to her—to adapt to them. She had no evidence for her theory, of course, but she didn't worry about little things like science. It didn't work anymore, not there. Not on Orbis Alius.

It took her nearly a month to work up the courage to find Yasmin. Cleo packed a pressurized backpack: sweetbread, mauby, fish cakes and bakes, and all the comfort foods she could fill it with. Then, a few auditive doses, just enough to shuffle off this mortal coil, or so that drug poet's proverb went. If Cleo was going to die out there, better to end it all in a bang of snare drums than in a whimper.

She loaded Shakes's back with half a ton of supplies: MREs, gallons of recyclable water, and a TPT (temperature-pressure tent—with the current environment outside, it might serve as a place to sleep). She could survive for months with these supplies, maybe more if she rationed, and that might be enough time to either find Yasmin or at least arrive at her capsule, resupply, and find out what happened to her.

But Cleo didn't leave that night. As deranged as she knew it sounded, she didn't trust the clouds. *Look at them*, their gray, lumbering bodies circling the capsule's ceiling window, a swarm of them wheeling around the aperture. Every time she had tried to reach the barrier where her drone had fallen, the wind or hail or something else would push her back. So Cleo waited two more days, then on the bright, sunny morning of the third day, she climbed into her space suit and made a hard, full-on sprint toward the barrier. Shakes followed, and so did the clouds.

The turn in weather was so sudden that it must have been visible from space. To the *Antilles*, it might have appeared like gray dyes suddenly darkening the empty skies. From Cleo's angle, it was like black tentacles sprawling overhead, curling down toward her. Dust and rocks bombarded the suit. But she was almost there, bounding against the light gravity, with a leash tethered to her rover.

Static shot into her earpiece, and she had expected it. The call from the *Antilles* was inevitable.

"Xavier?" Daniel called down. "You seeing this, or is it instrumentation?"

Not instrumentation; no, this was real. Claws of cloud sharpening into spirals and precipitation stabbing down on Cleo and her rover.

"Xavier, do you read? Over."

She had considered not answering, but if she didn't make it back, Cleo would want them to know what she was trying to achieve.

"I'm going to find Boston," she gasped between each floating stride.

"No." And it was a command. "Cleo, get back to your capsule. This is a high-category storm."

"You can't . . ." Cleo sucked in all the oxygen she could. "Stop me."

"What am I supposed to tell them?"

That's what he's worried about? Of course it was. He could tell them whatever he wanted, she thought, mid-step and stumble over the uneven terrain. Cleo was close now. She could see the border, blinking in and out of the wind, its fog thickening the closer she came.

"Tell them . . ." Cleo inhaled. "Something's wrong . . ." She exhaled. "This world is wrong."

"Why?" Daniel said, his voice rising an octave. "You think it's too good? Orbis is too good to be true? What happened to you? What happened that'd make you afraid of things actually going right?"

A lot, she didn't tell him. But she didn't respond as she pressed her body into the brunt of the wind, holding on to the tether between her and Shakes. The rover was doing its damnedest to press forward as a gust behind them began to suck them backward. But it was too late. They were there, feet and inches away.

"And if you don't find her?" Daniel hissed through a staticky feed.

"Radiation levels are rising," Shakes interrupted. "Advising we take the time in *revising*. This plan is truly *compromising*."

“Keep . . .” But Cleo couldn’t finish. Her feet lifted off the ground and she flapped. “Keep . . .” She gasped again, the world spinning, her grip loosening. “Move,” she instructed her rover. “Keep moving.”

Shakes disappeared into the fog ahead. She couldn’t see the rover anymore or even hear its signal through the static.

“Cleo, please . . .” Daniel’s words were mangled in static. But she could hear the cadence. He was panicking, and more than she was, it seemed. She felt for him then, as she could in her state. Floating and spinning, this would be her last human connection for some time.

“Sorry,” she said, a final endeavor to impart something. Her lips trembled, wanting to say more, but that was all she had. *Sorry*, and he wouldn’t understand all that silent animosity she had held for him—for what? He was so young.

Cleo disappeared into that black fog. But it wasn’t fog, no, this was an abyss. The closer she got to it, the darker it became, until she herself was a shadow. The fog flowed like ink, but not a gas and not liquid either. This was something else. She called for the god then, the one that had told her to come find it alive, but it did not answer.

PART TWO

SOLUS

10

When Cleo was a little girl, she ran into a vertical pool. It carried her upstream, thirty feet high. She couldn't stay afloat. She couldn't swim down or to the other side—Cleo couldn't swim at all. Mom had left her four-year-old daughter alone at the Aqua-tecture Park, diagonal water-rises, an opposite of waterfalls, as the current flowed upward. This water-rise was pigmented in polka-dot color dyes, and vibrant melodies pulsed through the waves. Cleo had thought she saw her mother in that upward cascade of jubilant young bodies. And she nearly drowned trying to find her. *Wow*, she had nearly forgotten that memory, and thirty years later, there it was, gushing so suddenly to the forefront of her brain. Maybe because the memory ran parallel with her present situation, that lifeguard pulling a young Cleo out of the pool, just as Shakes was pulling her now, out through the other side of an inky smog.

Cleo found herself hunched over, posed in the same doglike shape as her rover. She shook as her space suit tightened, adjusting to the temperature and atmospheric pressure outside. Her halogen spun backward, recalibrating to that same opposite in atmos. Her fingers squeezed into the dirt, knuckles getting a grip, like she might just fall upward. *Fall upward?* At first, Cleo thought that sensation might be water-rise flashbacks, the trauma overweighing on her senses. But no, that was something else. *Gravity?* A gravity that was barely there. And she dug her fingers deeper into the dirt, for fear she might fall upward off into space.

She panted, not quite out of breath but out of sync. Her heart and lungs were hitched on a seesaw. *Relax*, she told the little Cleo inside her, but not loud enough.

"Relax," she scolded.

But as she stood, Cleo nearly lifted off the ground in the weakened gravity. She stared up at a sky that she might just reach if she jumped high enough. And with her neck craned upward, she realized that there was something off about the clouds. *What the hell?*

A wartlike cumulus dangled overhead. Thousands of bluish sacs chandeliered the sky. Something glimmered inside each of these pouches—electricity, maybe? It snapped like yellow fireworks, but smaller, shorter bursts that shook individual sacs of cloud. The acned sky appeared to stare back at her. She couldn't explain that feeling, but it was there in her gut—all those celestial warts and zits might pop and spew pus over the rotted landscape.

"What . . . happened?" she finally said, and felt the dryness in her throat. "Shakes?" She spun around, searching for the rover. "Shakes!"

Her rover stood loyally behind her. Its single eye flashed over her, X-rays scanning Cleo's body, likely checking for anything broken.

"What happened?"

"We emerged from that foggy *boundary*. And oddly *soundly—unharmed.* So no need to be a-*larmed*."

The cadence in the rover's voice eased her an inch. She rested her hand on its titanium body, and soon enough, the rest of her weight followed. She propped herself against the machine. Shakes was her crutch now, the hiss of static in her earpiece a constant reminder of that. Cleo was off the *Antilles* map, like Yasmin.

But why was the atmosphere so different? And the smooth dirt that didn't leave much in the way of a footprint. And those spooky clouds. Where had all the weeds gone?

"Shakes, can you run a lateral scan on the landscape?" she said, rubbing her glove along the machine's back. "What's our easiest path forward?"

Shakes took its good time on that scan. There was a clicking vibration from the rover's back; she was still crutched against it, listening with her palm. There was time there for her head to wander across that same landscape. *You won't find her. Boston's not here, and neither's your mom.* Her breathing rattled inside again, and it was hard to stand steady. *What's taking this rover so damn long?*

"Shakes," she snapped, panic spilling in her voice. She cleared her throat. "What's the best path? What do you see?"

"What I'm gonna say, you may not *believe in*. But from what I'm *perceiving*—that landscape ahead is uniformly *even*."

"Uniformly . . ." She eyed the dirt. It did appear steamroller smooth. "What?" And then it was more than a glance. She couldn't take her eyes off the dirt. "Uniformly even? What do you mean by that?"

"I'm saying it's abnormally *flat*—and normally *that*—would have me formally *chat*—with the *Antilles*. I need to confirm the technical *side*—I'm feeling like a skeptical *guide*—But both paths out here are identical. *Tied*."

"Well, good . . ." She shrugged, but that wasn't good. None of this was good. How the hell could any natural landscape be uniformly flat? Even the swankiest road of Neo Oistins had cracks and the occasional pothole. Her moisturized skin had more wrinkles than that dirt. But still her lips folded in stubborn insistence. "So . . . uh, good."

"That response . . . it seems so *flawed*. When you say, 'Uh, good,' do you mean 'Oh *God*'? I believe we should go back *early*. Like a throwback *jersey*—"

"No." She cut him off, not wanting any truth right now. "You're programmed to protect me. Do your goddamn job, Shakes! Cuz I'm not going back. I said 'good' because if that's all flat, then there's no hills. No canyons. Barely even any gravity, right? This *is* good!" And with that, Cleo bounded ahead of her rover. "I'll show you how we'll do this."

"Okay. I'm holding out hope. *Truce*. I'll let you show me the ropes. *Noose*."

They journeyed slow across the flat earth. Every step for Cleo was a bound several feet into the air, followed by a gradual, gradual descent in apathetic gravity. Shakes spun leg spikes into the dirt to stay grounded. With each step, a spinner from the rover's heel punctured the ground, then released. Cleo tried the same, releasing one-inch cleats, shaped in the Nike swoosh, from the bottom of her boots. But those didn't dig quite deep enough.

The landscape was abnormally flat—mindbogglingly so, like every earth-tone wrinkle had been ironed out. No rocks or pebbles, not even a crumb of dust. Cleo splayed her fingers against the dirt, and though she couldn't feel the flatness of it with her fingertips, she could measure the smoothness. There wasn't the slightest vibration as she ran her palm across the ground. Flatter than a concrete road or even her dad's old mahogany tables.

The only uneven element was this strange peeling, like dead skin flaking off. Paper-thin layers of film flayed from the ground. But as thin as this peel was, the wind didn't move it. Then she realized—there was no wind. She tilted her ear skyward, trying to filter out Shakes's spiking feet. She waited until the rover's percussion faded ahead of her. There wasn't even a whisper of wind. Nothing.

The deeper they ventured, the more Shakes coaxed her to turn back. Cleo couldn't—not yet, at least. She'd give it a full day's effort. Still, she couldn't remove her mind from all this strangeness. She had just stepped through a stampede of wind and debris, murderous weather, and a moment after passing through that fog, that gaseous goo, there was even the gentlest breeze. And how could the gravity have changed that drastically? The clouds too, right? She peered upward. Those sacs of . . . what? Something, a thousand testes hanging from bluish clouds. This place was like a . . . a different planet.

In the hours that followed, Cleo would regret having imagined up that mad possibility. She knew it was impossible, a different world, but the idea stuck to the walls of her brain, and it festered. It was the only answer to every question she had. Her preadolescent fantasies about portals to new universes and different dimensions reinvaded her adult mind. A different planet?

"Shakes . . ." Cleo started, but she didn't know how to finish. She sucked in a mouthful of recycled air and continued, "Shakes, do you think we could be on, uh . . ." She was embarrassed to say it, even to an IU. "That this could be, uh . . . different? You know, a different location, maybe? Like . . . a different part of a . . . or a different place altogether?"

"What you just said came out very *messily*. *Ineffably*. I'm not programmed with *telepathy*."

Smart-ass. Cleo rolled her eyes, but that was insecurity moving her. It pursed her lips and wrinkled her nose. Because the IU wasn't lying. Cleo wasn't expressing herself clearly. What she wanted to say was juvenile: *Did that fog transport me to another planet?*

"Never mind," she said, staring up at that terrifying sky. If she could see those familiar stars beyond the clouds—the Big Dipper, Lyra—if she had some clue that she was still on Orbis Alius, Cleo might ask the question in confidence, but not yet. "Never mind, Shakes. Let's keep going."

It would be another hour before she spoke again, an hour spent winding around the spiral in her head. Therapy sessions with Olivia Noah warned her away from too much self-reflection. *It's the mental equivalent of mirror gazing*, Olivia had said. *Staring at the reflection in your own head. Open up, Xavier. Communicate.*

But she would never say what was on her mind right now. Fantasies of God and other worlds. If she spoke up, it would probably worry her rover into a malfunction. But there were questions she could ask, like what the hell was that gaseous goo they'd passed through to get here? Wherever "here" was.

"Shakes." The rover was a few paces ahead, and she skipped to catch up. "What was that fog that we stepped through back there? That gaseous gooey thing behind us?"

"Not just behind *us*. That gaseous goo encircles the landscape like a bubble. Like a belt with no buckle. And wraps all the way around—*thus*, it surrounds *us*."

"Bubble . . . You're saying that it's wrapped around this whole landscape? Like a gaseous wall, but one that we can probe?"

"More like a snow globe. It's above us too. Beyond the *shrouds*—of those saclike *clouds*."

"So right now we're walking toward another wall of that . . . stuff. What is it, Shakes? It's not a fog. It's not gas or goo. What's the chemical makeup?"

"Clee, I got no science for this. It's like sorcery, and that's *tragic*. Cuz I'm like Larry Bird, I don't like black *Magic*."

"Black magic?" She nearly smiled as she stopped and turned to her rover. "And sorcery? You're a Cambridge-model IU, Shakes. You sure you're not broken?"

Now Shakes stopped and aimed its cyclopic eye at her, almost as if the machine were offended.

"No, I'm not un-*stable*. I'm not Cain. I will not diss *Abel*, Clee. So do not mis-*label*—me!"

"Sorry, Mr. Sensitive," she said, grinning. "But I interrupted you. You were saying: 'Don't mislabel me . . .'"

"That fog's an isotropic stable, *Clee*. Nonliquid. Not gas—nothing on our periodic table, *see*?"

She saw. Nothing on the periodic table . . . Might as well be black magic. Then maybe another planet wasn't so far-fetched after all. Cleo made a face like she was kissing sideways as her thoughts spun in circles. To hear a mind that was literally from science talk about sorcery and black magic was a bad sign.

"'Kay," she told herself. "What about the ground?" She kicked up some of the flaky residue with her boot. "Can you figure out the chemical makeup of this stuff?"

"SiO_2."

"Quartz." She knew that one, and a sudden perk of pride lit her face. The memory of Dad teaching her in the back of an oxtail eatery. "Crystals, right?"

"Big crystals. Imagine a farm of *gems*. All across this landscape: a swarm of *them*. Like cornfields but with diamond charms as *stems*. They grow, evolve, *then*—something out here dissolves *them*."

Cleo stared at the ground, trying her hardest to imagine crystals growing out of this dead, flat, salt-fed earth. She had to squeeze her eyes just for the shortest snapshot of it. Cornfields of crystals, amber shaded or violet, threatening their jagged ends. Tens of thousands of them looming high in the passive gravity. Then something dissolved them into these flaky, wafer-thin sheets.

"Crystals?" Cleo pointed to the flat ground, then again bent down to run her palm against the loose film. "This is the remainder of crystals after something dissolves it?"

"Something . . ."

"Something? That's all you got?" she said jovially. "You're just as lost as me, 'Intelligence' Unit. If I didn't love you, I'd be upset right now."

"Aww," the IU said in sarcasm. "It's a Roman *tragedy*. She's mad at *me*. Check the data, *Clee*. I'm operating at maximum *capacity*."

"Max capacity?" she said and smirked. "And you can't even tell me what's dissolving the crystals."

"Wow, this is a massive *attack*, can't do nothing to *please her*. I feel stabbed in the *back* . . . Julius *Caesar*."

She smiled again. Not wide and gummy, but just enough. She was glad for Shakes now, especially in this place. The rover had the programming to joke more often when Cleo appeared nervous or during bouts of anxiety. Which meant she must have seemed to be in a state of fright. Shakes continued its joking each mile it poled on, and she realized maybe she had been taking the rover for granted. Maybe she should listen, return to her capsule, and tell Austin and Daniel what she'd seen. Get the AST to postpone the new arrivals. But the farther she ventured, the stranger this world made itself, and the more her rover made her laugh in fright.

"Shakes, can you run one more radial scan?" She pointed to the path ahead. "How close are we to that next gaseous wall?"

"Four point four miles."

"And the gaseous wall behind us?" Cleo asked. "How far have we come?"

"Five point eight one."

They were closer now to the barrier in front of them. And still she glanced back—back to home base. Cleo eyed the monstrous sky overhead, clouds tensing up into muscular knots. Something like veins sprawled between the globular sacs. *What are you doing here?* That vigilant voice in her spoke with Dad's cadence. *Go back.* But she winced in pain as the thought of Yasmin somewhere out here alone hit her mind. *I'm a coward,* she thought, but that nasty voice sounded like Ava.

"Shakes . . ." It felt like she was holding her breath as she spoke. "I think we should—"

"I'm picking up something on my *scan*. It's not clicking. I don't quite under*stand*."

There was a slight shallowing in Shakes's tone—a seriousness to it. Cleo stepped closer to her rover as if the machine needed to whisper its words to her. Her earpiece was how she heard Shakes's voice and how it heard her, and still she had to look it in the eye.

"What'd you see?"

"The atmosphere is *distending*. While the clouds . . . they're *descending*."

There were no more hints of sarcasm or playfulness in Shakes's tone. Its single eye fixed on the skyline; the clicks of X-ray and radio-wave vision vibrated through its internal lenses. Cleo followed its gaze and rolled her neck upward at the clouds. Whether it was Shakes's warning or her own misgivings, the details of those clouds did appear clearer—closer.

"It is descending," she said, like she was the one to figure it out. "The sky's falling."

"Clouds," Shakes corrected her.

"The clouds," Cleo snapped back. "Whatever. How fast is it coming down?"

"Checking the graph barometer, and it's *dour*. Its descent is half a kilometer per *hour*."

Cleo tried to do the math of that but couldn't, not in this rising panic. But those clouds were no more than a couple of kilometers up.

"And it's accelerating . . ."

The hell with waiting.

"Two hours and it's *down* on us, *drown*ing us."

Shakes was spitting its lyrics faster than ever. Cleo peered up at the clouds and squinted, trying to make out anything she hadn't seen before. "What's in them?" she asked quickly, matching the IU's word speed. "The composition of the clouds. Can you tell?"

"Sorry, Clee."

Cleo squinted deeper into the cumulus. Something made of light slithered inside those clouds. What she had thought resembled veins from farther away now seemed like crawling tree branches—not foliage, just the naked skeleton of the plant. It was a massive thing many miles long, sprawling treelike through the cloudscape. Then she realized it was crawling above her, making circles around her position from the clouds.

"This is what dissolved the fields of crystals," she realized, glancing at the paper-thin residue on the ground. "We're heading back to the capsule, Shakes."

"To *escape* it? No, you won't *make* it."

They had come too far. "So, what? We go forward instead?"

"Yes," Shakes said. "To the gaseous wall ahead."

She was breathing like a marathoner but hadn't taken a single step. She was frozen in her exhaustion. What the hell were these . . . carnivorous clouds? Clouds that dissolved fields of crystals—what type of ecosystem was that? And how hadn't they seen any of this from the *Antilles*? Questions within questions, and she couldn't answer the simplest of them, forward or back . . .

Something hissed underneath her. She glanced down to see a raindrop evaporate a tiny patch of earth.

"Shit, the sacs are bursting."

"Stop *cursing*. Are we moving forward? Or *reversing*?"

"Forward. Like you said," she shouted, glancing back one last time, but the path to her capsule was too many miles behind her. "Forward, to the wall of . . . whatever it is. Gas. Goo."

The slow bounce in that low gravity wouldn't make for fast movement, and Shakes released its cable. Cleo grabbed hold. The machine trotted quickly as its legs spiked and unspiked into the dirt after each step. But it wasn't happening fast enough. The carnivorous clouds curled down, descending a meter a minute (according to the rover). The clouds were too close, just a mile above. And that colossal barbed thing twisted feverishly inside the clouded mass. Closer now, it more resembled a gargantuan crown of thorns in the way it spiraled around the yellowish cumulus.

Acidic rain bled out from those sacs in a dramatic snow-like slow motion, the leisurely gravity guiding it at a quarter tempo. The precipitation didn't muddy the soil but slicked the path. The rover's back was matted in corroded scars under the rain, but the alloys would sustain, hopefully. This drizzle wouldn't injure the rover; Cleo's space suit, though . . . it wouldn't survive. It would burn—it *was* burning. The logo on her arm read "tarbucks" as the *S* died an acidic death. Fortunately, only the top layer of the suit had worn away.

She had the good fortune that the halogen's atmosphere deflected most of the raindrops, but she had to square herself a bit, tuck herself in as she moved. *Fold your shoulders in. Straighten your back.* And the halo helmet's atmosphere acted sort of as an umbrella.

"We won't make it," Cleo shouted, though the IU could hear her loud and clear, even if she whispered. But every word was a scream in this panic. "Are you okay . . . ?" and "Stop the blasted-well rhyming . . ."

But the rover couldn't stop rhyming. That was its programming language. It would be like asking a native German monoglot to sing in Korean.

Pebble-size crystals were gradually spiking up from the ground, and it had to be the precipitation that was spurring this reaction. There was a complexity to this strange ecosystem. So alien. So beautifully malignant. And it was trying to kill her.

Above her, the clouds were peeled back like a foreskin, and the crown of thorns emerged. Miles long, the branches appeared skeletal, a calcified structure that itself was gaseous. Electrical signals flashed through these vaporous limbs, and the true acid deluge came with it.

"That acid will tear you asunder, *Clee*. Get under *me*."

Cleo embraced the rover's torso, swung downward, and angled her way underneath its belly, pregnant with all her supplies. She crawled low to the ground, floundering at a mad pace to keep up. She appeared to be almost paddling in the loose gravity, kicking and clawing at dead dirt to stay grounded. Shakes's powerful spikes stabbed into the ground on either side of her. She feared one of her limbs might be amputated.

Then she saw it from underneath the rover's belly. *Look, right there*—the gaseous goo. It was like a murmuration of black liquid crows flapping a million wings. It was waving and roiling on itself.

"Go," she gasped, choking on knots of saliva and oxygen.

They were nearly there, but carnivorous clouds were there too. Right on top of them. And for some reason, Shakes was slowing down. She heard the hissing of acids eating away at the rover's back. The acid ate everything—the air around her, the kicked-up dirt from Shakes's spikes. The acidic deluge consumed it all, but not the gaseous fog. The clouds couldn't get their teeth into that. So that was where they went. Back into the void.

11

Passing through that gaseous matter felt like drifting into a dream. The substance flowed through her as she flowed through it, and for an instant, or an infinity, Cleo was not conscious. Then she woke up in a crawling prone. Cleo dragged herself on all fours across a monochrome landscape. She couldn't identify what felt off, but there was an ugliness she couldn't put words to. Then she noticed the logos on her EMU. LEGO's yellow, Boeing's blue, and Google's rainbow of color patterns all appeared as varying shades of gray. All of Cleo's blinking and squinting did nothing to restore color. This world was colorless, and not just her—the terrain had been watered down to blacks and whites.

The topography itself was saturated in a mist as thick as ash, but there was more light here than there had been in the previous landscape. Beneath her, tortured rocks threatened with their barbed edges. Colorless stones were shaped like dry coral. Remarkably low-hanging clouds hugged the hills and slopes, and somehow, light flooded through all that haze. There was something different about this light. A different sun, maybe—a different world? A third world. Not Orbis. Not anymore. And not the flatlands of the carnivorous clouds. She had entered into a truly otherworldly space.

Emerging through that gaseous substance had a disorienting effect. Cleo arched her head away from the ground to prevent the halogen's spin from clipping the rocks beneath her. Then she tried lifting herself up, but after all that crawling, she didn't have the strength.

"Shakes . . ." Cleo started to say, but found the rover approaching from behind.

Shakes was in surprisingly good shape; her companion looked like shit, yes, but functional shit. The rover's titanium alloy skin was a leprosy of acid scars, but all of its processing "organs" were safely untouched by the sulfur. Cleo's suit, on the other hand, was peeling at its seams. *Cheese on bread*, she imagined Dad saying, mimicking the old country's adages and accent. He smiled out from her memory, crooked teeth and all, but she couldn't smile back. She was lost, hungry, and the skin of her suit was peeling like an eczema for fabrics.

Cleo attempted to lift herself up for a second time but struggled. Her feet didn't cooperate with her hips, which were incoherent to her backbone. She was worn out from her crawl, and it took all the effort she had just to get into a stooping position.

"Slow down," Shakes warned. "Don't move too *erratically*. Or this mad *gravity*—might crush your *anatomy*."

Oh, Cleo realized. That was what that was. That elephant on her back was an increase in gravity.

"What's the gravity compared to Earth?"

"One point five gs' worth," Shakes responded.

"Manageable." For now, at least. Cleo was never the best in the mathematics or medicine training required for this mission; she'd barely passed. But she wagered her heart would need to pump 1.5 times as hard to get the blood from her toes back up to her brain.

Understanding that it was the gravity weighing her down, Cleo tried standing a third time. She balanced herself first, widened her stance, imagining a barbell on her shoulders. Then she stood with her hips and knees. Her legs wobbled unsteadily underneath her, but Cleo managed to dance up to her feet.

"Okay," she said and kept repeating, "Okay, okay," trying to think through her next move. But her mind couldn't anchor to anything. She kept drifting, first thinking of Yasmin, poor Yasmin, likely suffering a similar plight. Then she wondered if Austin was now searching for her. Next, Cleo considered that maybe she'd had some luck. This world could have pulled at ten gs. She could have come through the other side of that barrier and been flattened, a pancake—oozing syrup. And she imagined it: pancakes, syrup, melting butter. Now she thought of food. But hunger wasn't the priority. Not yet. It hadn't even been a full day of hiking, and she needed to ration. "Still, though . . ." she whispered to herself. "Pancakes."

"You're talking to yourself—talking in *stealth*. But I've been stalking your *health*." Shakes stepped closer, and its magnified lenses looked at Cleo's eyes. "How are you *feeling*? The suit is *peeling*. Dilated pupils: your heart's *reeling*—from this gravity's unyielding *weight*. And you're not dealing *great*."

"I'm just hungry, Shakes," she said. She pressed her hand against its X-ray lenses. "But it's fine. Need to ration."

"Agreed," Shakes said.

"Right now, I need to know what the hell's going on. Those carnivorous clouds back there . . ." She pointed to the gaseous barrier behind the rover. "Its gravity, temperature, atmosphere—none of it's the same as Orbis Alius. And this gravity isn't like Orbis or the carnivorous clouds. So here's my question: Could that gaseous liquid-frigging-thing be taking us . . . elsewhere? Or are we on, uh . . . another planet, more specifically?"

"That's not very scientific, Clee."

"Then what is it?" Cleo said with a shrug worth a dumbbell press of effort. "What's the rational explanation?"

The rover appeared to pose in a stance of bewilderment, in the way dogs twist their head in confusion—it did that, contorting its cranium and staring at something miles out. She followed the rover's gaze to a spot where a bulge squeezed the mist. What was that? The terrain appeared to flex its rock and soil into muscular ranges. Maybe mountains or volcanoes, but so deep into that mist they were matchsticks swallowed in their own smoke.

"Those mountains there extend beyond the *cloud head*. Let's climb to a space where the stars aren't *shrou-ded*. Or *crowded*. With any dark *haze*. Then we can search and star*gaze*. And chart the star's *rays*."

Now that was the logical thing to do. Not panicking and imagining one high-fantasy theory after another. *Think it through to the solution*, she told herself, *like Dad taught you*. There was a little bit of Dad in Shakes, and she wondered then if the engineers had dripped a percentage of her father's personality profile into her IU.

"What are you thinking, Clee?"

She was staring at it—at him. "Sorry," she said and glanced away. "That's a great idea. We map our location via the stars. Smart, Shakes. Really damn smart."

"So you *are* seeing *this*. That I'm a star *genius*. And it's so far *meaningless*. To doubt *me*. Without *me* . . . Forget it—*wow*. And you're so indebted—*now*. You'll be so *broke*—no *joke*. Even with that cash from Co-*Coke*—"

"Okay, stop! Never giving you a compliment again," Cleo said, and a smirk slipped unexpectedly into her cheeks. Nothing as audacious as grinning teeth, but in these circumstances, any joy was its own miracle.

Her smile faded fast as she considered how far out the mountains might be. She'd have to trek all that way, and in this gravity. Then they'd have to ascend many more feet until they passed the curtain of clouds. Only then could they map the stars. Her breathing had already started to quicken. She didn't know if her feet would allow it, but right now, it was a better idea than anything she had in her head, which at the moment was mostly pancakes.

Shakes kept the pace brisk while warning about the dangers of having a misstep in this gravity. But Cleo already felt the threats against bones and cartilage. Every step needled at the soles of her feet, her still-ailing knees, and tailbone. She took measured steps, lifting her legs slowly and descending even slower, letting her legs feel the way as she wandered into the wilds of this world.

Farther out, the terrain was more uniform than anything on Venus. The flatness gave the ground an almost pavement-like feeling. The layers of condensed rock resembled smoothed concrete, but with fissures stretched across the surface. The heavier gravity seemed to press in on everything, squeezing the crumbs of rock and gravel into one over the centuries. That was why the clouds were so low, wasn't it? Escape velocity for this world had to be almost double that of Venus.

Then how, she wondered, had that mountain in the distance grown so damn high?

That first hour stretched longer than Cleo thought possible. Shakes agreed, describing it as a mock rubber band stretching on the clock's upper hand. But she kept her eyes on that mountain. That colossal target would help her focus. Everything else was in the peripherals. But the closer she got, Cleo realized that the hypnotic tower of rock was not a mountain; this was some new terror.

"What is . . ." The words caught in her throat as she stumbled back. The sudden, clumsy movement stung her knee, and the pain rang out in every direction—ankle, back, shoulders, neck. "Ah, damn it."

But even the discomfort couldn't shake her eyes off the thing. It was massive, a gargantuan structure that broke the horizon in half. To her, it appeared like a mountain-size sphere—a dwarf planet, maybe—that floated just a couple of miles off the surface. It was so massive that the top of the thing was hidden in the clouds. At first glance, the sphere was like a full moon too close to its mother planet. But as she gathered the nerve to waddle closer, Cleo realized the object was too geometrically symmetrical to be a natural phenomenon.

The sphere had made a crater of mountain ranges around it; they encircled it as if the sphere's own gravity propelled the mountains into being. They were like a jagged crown for something that could be best described as a perfectly spherical head.

"What is that?" Cleo asked her rover without as much as a glance in its direction. She was hypnotized by the thing. The shape of it fit perfectly inside her irises. "Shakes . . ."

"Don't know what I'm looking *at*. I'm just as shook, in *fact*."

"Thought you were the star genius?"

"No point in demeaning *us*. It's meaning*less*."

Shakes turned to gawk with her. The rover's ocular aperture bloomed wide open in robotic awe, though that was likely its lenses probing the sphere's glossy reflective surface at every wavelength. The sphere didn't appear like a natural phenomenon, and yet there it was, floating in its own gravity, strong enough to bend the space around it. The mist curved around its frame; stones and pebbles hovered between the ground and the base of the globular goliath.

Wow, she marveled, just . . . *wow*. Cleo felt dwarfed into insignificance, squished down like a germ against the face of this thing. It was rapturous, watching shades of gray reflect and stretch around the globe. The terraformer inside her gawked, humbled and hallowed at the majesty of the thing. But Shakes trotted ahead, reciting a simple rhyming couplet about getting out *rapidly* because of the *gravity*, and leaving her behind. But Cleo couldn't retreat. She was paralyzed by awe. She was imagining the ecosystem, maybe based on gravitational elements or how the light and color interacted with tidal forces. That was the Xavier side of her—Dad's little terraformer.

But Shakes would eventually coax her onward. The IU rhymed about the crew as a *whole*, Boston in particular, wasn't she the *goal*? The guilt was effective enough, if not downright manipulative. And the gravity was taking its toll too, especially as the terrain curved uphill. Pinches shot through her left leg every other step.

Yet there was a familiarity to this path, not that she had walked it before, but seen it maybe. Oh God, she had dreamed it. This gravity and that globe, this world reminded her of that feral god—like this was the road that led to Him . . . to Her, the plural deity. She couldn't understand the words in her head, but they were there, brooding: *My pheromones are dead. Find me alive.*

The climb steepened quickly, and pinches cut deeper. *Breathe*, she told herself, feeling the gravity now as much in her lungs as it was in her knees. Every step was a lunge of athletic effort. So much blood had gunged up in her swollen toes, and it left her lightheaded. She had to stop or risk collapsing.

They rested a quarter of the way up, right on the proscenium of the sphere's theater. It imposed itself onto the vista as a black-and-white sunset rested against its back. This journey to chart the stars above the cloud line was moot; they were not on Orbis Alius anymore.

The way up the mountain was painful. Too much weight bore down on her joints. Every step flattened her just a little bit more. Now she couldn't even think of pancakes—her gut was pulled down on her bladder. She had this constant sensation of urinating, even though there was no urine, nothing in her to squeeze out. The rover's back was a complication of supplies, but Cleo found her inch of ass space at the back, and Shakes carried her too. Her legs hung and felt like stretched elastic, but at least it was a relief from walking.

All that weight was devouring the rover's battery, but Cleo couldn't abandon her post on Shakes's back—not yet, at least. Just one more hour. She hadn't slept in a day and a half now, and her heart reminded her of that. Full-on cardio fists boxed against the inside of her chest. But they were in the clouds now, a couple thousand feet high. Her space suit adjusted, inflating slightly, and the halo increased its quiet spin. The first stars winked through the cloudscape, and she laughed. A strange reaction, but her mind was unbalanced. She had been lightheaded for an hour, heartbeats trampling on her chest, lungs overextended.

I need to stop.

But her body would stop for her. Eventually, Cleo climbed off Shakes's back. She didn't see the cavity in the dirt with her head tilted up, trying to distinguish snowflakes from stars. And in that next step, a ligament in her knees stretched, then snapped. *Shit!* But Cleo couldn't fall. *Don't fall.* How many more overstressed bones and ligaments would shatter in that collapse? She lurched forward, then slowly bent her good knee to the ground, both arms reaching down like she was going into a push-up position, and Cleo rested against the dirt.

Oh my God—it hurt. "Goddamn it!" She rolled onto her back, keeping her head elevated, preventing the halogen from skidding against the alien dirt. "I can't . . ." she said, not sure of what she couldn't do. "I pulled something . . ." Cleo clenched the side of her knee as if her hands were all that held the joint together. "Jeez—ugh." She groaned, wanting words but only grunting.

"We're almost there, *Clee*. Near-*ly*. Bare-*ly* ten minutes from viewing space clear-*ly*. Let's refute that weird *theory*. About being on some other *planet*. *Damn it*. This isn't how we *planned it*, but—"

"Shut up," she snapped. "Please. Go . . . Find out where we are, then come back."

"Copy that."

The rover's footsteps faded like distant raindrops rising up. Quiet settled over the mountain range, and Cleo was forced to listen to her rapid heartbeat. And the heartbeat strained her lungs, making it harder for her to breathe. And that breathing, or lack thereof, made it harder for her to keep her eyes open.

"Stay up," Cleo told herself. "Focus . . ." *On what?*

There were only clouds at those heights, and so she focused on that—dreamy, sheep-shaped clouds. The one directly above was shaped like her own product placement—the Nike swoosh. Another was like an ugly squid with only nine tentacles. One cloud bent its features into a young woman, and there were piercings on that woman's face, dotted along her ears and lips. Those piercings were the stars puncturing the canvas of cumulus. And a few of the brightest stars were all too familiar.

She squinted at a familiar row of stars, three of them, almost in a straight line. Then she saw four other stars that she could trace a square over their positions. With the seven stars together, she saw a big spoon, one for dipping into syrup and pouring it onto pancakes.

"The dipper . . ." she whispered in disbelief. "Big. Dipper . . . But . . ." But that would mean she was still relatively close to Earth—like she was still on Orbis Alius. But no—she shook her head. "No."

Cleo staggered to her feet and dragged her legs up the mountainous path unsteadily, panting and wheezing, hoping for a better look but finding something else. A sudden snap of static cracked over her headset. An avalanche of noise poured through her earpiece. But there shouldn't have been static on a signal that close. It had to be a long-range feed.

"Is that you, Shakes?"

"Swar . . ." Words formed out of the static. "Nest . . . I am inside . . . for a nest . . ." It was barely audible, but she knew that voice . . . "And beware the octonary, Cleo . . . Beware the octon—"

"Yasmin!" Cleo hollered. "Yasmin—Yas . . ." Nothing else came to mind except that name and the joy of it. It kept bursting out of her. Yet as Cleo shouted her name, Yasmin kept speaking over her and repeating the same puzzling words and in the same order.

"I am inside . . . for the nest . . . And beware of the octonary, Cleo . . . Beware the octonary."

"Yasmin? You copy?"

The signal blazed out; every word burned in a fire of static. It was a recording, for sure. A signal she'd sent out from somewhere high, or maybe she'd returned to her capsule. Cleo considered climbing higher for a moment, but she was breathing so heavily she was suddenly on her knees.

Her eyelids were heavy in that gravity, and she was nodding off. As her head dipped, the halogen hit the dirt like a tire skidding against gravel, and her head skidded with it. That woke her up, or did it? Everything was starting to blur together. Sleep and consciousness. Shakes was suddenly behind her, and it was saying something. Not behind her; now the rover was underneath her. She found herself on Shakes's back, strapped down like cargo. But she was skipping in and out of consciousness, and moments were missing in between. Shakes said something about a star and uttered, "I know where we are."

"Say it . . . again. Say it again, Shakes . . . ?" But only half of the sentence made it out of Cleo's lips, and only half of her lips moved. Only half of her body could move . . . *Oh no.*

Her right arm clenched up. Her fingers squeezed into a partial fist, unable to close. A numbness needled across her left half. All her nerves were rerouting, all her internal wires crossed. Sensation wasn't carrying like it should. She wasn't even breathing, was she? Cleo blinked, so slow that she was elsewhere when her eyes opened again. Not on the mountain anymore but approaching that black gaseous swirl, inviting her into the darkness.

12

Cleo balled up her toes. Clenched fingers rolled into fists. She hugged her legs toward her chest, and her head bowed to her knees. She was a circle. There wasn't an edge on her, and still she shivered inwardly, coiling in on herself. There was a strange cold slipping into those spaces between her limbs. *Weird.* And it was the cold that woke her up.

Her halogen had been demagnetized on its collar, and she had taken it off—much of her EMU (gloves, boots, chest plate) had been disrobed. Her skin felt liberated, like she had shed an entire layer of herself. She could rub her languid palm against itches on her scalp or the knots of her eyes and dig deep in her nostrils. She would eventually climb out of the rest of it, even the LCG—the skin-tight pajamas worn underneath the EMU. And somehow she did it all through heart arrhythmia and maybe onset seizures.

Cleo was in the pressurized tent, and she smelled it before she saw it. The hydroplastic polymer had that fresh sealed scent, like unopened sneakers or the inside of a new car. Part inflatable, part polymer, the tent was designed for Orbis Alius's temperature, atmosphere, and gravity. It would not have survived in that last world with its gravitational extremes and pressure, which meant Cleo was on another world now, and a more temperate one.

The tent was large enough for her and the rover but small enough that Shakes needed to stand over her in a bowlegged stance. Or was the rover standing over her because of the IV? She saw it now as her eyes winked open. A needle punctured her forearm; something dripped down. Now she saw a light bulb at the center of the tent feeding off Shakes's battery. The heating too, that warmth that swathed around her bare shoulders, was pumping from Shakes's nickel-hydrogen heartbeat. She needed to pull herself together before she killed the only ally she had.

There was a rustling outside the tent. A sort of expanding, then contracting, but Cleo had never heard anything like it before, so the noise was hard to place. What she was sure of, though, was that it sounded cold, and Cleo herself couldn't explain what the hell that meant. That same coldness had woken her up. The noise didn't just grip her ear but slithered icy along her neck and arms, around the curving of her body. This noise was literally squeezing and prodding at every part of her body.

"What's this outside the, ugh . . ." Cleo's words dried up at the end of her dehydrated lips. The drought in her throat burned, and she coughed out the rest of it. "Shakes. What's . . . what's happening?"

"You had a rough go at *it*. But you're tough and showing *it*. Growing *fit*, every *minute*, every *hour*, your health grows less *dour*."

"But I feel . . ." She reached for the rover's leg, too tired to lift her head and look it in the eye. "I just feel scared."

"Or just feel weird. Just rest, even though you feel strange and *highly*. It's cuz you're tipsy, you're *wily*, you're drunk on poison *IV*, the purest—the *cleanest*. You're sipping on that intra*venous* . . ."

And the rover's lullaby went on to Venus, then something about *redeem us*. But Cleo's eyes had sunk into her subconscious, the rover's cadence easing her back to sleep. The IU wanted her to rest, and physically Cleo wanted that too. But the anxiety rang like alarms in her brain and kept her conscious through that familiar dream. The recurring one—Mom floating dead in the vertical pool, and the nightmare fuel: tentacles slithering out from their seashells all around her. But now that high-gravity sphere dominated the skyline and the stars that Shakes was supposed to chart.

"Where . . ." Cleo murmured, eyes blinking open. She tried lifting herself off the ground, but her body was heavier than she thought. Drug weight. "Not resting until you tell me."

"Don't protest, *Clee*. I know you're trying to show *testes*. But don't test *me*, just lay back and rest, *please*."

"Testes?" Cleo lifted herself onto unsteady arms. "Now I need testicles to show strength?" But her elbows caved in, and she fell back into her sleeping bag. "Didn't we talk about the chauvinism?"

"I was speaking *relatively*. Don't be so sensitive, *Clee*. What's offensive to *me* is your defensive *degree*. You programmed my code's cluster *lines*, with LL, Big, and Busta *Rhymes*."

"Whatever." The rover was right, but she wasn't admitting it, not in this mood. "You mapped the stars last night?"

"That's right."

"Then what planet is this? Or where were we before? The world with heavy gravity, where was that?"

"You have injuries of sheer *variety*. Internal, external, yet you sit there *defiantly*. I'm not lying, *Clee*. Right now, you don't need the *anxiety*."

"Why would a simple answer cause me more anxiety?" Cleo asked, her blood boiling now. "My anxiety . . . it's thinking about Yasmin out there by herself." She could feel her heart pounding in her chest, warning her to calm down. "But the combination of you avoiding the question and then rhyming about it is pissing me the hell off. The little rhyming makes this whole thing sound playful, but this is life or goddamn death!"

"Wow. That sounds so damn *Clee*! Look, you programmed *me*. I carry meds and food, no sal-a-*ry*, not even *flattery*, just verbal *battery*. So frustrating, but I can't *show it*. Just an unappreciated techno-*poet*. You call me sexist, you techno-*phobic*, retro—"

"Okay. Okay. Stop," Cleo droned, headache creeping back in. "God, who's sensitive now? Okay. I love the rhyming. It's in your programming, and you're the GOAT. But you need to tell me what's going on. I want to know everything, even the worst."

"Eat first."

She didn't feel hungry, and that was a bad sign. It had been about a day since she'd lost consciousness. That meant more than two days since she had her last meal. And all the excursion, the hiking, the gravity. Cleo understood the need to eat intellectually, even if the urge wasn't there. She grabbed an unopened MRE.

"Fine," she said. Her cold, unsynchronized fingers floundered around the Tear Here marker on the package. Sweetbread was her first choice. She hoped her favorite food would spark her appetite. As Cleo tore it open, the magnesium base in the MRE reacted with the oxygen and an instant warmth burned into the foods. The aroma steamed to her nostrils, and *oh God* her appetite reignited.

She barely chewed. Her esophagus did most of the work. She licked her fingers. She sucked between her teeth and bit the crumbs lining her fingernails. It was a carnal sort of consumption. The type of fixation that vanished the world around you. That tent, the cold, Shakes, and all the noises outside bled away—and that blood drained to her gut.

It took a few minutes for the proteins and flavonoids to stoke the brain cells, but the fog was lifting, and the migraine with it. It was quiet for a moment, just a single moment, and that was all it took for the noises outside to ebb back into the tent. To press down on the hydroplastics—push through and rub cold noises down her spine.

What the hell was that? she wondered. *The drugs?*

"I mapped the stars via G-radio *gauger*. I mapped the Big Dipper and much of Ursa *Major*, Orion's Belt, so it's fair to *wager* . . . from that *radius*, if the math isn't *failing us*, that we are still on Orbis *Alius*."

Orbis? "How? That can't be right."

"Take a second to digest *that*, rest *back*. I know where your head's *at*, probably *spinning*. Well, buckle up, Clee, that's just the *beginning*."

"'Kay," Cleo said. "But before you go on . . . you're sure? We're still on Orbis? Even now?"

"Yes," the rover said plainly for once.

But she knew that. She had seen it too, squinting through the cumulus on that heavy world and finding the Big Dipper like piercings in the clouds.

"Big Dipper," Cleo admitted, somewhat buying into the possibility of it. "I might have seen the Big Dipper that night . . ."

"That's right," Shakes continued softly, gently, easing his words in. "We are still here, in Orbis's *verse*, for better or *worse*. Blessing or *curse*."

"But how to explain that fog, then?" Cleo asked, trying to think up the answers herself. "And the different environments?"

"The black fog that passes us *through*, that gaseous *goo*. It might act as a sort of *border* or *warder*, a force that keeps things in *order*. But we crossed through it like a *corridor*. And now you're a *foreigner*. In strange lands that don't purport to support *you*. That fog is not a portal to export *through*, just a barrier to thwart *you*."

"The gaseous goo . . ." She hated using such an unscientific term. "It separates different environments. Different biospheres. Why?" Cleo asked herself. How could that barrier separate regions with different weather, climates, and especially gravity? "How?" Now she aimed her words at Shakes. "Separate climates, sure—even pressure, maybe—but gravity? How's that possible?"

"The 'how,' I don't *know*. The 'why,' I might, *though*. Remember the discovered *sphere*, all that just hovered *there*?"

"The high-gravity world." Cleo nodded, then she remembered it wasn't a world. "That biosphere." She corrected herself before Shakes could. "What about it?"

"I picked up a signal at the mountain's *peak*, like I heard the mountain *speak*—"

"Signal," Cleo interrupted, a memory snapping up from her backbone. *How did I even forget?* "Me too. It was Yasmin. She's alive, but it was a recording playing."

"And what was she saying?" Shakes asked.

"Something about a nest?" she asked herself. "Too much interference."

The rover lowered its head. The entire conversation, Shakes had been leading up to saying something. And it hadn't said it yet. Still being on Orbis Alius wasn't the big reveal. There was something else her IU hadn't yet said about that signal it'd received.

"Shakes," she said, leaning toward her rover, "what did you find on top of that mountain?"

"I found a pattern in the noise. A pattern that employs advanced *design*, a pattern which aligns with itself, that very static is the *sign*—their signal, and it's not *ours*. I've scoured for *hours* . . ."

"Wait," Cleo said. "What do you mean 'it's not ours'?"

"It's a signal from other *powers*."

Her lips broke to speak, but she didn't know what to ask. What was the rover saying? Other powers?

"The signal has a pattern in it?" Cleo asked, hoping to get the story straight. "Right? That's what you're saying? That the static is not just noise, it's a . . ."

"Language," Shakes finished. "But a language that's hard *to speak*. All my computing power was far *too weak*. I can't understand or *respond, Clee*. This thing's *beyond me*. I compare it to a *wand, see*. Cuz it's like magic. All this static? It's data encoded in *gravity*, *my God*! Mathe*matically*, *I laud*. That *strategy*—"

"Shakes!" she cut her rover off and eased back to take in the whole scope of the machine. This wasn't like Shakes. "What's wrong with you?"

"Nothing's wrong—it's true."

But there was something wrong. Shakes's voice patterns were off, and even its rhyme scheme felt foreign. There was almost an unprogrammed excitement in its tone. But it was what Shakes was saying that was even further amiss. It was implying that the static's signal was from something else.

"You're saying . . ." She shook her head. "What? Data encoded in gravity. It's beyond us. What is?" *Go ahead*, she thought. "Say it . . ."

"Say what?" Shakes responded.

"What you're thinking. What that signal implies."

"Something here is *alive*, and they are *wise*—no *lies*. So *wise*, *Clee*. They outsized *me*. All-*mighty*. Communicating through *gravity*. *Rapidly*. So fast I can't *follow*. Encryption so vast that I can't *swallow*. It's a perfect *vision*, a found *religion*, it's *unflawed*. I'm *awed* . . ."

"You've found life?"

"God."

Shakes's decapitated skull lay on the tent's plastic floor. It was hard to look at, but she had to. The light on its digital display, which always sort of resembled a bright cycloptic eye, was now an empty black shell of metal. Its steel skull was screwed open at the scalp, black and red wiring oozing out. But Cleo cringed through it. She squinted into liquid batteries, coolants, and crown processors searching for that one glitch, a single wire out of place or a burnt fuse—a loose screw, even—something, anything to make it all make sense.

She didn't believe her IU, but she believed in it. This planet was mad. Gaseous barriers, variations in the gravity and atmosphere, a floating moon, and carnivorous clouds. This was a mad world, no doubt of that. But life? She scowled as she thought of it. And not just life. Shakes was asserting intelligence—an intelligence beyond humanity. A god . . . And that frightened her, because there was a god in her head too.

But why not? Cleo wondered as her fingers descended into the wired dreadlocks of Shakes's brain. *Why couldn't there be life here?*

"Why not?" Cleo said, giving voice to the noise in her head.

But maybe she knew why it had to be impossible. *You do*, Dad's voice said to her. The hints of it were in her name, not Cleo but Xavier. Because this doubt was less about science or theorems and far more concerned with Cleo's own inheritance. She was a Xavier; her grandfather was part of the team that had made the discovery: *We are alone*, he had declared, *isolated in the universe.* That was at the heart of her denial, the deconstruction of the rover's body, and its IU brain spilled between her fingers. She would be the one to discover life and destroy a family legacy, just like Ava had said. *Not so birdbrained after all,* Ava's voice whispered from the deepest part of Cleo.

She found nothing wrong, and all her movement was now in reverse. Cleo put the rover back together. She fastened the machine's neck onto its body. She replaced the screws, the magnets, and clamps. Right now, she needed to hear another voice to block out the others.

"Are you there, Shakes?" Cleo asked, leaning toward the lit screen on its head. "Shakes . . . You there?"

"Here," the IU said.

"Is everything okay?"

"I should ask you. You should *tell us.* When I said 'God' before, you seemed *jealous,* but honestly, maybe I was over*zealous.* Look, I'm not trying to oversell *us,* when I say we're a good duo, but with all we've been through, *though,* this lobotomy has gotta be, a new *low,* you *know.*"

She smiled. At least Shakes still held on to its sense of humor. "Had to make sure," she said. "Nothing you said made sense. I'm just getting a grip on us being on Orbis Alius. I'm barely over that. So let's take the rest of it slow."

"Sure," Shakes said. "But that *is* what I said before . . ." That part it said under its breath. "That whole thing about rest, taking it *slow,* hearts out of *flow.* Hate to say it but—"

"I told you so?" She heard it coming. "And I still want to know everything, smart-ass." Cleo sat up so that she would be eye to eye with the rover. "So let's go through it again. You went on top of that mountain. You caught hold of a signal, right? Not one of ours."

"Other powers."

"Yes. And you think it's other powers because of the complexity of the pattern of that signal."

"Correct."

"The complexity is beyond us, you said. You mean more advanced?"

"Beyond me," Shakes clarified.

"Right. But you can't understand it—the signal. All you did was come across a pattern of complexity that you can't understand. It could be anything . . . couldn't it?"

"It could not. Why are you trying to de-*ny us*? What's with the *bias*?"

My name, she thought, but then Cleo shook her head deliberately, forcing the idea out of her mind. She felt sick, like all those recently digested sweetbreads and fish cakes were about to come back up. She'd barely accepted that they were still on Orbis Alius and Shakes wanted to make a bid for life.

"There's no life anywhere," she said, reinforcing the terraformer's edict. *Old ideas fight desperately to survive*, Dad had told her once, but that was a conversation about religion. This was science. She was defending hard, cold mathematical fact. "It's universally accepted science." She spoke more confidently now. "Every hoolgirl knows that. Even the religious folk admit it now—the Apostles, everybody. We're alone in the universe."

A spell of dizziness shook her. Cleo fell back. She caught herself on an unsteady hand. Shakes had to have seen that. Because the rover backed down. The IU realized it was upsetting her. It went quiet. She wanted it to feel sorry, to feel like an asshole, but the thing was an IU. They didn't think that way. They were logic machines. There was one thing Shakes still wasn't saying: How did it know for sure that there was life on this world? Every IU maintains at least a 1 percent probability for error. That's a numbers-based logic system at work. For them, no theory could be 100 percent, unless it was blatant, undeniable fact.

"You're sure there's life," she said, breaking her stubbornness to the idea of it. "You know for a fact life is out there?"

"No doubt here," Shakes responded.

"How do you know beyond a reasonable doubt?" she asked.

"Because of what's *outside*. That's where the doubt *died*."

What? she mouthed as a coldness washed over her, a tingling down her spine. She trembled as that strange cold vibrated through her. "What . . ." she managed in a shortness of breath.

"Just beyond the tent is irrefutable *evidence* for nonhuman *intelligence*."

That strange cold stroked along Cleo's back and through her hair, around her hips, and down her legs. A sound was doing this. Fingers of noise prodded at her.

"What. Is. It?" she stuttered, hugging herself, tying her legs in loops and bringing her knees to her chest. That circle again. "A bird, a plane, what? Carbon based? What elements compose it?"

"Clee. This is life as we don't know it."

13

Cleo kicked her feet into the boots, stomping down to fit them faster, until the pressure eventually suctioned around her toes. She clawed into the gloves, fingernails scratching to get all the way in, until fabric swathed knuckles as she made a fist. Cleo dressed faster and more violently than she ever had, finally gripping the halogen in a boxer's fist. The halo helmet shook as she squeezed it. Fear resembled violence sometimes, and maybe that was what violence was—an escalation of fear. And was it violence pushing through her as if she had known it would come to that?

Shakes stepped in front of her, blocking the circular egress. But she was halfway glad for the IU's obstruction. Cleo was terrified to detach locks on the ferrofluidic seal. She bluffed hostility at her rover, huffing and rolling her eyes, shaking her head, and a tantrum of hair shook with it. But she was glad for its resistance.

"Move, Shakes," Cleo said.

"What's with all the *immediacy*? No need to leave *immediately*. Did you hear what I said *previously*? Clee, listen to *me*, there's more you don't *know*. Don't leave with some *faux*, need to just *show—out*, show *clout*, and leave no *doubt* that you're some *heroine*. In an era *when—*"

"Then shut up and tell me." That part wasn't a bluff. "What more do I need to know? There's something out there, and you were just going to let me sleep here while some . . . thing is stalking outside?" Cleo pouted and pointed to that imagined thing beyond the tent. Her imagination ran wild, conjuring up human-size centipedes or a hundred-eyed jellyfish swimming through the air. "Answer the question," she shouted. "Why are we still here? With that thing outside?"

"A few hours ago you were dying and *slumping*. And honestly, I was just trying *something*. Buying *time*, crying *rhymes*. Acting as your *clinician*. Remember, you are my only *mission*. And you were in no *position* or *cognition* to move of your own *volition*."

Something moved in her. Something like warmth rose up from her chest, making its way out through her eyes. It was something about how the IU said, *You are my only mission*. Logically Cleo knew Shakes was programmed to jump in front of a bullet for her, but to hear it was another thing completely.

"So," Cleo sighed, "what do you want to do?"

"Boston's signal, I *tapped* it—I *trapped* it, isolated then *mapped* it. I know it's hard to swallow my heed with *blinders*. But if you follow my lead, we'll *find her*."

"You tell me this now?" Cleo snapped, quickly crowning herself with the halogen. The spin of the thing blurred her eyes with determination. "Why wasn't that the first thing you said?"

"Look at yourself now, that's *why*. In your health, and you wanna go *try*—devote your life and devote *my* . . . *objective*. Doesn't take a *detective*."

"'Kay . . ." She shrugged. "Still, you shoulda led with that. Let's follow Boston's signal."

Now Shakes appeared to sigh. "They say a wo-man is man's *woe*. Leaving now shouldn't be the plan, *though*. You're hurt and there's no *transpo*. We can't just Van *go*, sans *ogh*. And my scans *show*, your heart is—"

"My heart's fine," Cleo interrupted. "So's my knee, especially in this gravity." But that was a half-truth. The stretching of muscle around the cartilage brought on a shock of pain. *But I can manage it*, she told the voice in her head that said otherwise. "Whatever that thing is outside. I can feel it. I feel it and I don't like it." She gestured for Shakes to move.

"We're getting out of this biosphere and following that signal to find Boston. So you can stay here or come and protect me . . ."

"Let me inspect, *Clee*," Shakes grumbled, seemingly to itself. "You don't respect *me*. Just neglect *me*. Direct*ly*."

Shakes gripped the circular egress with the retractable pincers on its head. It twisted at the lock, and the rover's head spun like a drill. The air from outside hissed hostile into their faces, and the tent immediately began to deflate. Shakes crawled out first, then Cleo scrambled out as the plastic ceiling melted down on top of her.

It was dark out there—that was her first thought. Really damn dark. She untangled her legs from the tent, and immediately that darkness weighed down on her until there was nowhere else for it to go but inside. It was in her head; all these shadows and she wasn't alone. Cleo tapped the retina light affixed to her left chest, a sort of flashlight that followed the direction of her retinas. Whatever her eyes spotted, it spotlighted, and even the motion of squinting squeezed the light beam into a sharpened brightness. Fifty hours of battery life flashed into the darkness, and its sudden spark of incandescence was like oxygen in all those shadows.

The light followed her eyes' circular motion, from the ground up the rounded wall to the rounded ceiling, then right back down to her feet. It was a tunnel.

"Are we in a cave system?" Cleo asked.

"Yes," Shakes responded. "Caves, but a *strange type*. These tunnels resemble *de-ranged pipes*."

The ground beneath her was moving. Cleo looked down, and the retina light moved in sync, aiming at her feet. She found a spongy white membrane stretching underneath her. *The hell?* She squinted. It felt almost like sand—almost, but without the graininess. There was this sort of ripple around her feet that followed each step. She squinted harder, leaning in, neck first, then her back, and finally her knees. *Shit, my knees.* But Cleo hid the pain.

The ground wasn't rippling but was made of little white stones that moved; no, not stones, but something shaped like teeth. They were everywhere, countless little calcified . . . teeth? There was no other apt comparison. And they moved, tiny incisors oscillating back and forth.

"Millions," she said as she looked, and the retina light aimed the beam down the tunnel ahead. "Shakes, what are these teeth things on the ground?"

Shakes took a moment to scan the geological incisors. The click, click, click from the X-rays echoed from its oculars. It was visually mining deeper into the shorter wavelengths of the light. Click. Click. Click.

"Not teeth but more like stones, and they're *alive*. Growing from rootlike pores, they *survive*—cuz they thrive in the *dark*. Your light is the *spark*, that enlivens their *mark*."

"They thrive in the dark? So is the light hurting them, then?"

"It's more like a drug high, the light is *filling them*, with verve to its nerves, but in the end, it is *killing them*. They'll be comatose from the *light stress*, cuz of the overdose of *brightness*."

"Like radiation to the human body," she said, not asking—she understood it. Her light would excite the tooth stones for a while but would kill them in the end. "But this . . ." She gestured to the stones. "This isn't the intelligence, is it?"

"No. Like grass on Earth, it's just a *requirement* of this species' *environment*."

"So . . ." Where was it?

But Cleo didn't ask, because honestly, she didn't want Shakes to tell her. Deep down she was hoping they could escape this biosphere without ever having to run into this tunnel-burrowing intelligence.

"Is this the right way?" she asked, stepping forward. But there were only two paths, backward and forward. "Have you mapped this mess?"

"Yes. The design has a quasi-*frequence*, like structures built in a Fibonacci *sequence*. Definitely intelligent *design*. Art and architecture *aligned*."

"That's nice, Shakes," she said with a bite of sarcasm. The IU seemed to admire the alien design. "This is the god species that you heard yester—"

Something like sound gushed out from behind, and it splashed against her flesh. And it was so cold. The noise penetrated her suit and rubbed across her skin, brushed through her hair, then penetrated again—inside the sockets of her eyes, it touched her kidneys and heart, her lungs, and all the vessels in between. Then exited out the other side of her.

"What the fu . . ." Cleo fell backward and shivered on the floor. Saliva dripped from her lips and mucus from her nostrils. It was like a ghost had walked through her. Cleo crawled toward the rover and grabbed its leg. Tears lit her eyes, but she didn't want to cry.

"Clee?"

"Go," she said. "Go."

And Shakes went, marching slowly forward as Cleo held on to its anterior like a crutch. Her skin was still crawling. Cold rushes washed down her spine. A cold sweat poured down her arms like her pores were vomiting.

"What is it . . . what is this species?"

"I don't know, Clee. Biology is not my *vocation*, though it appears to have a type of *echolocation*."

"Echolocation?" Cleo whispered to herself. "But I felt it . . . inside. It was inside of me. Passed through me."

"Like echolocation. But this is so far *advanced*, like it's sonar *enhanced*. Beyond owls, bats, or even sea *whales*, this thing penetrates in *details* that we wouldn't imagine, it might even go down to the atom. The echo doesn't bounce off your skin, it's *seizing*, then *squeezing*. It penetrates your flesh, touching lungs and *breathing*—stroking your heart, its beating; your throat, its *wheezing*."

Yes, she considered, *like that*. She had felt like something was ricocheting inside her. Groping at all her internal parts: clenching, then examining. Advanced echolocation that penetrated down to the atom. Whatever this species was, it had taken an interesting evolutionary path.

"This thing can't see," Cleo realized, thinking about the extreme dark. "It's blind." She nodded, agreeing with the little terraformer inside her. "Echolocation," she said as if it was an epiphany and Shakes hadn't just told her. "Right. And if it's intelligent, then it would have some sort of advanced sonar that penetrates skin, body—cells, even. It knows what I'm made of."

"That's probably just the *start*. This thing now probably has a gaudy *chart* with the function of every body *part*, from your uterus down to your shoddy *heart*. God, he *smart*."

"He?"

"Or she. Didn't mean to *offend her* or *misgender*. But I'm not some *supremacist*, I'm super *feminist*."

Was her IU trying to lighten the mood? Because it wasn't working. Her shoddy heart was beating like a boxer's speed bag. Somewhere out there was a highly evolved and intelligent mole or bat or cave fish.

"Let's move," she said, stepping forward ahead of Shakes. "If it wanted us dead, my guess is, we'd be dead."

"This thing is *intelligent*, and that isn't *irrelevant*, there's a chance it's *benevolent*."

Benevolent—Casper, the friendly alien, only if her luck changed. They walked for a few hundred feet more, and Cleo felt the cold echolocation rubbing against her from behind. The coldness shoved against her back and exited on the other side. It was behind her. She whipped around, and again, there was nothing there. *Is it camouflaged?* she wondered.

"Shakes, what are we dealing with?" Cleo said, attempting one more glance behind her and finding nothing. "Do you have a scan of this thing?"

"No. And I've tried. But it hides."

Cleo paced ahead with renewed vigor, skipping at a jogger's pace, running from the imagined monsters in her head. Her imagination chased her for hours, downward through every dark tunnel. But she would eventually slow down, and so would her imagination. Her brain slumped with the same fatigue as her muscles. Two hours became three, then four, and even with Shakes rerouting and remapping, it appeared that the original entrance that brought them into this biosphere had disappeared.

Cleo proposed endless possibilities as to what was happening. Most of her theories, the IU discounted, except one. Maybe these tunnels were under this entity's control. Her words quieted the rhymester. Maybe it was changing the structure of the tunnels. And still, not a rhyme from Shakes.

It's observing us.

Her loquacious IU kept its lyrics to itself for the first time in a long time. Neither denying nor confirming what Cleo had said, only prompting her to keep talking. And that was its plan, to have her talk herself to sleep. They reopened the tent for her to eat and rest. This time she slept more than a dozen hours deep.

—

"We'll find a way *out*," the rover said in modes of positivity. "I know you may *doubt*, how this plays *out*, but just rest while I stake *out*, the lay*out*, to find a stray *route*—straight *out*."

But after forty-eight hours trapped in the tunnels, the doubt was unavoidable. Cleo doubted they'd find Boston at all, even with the signal. She doubted ever getting back home. It was obvious that the entity wasn't an immediate threat; the creature just seemed to observe. She and Shakes were like ants in its farm, running a merry-go-round under this species' microscope. The invisible species probed through Cleo every twenty-one minutes and seventeen seconds. She had timed it. But why? There were so many whys. Like, Was this her feral god? *This is a broad cast*, it had said. *Find us a live*. Had she found it? Or was this something else?

On the third day in those tunnels, Cleo dreamed of the feral god again, and it whispered new verses into her head. Its dead pheromones floated through this labyrinth world too. And the feral god recited a map into her dreams. It was there that an idea sparked. A flash of dangerous ideas so blazing bright that it woke Cleo up. It was something the feral god had said. Spark a light to escape the lonely dark.

"I don't think this thing is letting us out."

"Was it a dream?" Shakes said in the dark of the tent.

"Yes," she said. "Where's your battery at, Shakes?"

Shakes paused, then rolled back on its hind legs and dipped its head. "Just under twenty-two *percent*. It's plenty to *prevent*, any—"

"'Kay." She cut him off to save any inch of power. "Twenty-two. I, um . . ." Cleo cleared her throat. "I had another thought as well. What's the atmosphere in these caves made of?"

The rover stepped back. "Silicon, argon, carbon, *primarily*. Sulfur, fluorine, and neon *secondarily*."

"That's what I figured. No oxygen. Not even in a chemical compound. Fire isn't impossible here. It's a chemical reaction that it would have never seen."

"I'm betting that I know what you're getting *at*, and regretting that I didn't—"

"Think of that?" she said, though *that* likely wasn't the rhyming word. "You said that simple light from my flashlight's beam was injuring the toothy stones. Think about what fire would do. And you have the oxygen."

"But it's *preserved* for our *reserves*."

"I don't think we have a choice. Your reserves of compressed air and mine could easily fill a corridor. And I've got the lighter. We blow a hole in this bitch."

"You light the match and then we *bail*? It's desperate, but if we pre-*vail* . . ."

"Drinks on me."

They strategized for another couple of hours. Shakes wanted to run the numbers, prepare for every feasible outcome: the cave's chemical makeup, internal combustion, and the chances of Cleo inadvertently incinerating herself. With a fire-retardant space suit, that possibility was low but not zero, it reminded her. The IU was thorough when it came to her life, and in realizing that, she didn't feel as isolated.

Shakes seesawed radio and X-rays until it had mapped the cavernous space. To hear the IU talk, it would seem there was a pattern in the shape-shifting nature of that environment. They weren't walking in circles, exactly; instead, it was more of a Fibonacci sequence of concentric circles. It was architectural music, as Shakes described it—effectual acoustics. The subterranean space wasn't as much shape-shifting as it was dancing—and dancing with them, it seemed. And she realized that the design of these tunnels might be a form of communication. It was a bonjour, or a foreign handshake with too many fingers to follow. It was a flirtation, the way this entity fashioned its environment in a provocative mathematical aesthetic and waited for them to respond. But she would never understand completely, because Cleo was about to introduce this oxygenless species to fire.

Cleo and Shakes hiked the shape-shifting corridor for the last time; one way or the other, this would be their final lap. It was an hours-long trek until the IU landed them at an area it estimated would be closest to the gaseous goo. The mysterious fog was right there on the other side of that tooth-stone wall. She just needed to cut through.

Shakes released its liquid oxygen and it immediately vaporized, hissing out from the output nipple by its rib. Cleo's recycler system had a cocktail of nitrogen, oxygen, and trace gases, but it was a better conductor of fire than anything in that tunnel, so it vented too. They concentrated all that oxygen on the curve in the wall, and all that air settled there better than expected.

She felt them behind her, probing with more frequency—an excitement in them, maybe. Those invisible entities were a river flowing through her with their mad echolocation. They must have known something was about to happen. And a part of her felt sorry.

He, they, whatever it was, it had never attempted to harm her. It was just holding her like a pet and squeezing too tight. *Sorry*, she thought in those last moments. Because for a species that had never known fire, this was going to be one hell of an introduction.

"All we *require*," Shakes said, turning to her then, "right here in the *pyre*. Oh, for a muse of *fire*."

And Cleo lit the torch. A flash of white snapped into the darkness, then orange flames raged in front of her, knocking Cleo on her ass in light-gravity slow motion. The features of the tunnel arose from the dark. That brown spongelike ground and the ivory teeth shrank down to rice-size specks in the fire. And the entities flashed in and out of the visual spectrum, exposing themselves to her—full-naked-monsters. Benevolent or not, those things were otherworldly.

A circular black shell of a thing opened into a whirlwind of appendages, like a fist opening into fingers, then those fingers closed back into a fist. Opening and closing, and each time, a wave of echolocation cold pulsed outward. Its spongy flamingo-shaded insides had bioluminescent hairs wriggling on the tips of each appendage.

What the hell? Cleo thought as her hippocampus vomited adrenaline and biochemical fear.

They didn't appear to have any intention toward her. Might have been the shock of the fire. Their bodies appeared flammable, and retreated into higher or lower spectrums of light. The walls of the tunnel were dangerously flammable and peeled away, revealing the gaseous goo beyond. But Cleo couldn't pull her eyes from true first contact. Wave after wave of evolved sound washed over her, and she knew then that she was the monster. They weren't just probing her—they were communicating.

"Move now, Clee," Shakes urged her, then something about *proudly* and *allowed me*, but she didn't hear it over her own panting echoed in her halogen's atmosphere. She was running low on oxygen. Cleo had exhausted too much. She stumbled toward the gaseous goo on the other side of the living walls, and Shakes helped drag her through.

14

Cleo and her rover emerged from that gaseous boundary on fire. Flames spiraled around her halogen, then quickly fizzled out. Google's *G* smoked, and the LEGO logo was a blur of singed ink. The duo smoldered in the sudden cold and new sunlight. But it was the moisture burning at the rims of Cleo's eyes that hurt the most; she was gutted and felt the urge to vomit. *What did I just do?* she kept thinking. That species. That whole world or biosphere, whatever it was. "What'd I . . ."

But as the water washed out from her eyes, Cleo glimpsed the terrain ahead. Beneath the soles of her boots, the ground was threaded like guitar strings, thousands of threads, overlapping each other, no spaces between. It resembled black hairlike follicles that stretched on for miles. Billions of individual strands sprawled across the landscape. No soil or stones, nothing like vegetation existed here, just endless black strings on the ground and a frenzied but distant pair of white stars above.

"What the hell?"

For a split second, the past washed to the back of her mind—she was fully present. *No time to mourn*, she observed as all those strings moved. Or maybe *it* moved? It was all one thing, wasn't it? One entity with a million parts? It moved under her feet. Individual strands wormed in and out of each other. Black noodles wrapping and winding around the spin of an invisible fork.

"What. The. Hell?"

Ahead, she saw large knots within the hair, a bushy, bundled-up collection of threads, like kinks in its tresses—like nodes. Were those nerve centers? Flashes of black light, if there was such a thing, streaming through the hairs, and all met at these nodes, swirling faster and brighter in rhapsody. Then wisps of the hairlike material flaked off at these nodal centers, like shedding skin.

"What is this?" Cleo whispered to herself, jaw ajar for so long that saliva had started to gather. "How does it work?"

"There seem to be *surges* in these *convergences*. What's emerging is a web of *channels*—a network containing *annals* of information and random communication."

"Convergences?" Cleo asked, pointing to the nodes. "Those nodes, you mean. There's communication between the nodes."

"Seems so."

Intelligence. "Again . . ." She stood like a smoldering statue as she pieced the puzzle together. There was intelligence here too. And what about that sphere—might there have been thoughts roaming within that floating leviathan? "And the carnivorous clouds," she whispered, weaving in and out of her head. If every environment changed, then maybe it was to support different forms of life. Different species. "But that's unreal."

"Even I'll admit that this vista's *moving me*. So I'm not speaking disap*proving-ly*. But we have to keep *moving*, *Clee*."

"It's all intelligent life," she said, pointing back to the gaseous barrier. "That echolocation . . . thing. The sphere. The carnivorous clouds. And here too."

"That may be true. But without science, it's just *subjective*. An opinion. And not our *objective*. Find Boston. Her signal is mapped, *see*. As simple as that, *Clee*."

Shakes sent the mapping information to the tablet on Cleo's wrist. Information that she already possessed, but this was just a reminder: Boston and for the collective, the mission statement printed across the space suit. And still she stood comatose, staring into the preternatural space in front of her.

"I know this is an amazing goddamn *find*. Maybe the greatest of all *mankind*. But don't let it make you so damn *blind*."

"Womankind," she said, hints of a smile swelling her lips. "Keep moving," she said mostly herself, and she would try.

Yet an hour across the terrain and her heartbeat flickered palpitations. She hadn't recovered completely. And the lift in her legs just wasn't there. Her feet dragged, and Cleo kept drifting farther behind the rover.

She knew it was best not to linger in landscapes she didn't understand. The signal was closer now—barely a hundred miles, according to the maps. The strings or wires or hair never bothered her, and she never bothered them. She tiptoed over their silky bodies as she and Shakes continued through that landscape toward the signal, beckoning louder. Then she saw the dank fog and they rushed across the barrier. Whatever this hair was, there was no toll to pay for crossing over, and thank God for that.

The subsequent landscape was a world of ice and the most Earthlike of any Cleo had surveyed yet. The gravity pulled just a few pounds higher than on Earth. Atmospheric readings suggested the air held just enough oxygen to keep Cleo alive for a couple of minutes without the halogen. And water was abundant, though trapped in the boundless ice. Snowflakes parachuted from pink-flushed cumulus down to an ocean of frozen water. The entire landscape in every direction was a consistency of ice.

The first thing Cleo noticed, though, wasn't the topography of sheer ice but the light. The cloud-choked sky didn't let in a blink of light, and yet there was brightness here. An incredibly soft glow beamed from deep underneath the ice, lighting the world with an overcast-day sort of light—an early-evening sort of shine. Bioluminescence? That was her first guess, but it was unlikely. The landscape was far too bright for bioluminescence that deep beneath the ice.

Cleo thought to ask Shakes, then realized that the distance between her and the rover was expanding still. She needed rest but couldn't. She stared zombie-eyed at her feet slithering across the glassy ground. Cleo held her arms out at her sides, mimicking wings to keep balance, and wondered if some deep childhood enjoyment was emerging. Like, why hadn't she released the cleats from her boots? She was very aware of this conundrum and still refused to do it.

"Shakes," she shouted to the distant rover, over a hundred feet ahead. "Slow! Down!"

"Your earpiece still works *perfectly*. So, it's *certainly*—unnerving, Clee. When you shout so *fervently*."

"Sorry," she said in a pant. "Now, slow the hell down."

"Pace up," Shakes beckoned. "It would be wise, *Clee*. I ran a scan to capture precise-*ly* why there's not a fracture in the ice-*y*, surface, to put it concise-*ly*. I'm nervous. Something's there deep in *ground*, creep-ing *round*, my radar's beep-ing *sound*."

The radar's image linked to Cleo's wrist tablet. It looked like a clock with a single hand circling. It clicked, not a beep but a choking crackle that crescendoed as the radar hand flashed on a red dot, followed by a coma of quiet.

Cleo gazed into the ice beneath her feet. Not a single fissure lay in its crystal-clear depths. The bizarre underground light didn't bend on a single imperfection. She could stare down for miles into fathoms of ice like it was solid air. She didn't like being able to see that deep. It was unnatural. If looking up to the heavens gave her peace, then gazing downward drudged up maelstroms of distress.

Cleo snapped the cleats at the bottoms of her boots and marched hard along the ice, gaining one foot on the rover every couple of strides.

"Keep moving," she said and waved Shakes on, telling him that she was catching up. "Don't slow down."

But there was a slight spasm in Shakes's step every few seconds. What was that? It took a moment, but Cleo soon realized the twitch matched the radar's clicking in her earpiece. That recognition brought her gaze back to the transparent ice, and right there, beneath her feet, she saw another devil.

It was hard to make out at that distance. The thing was just a dance of white somehow ascending upward through solid ice.

"Are you seeing this?" Cleo, out of breath, howled to the IU.

"I see *it*, al*beit*, I don't believe *it*, that I—That I . . . That . . . I . . ."

"I, what?" Cleo shouted back over the static. "Shakes? That I what?"

But it was the static, a whole hornet's nest droning into her earpiece. The closer that thing rose to the surface, the deeper the interference buzzed. And the more it appeared to interfere with Shakes's communications.

"That I?" she repeated, feeling that the point of its message was there.

The light was fading now. A glance down revealed that as this devil was rising up, it was eclipsing whatever light source was below. How big was this thing? Cleo stopped, kneeled, and bowed her head toward the ice. She saw it now. The thing wasn't swimming. Somehow this monster was vibrating its way through the ice, literally oscillating through a solid body of frozen water.

"Ice XI?" Cleo asked, Dad in her head. "What is it? Maybe Ice XIV?"

That was the terraformer in her. There were twenty-one observed phases of ice—Dad had taught her that. But at no phase should anything that large be able to oscillate itself through the ice.

Cleo sprinted, head down, one eye aimed at Shakes, the other at the leviathan rising beneath them. An unrecognizable disarray of limbs and spikes and something like eyes vibrated upward. Her loyal rover waited, likely rhyming something witty underneath all that static. She hugged the rover's back, breathless, heaving for air, barely enough strength left in her to hold on.

"Go," she gasped, releasing the cleats on her boots. "Go, Shakes."

Shakes stampeded ahead, Cleo's legs waggling behind it, a pair of tails slippery on the sleek ice. *Don't look down*, she directed herself, but the static crescendoed louder than even her own thoughts—barbed wire threaded through her ears. The leviathan was disrupting their signal.

Shakes's fast legs fumbled with a sort of intoxication, and it appeared to be the electric charge. Cleo's halogen too—it wobbled, demagnetizing, though not completely. Why? First the radio interference, now the magnetic connection to her halogen. What type of electromagnetic monster was this?

Slowly the world went dark. The creature had eclipsed the light completely. A high-pitched shrill whistled upward as it emerged. A dozen crab-like limbs oscillated out of the ice, reminiscent of helicopter rotors spinning faster than human vision. But these twelve appendages only vibrated—not rotating, just moving back and forth, back and goddamn forth, at unseeable speeds. They rose twenty, thirty feet high, encircling Cleo and her rover; it was like a birdcage growing up around them. Lightning snapped between each appendage, and the electromagnetism bore down on them both.

Cleo's halogen clapped down onto its collar. *Oh God*—she breathed the frozen air, and it kicked like cocaine ice. Her eyes rolled back. Saliva froze on her lips. The pressure squeezed in on her ears. She immediately lost her grip on the rover, bounced off the ice, then slid to a stop at the center of all those limbs.

She floundered, choking, grabbing at nothing, then crawled without direction—she couldn't find Shakes in the dark. The only thing she could see was a swarm of dead eyes glowing in the dark from underneath the ice. So many eyes, and watching without emotion—watching her die.

Shakes's headlights flickered on, aimed at the border ahead, as if showing her the way out. The static flared in her earpiece, words blanketed in an ocean of snow, but the static had rhythm—it said something—a goodbye, maybe, because a second later the rover exploded.

Not in the traditional sense of exploding, no smoke or flames. But an electromagnetic blast washed over her, a sort of wind that pushed out from the rover's body, sweeping the snow away in a spherical wave. And then the poor machine collapsed.

EMP, she realized. Somehow her rover had ignited an electromagnetic pulse, and the reaction was immediate. The tower of limbs spasmed their descent into the ice. Cleo's halogen unclipped from its collar and spun again, but at a wobbling rotation. That created some atmosphere, some warmth and oxygen. But not enough.

Blood burst from one nostril—plasma drizzled red and orbited the halogen's atmosphere. Something like brain freeze knocked her sideways, a brute migraine that rolled the world upside down, then right side up. And it kept rolling, even as Cleo dug her cleats in, clawing away at the ice. She propelled her compression-drunk body forward. Everything was spinning, but that liquid fog was within sprinting distance now. A mad dash—she could do it, escape all this screaming static in her ear. But she wasn't leaving this biosphere without Shakes. No way.

Cleo's balance spiraled, as did the aim of her retina light. She squinted through the spin, through the sprays of blood in her atmos, and she found her rover. Cleo stumbled over the rover and all the supplies on its back. She stripped the knife from her utility belt and tore the supplies off. A month's worth of rations, water, and medical provisions spilled out onto the ice. She left it all behind, holding only a single MRE in one hand as she shoved Shakes with everything she had. The rover's last dying motion had been to release its spikes from the ice and fold its legs so that its ultrasmooth knees rested on the surface. Like it knew Cleo would try to save it, or at least planned for that possibility.

It still took effort, though. Every fiber of muscle squeezed as she pushed Shakes's cadaver toward the barrier. She knew the alien's limbs would reemerge. The EMP had stunned the thing, but it was still moving beneath them. She groaned, breathless saliva gushing with sweat and staining the atmos, but she was almost there—almost. The machine disappeared first, and only the adrenaline carried her through that gaseous goo to a new world.

Sunlight slammed into her, a blinding blunt-force trauma, as she entered a green inferno. Her halogen magnetized against its collar, and suddenly Cleo was sucking on alien air. She blacked out in her panic and exhaustion as the world went black.

15

Boston's signal had originated here. It had ticked from some corner of this strange green environment. Shakes was incapacitated now, and truthfully, so was she. Cleo had curled inward against the cold, lightless hours, her wrists knotted into her armpits, her legs tucked against her chest. She was a spherical body—a globe, and every twist of her heartbeat pumped sideways, and the blood flowed counterclockwise. At least, it felt that way. It felt like she was rewinding to that fetal beginning and the nothingness just before it.

She wanted it to end, just a little bit, she thought, an intermission to all this living . . .

Later, she would blame that on the dreaming. Those weren't suicidal thoughts, she'd tell herself, just adenosine, the brain's natural drug of sleep. Not to mention the other voices in her dream, a Doppler of them whirring past her. Finn and his Rastafarian accent, and Austin too. Boston telling her to beware the nest, and Shakes and Dad talking over each other. Ava's voice was last—wicked things always came in her voice, even if she had never said them. That was just the part of Ava that had rubbed off on Cleo, the little villain inside Cleo's head. Then there was one more voice, the feral god. It was the loudest: "This is a broad cast, find us a live."

Cleo blinked awake. Alive. She unshackled herself from her limbs, and the breeze crept in. It wound around her and through the curls in her hair, unmaking her braids. There was something off about that, something her groggy brain couldn't piece together yet. What? Cleo fingered her hair, nails caught on its kinks, then she scratched down dry cheeks, to drier lips, and around the slope of her neck. *Oh God*—her halogen wasn't spinning; it had magnetized, locked on the EMU's collar. Cleo was breathing this atmosphere.

The air smelled green. Cleo unscrewed squinty eyes—light cut at her irises until they leaked, one tear chasing after the other. But she had to see this outbreak of green, from the sky to earth. It was everywhere.

"Where are we?" *But the rover is dead, remember?*

Cleo's heartbeat was noisy—completely out of rhythm with her respiration. That made it hard to get to her feet, but she put her hands on her knees, then hips, and climbed the ladder of herself. She wobbled, taking unsteady steps and finding her bearings as she eyed her wrist display. The map and signal flashed just a couple of miles out from where she was standing. Less than two miles away.

She nearly fell again as joy, exhilaration, misery, and hysteria all rained out from her mind and drowned her body in neurochemicals. She thought of the carnivorous clouds, that moon-size sphere and its mad gravity. Cleo thought of the invisible echolocation creatures, the black web, and a leviathan that vibrated through ice. She did it, and part of her didn't want to believe it. "But I do . . ." she whispered to that side of her.

Cleo ambled away from her rover, promising the machine she'd be back, and soon, and not to worry, and everything was going to be okay, and she kept on promising until the distance and alien flora blurred Shakes from her vision.

She journeyed uphill. Nike prints followed in the dirt behind her. The signal was at the top of the hillside, and that made sense. Wherever this beacon was, it needed to be on higher ground for it to transmit. But fatigue knocked her over on occasion, then the headaches shoved her face-first into the dirt. It would take half the day to stagger up those hills, but she would. She was too close now.

The plateau was dry, and plant life was sparse, only a few resilient weeds performing in the dirt. The view of the valley below revealed a lake and waterways so Earthlike that it all but confirmed Cleo's suspicions. This was her biosphere—Yasmin's. An environment made in her image. From the gravity to the freshest air Cleo had ever breathed, this world was built for the human anatomy. But what did that mean? There was a missing piece to the puzzle, and Cleo hoped that Yasmin—brilliant savant Yasmin Boston—had that piece.

Cleo arrived at sunset. The beacon's pole extended twelve feet high. A satellite dish crowned the shaft, and light twinkled there like the end of a fairy-tale wand. About five feet up on that pole was a touch-screen display with one flashing-white envelope icon. It was the message she had come all this way for.

Cleo clung to the antenna's pole like a crutch to catch her breath. She sucked in hard, ingesting mouthfuls of sweet, sweet oxygen. All that hiking and she was now, finally, tasting the ripeness of the evening breeze. But somehow her breathing picked up as her eyes swelled with tears. Again, she thought, *What's wrong with me?* She didn't miss them that much—Yasmin, Austin, and even little Daniel, all their silly smiles and goofy faces. Maybe. She could grope at the holes inside her, human-size holes, one shaped like Dad, one like Yasmin. Austin and Daniel had the same shape. And somehow even Ava's villainous voice was a vacant space in Cleo. Were these the puzzle pieces that she was looking for?

There was loneliness in her—there was—but she knew the biochemical recipes to numb it. *So numb it up*, she told herself in Ava's raw accent. *Get ya-self together*. And she did. Cleo sucked it all back up with a single sniffle. But hunched there in that disposition, she noticed a scatter of Adidas-logo footprints around the beacon, one of Yasmin's sponsors, and these prints were relatively fresh, no more than a couple days old.

Cleo twirled and tiptoed, surveying the panorama around her. "Boston?" she hollered, nearly tripping as she spun 720 degrees. "Yasmin?"

It was a long shot. She knew that, and still the disappointment stung. Cleo decoupled her right glove, reached for the touch screen, and saw hands anciently dry. It was like a shawl of dead skin and overgrown fingernails. She took a moment to admire her decay before tapping the mail icon on the screen. The vocal response was immediate.

"And beware the octonary . . ." Yasmin—her voice trembled over the speaker. "That one's here—the octonary followed . . ."

"Yasmin?" Cleo questioned the tremble in Yasmin's voice. She hunched, bowing her head toward the speaker.

"But I can't get out of the nest . . . I'm sorry," Boston replied and kept on repeating. "And beware the octonary. That one's here—the octonary followed . . ."

And it looped. The audio kept skipping on those last few sentences. Maybe the end of the message? It was a strange glitch, but one that allowed her to pinpoint this beacon. If the message had broadcasted just once, Shakes would have never detected it. Yasmin did it on purpose. Cleo tapped the interface and found the original recording, a file too large to broadcast in a loop. She rewound Yasmin's words, dragging its cursor back to the start.

"A zoo," Yasmin said in full conviction. "This world is a zoo . . ." Boston's words shuddered over the speaker, like that vocal shakiness just before weeping. "It is artificial. It's . . . a manufactured thing . . ." Her voice kept dropping into deep pauses as she seemed to search for the right words. "This world is unnatural. And it is not a world. It's a structure. It is ancient architecture built from the bones of civilizations. I tested the radioactive decay. This thing is the age of our universe . . ."

Radiometric dating—Cleo would have never even considered it. But Yasmin Boston was layers smarter than she was. Yasmin's prenatal enhancements had the genetic instruction to mimic the greatest minds of science. But even if you were to peel back that layer of cerebral privilege, Yasmin had stem augmentations, every year a new chip on a different cortex of the brain. But peel that layer away too and you'd find Yasmin's superior educational history, her work ethic, a natural inclination to the sciences, all of which far exceeded Cleo's bare-average scholastic aptitude.

"I investigated beyond my biosphere but didn't get far. I encountered this field of octahedrons. Silicon-based life; hydrocarbon veins; liquid methane, maybe. It had these crystal-like roots that pulsed in a rhythmic pattern. In another biosphere, I saw something like balloons, but without pigment, see-through. I could see their electric organs, and current exchanged between them. Wait . . . I hear something."

Cleo thought she heard that something too, and she pressed her ear against the speaker. But she couldn't hear much with the wind picking up, whistling, noisy, spitting twigs, dirt. Everything swirled, even the clouds, bushy-bearded grays sweeping fast across the skyline. Just the boulder behind her stayed in place—the only anchor for her eyes.

"Listen," Yasmin continued, "it's the nest. I don't know its intentions, but it has a way with . . . words. It's communicating. It's driving me mad. It's smarter than us. Smarter. Than anything. Than God. It's killing me. Its words are like a baseball bat. It hurts to listen. Don't trust them. I don't. But it knows things. Like the barriers between biospheres. It kills anything that crosses, except for us. We're the only species that can cross over. But I do not trust them. Do not trust the nest."

"Nest?" Cleo asked, expecting an answer or an explanation. Who was this species that could communicate? But the explanation wouldn't come.

"I came back to my biosphere to tell Daniel and have him tell everyone, but Xavier went to find me and . . . I don't think she'll make it. God, I'm sorry. I'm so sorry . . ." Yasmin's voice broke into pieces, and all that was left audible was the sound of panicked breathing. "It's my fault. I don't know that she can make it. Xavier . . . Cleo."

"It's okay," Cleo said, mirroring the tears in Yasmin's eyes however many days ago.

"And now," Yasmin continued, "Austin's in the . . ."

"Austin's in what?" Cleo asked herself.

"But something else followed me back. And not the nest. The nest is ambiguous. Good or bad. I don't know. I can't tell. But this thing is bad."

"What . . ."

"The octonary," Boston whispered now. "I feel like it's watching me at this very moment. Like it's letting me record."

The hairs on the back of Cleo's neck rose up, and reflexively, her head spun backward. It felt like something was touching her there. Behind her, a metallic sunset rusted a red and orange-brown corrosion across the skyline. The cumulus squirmed in visible discomfort. Thunder rumbled. But her eyes kept moving. What she was looking for was behind the wind, eyes made of nothing but blinking at her. She felt the touch of eyesight, but she didn't see anything other than that rock. But that rock was bigger now, or was it closer? That rock that was . . . Was it breathing? *Holy shit.* The slightest, nearly indiscernible flexing of gills on its sides.

"This octonary . . ." Yasmin's crackling voice continued, "it can camouflage itself." Cleo glanced back again at the breathing rock, breathing heavier—panting. "It's stronger than the rovers. So much stronger."

Cleo pretended to lean in, pretended to listen closer, but in fact her fingers were snaking around the back of the beacon to use it as an anchor to thrust herself forward. She positioned her heels against the starting blocks of rock and sand to push off into a mad dash.

"We're talking about a species for which dying is part of its natural life cycle." Chills ran down Cleo's spine. "A ghost species." She dug her feet into the ground. "That's how it passes through the barriers. It can't die." Ready to run. "It's already dead."

Cleo envisioned flinging herself forward, off the beacon's post, and in one simultaneous motion, pushing off the rocks into a full-on sprint. But that didn't happen. That rock—the octonary—as if knowing exactly what she wanted to do, exploded into a whirlwind of tentacles and eyes and propelled itself directly at her.

"Beware the octonary . . ." Yasmin's last words.

Cleo scrambled forward, immediately tripping, then pushing herself back to her feet. The octonary was hard on her heels, rolling like a tornado of limbs, what she assumed could only be eight. It was too damn fast; she heard it now like a fly buzzing past her ear—that close. Cleo veered right, but it was there before her, as if it was predicting her movement. So Cleo jumped, without aiming at anything but a thicket of trees beneath her. She jumped off the edge of that hillscape.

She fell through a tree line. Small branches bent and the larger ones snapped—no, that was her snapping—then she hit water, feetfirst, and still it knocked the air out of her. Cleo gasped a mouthful of salt water but only tasted blood. She paddled in her heavy space suit, but only one hand was moving—the other hand wasn't there. Cleo groped for what should have been an amputated stub on her right side, but her arm was still there, just bent backward, snapped out of the socket at the shoulder. And that was when the pain hit.

"Ugh, God . . ." she gargled, water choking. "Goddamn it."

A muddied shore was only about twenty yards out, but in her EMU and paddling on three limbs, the distance might as well have been a mile. She floundered, fighting the water—*Don't fight the water*, Dad told her, *it'll fight back*. And it did. She flailed up waves, submerging herself, and she was so out of breath that she choked on the water. The pond wasn't deep, so she hit the bottom nearly immediately. Cleo kicked her way back to the surface. She had swallowed a good half gallon of water before slithering ashore, using just knees and hips, her arm throbbing in pain. She belched water and then vomited it. She'd barely taken her first breath before another splash of water undulated behind her—*the octonary*. And even with everything broken, she found a way to run.

16

Cleo lunged upward, but her heart stabbed her back. Just a warning, but she kept moving anyway. She grabbed her chest with her left hand as the other dangled backward. But every step swung her right arm just enough, shooting razors through her shoulder.

Cleo pinpointed Yasmin's capsule on her map, another mile and a half. *Almost there*, she told herself, but not convincingly enough, as she was seesawing unsteadily on lactic-acidy legs, but eventually she saw its reflective exterior. The capsule bludgeoned the tree line with shrapnel of the sunset's reflected light. *Yes.* Cleo slowed her run to unsteady strides. She tapped the touch screen on her limp wrist and opened access to Yasmin's capsule. Bypassing the few overrides was easy enough.

"Open . . ." Cleo gasped in exhaustion, "the . . . door."

"Air-lock access denied," a female IU replied in a posh British accent. "Door lodged, unable to open."

Lodged with what?

Color oozed across the capsule's hull—biological graffiti emerged in an arachnid anatomy. The octonary, she saw in earnest for the first time. Its lizard-tail limbs stretched around the capsule's waist; its body, if it could be called that, was a gaseous solid, like pressurized hydrogen or something. A ghost drifting in and out of reality. And underneath that smoky, roiling body, a hundred eyes stared out at her. What goddamn genre of monster was this?

It slid off the capsule slowly and almost with technique. Each limb descended and touched the grass separately. It was almost elegant, an alien. This thing obviously could have taken Cleo at any point during her stumbling run, especially with all her injuries. It could kill her now—it should, because that overconfident species was standing in the wrong damn position.

"Test flash charge on engine two," Cleo whispered. She eyed the right engine, mere feet from the octonary. "Flash charge test on two," she hissed even quieter and faster. *It needs to happen now.*

"Confirming," the IU articulated in its glacial bourgeois cadence. "Flash charge to engine two?"

"Yes," Cleo snapped back.

"Warning—test charge on engine two."

Flash charges had no buildup, no sound, no warning, just a hot flash to warm up the engines, yet hot enough to tear a hole in a tank. But it took its sweet time. *Shit,* Cleo had forgotten how slow it was. If the octonary moved from its position in front of engine two, it would have been all for naught. So Cleo took a step forward; before the octonary could move toward her, she would move toward it. She wasn't a threat to the thing, and she was sure it knew that. She even picked up a small rock, which she hoped would make the octonary laugh. *Just keep laughing right there in that spot.*

"Ignition," the IU said.

The light hit first, blinding her, then heat. Even at forty feet away, it burned her eyes with sand and cinders. The blast took her off her feet, and she landed ass-first against the dirt. The octonary, barely a few feet from the second engine, was engulfed in fire. The alien was launched over Cleo's head and knocked sixty feet back, flames on every tentacle.

She picked herself up and limped to the door. She didn't so much as glance back. "Open air-lock doors."

"Opening," the IU said, but the door swiveled on the slow motion of heavy hinges.

"Open it," Cleo demanded, hobbling to the door and pressing the weight of her broken body against it. "Come on . . ."

Cleo squeezed herself sideways as the gap widened. The suit scraped against the two sides of the door. Finally feeling herself slipping inside, she dared to look back. The octonary writhed, whipping its tentacles into the dirt to snuff out the flames.

"Shut the door!" she screamed, not even fully inside yet. The hinges paused, the IU confirmed the directive, and Cleo cursed it out. "Yes, I'm goddamn sure."

The door spun backward, closing again. There was more than enough time for the octonary to slide its slithery ass inside. But it didn't rush the door. Instead, the monster appeared to dance. That elegant motion again, one limb lifting over another. Then it stared Cleo down through the squint of the narrowing space, half of its hundred eyes watching, until the door finally closed.

Breathe . . . Cleo rolled onto her back, resting on the mess of papers and empty MRE wrappers on the floor. Every part of her compelled her to stay there. Her body manipulated her, coerced her with cramps and spasms. Blood danced out from lacerations on her lip. The apocalypse in her eyes—the sand, the glass, the hot embers—cut every time she blinked. There was only pain.

Cleo propped herself against the capsule wall gently. "Easy," she told herself, trying not to swing her dislocated arm. She maneuvered through space with eyes closed, squinting only when she bumped into a chair or slipped on a half-torn notebook. Rotting foods that soured in the air. And a thousand strange equations had been etched on the walls, floor, and ceiling.

"Boston?" Cleo half shouted without a shred of confidence. She didn't even wait for the response before opening her watery eyes. "IU, bring up the display on external cameras."

"External cameras on."

A large 16:9 image appeared in thin air, containing four smaller rectangular images from outside the capsule. Cleo scrutinized the images through the blur of her eyes but couldn't find the octonary. She checked the infrared imaging and even X-ray imaging, knowing that it might hide in camouflage, but no, nothing. Equal doses of relief and angst filled her, but that'd have to do for now.

Unsatisfied but willing to multitask, Cleo kept one eye on the cameras, the other fixed on schematics for rover repairs. She and the Cambridge IU squabbled over the possibility of an electromagnetic pulse and if a rover was even capable of doing such a thing. They never agreed on the merit of it, but by the end of their argument, which the IU described politely as a tiff, a solution was proposed. First, a new battery—there was a smaller power unit for such an emergency, but it required a daily solar charge. Second, she would need to replace and rewire the smaller damaged circuits, most of which could be amputated from the capsule's body. Last was Shakes's memory; it was stored in the cloud in the *Antilles*, which made her wonder, What was the last moment saved in the cloud? Was it when they reached the mountaintop in the high-gravity world, or was it way back when they'd retreated from her own bubble?

Over the next hour, Cleo threw her shoulder back into place—with the IU's instruction, of course—and she washed herself as best she could. Then she read through some of Yasmin's notebooks. There were so many of them, and written too technically for her to digest.

But then she happened upon a book of Yasmin's illustrations that she could maneuver. Hand-drawn sketches of alien species covered the pages in amazing detail. She'd even labeled speculated organs and functions, yet another zone of Yasmin's genius. Curious drawings of a balloon species that floated, yet their veins were tethered to the ground and sprawled through the dirt like roots. Then diamond-shaped entities, twice the size of a man, with something swimming about inside them. Then pictures of fruits for some reason—pomegranates, mostly. The octonary was drawn six times with varying numbers of limbs. But strangest of all was the one page with the drawing of an ant nest. Yasmin had drawn a tiny little anthill with a few dozen of the arthropods crawling around it. This couldn't be the godlike "nest" that Yasmin had proclaimed in her recording. Not these childlike scribblings of ants creeping around a hole in the ground.

Cleo turned to the last drawing in the alien art book—her eyes averted, lips twisted, knotting down anything sentimental. The crew was depicted on that last page. Daniel, flight controls in his deft hands, Austin with the confident smirk of a commander, and a self-portrait of Yasmin between the boys, then Cleo, floating above them, that float chick, Nike prints on her toenails. Cleo smiled at those details; Cuban and Dominican flags, rovers portrayed as toys, and all that precision must have taken Yasmin many days and hours.

Cleo closed the book before she cried again and opened a diary next. As she read, she bit into a second MRE, and by the third, sloth had taken over. Her body wouldn't give anymore, it could only take. Cleo ended up on the ground, half naked, using her own space suit as a pillow, and she barely remembered doing it. Sleep invaded and she surrendered.

It felt like just a minute of sleep, but it had to have been longer—her dreams were already in their final act. The capsule was all shadows and icy air. It was vacuum quiet. Yet it was the smell that woke her, a scent like burnt rubber or . . . burnt something—the octonary? Had the monster gotten inside? Something had. The stench was excessive.

Then, lying there on her back, she saw it. Its camouflage was perfect in a way, and that was how she noticed it on the ceiling above her. The octonary had created a perfect match of gardenia white on the ceiling, but the smudges of Yasmin's fingerprints that Cleo had noticed before were gone. It hadn't re-created those imperfections.

Relax, bumblebee, Dad whispered up from deep inside her. How, though? A nightmarish voyeur species stalked above. It could have killed her while she slept. But the octonary was observant, an intelligent species. How intelligent? Because a nasty little plan was forming in the back of her own head, whispering to her in Ava's voice. It had taken Cleo no time to figure out that the octonary likely slithered its way in through the very engine that had blasted it—engine two. The exhaust valve for engine two remained open as it cooled; that was how it got in, and that was its only way back out.

Full goddamn launch on engine two, that villainous side of her chirped. *Kill that little shit.*

Cleo yawned artificially and stretched even more unnaturally, attempting to disguise her awareness of the monster above her. She moved toward the air lock as naturally as she could. Her plan was to step outside and lock the door behind her, thereby forcing the octonary to escape through that same valve. But as she reached for the air-lock handle, Cleo saw it reflected in the window of the air-lock door: something as transparent as glass slithering down from the ceiling—the octonary's camouflage at work. Eight glassy tentacles, nearly invisible, descended to the ground at her back.

Won't work.

This thing was smarter than her, and if she opened any engine valve now, the octonary would hear or feel the vibration, depending on its sensory organs. Cleo needed to distract it with something louder than an exhaust value. Music?

"IU, play 'Dollar Wine' by Colin Lucas," she whispered. "Ninety percent volume."

"'Dollar Wine' by Colin Lucas," the IU responded.

Trumpets horned immediately over the speakers, and the accompanying soca-style guitars and drums echoed rhythmically through the capsule. But would it be enough? Even at 90 percent volume, it might still feel the engine's vibration.

"Air," she said to herself.

Cleo typed the access to the holoscreen and turned the air-conditioning to full, and the vents hummed. Cool air hissed into the capsule. She spun the water to recycle. That hummed too. All the while, the octonary observed what must have appeared to it as a completely alien environment.

"Open engine two." She pronounced the words as delicately as she could over the music. "And volume at a hundred percent."

The lyrics screamed at full volume just as the engine hummed silently beneath her. Simultaneously, Cleo pulled and spun the air-lock handle, timing the opening of the door to match the engine's rumble. She couldn't feel the engine valves resetting—had they?

She held her breath as she stepped into the air-lock corridor; she could feel the thing ready to snatch her up. But it didn't. The first air-lock door snapped closed behind her. From the relative quiet of the air lock, Cleo could hear a hiss and rumble beneath her feet that wasn't the music. The charge on the engine was intensifying. *And if I can feel it . . .* Cleo whipped back to the air-lock door window and watched the octonary emerge from camouflage. It hit the air vent that led into the bowels of the capsule and its engine exit.

"Ignite engine two!" Cleo screamed, as if that would make it go faster.

"Engine two not fully primed—"

"Override," her vocal cords screeched. "Ignite now. Just—"

She didn't finish. She saw a flash outside the second air-lock door window. Engine two exploded, rocking the capsule sideways. Cleo bounced off the wall and hit the floor.

"Pull up the engine cameras," she shouted over the separate noises, clutching on to the railing. All three engine cameras emerged midair in front of her, and Cleo saw it immediately. "Two," she said, pointing to the second camera.

Four lizard-tail limbs whipped around the mouth of engine two. Color pulsed like fireworks across its epidermis. The thing was dying, trapped between the engine's vacuum and propulsion. Three thousand degrees of fire. She watched it fight for seconds more at temperatures that even Shakes couldn't survive in its titanium armor. Its limbs disintegrated into a strange glassy, gaseous state, then it faded. Cleo didn't take any chances—she kept the engine running until the fuel cylinders ran dry.

17

"Shakes . . ." Cleo whispered as if rousing a sleeping child, then pressed lubricant-greased palms against the rover's body, feeling for any vibration.

Shakes's surgical repair had taken all night. Changing the battery and applying the correct adapters had cost Cleo an extra miles-long round trip back to the capsule. Her fingertips were scarred with paper-thin cuts. But now every chip and cable was in place. Now it was done, and the lights in Shakes's eye lit the night.

"Hello, *Clee*," Shakes started. "Long time, *no see*."

She tilted her head to its voice and wanted to somehow coil herself around the machine, but Shakes was awkwardly shaped for hugging. She instead kept her palm pressed against the cold, dewy metal.

"Shakes, what's the last thing you remember?"

"You . . ." Shakes said softly and leaned in to her. "Dying."

"Dying?" Cleo shook her head.

"You were struggling with *death*. Your lungs juggling your *breath*."

"No," Cleo scolded the rover. "That didn't happen. You hacked your own battery to create an EMP blast. You don't remember that?"

"Oh . . ." The rover cocked its head in confusion. "No."

Shakes was malfunctioning. She could even see it in the slant of its posture. But that was to be expected, wasn't it? The poor machine had, in essence, kamikazed itself. Cleo was no engineer, and had rebuilt the thing as best she could. This was as good as it was going to get, the rover carrying her supplies.

"Then what I said was *over traumatic*—just a little *rover dramatic*."

"It's okay," she said, touching the rover's head again. "It's, uh . . . fine. How are your motor functions?"

"I'm feeling plenty *nimble*. If this is any *symbol*."

Shakes scratched one leg against the dirt like a bull ready to charge, then charged forward and headbutted her playfully.

"That's a *bull's tenacity*. I'm at *full capacity*."

"Good," Cleo said, forcing a smile. But that goddamn headbutt hurt like hell, enough to leave a bruise on her hip. "We, uh . . ." She rubbed her hip. "Need to find Yasmin. She's not in her capsule. Has all this mathematical graffiti on the capsule walls."

"Well, she's with her IU *often*. Find the rover—might lead right to *Boston*."

"You know where her rover is?"

The rover nodded. "*Yup*. First signal I picked *up*."

The march to Yasmin's rover was leisurely and mostly quiet, and that was by design. Cleo wasn't squandering a single amp on any rhymes or rapid movement. Shakes was still recovering from that battery transplant, and she hoped time and rest might work out the rover's kinks.

Dew-wet stones bit into the grassy meadow, creating a natural cobblestone path. A quiet stream escorted them along nature's promenade. Dead nettles, evening primroses, and other night-bloom flowers hugged either side of the road, exposing naked pollen to a faux moon. The hillside arched its hips, cleavage against the coming sunlight. *This landscape* . . . she marveled; it was seductive, if not downright terra-erotic. The breeze carried sugary aromas in the air and pulsed gently against her skin as if it were air-conditioning. Yasmin had said Orbis Alius was a zoo, and if so, then this was their cage—a human cage.

The brush thickened as she closed in, and thorny undergrowth aimed their knots at her heels. She stumbled. The signal pulsed louder under the shade of verdant sycamores. It was close. But she knew something was off, that sticky feeling that had been with her for a while now. This wasn't right. And as they ascended a weed-webbed incline, they found the foreleg to Yasmin's rover lying under the tall grass. Farther up, a hind leg spasmed in the dirt. It was a trail of metal entrails: lenses, then glass, and other sharp organs lay like breadcrumbs to the inevitable—Yasmin.

A notebook's worth of pages scattered about in the breeze or were caught in stems or thorns or just lay obstinately in the dirt, disinterested in the shape of the wind. All her last thoughts on the ground, and Yasmin Boston hung by her neck and the branch of a willow. She hung flaccid, a beautiful piece of meat on a metal hook. Yasmin didn't swing. She was an icicle—pale, cold, and stiff. Boston was dead. Cleo had suspected her passing for days now, but maybe in an accident or at the hands of the octonary, or its tentacles. Cleo had imagined Boston slaughtered or eaten alive . . . by something. Not suicide. The rover's metal cable had been tied into a diamond knot and threaded around Boston's windpipe. And that meant it was Boston who'd destroyed her own rover, because it would have stopped her if she didn't.

Cleo spun away like someone had twisted her at the waist. She couldn't look but couldn't get the image out of her head. She stumbled away from her friend's cadaver, dizzy at first, queasy in the next moment, until both she and her indigestion ended up in the dirt.

Why? "Why'd you do that?"

Shakes said something, but she was crippled and crawling away. She wasn't crying yet, but she breathed like she was. Her mother had drowned like this too, except Yasmin drowned in a dry noose. Mom dried in a noose-shaped pool. But both suicides, all the same. Both of them floated—in water, in rope—and Cleo would never be able to wipe them from her mind. And now she cried.

"I didn't . . ." The gasp gnarled her throat. None of the words came out as they should. "Didn't get here in time."

She closed her eyes and pressed her head deeper into the vomit-soaked earth. It was all for nothing. Everything was for nothing.

"Do you hear me, Clee?" Shakes finally broke through.

But no. It was like the senses were numb, no scents or sounds penetrated, and maybe so that she could feel everything.

"Let's head back, it's *damn chilly*. Then we connect with the *An-tilles*."

"Connect with who?" Her lips rolled against the soil, her nostrils filled with dirt. Since Mom's suicide, Cleo hadn't connected to anyone. That was how all the psychologists had explained it. And here she was again, Yasmin floating above her, because Cleo hadn't found her in time. "Connect to who?" she kept saying. "Connect to who?"

"Clee, I don't think—"

"Wait . . ." she said and paused. The epiphany hadn't quite fully formed, but there was something the IU had said. The first signal Shakes connected to was Yasmin's rover, and then it said all those weird things about Cleo dying. "Shakes," Cleo said, lifting her mud-coated face from the dirt. "You said her rover's signal was the first thing you picked up."

"Yup."

"And when I asked what was the last thing you remembered, you said . . . what was it?" Cleo couldn't quite recall the rhyme but remembered the idea of it. "My dying breath or—oh!" She remembered now. "My lungs juggling breath. Struggling with death. Right?"

"I can't remember, it *seems*. The memory faded like *dreams*."

"I remember—but it wasn't me juggling my breath. It was Yasmin. You were seeing the last images from her rover. She was . . . choking. Juggling breaths. Struggling with death. You don't remember that?" she asked in tearful exasperation.

"Maybe," the rover said. "Vaguely."

"What does it mean?" Cleo asked as she wiped her eyes.

Shakes didn't have the answer. But Yasmin's last words were all around them. Loose notebook pages were torn out, and many torn up. "I don't trust it," one balled-up page had etched on it. "Don't believe them," another sheet of paper read. She was trying to say something in the end, but Cleo wasn't sure what. And from the looks of it, neither was Yasmin—she didn't know what she was saying either.

There were hints, though, like why the discrepancy between torn-out pages and the few pages left in the notebook? Did these pages have more credence? Cleo glanced through the notebook pages after minutes of wiping her face clean. The read didn't take long either. Of a maybe two-hundred-page notebook, only twenty-three pages remained, and only eleven were written on.

The central thesis of Yasmin's mad scribblings was the idea of evolution and growth. And how the growth of an intelligent species was related to energy consumption. Progress, she wrote, if continued infinitely, relies on infinite consumption. Yasmin attached this idea to human progress and human expansion to Venus, Mars, and the rings of Saturn; it required a larger appetite for energy. Extrapolating that idea over deep time, future humans would have to consume far more to "progress." There is no progress without expansion. There is no expansion without consumption.

There was no structure to Yasmin's writing. One big idea after another, but not necessarily connected. The last pages, though, connected back to the idea that this planet was a zoo for intelligence. And within this zoo, there were two apex predators: a god, maybe the same as Cleo's feral god, and its opposite, which, for lack of a better term, Yasmin had dubbed "the devil." Beyond that, the handwriting slurred to the point that everything was incoherent. A few words floated to the top of all the scribbling.

I had to—for the collective.

Cleo buried Yasmin in the shallowest of graves. Her hands were shovels. Overgrown fingernails bent backward.

"Yasmin, I'm sorry. I . . . wish I got to know you. I wish we met in another . . ." Cleo didn't have the words, and she turned to her rover. "Say something. Like a eulogy. Give her a eulogy."

"Well, I don't usually—"

"I don't care," she interrupted. "Say something."

Her rover stepped closer to the shallow grave—too shallow. Wisps of Yasmin's hair were still visible, and her big toe too. Shakes kicked a spot of dirt over her toe, then lowered its lens to Yasmin's buried chest and whispered—

"Yasmin, you're the *best of us*. And the *rest of us*. Are *blessed to just*—call you *friend*. And to that *end* . . . there's a surge of *regret*. That urge to *reset*—everything that *has been*. But, *Yasmin*. Know that you're a nova among *stars*. And even my *bars*—are not quite *flexible*. In describing the *ineffable*."

"Okay," Cleo said, pressing the tremble of her palm against Shakes's back. "'Kay . . . Thank you." Her feet trembled too. "I think I need to lie down."

18

They arrived at the capsule just at the tip of daybreak, and they couldn't have planned it better. Light gleamed off the rounded metals like a lighthouse between the waving trees. They spilled inside. She lay down but didn't sleep, making sure Shakes reran its diagnostics while charging the new battery. The *Antilles* was a few minutes from veering around the curve of the planet, and that was how long it took for her to fall asleep.

She slept an hour. Dreams of Daniel's commands spooled around her head. Even as she dreamed of drowning, that water-rise pulling little Cleo upward as she tried to swim down, Daniel stood there too, calling to her, transmitting over space and the subconscious.

"Boston," he shouted over the receiver, his cadence barely recognizable. "Is it out? Over."

"Daniel . . ." Cleo grumbled to herself, hoisting one eye open.

"Are you there?" Daniel continued with wild desperation. "Do you read? Over."

"Why'd you let me sleep?" Cleo asked her rover. "Didn't wake me up?"

"You had a full *head of sheep. Dead asleep.*"

The rover turned away from her as if there was shame in its programming. It was broken and required professional repair. It had already rerun its software through Cambridge systems, reset itself, rebooted, and still it seemed that parts of Ripley, Yasmin's rover, had copied onto it.

"It's fine," she told the rover as she rubbed the sleep from her eyes and cleared her throat of an hour's worth of drowsiness. "Cambridge, open transmission channel to the *Antilles*," Cleo now said to the capsule's IU.

"Transmission channel open," the British-accented IU responded.

"*Antilles*, you read," Cleo said. "This is—"

"Boston!" Daniel exclaimed in relief. "Did you get it out? Over."

"No," Cleo said. "It's me. Cleo. Over."

"Xavi . . ." His voice trembled. "Cleo?"

"Yes. I'm in Yas—I'm in Boston's capsule."

"You . . . you're there? So, where's . . ."

She waited for him to finish, to say her name. Yasmin or Boston, or to say anything at all. But he held the name in the back of his throat, almost as if keeping it safe. She knew that strategy, remembered little Cleo wondering what happened to Mom but never asking.

"She's dead, Daniel," Cleo said in a pedestrian tone—too pedestrian, and the regret of it winced on her lips. "She, uh . . . passed peacefully, but . . . she's gone."

But Daniel was quiet. So much so that Cleo rechecked the connection. The signal pulsed as strong as it ever had. He was there. She imagined his body crouched in front of the *Antilles* console. Watery eyes. A clenching at his throat. Slender piloting fingers crooked into knobs. There he was, shrunken in front of her mind's eye, and then she imagined him looking at her. *Where's your grief, Cleo?* Where were her tears? The little girl who couldn't cry at her mom's funeral wasn't crying again.

"I'm pretty upset too," she said softly, performative. "Truly. I just had some more time to process it, and so . . ." The quiet was choking her, squeezing confessions out from her throat. "Are you there?"

"Here," he said.

"It's a lot. It is. Everything. This place. It's . . ."

"Yeah. It is."

"How are you holding out up there?" she asked with genuine curiosity.

"I don't know," he responded, sounding equally as genuine.

"Do you need some time alone, maybe—"

"No," he responded faster than she could finish. "Just don't disconnect."

"I won't."

And right then she knew it was loneliness. Daniel had scored the lowest in the deprivation tank examinations. He wasn't good at isolation. He was social and friendly, the normal type of person who would be ideal for any other work environment—spaceport, university, or telecom. But not here, three billion miles into solitude.

"I'm happy you . . ." He sniffled, then cleared his throat. "Happy you're all right, though. Are you? You're okay?"

"I'm . . ." *beaten to hell but* . . . "I'll survive."

"Good," he said, and his tone was rising, indicating a longer sentence to come, so Cleo spoke quicker.

"Daniel, I need to know what's been happening." She glanced around at the scribblings on the capsule walls. "Everything—what happened to her."

"To Boston," he said and sort of asked altogether.

"Yes."

"Sure . . ." Another deep breath steadying his voice a bit more. "Where to start?"

"The beginning," Cleo cut in. "What did Boston tell you—"

"At the end," he said in stark contradiction. "I should tell you about the end."

She waited for a few restless seconds before giving in to her impatience. "What happened in the end?"

"At the very end, the last transmission I had with her—she was afraid of you. But not like you'd think. It was like . . . she was scared *for* you. And you specifically, because of some nest? But I honestly think she had lost it by then. She's been messed up for a while. Especially since she returned to her . . . biosphere?" he asked as if he didn't know what it meant. "She was calling it that. A biosphere. And she was convinced that something on that planet had followed her back there. Some living . . . thing."

Octonary. Cleo mouthed the word but wouldn't say it. Because Daniel didn't seem to believe any of Yasmin's claims. The octonary, or the idea of biospheres—he didn't trust any of it. And that made sense; he was in orbit, in the literal dark, and with the MCs in his ear, this would all seem like some dark fantasy.

"Wow," Cleo said, acting out her surprise. "A living thing? What else did she say?"

"A lot. She was sick, Cleo. A fever, I think. It might be something on the planet. Something that causes delusions."

"Right," Cleo said, wanting to hear those delusions. "Did she say anything . . . useful?"

"No. She was going on about Orbis Alius not being a planet but a type of machine. The ideas in her head . . ."

But what type of machine? She couldn't ask. Daniel didn't believe any of it. Orbiting up there in that shadowy vessel, the last thing he needed to know was that monsters do exist.

"Orbis is a machine . . ." Cleo searched for the right words. "That's not possible."

"Right?" And his voice gushed with relief, with volume, feeling, and exhalation. "Like . . ." Now he was trying to find the words. "Because Austin was on about it too for a while, and I thought all of you were . . ."

"No. Not all of us." *But good*, she thought. *Austin knows it too.*

"I agree," Daniel said. "Things don't add up on this planet. Sure, but don't jump off the deep end."

"How about Austin? You said he was saying things," Cleo whispered, unaware of when she had started lowering her voice.

"Austin's . . . he's getting better. We're working with him. The MCs brought in experts. He's taking meds now."

"Huh," she said, full of thought. Austin would just forget what he had seen. But he probably knew what Cleo did, that Daniel couldn't handle the truth, and therefore it was better to hide it. Just a few white lies in the dark. "Before Austin got better, though, what sort of things was he saying?"

"Why?" he snapped at her.

"I'm just . . . curious."

"No, Xavier." He called her by her surname, not Cleo anymore. "Why's that all you want to talk about—Austin's and Boston's schizophrenic breaks?"

She had lost him. Daniel's responses diminished to an infrequent yes or no. She would push the subject sideways, and conversation capsized into a monologue. Just Cleo inventing stories about an uneventful journey to Yasmin's capsule and how she discovered Yasmin's body resting in a meadow after a blissful drug overdose. Cleo even made up a poetic suicide note with themes of hope. And that seemed to do the trick.

Daniel's voice cracked in the speaker. "I indulged her in the beginning. I . . . listened to her madness. I played in to her reality. I double-checked those gravitational equations she would send, and . . . I hid it from Mission Control."

"It's not your fault," Cleo said, finally understanding. He was blaming himself.

"It's . . ." His voice hiccuped, seeming to choke on the guilt. "My job is to maintain a level of sanity down there . . ."

As Cleo listened to him weep, an indignation started building within her. Like, what right did he have to be this far gone? Pull it together. But she held her tongue. Cleo had trekked through the abyss of alien worlds and done it all alone. *Jeez, listen to you. You're so weak.* And maybe she would say that, because the frustration was in her face now; her scowl was squeezing down to the spout of her lips.

But be nice, bumblebee, Dad told her. Cleo had never had enough friends for his liking. Be nice. But truth be told, Daniel withholding all the mad things Austin and Boston had said was his way of protecting her. He was trying to keep her safe. *Shouldn't you be doing the same, bumblebee?*

"Cleo," Daniel whispered at a boyish volume. Cleo had gone quiet as she tried to muzzle her temper. "You there?"

“I’m here,” she said, in what she assumed a motherly tone might sound like—Ava had never taught her. “I’m always going to be here. What happened to Boston won’t happen to me. It’s like they said, I’m immune to loneliness. Remember? We’re gonna be okay.”

“You don’t know that.”

“I promise.” That sounded like a lie—it was, but she needed to convince him. “I’m gonna be okay down here because I know you’re watching after me up there.”

“I . . .” he said, his voice rising high, sharp, then disappearing.

“Take your time,” she said.

“Sorry . . . I’m good.”

Now ease back in to it, she thought. “Good. So, Austin’s getting better?”

“He’s good. Spoke to him last rotation. He’s on meds now, including auditives, which . . . you know.” She knew and smiled, and she imagined him smiling too. “He hasn’t left his capsule, fortunately, but he was talking with Boston a good bit.”

“They were communicating?”

“On a private line, I think. I don’t know how. And she got in his head. They were working on gravity equations together. Austin has a background in—”

“Gravitational waves,” she cut him off, her curiosity showing. “Sorry. Daniel, I’m not buying into any of this, but do you mind telling me what they were trying to figure out with the gravity?”

“Not sure,” he said. “They thought Orbis was a construct and that they could use gravity to trigger something in a planet. A fail-safe. I’d ask Austin, but I don’t want to upset him again.”

“Of course,” she said.

“He’s not that far from you either. Through a few of those dark zones. I’ve been trying to connect to him, but he’s off-grid at the moment. It’d be good for him to see someone else.”

Dark zones? He was likely seeing individual biospheres as dark zones. And if Austin was just a few alien worlds away, it might be worth the risk to venture out there. He had all the missing pieces.

"Send me the coordinates."

"Copy," Daniel said. "Sending coordinates to your rover."

Shakes perked up with a revelation of digital information.

"Got a ring from the *Antilles IU*. That's a proposal, and *I do*. Downloading map to site *two*."

"Thanks, Shakes," she said, hopeful the rover would uptick in function just a few days longer. It was more hit than miss at the moment, and that would have to be good enough.

"I forgot your IU raps," Daniel said. "That's fun . . . This was supposed to be fun—"

"Clee . . ." Shakes interrupted. "Now that the cameras have *access*. I've started to *track this*—crystalline growth beneath the engine's *axis*."

"What's it saying?" Daniel asked.

"Hold on. Cambridge, pull up holoscreen visual."

The holoscreen flashed in the dark, lighting the space in front of her. The image was from underneath engine two. A large crystal-like structure stood below the booster nozzle. It was like a diamond or gem statue of a hand reaching upward, but a hand with eight fingers . . . or was it eight tentacles? Inside that glassy prison, something was throbbing, like a heartbeat. This was some sort of crystal cocoon.

Cleo dropped to her knees and rifled through the mess of Yasmin's many notebooks. She found the book of artwork and flipped to the sketches of the octonary. "Death and resurrection cycle," Yasmin had written. "Dying is a natural part of the octonary's life cycle." Yasmin wrote about the octonary's evolution and how it had conquered death.

"Shakes, we're leaving," Cleo said as she started foraging for supplies, notebooks, MREs. "Cambridge, shut down all systems after we exit. Daniel, I'm sorry. We'll have to reconnect when I get to Austin's capsule. Tell him to wait for me. Tell him I'm coming."

"You have to leave now?" Daniel's voice sounded as soft as a child's. "Can we talk . . . just a little while longer?"

Cleo hardened herself. "Sorry. I can't—" Too hard, maybe. "Look, I need you to be there for me," she said quickly. "We can't do this without you, Austin and I . . . we're counting on you."

His response was a request for a video call. She hesitated but eventually tapped in, and Daniel's broken image flashed on the holoscreen. It lit her face like a vanity mirror, there was so much light. Daniel had every bulb at full shine, and not just the cabin lights—the UV lamps too. The yellow-orange artificial sun beamed down on Daniel. And even a pair of flashlights floated behind him. So much light that she had to squint into the holoscreen.

He was unwell. His mahogany complexion had burned many shades darker, tanned under UV lamps meant for the veggie garden. His eyes were strained to sangria red, intoxicated in all that counterfeit light.

"It was too dark," Daniel said softly. "Sometimes it looks like it's moving, ya know . . . the shadows. Like out of the corner of my eyes. Then I turn to them, and obviously it's just in my head, but—"

"Daniel," she interrupted, not sure what to say next. Ava would cuss his tail. Dad might coddle the young man. But Cleo would aim for the median between those two roads. "Daniel, you're a little younger than me. Just a few years, but nonetheless, I'm older. Still, I've always admired you, in that looking-up-to-you sort of way. You're one of the top ten pilots in the world. I'm not top ten thousand anything. I need you looking out for me up there. For me and Austin . . . and everybody back home. For the collective, Daniel."

She almost cringed reciting that slogan, "for the collective," but she didn't want him seeing her in a disingenuous moment. She didn't believe in their motto, mostly because she was the opposite of a collective. Cleo was pure, 100 percent individual.

Daniel nodded, though it seemed forced. "For the collective," he said in the way a pert thirteen-year-old might. "I'll try."

"That's not good enough. Daniel, none of us are getting back into orbit without you. You understand that? How important you are to everything? Promise me you'll be there waiting when we call. I need to hear you say it. Promise me . . ."

The lights in his eyes seemed to finally flash momentarily, and maybe something like a smile rounded his cheeks, or was that her wishful thinking?

"I promise," he said and nodded firmly. "I'll be here. I will."

"You feel lonely, just think about me trying to get back to you. Because I'm thinking about you all the time." Now she forced a smile but meant what she said with every fiber in her. "Goodbye, Daniel."

"Not bye, right?" he asked. "See you later. See you soon." And he signed off.

Good job, bumblebee. And she beamed with Dad's pride. Traveling three billion miles into space was nothing compared to what she'd just accomplished. Connecting. That was so unlike her—it was alien. That positivity talk, the motivation and cheerleading—leading. *So that's what it feels like.*

Cleo loaded MREs and a tent into Boston's smaller vacuum pack. Finally, and maybe most importantly, she grabbed Boston's small notebooks, an entire volume of them, filled with sketches and scribbled bilingual English and Spanish notes. She moved to the door, but the rover was still, eyeing all the equations scribbled on the capsule walls.

"Shakes, we need to leave now . . ." Still nothing from her rover. "You copy, Shakes?"

"Copy this, *copy that*. I'm just a *copycat*. And I *mime*—your polyfat *mind*. Why is *that*? Me . . . a quantum *cat* (Schrödinger). Follows a quondam *rat* (Koedinger)? That's *backward*. Like that *bird*—"

"Stop," Cleo interrupted. "Shakes . . . ?"

She turned back toward the rover, an over-a-sore-shoulder glance, and it stared back. *What was that*? The rhyme wasn't like rap per se but something far more solemn—sinister, even. And somehow she'd have to ignore it. Cleo needed the rover, and Shakes had that type of wit, *didn't he*? That sharp, biting sarcasm. *Yes*, she decided, and there were only a few biospheres between her and Austin. Hopefully, Shakes would hold up until then.

19

Lightning stabbed down from golden clouds, and the swirl of vengeful weather struck lightning vindictively back upward from the planet's surface. The lightning strobed in its frequency. And the wind was a visible thing in this biosphere, bright yellow, almost gold, and powerful as all hell. Shakes's spikes were the only things keeping them grounded as a sulfur desert swirled like waves. This world was a yellow ocean. The rover's cable was attached to Cleo's utility belt; she kept the line short, just a foot's worth, as the wind kept lifting her off the ground in an involuntary dance on her machine's human leash.

The intelligence in this biosphere was an immobile egg-shaped thing, and more than ten feet tall. The exterior of the species was calcified in thick, impenetrable stone—according to Shakes, at least—but inside that shell, it was all brain. It had run an X-ray scan. The theory exchanged between it and her was that this supremely intelligent species and its ten-foot brain dreamed its whole immortal life, no eyes or ears to hear or see, nothing to smell the stink of the outside world. It was a living coma, with creativity and invention far beyond their wildest dreams.

And there was more than one shell encasing a brain. An entire network of them sprawled across the landscape. Something resembling radioactive mushrooms grew from their shells, and bioluminescent light was their seed. It pulsed through the winds and carried unconscious conversations to other egg-shaped monoliths miles off.

They weren't unaware of Cleo, but she marveled at them. The entire ecosystem confounded her. But her intrigue weakened through the course of her journey. It was a days-long trek, with no opportunity to rest in those violent winds. Cleo lost consciousness while on her feet, and more than once.

The subsequent biosphere's mild pressures and temperature allowed for tent usage and rest. Cleo needed nearly a week to recover. She had overexerted herself, and done it without sleeping or eating for two straight days. And every day she woke up, Cleo thought of Daniel, waiting for her in the dark. *Just hold on*, she thought. *I'm almost there.*

The rover adapted its solar panels to charge on red sunlight; its dead battery was its pillow, and it slept. It was only then that Cleo had the audacity and strength to read Yasmin's journals. In the first couple of notebooks, she found little about the secrets of this planet. Yasmin wrote instead about home. She wrote about yachting jaunts to Isla de Mona, gourmet mofongo or kipes, and so many Dominican eats that it took half the page. Cleo managed a smile at that. She did come across the word *nest*, but it referred to when a six-year-old Yasmin had stepped into one of the many ant nests in the Dominican highlands. She was hospitalized for the bites.

But mostly, Yasmin wrote her regrets, and many dealt with the finances of time, investments of days and hours with strangers—misspent years without her siblings and her perfect baby niece. She regretted her pursuit of wealth, as she, born in a nation of poverty, did little for the people. Spent it all in London or Paris or Lagos, she wrote, on banks and lawyers, and every billion-dollar brand. How someone so connected and social, extroverted, and followed on every media platform was, in her way, disconnected. She felt alone in those crowds, and in that way, Yasmin's disconnect connected Cleo to her.

"I should have never come" was the last thing scribbled in that particular notebook. "Should have listened to you." Cleo never found out who the letter was to. It strangely never mentioned a name. And it may have just been an outlet for loneliness. The voice that emerges in the dark and monstrous quiet.

The notebook Cleo was looking for, the one with gravitational equations, she could barely make it through the first page. The math was as foreign to her as Portuguese, but the handwritten notes on the side were simpler: Trigger the fail-safe, break the construct.

"Trigger the fail-safe with what?" she asked. Gravity? The honest answer to all of Cleo's questions was that they were utterly lost without Yasmin Boston. As good a mathematician as Austin was, he couldn't hold a candle to her. And Cleo was inept at all of it—math, physics, med training, star charting. Her only expertise was music and childhood trauma.

After eight days of recuperating, the fatigue lingered, but Cleo mustered enough strength to continue on. The following biosphere was a mountainous world under the spotlight of two suns. The stellar bodies swing-danced overhead, and her shadow split to dance with them. But the closest of those two stars orbited farther than the Earth's aphelion with its sun. And both were red phase sequence stars—cooler, relatively speaking, warming the planet only to an ideal ninety-degree day.

An aerial intelligence roosted in something that resembled a floating rose petal, a techno-organic chandelier positioned in the upper atmosphere. The low gravity and high altitude, plus something beyond her technical grasp, kept their aerial structure afloat. The avians were naked in their see-through flesh, a flat-bodied species, like manta rays but as colossal as whales. Underneath that translucent skin, three pairs of pitch-black eyes absorbed every ounce of light. They stared in every direction—up, down, left right—its body as clear as glass. Every organ was exposed, including a pair of wrecking ball–size brains. Smarter than her, she was sure of that. And as much as Shakes scanned and analyzed the avians, she was sure that they knew more about her than she did about them.

Though the creatures didn't appear hostile—quite the contrary, the avians' contortionist aerial motion and synchronized ballet seemed more like a performance, like she was their alien audience. An amicable intelligence? They would be her first. They pirouetted around each other, organs flashing true brightness, their heartbeats like floodlights, and something like urine poured out from their fins. Though it was more like liquid fireworks, and highly radioactive, according to Shakes. The urine descended in concentric patterns that left crop circle–like graffiti on the ground. It was alien pageantry. And it was for her, she decided. They danced their alien dance for her.

She set up the tent after just a half day of hiking. The duo had lost the other half of the daylight marveling over the aerial display. But Cleo couldn't sleep, partly because of the biosphere's twin-sun day cycle. The smaller star still roamed the sky, and there was only a half hour of true night before the second sun rose.

But the true reason for the insomnia revolved around an idea. Could all that jet-stream dancing be more than performance? Might it be communication? That led her down another rabbit hole—the octonary's own exaggerated movements. Had the octonary attempted to communicate? A species without a vocal or auditory apparatus might evolve to communicate through movement.

She spent the night scrutinizing video footage from Yasmin's capsule. The octonary was moving in a pattern, and somehow it was familiar to her. She struggled to find meaning in all those flailing limbs, but nothing sparked, just vague familiarity.

Then, at the edge of sleep, it happened in the most knee-jerk manner—or knuckle-jerk, because with each whip of the octonary's tentacles, Cleo's knuckle tapped against her lap. Her finger tapped, over and over, until she felt the rhythm. Music. The octonary's language was percussion. The music lover in her arose, and she leaned in to the video screen. She heard it immediately: C, D, G-clef. The musical alphabet. It was a communication through patterns not formed by math, but by musical notes.

Not that it was worth anything at this point, just some pride, a smile of self-affirmation. She was probably the only person on the mission capable of figuring it out. *You're engaged in terraforming, but in an affair with melody*—Dad had told her that before launch. *Got that from your mother.*

Cleo slept in the next morning. Shakes urged her to wake, but this was her reward for learning a new language. When she did wake up, the weight of exhaustion trampled on top of her. She wasn't going anywhere. She sat in a daze or dozed or scoured Yasmin's notebooks for mentions of the octonary. But the stream-of-consciousness scribblings revealed little about any alien. Every word spelled out more of Yasmin's personal life: false charity work, tax evasion, cheating on her many lovers, unmemorable men, experimental women. It was confessional, divulged to the page. She was a lonely girl, surrounded by hundreds of friends and a billion followers, but Yasmin was an isolated Idol.

It was at that half hour before midnight when both suns had set that she decided to move on. "Hitchhike in the shade," Cleo told the rover. But it wasn't even a mile until she noticed Shakes's limp. Barely a hundred pounds of supplies weighed on its back now, but the poor machine hobbled in a sad, unbalanced dance. She'd have to put it down when they arrived at Austin's capsule. It was too far gone for repair.

They limped across the barrier together into another biosphere. Its starless sky was crowned in a viscid dark that appeared to glow. That was the best way she should describe it, a darkness so deep it vibrated against her eyes. But the truth of that atmospheric darkness soon revealed itself, snowing down in the form of strange dandelion-like flakes. They floated through the beam of her retina light and still glowed in a sort of radioactive black. Those dandelion petals drifted toward Cleo even as she backpedaled. It was like they were magnetized to her.

Then somehow the black petals passed through her, through Cleo's suit, then her skin. Their black light was visible as they washed into her veins. They coursed through her bloodstream, flowing black-bright down through her neck, then cascaded over the falls of her chest into pulmonary arteries. They coursed faster through a panicked heartbeat and gasping lungs—she was breathing it now. It was inside her, but on second thought, Cleo wondered if she was inside it.

PART THREE

A CURE TO ISOLATION

20

Cleo steps through a field of proud sunflowers, their regal postures thrusting them shoulder high as their gold crowns tilt toward the sunlight. Flowers so vividly yellow they seem like suns unto themselves. She had been to a sunflower field like this with Finn on their anniversary, five years ago now. That long. But there is something different here. A strange breeze shushes between the stems. The flora sashay in place. That sea of yellow stretches all the way to a golden blur on the horizon.

"You seeing this?" Cleo shouts to her rover.

But as she spins back, Shakes isn't there; something else is. The thing isn't that far away, just blurred in a strange haze of static. It's elevated above the flowers, something like a bronze edifice with the shape of a person on top. It moves like a person, at least, but the longer she stares, the more it resembles a puppet, maybe, or a machine balancing itself on the uncanny valley.

It's all too surreal. The colors too vivid, the scents of Venusian breezes too rich. This world is like a dream, but not her, no, Cleo is wide, wide awake. Logic can't survive this deep in the subconscious. It's this world that's the dream, and she tiptoes forward, worrying she might wake it up.

The wind pushes at Cleo's back, ushering her toward that thing and its altar. But now she resists, digging her heels into the rich, soft soil, because as the blur comes into focus, she sees a throne.

"It is," she tells herself. "That's a . . . throne?"

The thing seated on the throne has a human form. Its arms and legs are rubbery and boneless, like the hollowed-out sleeves of a sweater. Its empty legs are flapping in the wind. And the details of fingers, toes, or skin just aren't there. There are no eyes either, nor lips, just flatness where a face should be. But there is something like a crown growing out of its bald skull.

"Sit down," the thing without a mouth says. It sounds old. But Cleo just stares, her jaw unhinged in the awe of it. So the thing speaks louder. "Sit, please," it chants. "Sit, Cleo."

"You . . ." Cleo finally responds. "What are you?"

"Sit down," the thing says again. "Please sit."

"No," Cleo snaps back, resistant but also afraid. There's something about the way the thing is talking to her—there's an echo that shouldn't be there, an echo that reverberates through her.

"Sit," the thing says, softer, as if sensing the fear. "Please."

"I said no, I'm not . . ." But as Cleo glances down at her lap, she sees her knees hanging off the edge of a comfortable cushioned seat. She is sitting. "The hell . . . ?" She gapes at her own body. "I'm . . . dreaming." And just saying that one word aloud relieves her. A dream, that's all.

"Dreaming," the thing echoes. It speaks with an ancient tongue, but at the same time there's an infantile intonation, like it has just learned to form words.

Who is this? No part of her subconscious resembles it. No individual she has ever encountered, no relatives, not even Ava's nasty voice could bend into those alien shapes. "You're real," Cleo says.

"I am real," it says and bows its bald head.

As the thing lifts its head again, she notices it does have a mouth. How'd she miss that? But it is more like a rubbery slit on its rubbery face, without the detail of lips and gums.

"Are you a species of alien?" Cleo asks and assumes all at once. "Is this a type of telepathy?" She leans forward in her chair, ready to stand. "You understand me? I understand you."

"I am a resident of this globe. This . . ." The thing searches for a word, maybe, as it cocks its head in that questioning gesture. "This . . ."

"Zoo?" Cleo offers.

"Zoo . . ." the thing repeats in its ancient voice. "Zoo?"

Steel bars emerge from the soil behind her and hold in place, forming cages. Within them, monkeys swing from verdant vines that wrap around the length of the bars. But then the vines themselves coil with movement, flexing into serpentine beings. Snakes emerge and the monkeys fall—but wait, now the snakes split—octuple, curling into tentacles around the bars and suctioning onto the metal. Octopus or squid? It's all changing, one thing becoming another, like a flash of different memories all merged.

The cage fills with water, then overflows. The water bursts, geysering in every direction, and then comes down as rain. A young Cleo stands in that rainfall, three feet tall and pointing at an octopus with her eyes closed. Dad stands behind her, one hand on her shoulder, the other holding an umbrella and laughing. *My memory*, she realizes. That day she saw the monkeys, snakes, and the terror of an octopus. And it was raining that day, right? *Muddy, muddy bumblebee.* This thing is accessing her memories to interpret the word *zoo*; that was Cleo's first memory of the term. This specific memory is how it understood the word *zoo*.

"Ah." The thing nearly stands from its throne in excitement. "Zoo. Interesting word. Yes. It is like . . . zoo."

Then the memory disappears—Dad, the zoo, and every imagined animal fade between the stems of all those swaying sunflowers.

"You're that . . . thing—that voice. I heard you in my head when I was in my capsule. That was you."

"It was." The thing nods its empty head. "I have unpuzzled a path through that barrier, but only for signals. Words. I cannot cross that barrier. No species here can."

"So how come I can?"

"You are new. Your own biosphere is not finished. This construct has not figured you out. Biology. It is still solving your makeup."

"So how does this construct work? We call it Orbis Alius, but . . ." *Simple words, Clee*, she tells herself. "How does the globe work? Like, is it . . ."

"Like," it repeats before she can finish. As Cleo looks to the thing, she spots a blackboard in the field of flowers. She squints at the word written on it, but it is actively changing its spelling—*Sillier, Slime, Smile*—and she can't read it until the voices of children echo from between the flowers.

"Sim-i-le . . . Sim-i-le. Simile!"

And children keep repeating it. Cleo doesn't remember that day, but there it is out in the field of flowers. This is the root of her understanding of this word. This entity is learning a new meaning of the word *like. Like* means affection or love, *like* means *for example*, but it is also used to compare, like a simile.

"Funny word," the entity says as it lifts some fruit in its hand and begins peeling. "Like. This globe is like a pomegranate," it says.

"I don't want pom-o-gan-ate—" Cleo hears her own five-year-old voice echoing somewhere in those sunflower fields. That distant memory was her first time using the word.

"Think of a pomegranate," the thing says, holding a perfectly peeled pomegranate in its palm. "Each pomegranate bubble or seed is like one biosphere. Each one is a world unto itself but still part of Orbis Alius as a whole. And while you may believe your journey has been across the surface of this world, these bubbles are stacked upon bubbles, as with the pomegranate. You have traveled downward, diagonal, and sideways to reach us."

"Traveling down?" she asks, but the idea of a pomegranate helps her understand—she was delving deeper into this world of bubble biospheres.

Cleo nods. *Good simile*, she thinks, *especially for your first try at one.* Orbis Alius is like a giant pomegranate, with a thousand individual bubbles. As she glances to see memories taking physical form all around her—one for the word *biosphere*, a memory with Dad, of course, and all his schoolbooks—soapy bubbles float overhead, and it knows the meaning of *bubble*. And a lullaby whispers past her—"He's got the whole wide world in his hands," her mother's voice Dopplers past Cleo, and now it knows the word *world*.

This thing is picking memories from her brain like fruit from a tree, and it's using those memories to create a vocabulary. And Cleo lets it.

"Who are you?" Cleo asks.

"I am like you," it says plainly. "I am an intelligent captive."

Alien life, and she can't believe the words, even though she knows it is true. She is communicating with alien life.

"Who built it?" she asks. "Who created this construct?"

"This place is old," it says, but again is searching for a word. "Oh," the thing says with excitement as a sudden flurry of pages from English textbooks blows past them. "Primordial." And that word is written on every textbook page flying through the breeze. "I like this word," the thing says and licks its lips—lips? It has lips now, somehow, and a long giraffe-like tongue. It's as if it can taste the word. "Older than us. This construct is of a primordial age, but our belief is that it is part of the body of the universe. White blood cells that protect the universe from the viral intelligence."

"Viral . . . You're saying that intelligence is a virus?"

"Intelligence sprawls like roots. Like veins. They spread like us and like you. Your species are spreading—Venusian, Martian, Jovian, and in time, beyond this star, beyond the galaxies."

"No . . ." she thinks and says, and in this mind space, it's the same thing. "That doesn't make sense . . ."

But she does sort of understand it—the idea of it, at least. Humans would soon propel themselves across the galaxy, but Cleo imagines them more like monkeys swinging across stellar winds than a virus. But she needs more—more knowledge, more explanation. Cleo needs to understand it fully—fulfilled. It's like a thirst.

"Explain it to me," she says. "Intelligence sprawls like a virus—what does that mean?"

"The universe is a system of pure mathematics. It is a construction of perfect arithmetic. You might think of it as a gargantuan computer system. You split atoms. Crack the eggshell of quarks. Soon you will defy the laws of gravitation. And learn to sap your sun. Intelligences break down the system of mathematics . . ."

"Like a virus," she says, finishing its sentence.

"And this place is the cure." And it finishes hers. "Cure," the thing says with a childlike chortle, playing with its newest puzzle pieces of vocabulary. "Cure. An applicable word indeed."

"Cure . . ." She doesn't like the word's intimations. She breathes that fear in sharp, quick gasps, afraid to even ask what it means. But that peculiar thirst moves her parched lips. "Is that why, then?" Cleo finally asks, the question at the center of everything. "Orbis Alius, this construct, is why we're alone in the universe?"

"Yes," it says. "It ends all life."

"How?"

"A signal is released from this construct—a pulse. Then some worlds grow cold. Some stars go dark. It is dependent on the species type whether they are extinguished in a flash or a slow fizzle. And you too, and too soon, will be snuffed out."

"Snuffed out how?"

"Maybe a mass infertility event. I have witnessed it before for procreating species. No newborns ever birthed again. I cannot know for sure how it will happen, though it *will* happen."

"Oh . . ." she says, and that's all she can muster. The burden of this planet weighs on her, realizing that Orbis Alius has that type of ungodly power. It will wipe humanity out, like it did every other species, many of them more advanced than humankind.

She wants to cry. Feels appropriate, *right*? Dad, Finn, Auntie Deborah—*it can have Ava*—but all of Venus, every other world lost. But she can't muster the emotion. Cleo has never understood her malfunctions in despair. She would more easily weep for animated heroines than any real thing. A school counselor had once told her detachment is her defense mechanism. Maybe, or Cleo might just be a cold bitch.

Still, a helplessness like nothing before bears down on her. The weight of it suffocates Cleo, and she has to hunker over just to breathe. But this isn't the first time she has felt this variety of helplessness, is it? Overhead, a "doughnut pool" manifests, or its Aqua-tecture Park name: the pool-loop. It's a doughnut-shaped pressurized swimming pool, full of clams, seashells, and tiny, glow-in-the-dark octopods. Floating inside that circle is her mother. Mom stares at her, melanin-pale and dead-eyed—eyes wide enough for her to fall in. And Mom is trying to speak, her jaw shaking to open, but it's a mollusk that has made a shell out of her mouth.

Cleo's heartbeat somersaults. Why that sudden memory? Is it her inability to cry both then and now? Or is it the similar feeling of smallness—the helplessness of a child that she feels now too? Or is it everything, that these two moments, separated by thirty years and a billion miles, sound so similar? Is it because these moments rhyme?

She looks at her mother again and notices something—Ava's face. No, that's not right . . . But this isn't the alien's doing; this is the depths of her subconscious—the very bottom, dark and filled with seashells. The idea of a mother in her head had attached itself to another woman, Ava, and it's been feeding off Ava's features. Ava's sinister eyes had invaded Mom's face, then her pouty lips, the dyes in Ava's hair dyed her mom's. Every time Cleo remembered her mother, she subconsciously sprinkled aspects of Ava's face onto her; not in a clear, explicit way, but like a blurred mask, and Ava's face was always underneath.

She's at the bottom of herself—there's no air down here. Tears burn away the mascara from Cleo's eyes; makeup melts black down her face. She bows her head and buries herself in her hands. She has always been an ugly crier, and all the fancy makeup drips onto Cleo's palms.

"Don't cry, bumblebee," the thing says, crying with her, tears filling its beautiful chestnut-brown eyes and sniffling from two snotty nostrils. "Because every system has its flaw."

The thing's features are growing on its skull, like individual slugs emerging from a shell. A tongue laps awkwardly as it speaks, flapping at an opening that barely passes as lips. Its eyes blink on gears of wrinkled skin. Eyelashes hang too long, unnaturally stringy. A few threads of nappy hair crown the thing's skull. Is it learning how to shape a human face for itself, or were those details there the entire time and she just didn't notice?

"What's the flaw?" Cleo asks, staring into its beautiful brown eyes.

As the alien searches for the word, fire engulfs the flowers around them, and a man stands naked among the flames. He wears every billow of smoke like a cloak. His skin is redder than the fire itself, but it's the horns crowning his head that give him away. The devil—not in the literal sense, but a portrayal in this species' mental search for a word to describe it.

"A devil." The alien says the word just as Cleo thinks it. "It is an anti-god, trapped at the central biosphere of this pomegranate world. The most ancient of us."

Devil, Cleo thinks, remembering Yasmin's words. She talked about a fail-safe.

"What does that mean, 'a devil'? That's the system's flaw?"

A smile stretches across its rubbery face as something like eyes open, but like two black marbles, no whites of the eyes; just deep, black pits. Somehow Cleo hadn't noticed those features before. At first it appeared not to have a face at all, but now it smiles, now a bump swells where a nose should be, and now motes for eyes.

"Together," the thing says with its ever-brightening eyes and unshapely grin. "We fight it together. There are many flaws in this construct. The octonary, for example, a species where death is a part of its life cycle, and so, though it is killed every time it passes through the gaseous barriers, it is reborn and able to travel through every biosphere."

"And what's the flaw that will bring down the whole system?" Cleo asks.

"You thirst for all the knowledge," it says. "Ravenous."

"Ravenous," Cleo repeats.

Sunset bleeds wild colors across the skyscape. Cleo wipes her eyes, but all the fancy makeup smears across her face. The mascara and eye shadow slip into her nostrils and fill her lips. But that isn't makeup, and she can tell by the taste of it—what's smearing across Cleo's face is her own skin. Her facial features—like the eyelids, nostrils, and lips—are smudged. That's what's blotting out the sunlight. It's like the individual parts of her face are melting away.

"What's . . ." Cleo touches eyes that aren't swollen but shrinking into tiny dots. "What is this?"

"You are drinking me," it says. "And I am swallowing you."

Cleo runs her palms against a flattening face. All the curvature of cheeks and brow have been smoothed away, and in her last squint of light, she sees her features—eyes, lips, the bow of her nose, her entire face—on the head of that thing. It wears her like a mask. It blinks like her, its lips dance like hers—the way she rounds her vowels and pops her *p*'s—but that's not her.

"You're a . . ." She doesn't have the words. Nothing scientific, at least. "You're like a demon species. You're possessing me. You're infecting me."

"No. I'm infecting myself with you. I am pumping your consciousness intravenously into my system. You drink, but I swallow," it says in her voice. "What is that word . . . ?"

"Symbiosis," they say together, nearly in unison. "What the hell?" She even knows what it's thinking now, in the same way a reflection in the glass knows her next move. "Oh God," she gasps, and it gasps with her—like a chorus, like cognitive rhyme. "Oh God . . . Oh my fucking God."

It's swallowing her, this viral thing—an intelligent virus? Is that what it is? But it isn't just one thing inside her. A hundred corneas squeeze into Cleo's eyes, and they stare out of her. All their tongues slither around hers, and they speak with the newness of her voice. They are a hive species—therefore the sunflowers, thus the bees. And how many species has it consumed? Too many. Cleo feels herself knotting into a cosmic noose a billion years long, and it is choking her, squeezing her into its webbed singularity.

"You're drinking me," they all tell her, and Cleo speaks with them, her rhythm in meter and step with theirs. "And I'm swallowing you."

The Hive's memories start syncing with hers. A sundry of remembrances invade Cleo's mind. Flashes of ancient stars and dead nebulae, and apparatuses that Cleo doesn't have the vocabulary for—gravity dams, maybe—and nets for magnetic fields, culture and religion based around pulsars. Its knowledge has quenched her thirst, and now it's drowning her. She feels suffocated by its all-consuming weight—like its ocean is drinking her now. *Drink me and I swallow you.*

She remembers the Hive spreading across the various biospheres, one of the species Cleo has already encountered. Over the millennia, it has spread, somehow, from one pomegranate seed to another. Somehow it is the apex predator of this zoo. Nearly 20 percent of the tens of thousands of species that exist are already under its influence. And now her.

Though one very important detail of memory pulls on Cleo's attention—the length of time it takes for her to be submerged within the Hive. The species is a thinking virus, and when Cleo wakes up from this fevered dream, she will still be an individual. It will take hours, if not full-on days, for the virus to consume her—swallow her.

Now she started thinking for herself again, even as they swarmed her with their talons or spikes or tendrils, burrowing their roots into the nodes of her brain. "Oh God," the chorus of them chanted with her. "Oh God." They were an ocean, but she swam against a tide of bodies. And it hurt, like peeling back her teeth from the gums just to speak over their noise.

"No . . ." she tried, and now the chorus responded out of sync, echoing her objection many seconds late.

"No what?"

"When I wake up, I'll still be me . . . for a time. So you're gonna push your cells or particles or whatever it is you are out of me. You get out my head, or I'll end it myself."

"End . . . yourself. What is that word?"

"Suicide," she answered fast, nearly cutting them off. She knew the question was coming.

"Interesting word," it says. "Su-i-cide. That is an impossible word. I have only seen it on the mind of one other species before."

Is suicide a uniquely human trait? she wondered. "Not all species can commit suicide."

"Only one other has even conceived suicide as a concept."

"Well, you're in my head, right? Look. Look deep," Cleo said, and heard it echo, a thousand other voices repeating her words split seconds behind her. They were falling out of sync. "I don't do well in crowds. I'll do it."

"You will do it," it said now as it crawled through her memory.

"Fucking right," she said with all the rage she could muster. She couldn't bluff at this moment or second-guess. "Get out of my goddamn head."

"You have even tried it before . . ." the Hive said in a tone of fear. "You have tried it before . . ."

She felt them fading, separating their thoughts from hers, and not because they were letting her go out of kindness. No, there was something else at play—the Hive was scheming. They whispered beyond her awareness. They had a strategy in letting her go, but she couldn't hear it anymore. They were fading, but it wasn't happening fast enough.

"Get the hell out of my head."

And eventually, they did.

21

It felt like the ground was shaking underneath her, but it wasn't really. She was shaking—Cleo was convulsing. Saliva was a noose in her throat, and it choked her. Her fingers clenched in half curls, scratching at nothing but empty air. Her throat unclogged and she gargled up liquids, either blood or vomit, and likely both. Cleo's body was killing her, and all she could think was *hurry up*.

The convulsions and muscle spasms would eventually pass. Blood dripped from her nostrils. Her pores perspired until the glands went dry. Finally, her eyes opened, and it felt like the first time. Even the darkness around her was too bright. Fatigue was like paralysis; it softened her. She was rubbery from her legs to her wrists, and couldn't do much but lie there.

Her consciousness skipped like a stone over water. She blinked and an hour had passed. But everything still hurt, from her head to the soles of her feet, and her heartbeat, each pump stabbing deeper into her chest. And she wished it would just stop.

Something had tried to take her—some form of intelligent disease, parasitic or maybe fungal. It had passed like a dream or a high, but she could still feel its age inside her. Some of its memories lingered, others withered inside her brain and spilled out of her aural cavities. So much blood in her ears that she'd be deaf for the next hour. But what concerned Cleo the most was that the Hive was scheming at the very end, hatching some strategy to take her back. And that, she thought, was why it had let her go so easily in the first place.

Cleo rolled onto her side. Her rover lay splayed out on the ground beside her. Dead. There was no light here, neither sun nor stars, and Shakes couldn't charge its tiny battery without sunlight. But what this biosphere lacked in light, it made up for in oxygen, a healthy amount of it. The biosphere also maintained a Goldilocks level of warmth. Her halogen was magnetized to its collar, which meant the air pressure was just right. So she could lend Shakes her battery to the space suit, and she did. That simple attachment of two wires cost her nearly ten minutes of effort, but it was worth it just to watch the charge indicator light up.

"Shakes . . ." she croaked, but her tongue was more swollen than she first imagined. She moistened her lips and tried again. "How long have I been here?"

"Unconscious for two days, *Clee*. That's cra-*Z*. I thought may-*be*. You were pushing day-*Zs*."

"No, I'm good," she lied with her swollen tongue. "I'm fine."

Her rover disagreed. Telling her that she needed to start medicating or at least meditating, because it appeared her head was aching. Though *headache* wasn't a strong-enough word. There were trenches dug into her brain, and volleys of artillery launched from either hemisphere and cratered into the gray matter.

"But I'm fine," she kept lying, and even that took effort.

Cleo managed to sit up and crane her neck to the upper edge of the biosphere. A void as black as death, with little dandelion petals glowing even darker. She knew things now. Memories had rubbed off. The Hive had stained the walls of her skull. Just flashes, light at the backs of her eyes. But she knew now that the faux atmosphere above her was holographic information, a projection of the Hive's original planet. Like the moon and sun were holographic in Boston's biosphere, and every biosphere had an accurate projection of each species' original airspace. Cleo knew that now, like there was shrapnel of Hive knowledge wedged in her mind.

"But why's there no sun here?" she thought aloud. "No stars, nothing."

"There is a sun in that black *cavity*," Shakes said. "No light, but I can track *gravity*."

"You track its gravity. So where's the sun? On the opposite side of the planet? A brown dwarf, maybe?"

"Perhaps the sun doesn't shine up *there*, because an apparatus that siphons *flares*. It's possibly a world of Dyson *spheres*."

"Dyson sphere." The solar dam would seem inappropriate for an intelligence of the Hive's age, many billions of years old before Orbis Alius snuffed it out. This was just another thing Cleo remembered, another indentation, left behind from the Hive's trespassing. But just glimpses and vague half-remembered dreams. She knew the Hive species was beyond ancient. She knew its mind was comprised of many hundreds, if not thousands, of different alien races. Cleo remembered how the Hive, made up of a million tiny molecules, had tried to fly from this megastructure on Higgs boson wings, a manipulation of mass itself—magical mathematics, epochs and eons beyond her kindergarten physics. But this megastructure had magic of its own, and she knew that too. Orbis had inflated the gravity beneath the Hive and stunted the Hive's ascension, a dark-matter well that sucked the million dandelion particles back toward the ground. And Cleo knew there was no way of ever escaping this world.

"You're right," she told her rover. "Probably a Dyson sphere wrapped around the entire thing. Not a spot of light wasted."

"What's even stranger is, there's not another star in the *sky*. Orbiting *high*, my stellar targeting *tried*—tried . . . tried . . . tried . . ."

Shakes hiccuped there, seemingly unable to form the next word or the next rhyme. It stuttered itself into a glitch that jerked its entire body and was likely pulling heavily on Cleo's battery.

"It's a galaxy eater," she interrupted, and Shakes went quiet. "The species from this biosphere is a galaxy eater."

"Since you don't tell fallacies *either*. What the hell is a galaxy *eater*?"

"A galaxy eater is . . . Imagine a stellar dam—" But Shakes wouldn't know what a stellar dam was. She barely did. "Like a Dyson sphere, but billions of them, slithering like boa constrictors around every star in the galaxy. They siphon energy from every star in the galaxy and blacken the skies." Glimpses from other species flashed behind her eyes. "A hundred billion stars, made into an IV, a feeding tube straight to its gut. Maybe not even just one galaxy," she considered; this part was conjecture. "But the entire local group of galaxies. Trillions of stars feeding its Hive. Stellar dams pulling not only on light, but radiation, orbital and rotational gravity, magnetosphere netting. Sucking trillions upon trillions of stars dry. A stellar genocide. It would dye tens of thousands of galaxies in black."

"That's one hell of a theory, *yo*. Eerie, but I have a query, *though*. How do you really *know*?"

"I don't know," she said, but what she didn't say was that she remembered it. But Shakes didn't need any added stress.

The splinters of that god needled deeper every time she thought of it. So she stopped thinking altogether and had the audacity to try to stand. It worked for a while, but vertigo hit back. It took a few tries, but she would eventually walk, and Shakes would serve as her limping crutch.

"We have to move before my battery goes out too," Cleo told her rover. "Let's find some sun."

They found their suns. Big and blue or white and sometimes yellow. One shone on a low-gravity biosphere inhabited by what Cleo called fireflies. This species was fist-size luminous cores surrounded by a gaseous sac, so nothing like fireflies, but the name stuck. They hovered in the upper atmosphere, light linguists, communicating in a language of dark and brightness—ones and zeroes. Shakes recognized the binary code immediately like a proud native speaker. The dialogue ranged from a tedious once-a-minute blink to a nightclub strobe. Their brilliance lit up the alien skies.

Shakes found its charge in all that light but at the same time picked up a limp in its other leg. Her rover reported two more failing systems in its CPU; to compensate, it would start downscaling. Just background systems, it reassured her, but the truth was, her rover was dying, body and mind. That twitch in Shakes's limp prevented Cleo from propping her weight on the machine. So she walked on her own, her movement like a twisting branch, tortured limbs gnarled and buckling unevenly.

"Where are you hurt?" Shakes asked on more than one occasion.

Where doesn't it hurt? From the sores under her toes to the blitzkrieg in her brain, it hurt everywhere.

In the end, it was the headaches that overpowered her. They pulled Cleo's malnourished body to the ground, and she crawled into the pressurized tent. She had barely trekked a mile into the fireflies' biosphere, but something about being disconnected from the Hive hit her like withdrawals.

Her mind stretched against the lining of its skull like a rattlesnake hatching from its eggshell, and goddamn it, it hurt. What was this starvation in her head? A feeling that might best compare to insomnia—not the desperate need for sleep, but a maddening need to wake up, awaken to that higher consciousness. *God-fucking-damn it.* She squirmed against herself. The roof of her brain was too low, too tight, and the claustrophobia made her gag. Cleo shivered cold and sweat hot, burning fat and muscle, breaking down for days. Then, on the third day—or fourth, she had lost track—Cleo thought up a stratagem. She would exchange the Hive drug for more familiar narcotics.

She instructed Shakes to remain outside the tent and fill its charge, which the rover thought a strange request but complied nonetheless. In the quiet and relative darkness, Cleo hung the IV at the top of the tent. She plugged the line into her ear. It might not help with the pain, but it might distract her from it.

The drug genre was Opera Ecstasy, an impatient little conductor. It kneaded into her gray matter before Cleo could even set herself supine. Its timbre strummed flamboyantly. Her nerves were strings; the vibrato wriggled down her neck, along the backbone highway, down to her toes, then echoed back up. Suddenly, her feet tiptoed into her knuckles. Her ears wound around her navel. Her anatomy was a Picasso-made soup in a circular frame. Each drop from the IV sent ripples across her body.

But the auditives were not helping. Cleo's pulse was out of sync. The cardio percussion of her heart was still off. The arteries were gnarled up, and her heart kept stabbing in her chest, way out of rhythm. *What's wrong?* Cleo placed her hand over her left breast and made a fist.

And maybe it was the drugs—most definitely the drugs—but there in the dark, her heart responded: *I'm trying.* Her heart spoke with its rhythm, a sort of Morse code, tap, tap-tap. Ah, and Cleo understood it. *I tried*, her heart tapped again, *I really tried.*

"It is okay," Cleo said aloud, way too high and slurring her words. Her lips sagged. Her eyes glazed over. "It's not your fault."

She felt goose bumps on her breast and up the nape of her neck, and Cleo just knew her entire body was speaking to her now. This particular language was braille. And she was suddenly literate in the language of fingertips. Her body wrote in chapters, every organ writing at once: *Shakes is dying*, one wrote. *Like Mom drowned*, wrote another. *That's symmetry*—full circle, drown out the noise, turn up that volume.

"It is symmetry," she slurred. "It rhymes, one side with the other."

Cleo twisted the valve on the IV like a volume knob. And the volume did tick up. *Wow.* The full dose of auditives cascaded down the tubing. But it was drowning out everything else. It was even drowning out her. Suddenly, the rounds of her ears folded in, then opened like a heartbeat in her ears. Then, as the opera crescendoed, its sound galloped across her anatomy, trampling her organs under quarter-tone hooves. She was suddenly flatlining on an overdose; her senses squeezed together, into that last narrowing window to the world outside. Noise, light, scents were reduced to the same singularity of sensation—and then nothing.

22

Cleo saw her mother drowning in the doughnut-shaped pool—baby octopus in her mossy hair, another mollusk in Mom's mouth. Then Ava chirped about the shape of Cleo's nose or her jawline, explaining how Dad's bumblebee didn't have his features. And then Dad hesitated to call her his daughter one day at school registration. She noticed. So Cleo chose a high school concentration to prove she was more like Dad than Mom. *Prove it again*, she had thought, and Cleo charged into Dad's field of study—terraforming. And he smiled—look at him smile. *My girl. My baby bumblebee.* Those words were the purest high. And habit-forming, even. So she joined the Orbis Alius Program. She needed more of that high. All of it had led her here, to this primordial rock and Cleo's last epiphany: She was her mom. Screw the science and this terraforming bullshit; Cleo wanted the music and the occasional drugs. And the tattoos, God, she wanted to make a canvas of herself. She wanted the Sistine Chapel weighing on her back. What a waste. Her loneliness was the side effect of being a stranger unto herself, wasn't it? Being alien.

Is that what it all meant—your life flashing before your eyes? Cleo's eyes were open now, but the light was hollow and she saw nothing. And it was like the rounds of Cleo's ears had folded in, and the world was muted. Cleo was gone, and these final thoughts were just the cooling embers of neurons.

Something nudged her—Shakes, in all likelihood, a suspicion that was confirmed as its cold, steel forehead pressed against her naked arm. The IV was ripped out of her arm, and after a minute or an hour, she could hear the rover.

"Are you there, *Clee*? You hear *me*? Clear-*ly*? Bare-*ly*?"

The weight lifted. She breathed in, but it was like her nose was clogged. The heartbeat was shallow but still there. The blur of the world came into focus, and her rover stood over her, the IV under its paws and its head nudging her chest.

"Thank God," the rover said with an exaggerated exhale. "I see you *blinking*. But what the hell were you *thinking*? *Sinking*—to that level. *Suicide?* Clee, you just *died*. And you still *might*. Your skin's sheet *white*. And your heart just left—doesn't beat *right*."

Shakes ran its Doppler ultrasound, checking blood flow, X-ray scans, CT scan, and all the other checkups. She likely lost consciousness once or twice during this process, because it all seemed quicker than normal.

"It was a mistake . . ." she lied. "Didn't mean to up the dosage like that."

"Lies, but I can't *change her*. Out here acting like a *lone ranger*. But you're just a *loan stranger*. You don't give *back*. Can't forgive *that*. It's hard for you to communicate? So why *try*? Feel disconnected, no *Wi-Fi*. But you do need others to feed *through*. More importantly, what about those who need *you*? Dad. Daniel. And me *too*."

"I didn't try to kill myself," she said and gasped, still catching her breath. "I'm fine. I'm immune to this."

"And that was your only *miss*. You think you're immune to *loneliness*. No sense of community to *appease*. And maybe immunity is the *disease*. But I can see it in your broken *look*. You're an open *book*."

"Stop!" she said, barely able to catch her breath. "Please, just let me . . . Let me . . ."

Breathe, she wasn't able to say. Cleo didn't have enough air in her lungs to both argue and maintain consciousness. So she'd have to lie in that discontent for hours. Shakes's last word—that last rhyme—would have to linger. Immunity was her disease? Maybe. But her IU was wrong about the suicide. It was the auditives that made her do it. It was that acrophobic high that forced her hand. The last thing she'd ever do would be to end up like her mother.

"The last thing . . ." she whispered into the ether, then fell unconscious.

It'd take a few hours to get the feeling back in her toes, and another hour to get enough oxygen in her lungs for motor functions. She was dehydrated and malnourished, and she ate slowly. She slept long and dreamed even slower. It would take a full forty-eight hours more before Cleo dared venture back outside, and even then, she would need Shakes's help. But the Hive headaches were gone now, and she knew it was time to move on.

Cleo packed away the tent underneath the fireflies' nighttime sky. Her rations were low, which had the advantage of offering Shakes more balance in its twitchy gait. Shakes kept glancing upward at the lights and hadn't looked down once.

"What are they?" she asked, genuinely curious.

"This will sound *bizarre*. But each point of light is a browning *star*."

"Star?" Cleo craned her aching neck to the spectacle overhead. "That's not possib—" But what wasn't possible at this point? Cleo had witnessed everything she could never have imagined. The better question was, *How's that even possible?*

"It's in their *density*. These stars have full *propensity*—to fuse atoms due to tearing *them*. And fusing *deuterium*."

"Stars . . ." she whispered in absolute awe. Fist-size hydrogen fusion. Nuclear fusion was the holy grail of energy resources, clean and nearly unlimited. Humanity's greatest minds had attempted to harness it for hundreds of years and here it was, floating just above her head. "Every firefly is a . . . star?"

"Yes. They're stellar more or *less*. More *compressed*. With mind-blowing *peculiarities*. Like they die in *singularities*."

"They're so damn . . ."

"Alien."

"Yes," Cleo said, gawking upward at the stellar bodies. "Living stars? They're conscious, self-aware things. What is consciousness anymore, if things like this exist?"

"Consciousness is having countless inner *voices*. Finding consensus on individual *choices*. A hundred voices sing to *blur*. I know this because I'm sing-u-*lar*. I'm not self-aware in that *respect*. Consciousness requires more than one inner self to self-*reflect*."

Consciousness requires more than one inner self to self-reflect. She mouthed the words and considered this, thinking suddenly of Ava, that wicked witch who'd played a major role in Cleo's development. Like it or not, Ava was a part of Cleo. Dad's voice was always in her head. And Finn was a foundational part of her too. Even Mom. Cleo was her own sort of Hive. All her inner voices like a chorus inside her head. And in that sense, she wasn't that dissimilar from her IU, with Shaggy, Busta Rhymes, and Missy swimming in its imitation of a consciousness.

Cleo observed the four-legged philosopher. The rover's gait shifted like it was on a tightrope. Craggy rocks slashed into the footpath. Shakes hobbled as if turbulence shook underneath its feet, but she regarded its limp-like swagger. In that moment Shakes reminded her of Dad. And she wasn't wondering anymore about that missing piece of the IU's personality profile; Cleo was nearly sure they'd poured her father's algorithmic data into those empty spaces. So she touched the quadruped's back, guiding its aging feet.

The fireflies followed her through the night. Maybe attracted to her retina light, or perhaps Shakes's high beams communicated something. They flocked overhead in murmuration, and thousands of individuals moved in a single luminous dance. And maybe a Hive wasn't that different from what she deemed individuality.

She crossed into the next biosphere, an ocean world, with pressure so high that she walked on the surface of a liquid sea. There was nothing there, no life, though by the end of her journey, Cleo considered that the ocean under her feet was alive. In a subsequent world, a giant roamed, a thing with a clockwork exoskeleton. The goliath's limbs extended beyond the clouds with something that resembled the gears of a clock twisted around its joints. In the last biosphere, Shakes guided her to a world of Earthlike conditions—sunlight and air, evergreens, and primrose weeds. This was home. This was Austin's biosphere.

She had walked for days, and the Hive's scars and stretch marks in her brain had seemed to heal. The last thing she remembered was the Hive plotting to take her back, though she remembered much more than that. Light-years of primordial knowledge buzzed in her head, and though she only maintained a fraction of it, by the time she had reached Austin's bubble, something like an epiphany was dawning on her. *Light the match, blow the gravity*, she thought. Could it be that simple? And just like that, Cleo believed she might have a plan to unmake this construct.

23

Austin's biosphere was a red-weeded tundra. Knotty spots of turf caught her boots and kept her off-balance. Cleo's stride was already seesawing on her reckless limp; she'd fall soon enough. The day was overcast and damp, sunlight dripping in through bloated gray clouds. The air was breathable, but as she demagnetized the halogen, a rotting stink filled her nostrils. It was like the entire world was a corpse.

The capsule flickered in the sunlight, a lighthouse beckoning, and Cleo made a crutch out of her rover and lumbered forward even more rashly. No matter how she curved her foot, every step was a minefield of peeling skin, cysts, loose toenails, and swollen heels. Nearly there, that was her anthem, and she repeated it a thousand times before she got close enough to see the air-lock doors and the window on their face.

But the window was dark. Not a single bulb was lit on the outside either. Why? The sunset and overcast day should have prompted an automatic switch. None of the solar panel charges were lit up. And the air-lock lights, red for locked and green for unlocked, were both dark.

Trepidation crept in. After a journey that protracted all the sores and scabs, Cleo stood outside Austin's capsule and wouldn't venture a step closer. She was too afraid to see another empty space. Another dead body. Suddenly, the air tightened around her shoulders, stifling and nearly choking. *Please,* she begged, *turn on a light.* The day was overcast. That holographic sun was setting. It was too dark. *So just turn on a goddamn light.*

Shakes beckoned her attention, but Cleo wasn't listening. Her breathing was heavy, and she unlocked her halogen, hoping the artificial atmosphere would resuscitate her heaving lungs. It didn't. *Breathe*, she urged her body. But the halo's spin dizzied her. This was a panic attack. Cleo limped and hobbled over to a pocket of shrubs and shadow. She kneeled there, afraid to look inside, afraid that Austin was dead, more afraid that she was truly alone than she had ever been. *Breathe* . . .

"Xavier?"

Cleo spun around so fast that she nearly fell over. A shadowy figure raced toward her, and in the midst of her panic attack, she wasn't sure if it was real. It called for her again, closer now, and she could make out Austin's voice. He wore a sweater and sweatpants, and his arms were tied tight to his chest, shivering cold.

"Aus . . ." She couldn't finish; she was already limping toward him. She locked the halogen into its collar and tackled him, nearly bringing him to the ground. She fit her head between his shoulder and neck and shuddered in that human pocket. His skin cracked and flaked, a desert, and his beard scratched like cacti. Austin looked as disheveled as she had ever seen him. Even his blueberry eyes appeared sapped of their moisture. Handsome, proud Austin appeared nearly as broken as she was, and yet nothing could be more beautiful to Cleo in that moment than him, her crewmate warm in her arms.

"I'm sorry," she whimpered, not even sure what she was apologizing for. Words were just pouring out of her.

"Hey," Austin said, running his hand along her mess of hair. "It's going to be . . ."

He paused, but she didn't know for what. She brought her eyes to his, and their smiles fit between his loss for words. His dry palm caught on the kinks in her hair, and he mouthed the apology. He nodded and pressed his head against hers. They smirked and cried and raised their brows and shook their heads, all of it without a single word. She looked at him, and this was where their eyes interlocked. Warmth was all she felt. Then he leaned down, bringing his lips to hers—a kiss.

"No," she said, pulling away. "I . . ." *That's not what I meant.* "Sorry—"

"No," he interrupted her. "It's me. I'm sorry. I just . . . It's been so long, and I'm filled with . . . longing?" He smiled and choked on the word all at once. "Not that type of longing, I mean, just . . . feeling."

He kept going. Austin struggled to lift the words over his tongue. She saw the dryness in his lips and dandruff at his scalp. Loneliness was that desert at the bottom of the sea. It was a quiet, black forever. And that desert sand was in the corner of his eyes, crusty mucus there left over from sleep. Cleo wiped the salt from his eyes and squeezed his hand. And he squeezed back. And the harder he squeezed, the more moisture poured from her eyes.

"Thank you," Austin whispered too quietly, but she could read it in his lips. "Are you okay?"

"Hungry." She smiled.

"How about some cou-cou and flying fish?" he asked. "Maybe a slice of sweetbread?"

"Sweetest thing anyone's ever said to me." Cleo nodded. "Yes."

24

Over the past eight months, Cleo's sweat-slicked skin had soaked into the suit's polyfibers, and now it peeled like duct tape from her skin. As she stripped it all away, bumps erupted along her arms and waist. The skin cracked on her knee, and the blood dribbled from her. Every end was either bruised or rashed or split open. Her MAG underwear had raisined, the elastic waistband had snapped, and she didn't take it off; it just fell away.

Austin had pasted a bedsheet to the ceiling with thermoplastic tape. That was their version of privacy in the tiny capsule. The sheet had seemed thick enough at first, but now, hanging flat and backlit by ceiling lights, there was a transparency to it. She saw Austin's silhouette roaming busily between the food pantry and the coffee machine. Her silhouette must have shown similar clarity, but she trusted him, *right*? Or was she just in too much pain to give a shit?

The hiss of water sent a chill along her back. Just the noise of it gave her goosebumps. She wet a hand towel and started gently on her face, and still water burned the exposed sublayers of skin. Then she scrubbed the dirtier corners of herself. There was so much dirt. *No*, not dirt, in fact—it was her. Months of dead skin, blood, hair, and perspiration. Entire layers of herself came off in that towel, dead cells, and the white towel had browned before she even got down to her waist.

Look at ya-self, Ava would often say in that high-pitched loathing that only she could render. And Cleo did just that. She autopsied her own wrinkled anatomy, the bruises and scabs, and so much loose flesh. Her skin hung rubbery off her bones with no fat to fill it. Her rib cage protruded under her breasts. Her pelvic bones jutted out, as did her clavicles. She felt the shame Ava had taught her to feel. And almost instinctively, Cleo pivoted back to the sheet. Austin stood motionless on the other side, and so close to it his breathing pushed the sheet to sway.

"Austin?" she called, climbing into his T-shirt, stepping into his sweatpants. "Austin . . ." Cleo called again as she tightened the strings around her anorexic waist. Austin was eight inches taller than Cleo's own five foot eight, and she felt every inch of the gap in his clothing.

Cleo emerged from her curtain hideaway to Austin's white smile and the scent of coffee. He had brewed a cup like a professional barista, licking his finger and even taking a sip before offering it to her.

"It's perfect," he said.

"Me?" she asked, surprised—germaphobia was another one of her loner quirks. She even saw little saliva bubbles floating like foam. *Gross.* But she straightened the nauseated squirm from her lips and smiled. "Thanks."

The coffee was far too hot anyway. But Cleo bowed to the holy coffee bean nonetheless and held the steam to her face, exfoliating in its caffeine.

"Can't get over the beard," she said and pointed at Austin's bouquet of facial hair.

"It's growing on me." He smiled.

"Literally." And she smiled back.

"Can't imagine what you've been through. Ten months alone in the wilds."

"I'm . . ." She shrugged—to say an inch was to speak a mile. "It was something. And somehow you never left, as curious as you are."

"I'm cautious too. Running off into wonderland . . ." He shook his head. "Like you and Yasmin. Guess it's a girl thing?"

"She's . . ." She choked on the word. "Yasmin's not . . . She didn't make it."

"I know," he said and nodded. "Daniel informed me and, uh . . . I had assumed it, once she stopped responding. Boston was in a bad way at the end."

It was appropriately quiet for a few seconds, Yasmin's moment of silence. He sipped his mug of coffee and gestured to Cleo's cup, like he wanted to toast in Yasmin's honor. But what did he mean she'd been "in a bad way at the end"?

"What did you say about her in the end?" Cleo eventually asked. "In a bad way, how?"

"Some of the things she was talking about were . . ." He shook his head like he didn't have a word for it.

"What things?"

"In her last transmissions to Daniel and me, she talked about, what—seeing a nest? 'The nest,' she called it. She had these breaks from reality, afraid of finding an ant nest here on this world."

"It's in her notebooks," Cleo blurted out in Yasmin's defense. "When she was a kid, Yasmin fell into an ant nest and it was a traumatic . . . *memory* . . . oh my God."

The realization hit her like a bullet to the head. Cleo didn't quite turn away from Austin, but she did turn inward. She recognized in that moment that Yasmin had encountered the Hive. She had called it the nest—"a nest in my head," she had scribbled in her notebooks. Because of her childhood fears, she'd pictured the group mind as an ant nest. For Cleo, the Bajan bumblebee, she thought of it as a beehive. So Yasmin was victim to that viral intelligence too. It was swallowing her. Was that the reason for her suicide? And was Yasmin's suicide the reason why Cleo had been let go when she threatened to kill herself?

"You still with me, Cleo?" Austin asked.

"Yeah. Sorry. What was I saying?"

"I think you were trying to explain that Yasmin hadn't lost her mind."

"Right—there is alien life out there, Austin. Yasmin wasn't breaking from reality. You haven't been out there, and I don't know what you believe is real or . . ."

"I know," he said. "I've watched this world terraform itself to suit me, tailor-made head to toe. And I'm sure beyond my border, there's an environment adapted to another species. There is life here. There's no denying that."

"Good." She sighed relief. She could forgo all the undue explanation. But she wouldn't say more than she had to. The Hive, an intelligent viral, fungal something, and the primordial memories it left in her head—none of that needed to be explained.

Instead, they investigated the particulars of Yasmin's notebooks. The slurring cursive script and every chaotic scribble on the page made a bit more sense to her now. Not in the meaning of the words, but in the *why*. "Why write this down?" Austin eventually asked. And that was the question she hadn't considered yet. *Why?* Yasmin wrote these passages as the Hive, or *ant nest*, had colonized her mind because she wanted Cleo to read it. This was for them, her and Austin.

Cleo only had flashes, momentary glimpses of ancient memory. But Yasmin had everything. Her direct link with that viral intelligence gave her insight. Yasmin knew something, and they just needed to figure it out.

It was obvious that something within the Orbis Alius superstructure could be exploited. The term *fail-safe* was written seventeen times, and it dealt with one species so dangerous Yasmin described it as a "devil." A species so terrifying that its biosphere was at the very center of this pomegranate world, and even that wasn't enough. There was a prison made of gravity that held it in place. And according to Yasmin's notes, releasing the "devil" would bring about the deconstruction of Orbis Alius by way of singularities.

Austin appeared dubious about all of it. "A *space devil?*" he joked. "And a fail-safe that would destroy this megastructure? How would she even know all of this?"

But Cleo knew what he didn't. Poor Yasmin was being swallowed by a thousand species, both caught and connected in the spider's web of the viral intelligence. And in that sticky, webbed connection, those thousand species were one.

"I don't know how," Cleo said, "but I believe her."

Austin sighed. "I don't know . . ." He yawned, appearing tired from all the reading, even with the coffee mug at his lips.

"What's strange, though, is she said you agreed. In her notebooks, she said you were helping her figure it out. You and Boston didn't discuss any of this?"

Austin paused, like she had caught him in some lie, then he smiled. "I was trying to placate. Maybe I shouldn't have. Maybe she'd still be here."

Austin's gaze gave it away—a blue eye flit toward the capsule's dirty walls. Cleo sprang astride. She paced the rounded walls and tiptoed to a ceiling covered in an entire encyclopedia of mathematics and notations smudged in marker. Austin had written far more than Yasmin. There was even math on the floor.

"Mass over distance times gravity. These are Yasmin's. I know the equation; it's about the structure of Orbis." She tapped her finger against the equation in excitement. "A pomegranate world, set up in such a way that the bubble with the most gravity at the center . . ." She waited for his agreement, but he stared at his mug of coffee. "Austin," she called louder. "The equations are about breaking the devil species' prison of gravity."

"Sure," he said dismissively. "I tried it for kicks. Didn't work."

"We can work it out together," she said, dropping to her knees and kneeling in front of him. "And you're smarter than me, and I . . ." *I have some memories of a viral Hive intelligence in my brain.* "I can help. We can do it. Together . . . a team."

He smiled. "Teamwork," he said, like it was the first time he had heard her say it. But as he leaned forward, Cleo realized that she had moved too close in her excitement. There was this strange discomfort between them. Her white lies. His failed kiss.

"For the collective," she said and rolled back, off her knees and onto her ass.

"You believe that bullshit now?"

"Why's it bullshit?"

"Your words, not mine."

That's right. She had called it *bullshit,* that writer's-room-developed jingle, recycled through a user feedback loop, redeveloped, redesigned—even back then, the slogan was bullshit. She had also called it gimmicky, corny, goofy as hell. But out there in the cold, Cleo had a different perspective. It kept her warm somehow. It was light in all that dark.

"I think you should rest," Austin said, and he reached for her, gently, one fatherly hand on her shoulder, but Cleo recoiled.

"I know I look tired—hell, I feel tired. But I can't sleep. Too amped."

"Sure you don't want some coffee, then?" He seemed to be trying to make it up to her. He reached for the coffee and wrapped his fingers around it. "Still hot."

"No thanks," she said, averting her eyes from his.

"You are beautiful," he said, gazing into her.

Austin leaned toward her and she tried to lean away, but her back hit the wall. His nose touched hers, and Cleo flinched sideways.

"Austin . . ." She shook her head.

But he leaned farther. His lips pursed. He thrust his tongue at her. Cleo pulled away with one hand and shoved him back with the other.

"No," she insisted. *Not like this.* Had the loneliness done this to him? "I don't want that."

Austin looked at her, confused. He cocked his head like she was upside down. "Are you not attracted to me?" he asked.

"What the hell are you talking about?" she snapped.

Austin appeared to be thinking about something else, even as his eyes lassoed around her. He stared at her, angrier now; she could almost hear a wolflike growl rattling at his Adam's apple. *No*, she realized, it sounded more like the gargling of saliva in his throat. And right then, Austin snapped forward and spit at her. She twisted away, and wet phlegm sprayed yellow on her cheek.

"What the hell is wrong with you?" she shouted, wiping the stickiness away.

His response was a heavy sigh. She saw the frustration in the long, cold air that chimneyed from his lips.

"Austin . . . ?"

"Fuck it."

He lunged at her, knocking Cleo on her back. He squirmed his body around hers, his legs pinning hers to the ground. His heavy gut pressed into hers, and he gripped her wrists. He had gone mad, giggling and spitting at her again and again. She turned her head, and his saliva stuck to her hair. It stuck to her neck. With her head turned from him, Cleo then felt his tongue finding its way into her ear. And that was when she saw it—a notebook underneath the stool. Yasmin's missing notebook. *Oh God*, she thought, and kept on thinking, *Oh God.*

"Oh God," she blurted out, as she squirmed from Austin's grip.

But Austin slammed his weight down onto her. He was too heavy. Her arms were tiring as his tongue descended the curve of her ear.

But it wasn't him—this wasn't Austin. If he had Yasmin's notebook, then he had traveled beyond his bubble. He was lying. Then the coffee he wanted her to drink. The spitting. Austin was trying to get his genetic code into her. He was part of that goddamn Hive.

His lips over her now, Austin coughed up his fungal phlegm and spit it into her ear. *He missed.* She twisted her head away, cocked her neck back, and headbutted him in the nose. The force dizzied her, but it dizzied him too. *One more time*, and she hammered her head against his nose again. He recoiled and stumbled backward. Blood gushed from his nostrils and dribbled onto his lips.

"Blood . . ." he said, the blood pouring into his mouth. "This works too."

He was a dragon then, spitting blood like fire, and it hit the back of her neck as she twisted away.

"I got you," he said in a playful singsong tone. "Blood on your lip."

Did he? Cleo wiped her mouth as she scrambled backward to the air-lock doors, tapping wildly at the buttons. *Shakes*, she mouthed, but her earpiece wasn't even in. She reached for the doors, but he was already on top of her. The math of it played in her head. He was eight inches taller than she was and maybe fifty pounds heavier. He was in the military, while she hadn't slept in two days and hadn't eaten in almost three. She couldn't win—every part of her body hurt right now.

"What do you want?" she gasped.

"You."

"But—"

"Digested," he said, cutting her off. "I want to digest you."

"I *will* kill myself," she threatened.

"I remember." Austin nodded and grinned. "But now. Here. I can stop you. I can tie you up. I can sedate you. Auditives, right? Drug you until the infection is complete."

A realization hit her faster than it should have. The reason the Hive was so willing to let her go was because it or they knew she would come to Austin and he would infect her—secretly, if possible—and Cleo would fall asleep and never wake up. The strategy felt so familiar to her that it was as if she had thought of it herself. That was the strategy that had slipped her mind like a half-remembered dream.

"Wait," she said, pulling backward. "Just one question. And then I won't fight. I know I can't win, but . . . one question."

He hesitated. "What question?"

"Austin?" And it almost sounded like his name *was* the question. "Is Austin in there?"

Austin paused and his face softened, as if this was the question he was waiting for. "I am," he said, taking a step back, demonstrating he wasn't a threat. "I am in here. *We* are. When you assimilate with the Hive, you don't die, Cleo. You become part of a whole—a biological singularity." Austin opened his arms in embrace. "Already, twenty-eight percent of the species on this superstructure are part of a community. Many were so isolated after thousands of years that they came willingly. You don't have to be alone."

"It won't hurt?" she asked, taking a half step toward Austin's open arms, but this was all a performance.

From the first words she spoke—*Is Austin in there?*—that was a line Cleo had written for herself. Because as she spoke, she was typing with her left hand, which was concealed behind her back. The holoscreen was positioned behind Austin's head. She had already muted the IU's volume, and now she was working on pulling the oxygen from the air lock.

"It won't hurt," Austin said. "Truth is, most intelligent species eventually reach a Hive state. Yours too. I see it in your technologies where you watch other lives. And your first technology—storytelling, language—is an evolution of empathy. A desire to live vicariously through the stories of others. And empathy will continue to evolve. Humanity would eventually find its Hive state after some hundred thousand years. This is inevitable. Even the devil species is its own twisted Hive form."

"Devil . . ." She paused. "What is it?"

"In a word, loneliness," Austin said, stepping forward and reaching for her. "And I'll show you. I'll show you everything."

Time's up. The air lock was emptied of oxygen; that emergency measure was created to pull any noxious fumes that might accumulate in that space. *Now or never.* He hugged her and opened his mouth. Blood dripped from Austin's gums as his tongue slithered out.

She punched, right-handed, and in the same motion swung her left hand to the air-lock door release. But neither connected. *Shit.* He grabbed Cleo from the back and dragged her into his embrace.

"No," Austin told her.

He had her arms shackled in his, so she kicked the air-lock release. It hissed open. Austin leaned forward to close it, and that was just enough freedom for her to untangle herself. Cleo stumbled into the air lock, and he lunged after her, tackling her inside its narrow passage. The air-lock door closed.

You lost, she thought, and part of her wanted to announce that to him—all of him. She wanted to boast her outmaneuvering of all those species. That would be her version of spitting in their faces. Instead, Cleo bowed in a humble egg-shaped posture, hands over her ears, while her eyes and lips squeezed shut.

He poured himself on top of her, pulling at her elbows and trying to peel her open. But he was wheezing and hadn't noticed it yet. Cleo locked her limbs tighter as Austin lost his grip on her. That must have been when he understood it, her trap, because that was when he went mad. Austin slashed jagged fingernails into Cleo's skin, like he was trying to bore a hole into her—*Oh shit,* he was. Blood spurt from her forearm and wrist, and he spit until there was no moisture left in him.

Then, just as suddenly as he started, Austin stopped. She could hear him drowning, then she heard the thud of his body hitting the floor.

Cleo hatched from the fetal posture but found that Austin wasn't out. He snailed across the floor toward the air-lock door. She stood over him and kicked him over onto his back. Austin peered up at her and smiled. His lips fizzed with saliva as he tried to spit at her once more. He blew the spit pathetically into a froth over his own face. And then Austin, and the all-powerful Hive, blacked out.

25

Austin slept peacefully, and almost inhumanly so. Cleo had used the entire roll of thermoplastic tape on his wrists and ankles as he had lain oxygen-deprived. But two hours now and his baby-faced sedation gave her pause. Was it a ruse? Was he pretending to sleep so that she might creep closer and he'd spit in her eye? Cleo's sleep-deprived brain was a cesspool of paranoia. Thirtysomething hours without sleep weighed on her, and she worried she might just doze off and that was exactly when he would open his eyes.

"Austin," she whispered. "Open your eyes," she said and waited, but the monster didn't stir. "Austin. I know you're not sleeping."

Nothing.

Then she'd wake him up, sleeping or not. A splash of coffee in his face should suffice. But Cleo checked on her rover first. She remained outside, plugged in to the external battery port. Shakes would be no good to Cleo inside anyway; the rover was programmed not to harm any member of the crew, so it would stand neutral in a fight between Austin and her.

Shakes reported a full charge. "But stay outside," she told it. "I have to try and interrogate a goddamn virus."

Or fungus. Whatever the hell it was. Though Cleo had a theory. The virus itself was just the web that attached all these minds. It had no intelligence—this persona or identity was an amalgamation of every alien mind and one sleeping human.

She brewed two mugs of coffee, one for her, the other for Austin—more specifically, Austin's face. She sipped hers first; the caffeine buzz hit like sunlight, and everything lit up a tone brighter. Insomnia's paranoia drifted fast, and a confidence rose in her. Daniel was just about an hour from swinging back into signal range.

"Cleo . . ." Austin said from behind her, yawning and squinting at the coffee. "Is the other cup for me?"

Angst stiffened her for a moment, but she forced herself to recover. She couldn't reveal a hint of weakness. There were too many minds in his eyes.

"You know," she started, not sure what to say next, "I thought it was weird that you were calling me Cleo instead of Xavier. Not like you. I thought maybe it was the loneliness thing, but . . . now I know."

"Which do you prefer?"

"Obviously, I . . ." *Was it obvious anymore?* Two names, one given by her mother, the other taken from Dad. A year ago, Xavier was far and wide more to her liking; now they seemed to be balancing out. "How did you get to Austin?"

"I am Austin—"

"You know what I'm asking."

"On Austin's venture to Boston's capsule. He found us along his path. He stepped into our biosphere, thirsting. And we drank together."

"Then Austin gave it to Yasmin . . ."

"Yes. We made love. A pleasurable thing."

Her face squirmed as she considered the horde of thousands of species experiencing sexuality through Austin.

"Pleasurable," Cleo scoffed. "Is that why she ended up killing herself? Because you were taking over her mind?"

"It's less taking over and more of a dance between partners."

"One dancer with ten thousand. That's not dancing, that's . . ."

"An orgy?" Austin smiled at her. "We almost had Yasmin Boston, just minutes and hours away. Yasmin sat staring at a white wall in a daze—that final beautiful daze. But then you entered her biosphere,

Cleo. You woke her up. She saw you. Her drone circled overhead. And she knew that by the time you reached her capsule, she wouldn't be there anymore; we would. So she hung—"

"Fine," she cut him off. "Just stop talking for a second." *Stop talking about her*—that was it, wasn't it? Yasmin Boston had sacrificed herself because she knew. Once the Hive swallowed her, they would use her body to take Cleo. And the longer she thought about it, the more emotion bubbled in her chest—and the more her facial demeanor bent.

You can't cry in front of the horde, she told herself.

"What are you thinking?" Austin asked. Or them—*they* asked.

"I'm thinking that the real Austin *was* working with Yasmin to understand this superstructure. Right? Cuz it says so in her notebooks. Earlier, you were pretending that everything I said was crazy, because you don't want me looking into this. And that means . . ." Cleo considered, thinking it all up as she was saying it. "That means Yasmin was right. It could work. This superstructure's fail-safe can be exploited."

"By breaking a devil out of its gravity prison." They said it like a warning. "You are beyond your depth. Mentally unequipped. I'm sorry. Even if the superstructure is unmade, every other species on this world goes with it."

"This graveyard world? This museum. It's no way to exist—being a sad memory of what they were."

"But you want to save your species," Austin said, and his eyes opened in discovery. "But you can't release the devil anyway. It's locked under the restraints of gravity. I've seen your spacecraft in Austin's memories. You mimic gravity by spinning it in circles." They chuckled. "Your physicists haven't unlocked the graviton nor its undiscovered quark. Humanity is ten hundred thousand years away from mastering gravity. You couldn't begin to comprehend the gravitational force needed to break something like that out."

"*Like that*—the devil species?" she asked, placing her coffee aside. "What is it?"

"Ecophagy," Austin said and smirked. "A term from Austin's mind that I doubt you're familiar with. But maybe you have heard of gray goo?"

"Gray goo . . ." Cleo said, and it sounded familiar but . . . "No. What is it? What's the devil species?"

"Less a devil, but more of an anti-god. Imagine a cloud of gas half the size of your galaxy absorbing anything in its path—planets, peoples, suns. Its individual parts are microscopic, countless tiny machines that devour any matter and convert it into itself. It spreads across the universe and replicates itself over and over and over and . . . infinitely. Imagine a black ocean washing over every star in the night sky."

"Anti-god?"

"It's the best your vocabulary can describe. It is an opposite to creation. It just consumes."

"Isn't that sorta what you do?" she shot back. "Just consume?"

"Far from," they said, appearing annoyed. "Austin's body remains, doesn't it? I just attached to his mind. You describe me as bees or ants, but I liken myself to a centipede, and each mind is a leg that allows me to step across this world. That devil—anti-god—would convert all matter into its cloud: the rocks, the dirt, the oceans, skyscrapers, entire planets and stars."

"That's why there's a fail-safe." Cleo nodded. "This structure won't allow that species to get out. It would destroy everything to keep it contained."

"You know we have a theory. That space devil trapped in the center of this pomegranate world is the original intelligence. As in, it is the first and oldest of all intelligent life. Who knows where it started, but it evolved to that point. And the destructive nature of that species is the very reason this superstructure exists. This construct was created to prevent anything from evolving to that point again."

Cleo sat in the center of the capsule, a safe distance from Austin. That was it. All she wanted to know. She knew what she needed to do. Carry the baton that Austin and Boston had laid out for her, find a way to release that alien species and trigger the superstructure's fail-safe. And strangely, or even arrogantly, Cleo believed she might know how.

But what to do with him—*them*? If she had any sense in her, Cleo would murder the thing. Nail gun to the temple or, what was more realistic, simply suck the oxygen from the room while she breathed through her halogen, no blood on her hands. But that thing wore Austin's face so well, especially in the eyes, staring out with all that blue empathy.

They smiled wide, acres of incisors, it seemed like, stretching across Austin's cheeks. "How much of me rubbed off on you?"

"Not much," she said before even considering the question. "But . . ." she went on, actually considering, "I have this memory of one of your worker bees. One of your minds. I don't know what you call them, but it's an old memory. Many times the age of our sun. This intelligence was advanced; it could fly, so you absorbed it. You—they—flew upward, wings of fire, trying to get off this world, but the superstructure intensified the gravity underneath it and dragged you back down."

Austin smiled reminiscently. "Why that memory?"

Because that memory—that winged species rising against gravity—it evoked some of her own trauma. It parallelled the day little Cleo tried to swim upward against the current in that vertical pool. The pull of the gravity and the drag of the tide knotted up somehow, the trauma of it intermingled. She remembered something they didn't intend her to, but Cleo wasn't going to tell.

"How, Cleo?" they pressed. "How did you find that memory? Something so ancient?"

"Was I not supposed to?"

"I rubbed off on you," they said, grinning. "More than I imagined. So much colonial residue. But I also have the splinters of you in me. I retain an exact memory of who you are, Cleo Patricia Bynoe, down to the last particle. Every memory was copied. Same as Boston. Her memories are archived too. And if Austin's body dies, I have a memorial copy of him within me as well."

"So what?" she said, but Cleo knew what they meant.

"I know what you're thinking, down to the ninetieth percentile in accuracy."

"So why are you the one shackled in tape, then?"

"That ten fucking percent." They smiled. "But I pulled on the strings of your vocal cords. I skipped synapses of your brainstorms and coursed the currents of your bloodstream. You are on the tip of my tongue."

She maintained a flat, expressionless gaze. They were trying to get back into her head—not biologically, but with these idiosyncrasies of psychological warfare. And they were winning. It was the age of the thing that overwhelmed her. A duration so vast that it was like the trenches of an ocean, and to simply remember was to drown and never resurface. But Cleo couldn't give them a hint of her angst, and so she squeezed gritty teeth into a smile.

"Are you done?" she asked, but didn't wait for the answer. "Because I am."

"No, Specialist Bynoe," they said, utilizing her mother's maiden name. "You're not done. You can't break the chains of gravity. Even Austin and Boston, for all their erudition, didn't come up with a solution for that. But if you play nice, maybe I'll give you a hint of how to—"

"I know how to do it."

They raised Austin's eyebrow. "Bluff."

No, but *maybe*. Cleo did have a strategy. She just didn't know whether it would work. There were too many variables. And she would need Daniel's help for it to work. That lack of confidence must have wrinkled somewhere on her face, maybe just a flinch under her eye, but they saw it. They changed the look in Austin's eyes.

"You *are* bluffing," they said, and it seemed like frustration. "You don't know anything."

"I do," she tried in a confident pitch. "I know how to break the grav—"

"Liar," they shrieked, then they grumbled something with a petty twist of Austin's head.

Am I winning? she wondered. Was she beating the Hive at their own mind games?

"What's that?" Cleo asked, tilting her head and resisting a smile. "What did you say?"

They grumbled again, something indistinguishable, but she heard the end of it, something about *here nor there*.

Cleo leaned in closer, cocking her ear toward Austin. "What?" And they spit the answer at her, thick phlegm hitting her ear and neck.

"Shit!" she screamed. *Did it get in?* She leaned her ear to the side and wiped the sticky saliva from her skin.

Laughter was all she heard at a muffle with the liquid in her ear. And she realized that entire conversation had been a lure to draw her in closer. Cleo was three feet closer to Austin now than when she'd started the conversation, and it was all subconscious, creeping inward, leaning; she hadn't even registered it. It was that feeling of winning that had intoxicated her with confidence, arrogance, and it was all a part of their stratagem.

Did it get in?

"Hole in one," they said, speaking in her accent again. "Swish—*thwack*, like Tatum's step *back*."

"It didn't get in," she said in defiance, though she didn't know.

"Oh, I'm in," Austin said, nodding like they wanted her to nod with them. "I'm in your head, Cleo. Maybe not biologically, but in a cerebral, mind-fuck sort of way."

Cleo wiped the last of the phlegm from her earhole. The sticky yellow mucus streaked the length of her shirt. As she climbed out of the shirt and tossed it on the floor, they squeezed Austin's lips into a whistle.

"You look deathly in all those bones," they said.

She picked up the helmet for Austin's space suit and cocked it back, ready to knock his teeth out. But they flinched—*Austin* flinched. And she saw him for a moment, his face there in between a legion of monsters. Poor Austin appeared frightened just long enough for Cleo drop the helmet.

"What's wrong, bumblebee?" Austin asked, the smile returning.

"Shut up."

"Baby bee, baby Clee." They smiled at her as they mimicked Dad's old sayings.

And suddenly, Cleo didn't give a shit about hiding her goddamn temper. She picked up the helmet again. She aimed it Austin's head and pelted it like a cricket bowler. She missed, and it might have been on purpose.

"The hell are you trying to do, huh?" she screamed, but they only responded in grins and chuckles. "You are not in my head. You're just pissing me off."

"Oh, I've already been in your head, Cleo. Xavier. Bynoe. Who's my real dad? Daddy, I wanna be like you, but I'm nothing like you. Your conscious mind thinks about terraforming, but you dream of drugs and soca at night. Your nightmares are of octopuses in the deprivation tanks. You're all fucked up in there. Of all the hundreds of minds within me, I feel like I've been infected by you. *You* and your adolescent traumas are like germs on my tendrils."

"Stop," she said. Her voice cracked, and she knew they heard it.

"You're a drug addict. A suicide failure. You are your mother's child and your father's disappointments. Let's not talk about your awkward attempts at masturbating, at shame. Isn't it like a loner that the only person you can find to have sex with is yourself and can't even find the spot."

"Shut. Up."

"Me tied up and you standing there with deadly helmets, and you think you're in control? I will eat you alive in here. You will beg me to take you in before the night is out. You should kill me now, and I only say it because I know you are incapable. I know your next move, Cleo. Every nervous twitch running through you right now, I can predict. Go ahead and wipe the spit away."

And she nearly did—not by their command, but that was her nervous tic. Always scratching at every goddamn itch. And there was something trickling down the side of her neck. *Phlegmy residue?* They knew her so damn precisely. Everything they'd learned about her was still stored in their spider-webbed memory.

"Whatever," she whispered, unable to meet their eyes now. Cleo turned toward the monitors to check on Daniel.

"We are not just a Hive," they said. "We process information thousands of powers faster than your rover. Most other species have adjoined us willingly. Because we are the perfect organism. And if that devil out there is an anti-god and we are its opposite, what does it make us, Cleo? Together we will escape this zoo, but only together. Go ahead, check on Daniel; he will be in signal range in a minute or two."

"I'm not willing, and neither was Boston or even Austin. Humans are singular beings."

"No. Your mother and father wrestle inside of you, Cleo. Ava comprises your hostility and aggression, Finn your intimacy. You are a puzzle of personality with many pieces. You are your own sort of Hive, Cleo . . ."

"Captain Zachariah," Daniel's voice came over the speaker, saving her from any more of the conversation. "Austin, this is the *Antilles*, on station. You copy? Over."

The rectangular holoscreen requesting a visual conference flashed in the air in front of both Austin and Cleo. There was a calming beep that stoked through the quiet.

"Should you get it, or should I?" Austin asked.

Cleo mulled it over for a moment. Austin was still tied up. His lips swollen, bloodied, and bruised. Blood on his shirt. Blood on the floor. She couldn't answer Daniel's call, not with everything in the capsule lying in such disarray.

"Austin . . ." Daniel chuckled nervously on the third beep. "You on your poop throne or something?"

What worried Cleo was that Daniel had access to the camera system within every capsule. He could override the controls and peek in if he wanted. He shouldn't, of course—there were privacy protocols—but in his broken state, who knew what he'd do if she didn't answer.

"Can't wait to hear you explain this," the Hive said, lifting Austin's duct-taped wrists. His smile shone knowingly; they had been expecting this. They'd known the call was coming.

Then another buzz rang in her earpiece; it was Shakes. Cleo twisted away from Austin and whispered to her rover.

"Not now, Shakes."

"I know, Clee. And I want to *abide.* But there's real problems *outside.*"

"There's problems *inside*, Shakes," she snapped back, then remembered she should be whispering. "I have bigger problems. Stay off the damn line."

"Austin . . ." Daniel's desperate voice echoed through the capsule. "Are you okay, man?"

"Poor guy," they said in Austin's most sympathetic tone. "You gonna pick up, Clee?"

A dry, bloodstained smile erupted across Austin's face. Glee, childish and sinister in equal measure. Blood dyed the white collar of his shirt, like she had taken a knife to his neck. The thermoplastic tape rashed and reddened along his wrists and ankles. It looked like torture. She couldn't answer Daniel's request, especially in his current state of mind. And as Daniel's call-in request pulsed outside, she felt the faint vibration of the earpiece. Her rover just wouldn't quit.

She tapped the earpiece again. "What, Shakes?" she whispered in exasperation. "What's the problem?"

"It's the octonary. It's spilled-blood-*hounding us*—nine limbs *surrounding us.*"

"Well . . . *shit.*"

26

"Just gimme a minute," Austin said to Daniel, but under the duress of Cleo's instruction and the muzzle of the nail gun. The excuse for his tardy response was oversleeping. The reason for no image on the camera was the need for Austin to get himself together. "So just gimme one minute," Cleo told *them* to say, even though she needed at least two.

That was the time she gave herself to cram Austin into his EMU suit. Her rush became unintentional violence as his knuckles bent gymnastically into the fingers of the gloves. His nose stubbed against the glass of the helmet as she forced it over his head. But as she knotted the suit's wrists together in rolls of duct tape, Cleo suddenly realized there was no resistance. They just watched her do it. Austin's blue-eyed fixation observed her every move. *Why aren't they fighting back?*

"Take your time," Daniel replied, relieved just to hear Austin's voice, it seemed.

Cleo grabbed her own EMU, a backpack full of rations, the nail gun. *What else?* Her gaze swept across the room. There wouldn't be any coming back after she blew this capsule and the octonary off the face of the planet.

"What else?" she asked herself again.

"What else, what?" they asked, a smirk swelling on Austin's cheek. "All that self-talk. Like there's a congregation in your head."

"Quiet," she said, picking up a syringe. It had been used, but she shoved it into the pressurized backpack all the same.

"It's been a couple minutes now," they said. "Should I respond or . . . ?"

"Not yet," she snapped and threatened them with a thrust of the nail gun.

"Shakes," Cleo whispered as she climbed into her own space suit, "the octonary comes from a species that communicates through movement. That dance it does with its tentacles, those are words. There is a rhythm to it. The scales are similar to music. I'm sending you a surveillance video from Yasmin's capsule of its movement patterns. See if you can decode its singing movement, understand some of what it's saying. Maybe even sing back."

"You want me to *commun-i-cate hymns*," Shakes asked, flabbergasted, "with something that *communes with eight limbs*. Yo, I'm *short four*. What, should I *contort more*? Or maybe you ride me like a *centaur*."

"I know I'm asking a lot," she said and meant it. Learning the sign language music of an alien species, even for quantum processors, was impossible. "But at the end of the day, it's just a distraction ploy. Doesn't have to be perfect, Shakes. Just a distraction. Something to keep it occupied. I'm going to rig the capsule to explode."

"Copy that," Shakes replied.

"The octonary is outside?" Austin said and smiled.

Damn it, she hadn't whispered that last part.

"An interesting species," they continued. "Death is a part of its life cycle."

She could see the viral intelligence yearning for the octonary's mind. Excitement flashed across Austin's wily eyes. The Hive truly wanted everything: her, the octonary, every species on this artificial world.

"Okay." Cleo nudged Austin on the shoulder with the nail gun. "Tap in with Daniel. No video. Voice only."

"You blew up the octonary once already. It won't fall for that again."

"Call Daniel," she insisted.

"It is a highly intelligent species."

"So's my rover," she said. "Call Daniel." She aimed the nail gun at Austin's head and, therefore, his helmet. "Call him!"

They nodded their compliance, but that bloodied smile stretched across Austin's face without a wince of intimidation, even as she pressed the muzzle against the glass.

"Daniel?" they started, bending Austin's cadence into a playful Barbadian accent. "Cheese on bread, brother-man. Sorry, I overslept. It's been a really . . . interesting day."

"Careful . . ." Cleo let the weight of the nail gun press heavier against Austin's shoulder.

"Keeping your camera off, I see," Daniel responded.

"Feeling kinda rough, you know, and it shows. I just want to keep the camera off for a bit."

Not bad, Cleo thought.

"Hey, I get it."

Cleo maneuvered her way behind Austin and pressed the nail gun against the back of their head. She tapped the holoscreen, flipping through external cameras two to four to six, searching for a dancing rover. *There*—she couldn't help but point. Her rover could be seen on external camera four, approaching the dancing octonary. The alien stood over her rover like a spider might an ant.

The download of Boston's surveillance images had finished a minute ago. Shakes should have it all now. The octonary's movement and language should have been analyzed at least to a remedial degree. So what the hell was Shakes waiting for? *Dance, move, communicate something.*

"Shakes?" she whispered, even with Austin immediately in front of her. "Where are you at with the language interpretation?"

"Download is complete. So stop *stressing*. I'm *processing*."

"Well, process faster."

The conversation between Daniel and Austin kept rumbling in front of her. But it was all in one ear and out the other. She didn't have the bandwidth to listen, not with her fingers like pincers zooming in and out on the octonary and rover.

"Hey." Daniel's voice echoed through the capsule. "Why you all a sudden speaking real-life Bajan now?"

"You remember," Austin said, "where I said I visited last time?"

"Oistins."

"You remember what that means . . . Oistins?"

"Oh . . ." Daniel lowered his voice a pitch. "You're saying—"

"I'm just saying, it's like Oistins in here."

On the holoscreen, Cleo watched the octonary's body tighten as its limbs spooled outward. One limb at a time, then another, then a third. Its tentacles were speaking in tongues. And there was rhythm, meter—cosmic song. And she couldn't take her eyes off the octonary's elegant ballet. She tapped her feet to its rhythm, feeling its artistry through her own body.

Austin mumbled something then that she didn't quite catch. It was at the bare limits of her perception. She turned her back to the conversation.

"I get you," Daniel responded.

"So that's all. Feeling under the weather, like that day in Oistins. That's the only reason the screen's off. Just need some breathing room."

"Right," Daniel said. "I understand."

Cleo had lost track completely of the conversation. The octonary's dance continued to beguile. There was a violence to its dance, but it balanced it with supple pirouettes and gyrations that nearly brought a smile to her face. A truly intelligent thing, but did Shakes understand any of it?

"You getting any of this?" she asked her rover.

"Its dance is quite *radical*. In that, the mathe*matical*. Is sort of gram*matical*."

"Mathematical grammar." *Wow*, she thought, both of her rover's understanding and the concept of using mathematics to command the verbs and gerunds of its language. "So you understand?" she asked, but too loud—too much excitement. "Do you know what it's trying to say?"

"No. But its limbs are *nine now.* I think that new growth de*fines how*—after each death a new *twine bows.*"

"Nine limbs." She expanded the holoscreen but couldn't distinguish the ninth limb. Every appendage was too fluid and in motion. But she didn't care about extra limbs; Shakes just said it still couldn't understand. "So is communication impossible, then?" she asked and twisted back to Austin to see if they heard her. But they were too invested in the conversation with Daniel to care.

"Got it?" Austin said to Daniel.

Got what? Cleo tapped Austin on the shoulder and gestured for them to cut the line. Two fingers scissoring along her own neck. There was way too much talking. Austin seemed to understand, nodding in compliance.

Cleo turned back to the holoscreen. "Sorry, Shakes," she whispered into her earpiece. "What was I saying?"

"Is communication impossible?"

"Is it?" she asked.

"Yes—for any other *team than us.* But remember, I'm the *genie-us.* Your wish is my *devotion.* So for now I'll copy the octonary's *motion.*"

"You're mimicking him, it, whatever?"

"And so far it's worked *great.* A distraction instead of a way to *communicate*—could buy you time to *use as bait.* A *ruse to wait* . . ."

"Keep it up," she said. "Just buy me a few more . . ."

Cleo noticed something then—the hollow static. The conversation between Austin and Daniel had ended, but that staticky fizz of transmission still hissed in the air. She peered down at her alien prisoner and noticed Austin holding up five fingers.

Five what? she mused. Then, as five fingers became four, it hit her. *Seconds?* Three fingers, then two . . . one. Then it really hit her.

The lights went out, likely Daniel shutting them down from the *Antilles.* They lunged upward with Austin's shoulder and slammed into the bottom of her jaw. She staggered backward in the dark and stumbled. Before she could make out where she was, they were on top of her and headbutting with the Mylar-sheet glass of the helmet. She nearly blacked out, but not from the headbutt. Somehow she was already lightheaded. *Oxygen?* Daniel again, he had turned it off at the *Antilles*'s master controls. *Goddamn copycat.* And she had stupidly put Austin's helmet on over his head. And he was breathing fine.

"Lights on, *Antilles*," they said in Austin's triumphant voice, and the lights flashed on.

They sat on top of her, Austin's two hundred pounds straddling her malnourished rib cage. Saliva frothed on Austin's lips and dripped onto the glass of the helmet. *Think, bumblebee.* Dad's voice. But nothing came to mind. Then, surprisingly, Ava's nasty voice came into her head. *Nail gun, bitch!*

Cleo's arms flung to her side and gripped the nail gun. She rammed it at the side of the helmet and squeezed the trigger. The glass popped and suctioned inward on Austin's face. Glass washed into his lips and nostrils, and they tumbled off her.

"Daniel?" Cleo shouted as she rolled over onto Austin's choking body and slammed the nail gun's muzzle against his forehead. "Turn your video feed on. Watch me." She jabbed the gun against Austin's head, threatening with that gesture three times. "Turn the oxygen back on." Her finger trembled against the trigger.

"Oxygen's on, Cleo," Daniel said. "Cleo, please . . . it's on. Don't do that. It's going to be okay. All right? Everything's okay now."

He probably thought she had lost her mind, and as such, Cleo couldn't explain herself. If she did tell him the truth—*a viral intelligence, an anti-god species*—it would remove all doubt that she had gone completely stark raving mad. So she could only tell Daniel the one thing that mattered.

"Daniel, I don't have much time," Cleo said. "Austin and I are going to leave now, and I need you to do something for us."

"Cleo, listen—" Daniel tried, but she cut him off.

"You listen! I . . ." *Calmer*, she thought. *You're going to lose him.* "I wish I had spoken to you more. Three years to get here and we only spoke, what? A few dozen times? That's on me. You made an effort, I remember, but I . . . I don't know. I need you to trust me now. I'm going to ask you to do something. It's going to sound insane. But the lives of all . . ." She couldn't explain everything, that was a bridge way too far. "Our lives. All our lives depend on it, Daniel."

He was quiet for a long time. And maybe it was just a few seconds or so, but for her and in that moment, it felt like forever.

"You there?" Cleo's voice trembled. If he didn't trust her, then none of it would work. "Daniel . . ."

"What do you need?" he asked.

"Land. I need you to touch down at these coordinates." Cleo's fingers tapped quickly at the holoscreen before he could cut her off. "Here. Land the *Antilles* here."

"What?" Austin interjected with such disgust that saliva sprayed from his lips. "Why would you want him to land there?"

"Shut . . ." She started to press the nail gun harder against Austin's forehead but remembered her audience. Putting a nail through Austin's skull wouldn't play into her strategy of getting Daniel to trust her.

"I'm not landing," he said.

"Daniel, please—"

"I'd be jeopardizing the entire mission."

"Daniel . . ." She shook her head in disbelief. "This mission *has been* jeopardized. It's over."

Quiet again, but she couldn't rush him. Cleo couldn't seem frantic or unhinged. She lifted the nail gun from Austin's head and waited. Daniel dallied nearly a full minute before responding.

"Why do you want me to land there? What's there?"

"The devil," Austin whispered. "The anti-creation species."

"I will be there. And Austin will be there. Land in two, three days, maybe. We'll arrive there."

"No, Cleo, I can't."

"You can," she assured him. "You can do it."

"No. The MCs will lose their shit. I'll be reprimanded and . . ."

His voice broke. Daniel looked so young there. So small on that holoscreen, with tears so big, pouring out of his eyes.

"I believe in you. You will come. You will land. And you'll save us."

"I . . ." Daniel's voice warbled. "Can't."

"You will." Tears dripped from her eyes too. "You will. We're stepping outside now, and I want you to look at our external cameras before they go out. You're not going to believe what you see. But it's real. The octonary. In the coming days, think about what you saw. And we'll be there waiting for you in three days. I know you. You'll come."

"Cleo, please—"

"End transmission."

"Transmission ended," the capsule's IU said.

She exhaled. Her breathing had been clinched the entire conversation. Cleo could only hope now. Hope that loneliness might coerce him. Hope that the infinite weight of solitude might compel him. That was her gambit because she knew that weight better than most. But all she could do was hope, because if Daniel didn't land at those coordinates, it was all for nothing. *So save us, goddamn it.*

"Wipe your eyes," they said as a glassy nosebleed ran from Austin's nostrils and shards of the visor lodged in their gums.

"Get up." Cleo grabbed Austin by the collar and yanked them up. "I'll get a halogen for your busted-ass head."

"I don't know what you're planning or why we're going to the anti-god's biosphere. What I do know is that Daniel will not land."

"You don't know Daniel."

"I know him better than you do. Via your memories of him, and Austin's memories, and Boston's. They slept together, Daniel and Yasmin. Did you know *that*?"

She didn't, and it caught her off guard. But soon a smile rose up in her cheeks. "I'm glad they had each other in all that empty space."

"He won't come."

Cleo grappled Austin's collar. Their neck jerked. And she twisted hard to release the cracked helmet from their collar. She lifted it off and crowned Austin with a halogen. The magnetic collar clicked, then magnetized into place.

"Why don't you leave me here?" they said. "Kill me along with the octonary?"

"You would like that. Break your restraints. Somehow get your virus into the octonary's veins. I saw your eyes light up earlier. No. I need you for something else."

"And what's that? What are you planning?"

Wouldn't you like to know. But she shook her head. "That's not today's problem," she said, shoving him toward the air-lock door. "Right now, the plan starts with killing the octonary."

27

The octonary was barely a dot out there in the distance. A shadow buried under deeper shadow. *Has to be at least half a mile out*, she figured. She leaned in the air-lock doorway, fatigued and squinting into the distance. The octonary was too far away for the explosion to affect it. She scowled at all that dying dirt lying between herself and the octonary, and her tiny rover too. *Hang in there, Shakes.*

She would have to draw the alien in closer somehow. At half a mile, it would barely incur second-degree burns. At the same time, Cleo would need to get underneath the capsule to unbolt the valves to the engine. The liquid hydrogen would spark in the ignition and light up anything within a thousand feet.

"The kill zone is just over two thousand feet," Austin declared, as if she didn't know. They stood in front of her, their space suit's collar in the grip of her fist. They lurched back, meeting her with that bloody grin. A glass shard punctured his lower lip, and it bled when he spoke. "You won't kill it at that distance."

But Austin got nothing from her besides an inquisitive raising of the eyebrow. Cleo was considering something else now. If worse came to worse, she might have to sacrifice Austin's body. Maybe that would lure the octonary in. *Maybe*. And the pause—that *maybe* she mouthed—caught Austin's eye.

"Maybe what? Maybe you can't win? I've run the probability matrix. The octonary is a warrior species. It will tear through your rover like toilet paper. Then it will murder both you and Austin's body. I offer you everlasting life. Beyond the physical. Drink of my blood. Eat of my flesh."

"Move," she said, shoving them forward, out through the air lock and into the vulnerability of that withering world.

Above, wrinkled clouds drifted beneath the quarter slice of moonlight. The winds had picked up, and they came in spurts. Dried dirt dyed the breezes gray, and it appeared almost smoky as they swirled.

This biosphere was dying, at least it seemed to be, and Cleo decided that it was because Austin had been dead for many months now. The world was unadapting to its human host. She didn't know that for sure, of course, but the theory felt sound enough, and the fewer questions she had in her head, the better.

She ushered Austin beneath the capsule's four-foot underbelly. She tied them against one of the lander's auxiliary struts with the coaxial cables, then more thermoplastic tape for good measure. Then Cleo got to work unlocking the main fuel valve, unbolting the massive locks by switching the nail-gun head on the pistol grip with a wrench.

"Shakes?" Cleo said into her earpiece. "Are you any closer to figuring the language out?"

"I can't quite grasp *the meaning*. And what's *demeaning*—is even with all my data *streaming*. Left and right CPUs—I'm double-*teaming*. I won't figure this out, it's *seeming*."

Goddamn it. Cleo sighed her frustration into wisps of cold air. "You're saying you won't be able to figure the language out?"

"My grasp of the language, it's a bit *murk-y*. Too much guess-*work*, *Clee*."

She couldn't see anything from her position beneath the capsule, just the maw of the rockets and swells of dirt. Cleo imagined the scene out there—the octonary standing over Shakes's brittle reinforced steel and titanium, swinging its limbs in a schizophrenic ballet, trying to communicate something. And if Shakes didn't have something coherent to respond with, the octonary would just tear the rover to pieces.

The whir of her pistol-grip wrench buzzed as she unlocked the first bolt. It wouldn't take long, she thought, but what was the use of any of this work if the octonary was out of range? She had to get it closer. *But wait*, Austin just said the octonary was from a warrior species. And there was something familiar about that. Something sparked—a migraine-inducing flash of memory. Cleo remembered something like a see-through flower; the petals were transparent and all rotating like windmills within windmills.

These weren't her memories. And every flash and image was accompanied by a sudden stab of razors migrating across her gray matter. Cleo fell over in pain, hitting the dirt, and somehow she kept on falling deeper into those stowaway memories. Her eyes cracked open like eggshells and a hundred yolks spilled out—a hundred eyeballs. It was like headbutting a kaleidoscope. She saw in every direction from a species with as many eyes. Some eyes saw in infrared, others in ultraviolet. A thousand new dizzying colors stabbed her forehead with nausea. She saw underground networks, like cities, and yet unlike them in many more ways. And she saw that five-petal flower again—but it wasn't a flower, was it? That was a baby octonary. Its petals, or tentacles, were transparent before its first death. She saw the dance—a warrior's dance, full of hate and mockery, but with its own aesthetics of movement. And that was why they fought—to evolve. Death was a necessary development in their culture.

Cleo fell one last time and, splat, the vomit spilled out of her. She woke up, lightheaded and kissing the dirt. Liquid bile spooled out around her lips and nostrils, and she snorted up her own vomit. She sneezed, coughed, and nearly pissed herself. She tried to roll over and catch her breath, but the nausea hadn't retreated and she lay on a pillow of her own excrement.

Get up, Cleo told herself, climbing up from her subconscious first. Then she grabbed on to the struts and lifted her muddied, muck-stained face from the dirt.

"Shakes," she groaned. "You there?"

"Copy."

"Odds and evens. The war dance has something to do with odd and even numbers. I'm not sure what, but . . ." She took a breath, trying to make sense of what she had seen. "It's all a war dance. It's meant to be bellicose and disrespectful. They're a warrior species, and for them art is war. So the movements should be elegant, with an artistic aesthetic. Oh"—she remembered or realized—"the octonary species are born with five limbs. So the war dance is on a pentameter scale. Maybe you use your head as a dwarf limb? I don't know, but you only need five."

Her head dropped back into the muck. It was in her hair now. *Great.* What she saw and felt would haunt her. These weren't just things of nightmares; these were ancient memories, long before any life breathed on Earth. The only thing worse than seeing the monster was seeing through it. Seeing through that many eyes and at those extremes of light. Breathing phosphates and other nasty gases. She spit, still tasting the primordial arsenic on her tongue.

"Shakes, each time they die, they're reincarnated with one new limb. But the language base is five . . . like speaking with five tongues and at the same time. Does any of this help?"

"Helpful? Clee, that's the *cipher's writ*. I think you just *deciphered it*. Pentameter movement. It makes *sense*. Past and future spoken at once? That's *in tense*. More than helpful, this is *im-mense*."

"'Kay," she said. "How long 'til you under*stand*?"

"I've already translated every *strand*. Every musical verb, noun, or com*mand*."

"Good. Okay. Remember, the whole goal is to draw that thing in closer to the capsule. A couple hundred feet, if you can manage. You understand?"

"Get it all *riled up*. Let the anger *pile up*. Then lead it down the *aisle*, *yup*. Copy that."

"Send me the visuals and translate to me what you're saying."

A holoscreen flashed in midair in front of her. She saw what Shakes saw. The octonary towered over the rover, undulating as if it were underwater. That relative stillness in the octonary seemed to be it waiting for a response.

"Shakes, why are you just standing there?"

"Look, I'm not just *off resting*. I'm *processing* and *cross testing*. Do you want me to *die jesting*? Cuz I'm *digesting* everything it just *said*. Don't nag, gimme a second *instead*."

"'Kay, but goddamn it, process faster."

Suddenly, her rover spun its body backward. Then, in one fluent motion, it twisted onto its back and elevated its hind legs. It was communicating, but what was it saying? Then it flipped back onto its legs, crouched, stood, and crouched again. And it kept spinning in a five-limbed ballet of movement. *Translate*, she thought, and as if the IU had read her mind, Shakes spoke.

"Sending approximate *translation* of my nonverbal *communication*: The last of the octonary species, I greet you from *three feet away*. But don't get it twisted, I won't *retreat today*. Back down from *who*? *You*? A discount Cthu*lhu*. No. I didn't start this—but I ain't *diminishing, shit*! I'm *finishing it*! And I'm not *lying*. You were just reborn and now minutes from *dying*. Sounds like a midlife crisis, *squid*. But I'd have a crisis too if I was *mid*. Oh, God for*bid* . . ."

Shakes continued its verbal barrage for a full minute. And it appeared as if the octonary understood, the way its nine limbs dipped and bowed, like it was dancing. But even after Shakes's exchange was done, Cleo couldn't keep her wide eyes off the holoscreen. She had to keep reminding herself that this poetic ballet of a war dance was octonary tradition, because right now it sounded a hell of a lot like a rap battle.

"Does it understand what you're saying?" Cleo asked. "You're using words like 'spaghetti' and 'October.' How can it understand?"

"Five limbs are like *five tongues*. It's like I got *five lungs*. One limb is physical *rhyme*. Like beatboxing to rhythm on *time*. Another limb is the *etymology*—for my *terminology*. The third limb is context and the fourth is the *meaning—Convening* with the fifth limb that weaves it all into one digestible *sandwich*. And honestly, Clee, it's one hell of a *language*."

"I see . . ." Did she, though? Shakes seemed to be implying that in this language, each limb was having a separate conversation. *Maybe it was like in an orchestra*, she thought—one limb might be strings; others woodwinds, brass, and percussion; then a conductor limb that brought it all together. If so, there was a beauty to the octonary species—as combative as they were, the complexity and artistry in their language was unmatched.

She eyed the holoscreen again, reading the number for distance. Shakes had brought the octonary several feet closer to the capsule, but it was far from enough. *You gotta get it closer.*

Her rover had kicked up dust in all of that dancing. The octonary's limbs slithered out of that fog of kicked-up dirt like nine snakes, all with their own destination. Another round of vulgar gestures began as the octonary responded. But Cleo had her own job to do, and she had barely started. She grabbed the wrench and went to work unbolting the screws while Shakes translated the octonary's movement.

Shakes explained that the octonary's response was more noble than its own. There was an elegance to its verbiage—a regality, even. The octonary's war dance described Shakes's battery as a motor of decline. Then it expressed anger that Shakes had compared it to Earthbound squids. Then the octonary conveyed surprise that the rover followed Cleo, describing her as a subspecies. Finally, the alien communicated its prejudices, saying Cleo possessed child-bearer's cells. And therefore, she must be as fragile as eggshells.

"Fragile as an eggshell?" Cleo said, turning back to the holoscreen. "That's the best it could *do*?"

"*True*," Shakes agreed. "It speaks with this old *civility*. Like it glows *nobility*. But shows no *ability*."

"I guess . . ." She shrugged and returned to the panel above her. "Just keep it busy a little while longer."

"Its rhymes are weak," Shakes shouted into the earpiece. "It's soft. I should *finish him off.* Tear his *finn-ish limbs off.* Watch it *diminish, then scoff.*"

"No, Shakes, I need more time. And you need to draw it in closer. A lot closer. It's still out of blast range. Once you finish the verbal battle, the physical bout will start. We don't want that. Toy with it a bit more. Buy me more *time.*"

"Buy me more *rhymes.* Cuz I'm *running out.* Battery's in *stunning doubt.* Not sure about this second *bout.* Remember, this *diss track* is just a *distract.*"

"I know, Shakes. Just run it as long as you can."

Shakes continued its war dance response. It positioned itself in a horse's grazing posture, like it was bowing. Then it reared upward, but gracefully. It rolled, bucked its rear legs, then lay on the dirt and made a swimming motion with all four limbs. At about the tenth movement in, the rover began translating every motion into words.

But the whir of the pistol-grip wrench drowned out Shakes's voice. Cleo rolled onto her back to continue unbolting the fuel panels and, *God*, there were so many. Releasing the internal rocket fuel would take longer than she had first surmised.

Out of the corner of her eye, Cleo noticed Austin's hyena grin. Out of the corner of her other eye, she glimpsed the holoscreen. She saw the octonary's flesh wrinkled, every one of its nine limbs coiled in, ready to snap outward. It was seething. Its anger took shape in the sharpening of those bumps.

"Careful, Shakes . . ." Cleo whispered, stopping the wrench to hear herself speak.

The rover didn't listen. It continued to shape its body into the alien vocabulary. Describing the octonary as a *useless, Massachusetts, clam-chowder-looking ass and couth-less*. And each derogatory syllable enraged the monster more. Carnivals of color splashed across its epidermis—a grand kadooment of greens and blues and reds washed over its flesh in waves. It wasn't like an octopus anymore; its anatomy flailed like an inferno with nine tentacle flames. But Shakes's backward motion *was* luring the octonary closer in. It was working.

"Shaaaaaakes . . ." Cleo warned with the curvature of her voice. "Battle well enough that you're a challenge, but don't . . . Piss. It. Off. If it attacks before I'm done . . . it's all for nothing."

"May come to that, *either way*," Shakes said. "But I'll take a *breather, 'kay*?"

"Thank you," Cleo said. "I know your battery's fading. Just five more minutes. I'm almost there. Just gimme five."

"I've got hard-*drive limits*. I don't think we have *five minutes*."

"Fine, four," she lied. Cleo needed ten—fifteen, maybe. These valves weren't unbolting fast enough, and the octonary was closing in quick. "Just focus . . ." She had to hear herself say it. "Just. Breathe."

On the holoscreen, the octonary lifted itself onto all nine tentacles, bobbing up and down with violence. It stood on its head and spun as its tentacles stabbed outward like daggers. Its dance was like a shadowboxing routine. Shakes translated, telling Cleo how the octonary came from a warrior race and that it was a warrior's place to die an honorable death. And that almost humanized the monster for her. *Almost*. But the nine-legged worm on her holoscreen would never blend into an aesthetic she could identify with.

Her rover continued its response, twirling, thrusting, lifting its legs, and gyrating its back. But with each movement, it was inching furtively backward. She could see them now, five hundred feet out. The octonary was following her crafty rover, and nearly in range, but so was she. The liquid hydrogen started hissing outward into depressurized vapor.

"Shakes, I almost got it."

"Well *done*," the rover said. "Now it's time to get out and *run*."

"Not yet," she said as the smell of the hydrogen filled her nostrils. "We may need to use Austin as bait. I'm gonna keep him under here. The octonary will—"

"It won't work, Clee."

"Why?" she asked. "Why won't it work?"

"You know what I'll *say next*. This thing's a predator—*A-pex*. Ninety miles an hour *limb speed*. Even with a *slim lead*—that *grim steed*—would be on you in under a *minute*. I'm sorry. We just can't *win it . . .*"

"No . . ." she said, lowering the wrench even with just a couple bolts left. "Can't win what, Shakes?"

"I have to be honest—I knew this from the *beginning*. There was no *winning*. The octonary wanted you—*only*. *To own, Clee*. Its culture *instills it*. Because you *killed it*. Now it needs an *honorable vengeance*. To achieve a level of *cultural ascendance*."

There was something between the lines of what Shakes was saying. The rover was implying something.

"What are you saying, Shakes?" she asked.

"The octonary is smarter than us, *true*. But more impulsive *too*. Professing honor so *possessive*. And behaving far more *aggressive*. That's where I saw a *last chance*. A *passed glance*—*askance*. A desperate shot in its *war dance*. Don't you *see*—*Clee*? Now it's turning its hatred toward *me*."

So that was why the rover was communicating so aggressively—to turn the octonary's ire away from her.

"So you come up with your own plan. Disobeying my commands." She shook her head. "That's not how this is supposed to work."

"My orders are to *protect you*. *Respect too*. Where *respect's due*. But your plan had holes. So, I had to *correct you*."

"And what's that correction?" But she knew and asked anyway. "How do you stop the octonary?"

"Look. It's *deranged, wow*. It's *enraged now*. Get it? *In range now*. I got it—right where I want it. I'm on it. So, Clee—quiet any part of you that *says debate*. Don't—*hes-itate*. *Dec-imate*—this thing in *my honor*. Be a *sly bomber*. Like they *tried Palmer*. I *figure* I'm *done anyway*. My battery's all *liquor* and *rum*—*Henny sway*. So, pull the *trigger* and *run*—*Hemingway*."

"The trigger . . ." She shook her head, understanding in parts but unsure she had the full picture. "What are you saying?"

"You're gonna have to finish *without me*."

"No—"

"I don't *doubt, Clee*—that the *route we*—"

"Stop. Stop. Stop," she stuttered, not even sure what to say next. "Just . . . wait. We have time, right? We have time. Let's think. The octonary is . . . it's . . ."

"It won't just let us run *away*. It'll hunt *and prey*. But right now, it wants to *smush me*. Just need one more *damn push, Clee*. And it will *am-bush me*. I just have hit my *rap pinnacle. Cap lyrical.* Pull off a Christmas *rapped miracle*."

"Stop . . ." She sniffled, tears burning her eyes. "What are you talking . . ." But the words weren't coming. Just more tears.

"Don't be sad. I get to be a *rhetor* with my *flow*. What *better* way to *go*? I'm a *bettor*. Play the *dough*—and put it on *me*. Bumble*bee*. But *time's up, though*. You gotta *climb up*—*go*."

The last screw fell and clipped her collar, but Cleo couldn't quite pull away. She yanked at the valve, then kicked at it, but it wouldn't budge. *Shit*. But the liquid hydrogen was seeping through, dripping off her fingertips. *That's good enough, right?* It would have to be.

Cleo made her way behind Austin. They were still taped to the struts, but half of the duct tape was torn away. They were just a few minutes from making their escape. Austin's goddamn smile widened as they stared into her watery eyes. Cleo switched the pistol grip's wrench head with the nail-gun head. Then she pressed the gun's muzzle against Austin's shoulder. "We're moving."

"And am I supposed to make it easy for you?" they asked. "Help you to enact some ill-concocted strategy to release the anti-god?"

"Move," she cried, tears falling. "Please."

They stared at her defiantly. "No. Your plan to defeat this world will fail—*is* failing. Let me help you."

"Get up," she squealed, swinelike, her sobbing and hostility intersecting at the same hole of her throat. "Now." She pressed the nail gun harder against Austin's shoulder.

"Fuck. No." And they flashed another smile.

Their last smile, she decided. She tugged the trigger. The thwack of a three-inch nail ripped through flesh and threads of muscle, then cracked against the shoulder blade. They hollered—all of them, she hoped. Their voices echoed across the landscape.

Austin's body buckled against the pain. Cleo snatched them by the collar—the same side as the nail wound, and damn did they follow fast. The nail made the collar into a leash, and Austin whimpered every time she tugged at it.

They stumbled out from underneath the engine, and somehow she was already out of breath, biting at the air—devouring it. The air inside her whirled with sorrow, fear, and angst. The holoscreen followed her as she ran; it wobbled as she staggered unsteadily forward. On-screen, the octonary stood over the rover, but its tentacles veered in another direction—in Cleo's direction. Did it know she was running?

Shakes lurched forward suddenly and bowed. The rover's legs twisted, then it hopped and bowed again. Whatever that meant, it had an effect on the octonary. The rage at the alien's core undulated out and its limbs writhed—whipping mad. Then Shakes started its last translation.

"I got the soul of Biggie—the *dreamer*. Parts of Pun—and the whole of Missy's *demeanor. Between her*—I got Twain, Woolf, Nas, and Voltaire. *Sing!* I am no mere. *King*—I am so Lear. You're *in low gear*. You *incohere*-runt. No rhymes, you just *blare*—grunts . . ."

Shakes continued as Cleo and Austin stumbled in the dirt. Dried earth kicked up into gray plumes, and she lost hold of Austin. But the Hive didn't attempt to escape. They tried to cup their tied hands over their wound. Red splashed from between their fingers. For a moment Austin resembled his old self. And for that moment she felt sorry for him—but Cleo quickly remembered.

"Get up," she told Austin, tugging on that painful leash, and they listened. *Good boy*.

The two were still a ways away from exiting the blast radius. But Shakes was buying them time. The rover rolled and twisted in a techno-trance on-screen, translating every offensive word.

"Cuz you're *lacking*," Shakes continued. "You're under pressure and *cracking*, you *kraken*. Your species *boasts fighters*—but need *ghost-writers*. Cuz your lyrics sting a *dose lighter*—than *most spiders*."

The octonary twisted, limbs curling in like knuckles, digging its bodily claws into the dusty dirt. Its tentacles crawled across the dirt—tarantula motion. Shakes retreated backward, even closer to the capsule. But even then, her rover kept motioning—still communicating as it backed away. Her IU knew these would be its last lines, and it would make them count.

"I'm unmatched *historically*. Just look at me *metaphorically*. Imagine me covered in a *woolly coat*. *Pulley throat*. Imagine horns and hooves—like *woody spokes*. Get the picture? I *fully gloat*—that I'm the fucking *bully GOAT*."

Nine limbs swarmed around her little rover and brought it to its knees, like massive tires winding round and round and crushing inward. Shakes moved quickly to detach its two hind legs and maneuver itself out of the octonary's choke holds. It hobbled fast on two legs, closer toward the capsule's blast radius, even though it was already in range. And Shakes made it twenty or so feet before the octonary was back on top of it.

"Stop!" Cleo screamed. Her eyes were fixed on the holoscreen. She choked on her helplessness. All that pent-up attachment, every memory of Shakes, gagged out from inside her. She screamed until she was empty. Until she couldn't breathe.

"Move," Shakes shouted in staticky scratches. "You're still at a one-hundred-*foot debt*. You can't blow this thing to *soot yet*. You gotta move a *pace faster*. Cuz the octonary will *race after* and *erase vaster*, lengths of land than you can. The way it stretches its body and *spreads parts*. You don't truly have a *head start*. *Start—Start—Start—Sec—*"

The rover went quiet, its voice replaced by waves of static. Cleo stopped moving, stopped breathing; even her heartbeat felt like it paused. She listened to the static, not even sure what she was listening for. The interference buzzed like monsoons of sand. And Shakes died in her ear. She couldn't save him—her IU was gone.

In the end it was Austin that moved her. They staggered forward; with her fist still clenched on their collar, she was dragged along with them. She followed Austin now, with the virtue of her own orientation lost on that static. The duo ran, tripped and tumbled and rolled in the dirt. But they would eventually find their sync; the pattern of their footsteps came together. And they finally made some distance from the capsule.

"Love you, Shakes," she said to herself. "*Antilles*. Prepare to charge engines on my mark." But was she even out of range yet? *It doesn't look it.* "Shit," she cursed, hobbling forward. "I don't know."

Cleo spun back again to gauge her distance, and that was when she saw it. A helicopter spin of limbs propelled itself toward her—*the octonary*. And just like that, her head start had vanished. Cleo pulled Austin forward, but they pulled back, knocking her to the dirt.

Shit.

"IU, ignite . . ." Cleo choked on the words, gasping for breath, phlegm webbed in her throat. "Ig . . ." She could barely breathe. "Ignite all engines," she finally managed.

"Igniting engines," the IU said.

The flash of white was instant and blinding, a blizzard of light that consumed everything. Microseconds later, the speed of sound hit harder, blasting her eardrums off the hinges. There was only white noise after that. Finally, the blast wave gut-checked her, snatching all the oxygen away. It ripped Austin from her grip in one hand and the nail gun from the other and flung them in different directions. Then it picked Cleo up off the ground and threw her into the bright-white end of the world.

28

She lay beside Finn. His warmth wrapped around her like rope. His breathing burned hot along the nape of her narrow neck. She felt her own nakedness, and she held the blanket high on her shoulders. He whispered something that she couldn't hear. He had always been soft-spoken, and even softer now in their smoky bedroom. He gargled something about the engagement or the ring. She felt for the ring, reaching around her neck. *Why the neck?* Then she felt his hands there, holding her down as he kissed her. His long, wet tongue descended between her lips. But his lips were rough and tasted of bitter salts. His lips warped into the spiral of a seashell, and his tongue was the sea snail, barbed in barnacles.

"No!" Cleo shrieked, squirming away and opening her eyes to an apocalypse.

But the choke of air outside her dream burned like pepper spray. The sand particulates were spiced in rocket fuel, and she wept without the accompanying sorrow. Tears spilled down her cheeks from the simple act of blinking. She wiped her dreamy eyes and tried to remember what was real. *Oh, that's right—the explosion,* she remembered, *a nine-limbed octonary,* and *Shakes, poor Shakes.* And now, finally, sadness did fill in the gap between her blinking tears.

The smoke and saffron soil spray-painted the landscape. There was barely a foot of visibility in front of her. She couldn't breathe. Cleo reached for her halogen but dug the sand out of her hair and the rings of her ears first. Strings of saliva hung from her lips—Finn's kiss still moist on her mouth. She lathered the saliva away and cracked the mucus crusted in her eyes. Only then did she click her halogen into a spin.

Deep breath, her body told her. In through the mouth, then out through the pores. Artificial air never tasted so sweet. And at least she'd gotten a few hours of sleep in, Cleo told herself, feeling undeservedly rested. She was refreshed in a way that she shouldn't be. Alert and her head clear of headaches and the fogginess she had grown accustomed to. A glance at her wrist revealed the passage of three and a half hours in bright-green digits. She stood, and a strong posture anchored her on her feet. *Deep breath*. This was it. Her grand design to destroy this construct started here. She had to journey to that central biosphere and break the shackles of gravity that kept the anti-god species in check. To do that, she'd need Daniel to land, and she'd need Austin.

"Austin . . ." she said, frustrated that she had to find them again. She'd just had them in the grip of her fingers. "Damn it."

Cleo stepped through the mist with her arm in front of her, waving her hand like a windshield wiper. She was feeling for something that she knew was out there. Maybe a ten-tentacled octonary. Maybe Austin with a nail gun in their hands. Either might be stalking behind her in that particulate forest. Though the blast had hit Austin harder than it had her. Maybe the Hive was unconscious, or worse yet, Austin's body had died.

But Cleo didn't have to limp far before she found the nail gun. The red battery light flashed in the shadows, screaming out with dying brightness. She kneeled, picked it up, but found something worse next to it. *Boot prints.*

Cleo ascended slowly, a gazelle lifting its doe eyes from the graze. She remained hunched as she stepped forward and tightened her grip around the nail gun. She covered the battery light with her thumb, as it might give away her approach. She followed the depression in the sand. Each boot imprint treaded deeper the farther she tracked, each one a little less filled with the blowing sand. She was closing in.

The trail of prints ended, as expected, at Austin's flaccid body. Their limbs were strewn about in rubbery, boneless angles. The left arm and hand especially twisted twice over in the way a branch might reach out with its stems. Austin's neck was a rubber band, both stretched and twisted like the bone underneath was trying to peel itself out from the flesh. *Inhuman*, she thought, and still she kept the nail gun aimed as she tiptoed closer. *Inhumane*, she reminded herself, remembering the Hive within Austin. She kneeled on the left arm and pressed the gun against his temple.

"Wake up," she said and shoved the head of the nail gun into the skin. "Come on . . ."

Austin didn't move, and that frightened her even more. She spoke again and poked, again, but only stillness followed. And the fear built because she knew that she couldn't just leave Austin's body here. If there was even the smallest possibility that they were alive, she would have to put a nail through Austin's skull before she left.

"Austin?" Cleo pressed the nail-gun head in deeper. "Austin . . ." She pressed her finger against the trigger, not all the way; she'd check for a pulse first. "I know you're not . . ."

Dead? She didn't know anything. And maybe she wouldn't check for a pulse. It looked like the arm was broken, and even the ankle appeared twisted. If Austin was incapacitated in any way, then she'd have to kill them all the same; they'd slow her down. Austin wouldn't be able to make a three-day journey to the core of this pomegranate world.

Cleo magnetized her halogen, searched her belt for the syringe, and shoved it between the grip of her teeth. *Last call*, she thought. "Austin . . ." she muttered. Her whisper was muffled by the syringe and barely audible in the wind. Did she even want them to wake? *Stab the needle and fill the syringe with Hive blood*. "That's it."

"'Kay," she answered herself, aiming the needle at the median vein. "'Kay . . ." The word steadied her hand as the needle pressed against the skin, but right then, their eyes opened.

"Shit." She stumbled back, startled. "God. Damn. It."

They groaned with the sort of breath that implied injury. A long, guttural moan that ended in a whimper. She didn't take the gun from Austin's head, though. In fact, her arm steadied. She demagnetized her halo back into its spin.

"It's out," they said, licking their sticky lips with that wormy tongue. "It's . . ."

Austin's voice disappeared into another moan, and she pressed the gun harder still. Somewhere deep inside her, Cleo was willing the nail to snap out without her triggering it. *You don't need Austin*, she mouthed, thinking through the plan. A plan that started with Boston, then the real Austin, and now her. Cleo had to finish what they had started. *Crack the gravity well, release the anti-god, watch this world eat itself alive.* But she couldn't do it without Austin's body.

"My shoulder's out." They coughed spittle that bounced off her halogen's atmosphere. "I can't . . ." They finished the sentence with eyes that begged, and maybe it was the spots of sand swimming on the surface of Austin's eyes, but Cleo would swear that she could see a million beady eyes behind Austin's blink.

And that was all she needed to see to remind her of the monsters in her midst. *No*, she thought, then pulled the trigger. *Click*. And it was like the wind paused to listen. The sand rested to hear. But the nail didn't fire—the gun's battery was dead. The red light. She sucked her teeth and steups, as the old Bajans called it.

The shock of it took Austin's voice. They didn't breathe, not even to moan. It took a minute for them to find the words. "You . . ."

"I knew the battery was dead," she lied. "Can you walk?"

"I don't know . . ."

"You're not going to slow me down. Either you can walk at my pace, or I take your halogen and you won't be following past the next boundary."

"I can walk. It'll hurt but . . ." Austin paused as they noticed the syringe in her hand. "What's that for?"

"Get up."

"You want my blood," they realized. "That's why you need me? What is this plan of yours?"

She dropped the butt of the nail gun down onto their forehead. "Up. Now."

And Austin finally listened.

The duo journeyed to the borders of Austin's biosphere. The gaseous goo welcomed them with gyrations of spastic motions. But Austin's pace wasn't to her liking. The limp. The dislocated arm, which they would eventually thrust back into place. And something else—a procrastination, maybe, like they were intentionally buying time. *For what, though*? She shoved him and kept on shoving until they crossed over the threshold and into the fog.

The subsequent biosphere was a world at war with itself. The swirling blue storm above them was cannibalizing its own limbs. It rolled clockwise in the upper atmosphere, then somehow countered itself in the under-spheres, tearing off its spiral arms and licking at the nubs. That blowtorch sky burned at over a thousand degrees Fahrenheit in the upper regions, but at the surface it was only a scorching two hundred degrees. Nearing her suit's limits. And if the heat wasn't enough, the storm-swept sky propelled winds at six hundred miles an hour. Luckily for her, the ground winds pushed at one hundred fifty-five miles per hour. Though it wasn't the winds or temperature that worried her—it was the precipitation.

It rained glass, a naturally forming silicate bred in the upper atmospheres, and all of its shards rained sideways. The frail one-fifth G had no sway on this world; everything followed the direction of the storm, including her. Glass silicates whizzed past Cleo, slashing against her already tattered suit. It wouldn't last, not in this.

Turn back, part of her whispered in a fatherly tone—Dad's coddling wisdom. That was the last thing he had said to her before she launched, wasn't it? Something like, *You can stay, you know*. And he meant stay on Earth or Venus. *You can turn back, baby, no judgment*. But another smoky voice rose up from deeper inside her and interrupted. *Keep moving*, it insisted. *If you die, you die*.

Cleo listened to the latter, even if the implications were suicide-adjacent. The ground outside was nearly uniformly flat, with a concrete-like texture. She struggled to find grip even with her cleats. The thousand-year storm had smoothed it over the centuries, tens of thousands of years maybe. *Who knows?*

Cleo and Austin had lowered their bodies to the gravel, proning under the winds, crawling to avoid the full brunt of the gusts and blades of glass. The wind howled its magnetic fields. It screamed atmospheric shifts. All of its violent noise battered against the balance inside her ears and she crawled, dizzied by the ruthless winds. She charged the nail gun with her suit's battery, then punctured nails into the ground and reused them where she could. She would attach her belt's cables to the nailheads, keeping herself grounded while they dragged themselves forward, like climbing ropes on a horizontal Everest. It would be nearly two days of it, thirty-six hours of crawling under spiral winds, a trafficking of glass, and a radiation level just high enough to whistle warnings into her earpiece.

Austin's lips kept flapping, rounding into vowels and gritting the consonants. *Are you truly attempting to communicate? Now?* Every word they said was drowned out by that spinning blue vinyl screaming overhead. A Hive mind would actually be advantageous in their particular dilemma.

But there was some level of communication. Her hands gripped their shoulders, her arms grappling their torso. For now, the necessity of mass tied them together; they allied their weights against the rising winds and made gradual progress.

By the time Cleo's gaze met the eye of that storm, she finally recognized it for what it was—a stratospheric snail shell winding around in a Fibonacci knot. *Is the intelligence of this biosphere slithering around inside?* she wondered. *Is that where it is hiding?* Cleo waited for the thing to slither out, not blinking in case she missed it. But the spin was so hypnotic that she just gawked for minutes on end, forgetting to move. Exhaustion was a funny little hallucinogen. The drug-induced daze twisted her pupils like wine corks until they popped, and she dozed off.

The wind shoved her back. Whiplash snagged her neck and nearly broke it; at least, that's how it felt. It was the second time she had nearly fallen asleep and the second time the winds woke her immediately. This time, though, the palpitations beat out of rhythm behind her breast. Her lungs thrashed about. In the end it was a biological coup that would impede her: lungs rioting and her heart too. Her muscles surrendered to the winds. And all the medicines in her press pack might as well have been a million miles away in this tempest. Opening the pack would scatter it all into the air current.

"*Help . . .*" she said, or maybe mouthed; she couldn't tell anymore. The only audible thing for the past thirty some-odd hours was the shriek of that immortal storm.

Suddenly, her torso jerked against the wind current—it was Austin, dragging her toward them. Her body flailed in the wind and Cleo surrendered. Her body, the nail gun—Cleo's life lay in Austin's hands. It was on Austin now to fight through those last impossible miles.

The winds picked up at the end, and she finally heard Austin's voice, screaming against the gales. Though that may have been another hallucination. The ferocity of every gust wouldn't allow for sleep, and Cleo blacked out and then came to for seconds at a time. So it felt like no time at all as Austin dragged Cleo through the gaseous barrier.

—

The penultimate biosphere was a world of fire-breathing earth and flammable skies. Black ash capped the peaks of the thorny hills and hollows, a craggy flower bed of rock with volcanic blossoms. There was no sun, no stars, but magma rivers shone in the dark, sunless landscape. Ash descended slowly in the gentle gravity, settling on their suits like snow.

Cleo slumped on her knees and elbows, sunken in a paralytic stupor. Her limbs trembled even as she lay collapsed on the ground. She wormed onto her back, the swivel in her hips the only part of her with strength. Her arms and legs were completely hollow.

"Are you okay?" they asked, standing over her with their hand extended to lift Cleo to her feet. "Don't let your halogen hit the ground."

Cleo barely had enough strength to look at them; her halogen *was* just inches from the dirt. "Why'd you . . . back there . . ." She had to catch her breath from the simple act of forming a sentence. "You saved me. Why?"

"Your savior."

The Hive couldn't take her right now, not in this atmosphere and this heat; their halogens had to stay on. But Austin stood over her like they might try. The nail gun was gripped in their hand. *Take it*, she considered, in Ava's voice. *Grab the shit.* Cleo tried, frittering away her last ounce of strength, grabbing feebly for the gun.

"Stop," they told her, dodging the aim of her hand. "Your heart's sinking in those tribunes of blood running through you. Your body needs rest."

"Rest?" she said. "In other words, just give myself up to you?"

They watched her for a couple of seconds, searching for something in Cleo's countenance. *What?* she thought.

"I won't force myself on you. If I do, you would act erratically, attempting suicide or self-harm. I believe in you, Cleo. Believe that you will come to me, willingly. In time. Of course, if you had died back there, then you couldn't come to me. So I saved you. I will continue to save you. Because for me, saving you is, in essence, saving myself."

"Fine," she said, not believing a word.

Austin reached out with the nail gun, offering it to her freely. "Take it."

She did. Cleo attached the gun to her belt. She pulled an adrenal spray from the press pack and locked it into the oxygen valve at her chest. The manufactured adrenaline gusted into the halogen's atmosphere. The peppery musk burned at the backs of her nostrils. She sniffled. Her eyes watered a bit, but she could feel the weight of fatigue slowly lifting.

"Saving me is saving yourself . . ." Cleo repeated. "You give me the gun and say your little thing and you think, what? I'm just gonna . . ."

"You're my friend," they said, filling the gap as she was at a loss for words. "That's how Austin felt about you. Not a screwup. A smart kid. Our best problem solver."

"Kid . . ." She scoffed but smiled. "I'm thirty-three."

"And we're nearly twenty years your senior," they said. "You're a kid. One that takes a little too long to lace up."

Cleo nodded, still packing away and sealing the press pack. She recalled Austin calling her "kid" once, experimenting with nicknames that wouldn't offend her. He had nicknames for all of them that he'd mix up or replace. And she *was* slow at suiting up, what Austin called "lacing up." She met their eyes now. They crooked Austin's lips to smile, and it looked real. *God*, it looked like him.

"I'm still not letting you stalk behind me," she said, feeling the strength to climb to her feet. And she did, rising with a groan, then standing eye to eye with the entire Hive. "I don't trust you."

"I know," Austin said, nodding. They turned their back to her and walked forward, leading the way. "But still, onward we go."

There was something about the way they turned and marched forward that seemed sad to her. Like they had given up on taking her in. A rejection of sorts. She had expected more. More persuasion. More conversation. And now she wondered if she wanted that—to be taken in. *Lie better*, she thought. *We're nearly there.*

Cleo's musings left her a step behind, and Austin glanced back. "What's wrong?"

It took a second of staring wildly at Austin before the obviousness of it collided with her. *I'm lonely*. It was that simple. Cleo felt it like desperation at the back of her throat—a thirst to be part of something. Family. Community. Dad holding her to his chest and squeezing, bringing her closer to him and them being one, just for a moment. His heartbeat and hers in sync. Breathing in rhythm.

"Cleo?"

"What's it like?" She sputtered the words out through sniffles. "*Austin*. I'm only talking to Austin."

"I'm here," Austin said.

"What is it like in there?"

"What is it like to live within a collective? I would say . . . wholeness." That caught her attention, and now she met their gaze. "I think back on my human memories. I remember this feeling, even in the heights of success, the awards and promotions, but still feeling like something was missing. A hollowness in me, you know. As humans, we have this hole in us. But now that I am whole, I know what the hole is. Alienation. That disconnect, like our social Wi-Fi has been interrupted. But now the space is full, filled, and overflowing infinitely."

They had grown so eloquent. Even more so than before. Austin was well spoken, but not like this. Hints of poetry sprinkled into casual conversation. She didn't respond. *Why?* She wanted to hear more. More casual words. More poetry. Fill the empty spaces.

"My DNA," Austin continued. "It unwinds and lays out like . . . a bridge? If that makes sense. I am one voice in a god's chorus." They point to Austin's chest. "This flesh is my church. And my voice murmurs in a murmuration with billions of others."

"Stop talking like that."

"Like what?" Austin shakes their head.

"Like . . ."

"What?"

"Like . . . you're God. The words you're using . . . just stop talking that way."

"But I love your letters. How they commingle. A communication stitched together with the very essence of what keeps you alive—breath. For humanity, to commune is life. That is singular in the universe. Being part of us is being family. No hierarchy, just billions of brothers and sisters and others. It is a warm protective shell around you, like being in a womb."

Womb. And Cleo's mind went immediately to the sensory deprivation tanks. Floating in the black, soundless void. *No*, she told herself.

"'Kay." Cleo folded her fingers around the nail gun and gestured to the path ahead. "But no, thank you. Let's keep going."

"You truly believe he'll be there?" Austin said, their tone shifting, turning upside down. A nastiness returning. "Or does your scheme work without him too?"

They were probing, trying to unravel her. Language was a tool that they could now wield, and she needed to remember that. But the Hive knew Cleo wouldn't give them any straight answers, so that squint in Austin's eyes was another type of probing. They were scrutinizing every microexpression on her face. She broke eye contact.

"Maybe he won't be there," she told them, eyes on the dirt and gesturing forward. "Either way—we're going."

A wrinkle squirmed across Austin's face. "You have no concept of what you're seeking. The anti-god's world has radiation levels that will kill you in hours. Hours, Cleo. That's a bad way to die."

Cleo already knew that was a choice she would have to make. Survive alone or sacrifice for everyone else. *For the collective.* The mission had radically changed, but she believed in the cheesy slogans now.

"I don't think you're worried that my plan won't work," Cleo said. "I think your concern is that it will."

She pushed them forward without a response. The duo continued uphill. A downward draft pushed against them. *Short strides. Slow pace. What's your plan?* The question was driving the Hive mad. *How will you release the anti-god from a prison of gravity?* she heard them buzzing. But she and they were all only one world away from that devil's biosphere, so they would see her plan soon enough.

29

Oh no, she thought, and then tried to think quietly. *I forgot something. How long have I been following Austin?* Cleo glanced at her wrist. *Seven minutes—*

"Seven hours," she corrected herself, but out loud. *Don't speak out loud*, Cleo reminded herself. *Quiet.*

Paranoia. It was worming through Cleo's mind, making her dizzy. Or was that the fatigue weighing on her body?

They kept glancing back at her with fretful eyes. Worried she might collapse. She had fallen twice already. They had suggested that Cleo follow Austin's footsteps in the literal sense. And she stepped into the imprint of Austin's boots, avoiding the extra effort of lifting her own feet from the muddy soil. As the warm volcanic down pressure gusted against Austin's wide frame, he took the brunt of its currents, creating a pocket for her to amble within without wind resistance. Then there was the harness, tethered between Austin's belt and hers. They carried at least 20 percent of her weight on this uphill march. But there was strategy in this. Cleo wanted to wear Austin's body down until they were even. She didn't trust them and had to regain some measure of control. *So wear Austin down, and remember*. She needed to remember.

What'd I forget? That nagging feeling kept worrying her. *Something about Austin's footsteps. Something to do with their footsteps.*

She surveyed Austin's prints in the mud but saw nothing out of the ordinary. *Paranoia*, and maybe it was, but there was still something she had forgotten.

Austin glanced back at her. *Damn it.* She couldn't show that she was losing her mind right now. *Keep. It. Together.*

"Halfway there," Austin huffed in exhaustion. The walk was taking its toll on their breathing and posture. "Hang in there . . ." They gestured to the cable between them and smiled. "Get it. Hang . . ."

But she didn't have the energy for puns, much less a smile.

Another tear in the bedrock hissed open, gargling molten rock, and the entire world trembled. It spewed blood-fire a few hundred feet ahead. Cleo recoiled, stumbling back. Austin caught her.

"We're at a safe distance," they said. "Side winds will angle the lava jet eastward, and the natural curve of the valley will do the rest."

Austin's mind was a satellite connected to ten thousand super-intelligences calculating the perfect path ahead. Every step in the dance of tectonic plates had been foreseen and analyzed. Whatever this path was, it was the safest one. *But why?* They didn't know her plan, but they didn't want it to work. The Hive wasn't ready to face the anti-god. They couldn't allow her to even attempt to release it. *So why allow me to take this path?* Something was off.

Cleo kept her eyes down at the wide footprints she was following, and that was when it hit her. She wasn't trying to remember the footsteps in front of her, but the footsteps from two days ago. After the explosion in Austin's biosphere, she had woken up and followed Austin's footprints. But those winds should have filled in the prints, unless they were fresh.

"Very fresh."

Cleo licked her lips. The taste from Finn's dream kiss still lingered on her mouth. And maybe it wasn't Finn who had kissed her. Was the Hive already inside her?

"No," she had to tell herself. *Doesn't make sense*, she thought. *Austin would brag.* And she nodded in agreement. They would have gloated.

They were an arrogant little god. She turned her gaze to Austin; they were lumbering upward and hauling half her body weight as well.

"Should we take a break?" Austin said and tugged on the cable between them. "Pulling double duty here."

"Sure," she conceded, probably pining for that rest more than he was.

"You can see them from here," Austin said, pointing upward. "Agristellae."

"Latin?" Cleo asked. Though she understood the word meant "stellar farmers," it was strange hearing it come out of Austin's mouth. But then again, that wasn't Austin.

"That's the scientific nomenclature. Zoology. Astronomy. Even the name for Orbis Alius, right? Latin. You give new things old names. It's uniquely human." Austin returned their eyes to the heavens. "But you can't see them, can you?" Austin pointed upward. "Billions of Agristellae. Black jellyfish-like and unlike, floating on hot-air vents, farming sunlight to such a high degree that not one drop of sunshine lights the ground."

She looked up at the black, sunless, starless night, or maybe it was day. She listened to Austin ramble eloquently about the Agristellae, a hive species of their own sort. They went on about the predominance of hive species among alien intelligences and how humanity was unique in their individuality. Austin monologued for minutes on end; they liked the sound of their own voice, didn't they? *Arrogant god*, she thought, but she had to remember to think quietly. Hide her intentions.

But something was off with this conversation . . . What was it? The insomnia was dizzying, and she just wasn't thinking clearly enough to see it. But she knew something was very, very wrong here.

Austin paused mid-spiel and observed her. Maybe Cleo's paranoia was evident—blatant, even. *Think quietly*, she told herself, then nodded and smiled, feigning the interest Austin was craving.

"Keep going," she said.

Austin happily obliged, lecturing on about the rhythm of the Agristellae and comparing them to birds in migration. The Agristellae had migrated with the orbit of their planet's star, and that kept the planet in a forever night. Orbis's hologram sky offered the same proximation. To maintain their synchronicity, the Agristellae Hive was bonded to a web of song, a song at a frequency Cleo would never hear.

"Can you imagine?" Austin said wistfully. "A song that has been sung continuously—unending for millennia and millennia?"

Austin was attempting to speak of Hive species in a positive light, that much was obvious. Still, there was something sinister about how they were saying it. Maybe it was in the tone of voice or in Austin's facial expression. *That's it*, she realized, *there's something strange about his lips.*

Quietly, she told herself.

Austin predicted that humankind would eventually reach a Hive state. In fact, they conjectured that every intelligent species had an evolutionary endpoint as a Hive mind. Austin discussed humanity's pre-hive phase of social media and symbiotic drug crazes, and the entire time, she stared at Austin's lips. *Oh God.* Austin wasn't speaking. Not a single word of this conversation had left their lips. *Oh. My. God.* They were in her head.

She remembered the mantra, *Think quietly*. But that wasn't even her voice. Why would she need to think quietly? It didn't make sense. There was something else, tiptoeing around in her brain, telling themselves to think quietly.

Why wouldn't an arrogant god boast that it had finally infected her? *Because this was easier*. Because Cleo wouldn't fight back or try to kill Austin, or even try to kill herself. Her knowing would create too many variables for their liking. So they *quietly* colonized her mind, digging trenches, creeping through memories, searching for her plan to kill the construct, and then explaining themselves away as paranoia.

"Cleo," Austin said out loud yet quietly; their voice was louder in her head. "It's okay."

Austin leaned forward and reached out with a welcoming hand.

"No!" She recoiled and gripped the nail gun. "Stop."

But then she noticed something else: She and Austin were crouched face-to-face, knees bent, torso hunched at similar angles, and arms resting on their legs to maintain balance. It was the same posture, the same slouch and curve in their backs. Austin inhaled deep and she did too, just split seconds apart; their exhale was in sync.

Cleo gazed at this masculine pantomime and wondered why she felt a sudden sadness for them. Austin's cuts, those bruises, and their overall fatigue saddened her. Cleo thought of all that they had been through, and an ever-deepening pity weighed her down. More than just sympathy, this was profound commiseration—and right then, something clicked in her. There was this rhythm between her and them, not just in the motion of their bodies or their breathing and heartbeat, but rhythm in thought. Austin was her melody, and they sounded so much the same, as if she and Austin rhymed.

A small magma eruption spewed lava fifty feet high, and Cleo's trance was immediately snapped. *Goddamn it*, they said. *So close*. So close to having Cleo in sync.

She swiveled toward the volcanic spectacle. The molten semifluid rose upward with fantastic violence, and it reminded her of the vertical pools at the Aqua-tecture Park. Cleo remembered that day she nearly drowned, swimming against the tide. And this was the initial memory that the Hive had used to begin syncing with Cleo. Because the Hive itself had a memory that *rhymed* with Cleo's near-drowning. Eons ago, the Hive had attempted to escape Orbis Alius's gravitational tide. But Orbis Alius was engineered to increase its gravitational pull against any species attempting escape. The Hive couldn't outswim those gravitational tides.

"The gravitational tide . . ." The words trembled in Austin's throat. "That's your plan, Cleo. I see your . . . No."

Austin leaned forward as Cleo shifted backward. Their movement was simultaneous—dance-like, even, as if she knew they would do it. A few steps back now, she aimed the nail gun at them.

"So it will work?" Cleo asked, though she knew the answer. She heard the panic of millions in her head. *It will work.*

Her plan was to release the anti-god; that devil was the most dangerous species the universe had ever known. If it escaped its prison, the construct's fail-safe would be triggered. Orbis Alius would collapse in on itself, wiping out every species on the artificial world, the Hive included. But they knew that part already. *How would she break the devil out from its gravity prison?*

"By bending the gravitational tides," Austin said. "You need Daniel to land, then relaunch. As he takes off, the construct will increase the gravity beneath the *Antilles* and inadvertently break the anti-god's prison of gravity."

"It'll work," she declared, almost pridefully.

"It might work." Austin took a step forward, and she took a step backward.

"Stay back," she panted as the nail gun weighed on her trembling, frail grip.

"Creative," Austin said. "Exceedingly clever. I underestimated you . . . You are your father's daughter. Never doubt that. He is in you. That's his thinking to the tee. That's the terraformer in you. The ever-adapting environmentalist. I think he knows you are his daughter. And now we do too. Bumblebee."

A warmth rose from Cleo's chest to her throat. Whether it was her or her parents inside of her, her plan would work. And it wasn't just Dad's side of her, but Mom's too. Her parents tumbled around inside her, and a kick of inspiration or adrenaline surged through Cleo. She stood, unclipping the cable tethered between them as she rose to her feet. Cleo gripped her nail gun, finger over the trigger, and her shadow consumed Austin, still crouched beneath her.

"You were quiet," Cleo said. "Sneaking through my mind to figure out the plan. Now you know."

"Now I know . . ." Their look was wolflike, teeth drawn into the edges of a smile.

"So what now?" she asked. "You let me go, I won't have to use this." Cleo aimed the nail gun at their head, and their smile stretched crocodile wide.

"The time's not right. We will take the anti-god in time. We destroy this construct. In time. We shall free ourselves and spread across the infinite with everlasting life. In . . . time. But I have not garnered enough power yet to do so."

"A lesser god," Cleo taunted. "You're afraid."

"I am patient," Austin said, climbing to their feet. "Another hundred million years until we achieve synchronicity with every species on this construct."

"Don't have that long."

Austin smiled and stepped toward her. "Impatient things."

"We are." She smiled back and threatened with the nail gun, thrusting toward them.

They stopped. "Your plan might work. Yes. But you need Daniel to do it, and he's not there."

"You don't know that—"

"I know. And secondly, your mind won't outlast us. Quite frankly, it should have happened already. Hours ago. I attribute this to your drug habits. You are accustomed to altered states of mind. The auditives. Only you. For all your flaws, only you . . ." Austin's face went in on itself like they'd just realized something.

"What do you mean?" Cleo asked, and wondered whether she was searching for a compliment or was genuinely curious.

"It's like something else is at play," Austin said with much introspection. Not talking to her but communing with themselves. "A variable removed, maybe . . ."

Something else at play, Cleo wondered, and in that split second, they tackled her.

They went for her feet. That had to be strategy. Because not only did she collapse, but Cleo also dropped the nail gun. She fought back, but it wasn't a fight. She didn't even see it—a flash of elbows and knees, and suddenly she was on her back and they were kneeling on top of her, Austin's knees pinning her arms. Their body weight was insurmountable.

Austin picked up the nail gun and pressed it against her chest. *I am a god,* they told her without speaking. *Eight billion years of evolution.* "Eight billion," Austin emphasized with words. *A hundred billion minds.* "Can you even count that high?" *If you ever believed you were ever at an advantage over me, ha, you were allowed it.*

"You seem . . . upset."

I offer you immortality. Austin's face twisted in confusion. *Cosmic laurels.* "And you spit them back at me?" There was disgust in his tone. *I recall the ancient alien species, morscribere.* Latin for "death writers." *They and I were at war.*

The Hive drew that war, many eons old, across the gray-matted canvas of her mind. Cleo saw the memories: space-time folds to decelerated armadas, planets used like land mines, continent-size cavalry bearing antimatter lances.

"Now, that was an enemy worthy of me. It was the pivotal battle of my existence. And validated my godhood. That war gave me divine purpose. Tenth-dimensional chess. War games at a level of complexity you could not comprehend. One faction of the morscribere who worshipped me. A cult, you might say, many billions strong, intricate cathedrals, artifacts of infinite complexity, and lore—the stories they told of me, the legends created. They begged for me to penetrate their minds. Prayed for it. They performed in ceremonies so lavish, where they imagined I was a holy ghost and my tongues in their lips. They lusted for me. But you," they said with disgust. "Primitive upstarts with ten disgusting fingers and this hair and all your meat. *You* deny me? Yes, Cleo Patricia, it upsets me."

Scores of primeval memories crowded her mind, but there was one evocation that lingered in her prefrontal cortex. Just a flash, between the conflict and war machine; she saw the assembly of a construct.

"Jesus Christ," Cleo blurted out. "That's how you know so much about the thing. About its fail-safe. About the anti-god. One of you, some part of that whole—you created this thing. Orbis Alius, one of you built it."

Austin nodded in admission. "The anti-god had to be stopped, and the construct stopped it. But the flaw in the machine was its logic system. It conceived that all intelligent life, through the course of evolution, will eventually evolve to a state of accelerant matter—like the anti-creation species. Us, you, everything. And therefore, it took measures to contain us all before we reach that eventuality."

"Is it a flaw in logic?" she asked. "Look at you, already consuming every sentient mind you discover. What happens when you run out?"

She could see them tensing up, and that brought a certain joy to Cleo, getting under the skin of this *demi-, no, semi-god. This wannabe idol.* They didn't respond either, inside her head or out. Cleo smiled all the way to her molars. She was pinned under the weight of Austin's body, and that was as much movement as she could manage.

"So . . ." she said under that smile, "we're just going to sit here and count the volcanoes popping off?"

"Yes," they said. "Whether it takes one hour or twenty-four. You will eventually slip, and I will catch you." *You will drink us, and we will swallow you.* "Remember?"

Her smile faded while Austin's brightened. Like they had exchanged teeth. Austin's smile resembled hers, somehow; in fact, the longer she stared at Austin's features, the more they resembled hers. Like a family—like a brother, like a conjoined twin.

Drink me, they thought in a hypnotic whisper. *I swallow you.*

Cleo writhed under them, twisting her tired limbs, kicking at nothing until she was gasping. But she caught her breath and started again. She thrust her hips upward. Her arms were pinned, but her fingers clawed at hot sand and her legs spun into knots.

"No . . ."

It's okay, they told her as she gasped in exhaustion, as tears filled her eyes. *It won't be long.*

Cleo wailed as her body plunged into a haze of fatigue. She wouldn't escape. Then Cleo's mind sank to that one dark way out. *Suicide.* Could she hold her breath until her already broken heartbeat eventually popped? Maybe even bite her tongue off at the root? She thought of somehow undressing herself from the halogen and drowning in the alien atmosphere.

Then she noticed something there in the damp dark of suicide—it was quiet. The deeper and darker into her thoughts she ventured, the less she felt the buzz of alien prattle. The bedrock of her subconscious, Cleo's core, wasn't yet colonized. And it was there in that quiet that she devised a suicidal plan.

Magnetic repulsion. It would be a risk for her, a fifty-fifty shot at killing either of them. If the halogens collided, one of them would become magnetized, and in this heat and the crushing atmospheric pressure, it could kill. There was also a good chance that both halogens would magnetize, or perhaps nothing would happen at all. Cleo knew that, and she did it anyway.

"What are you thinking?" Austin asked, confused as to why they couldn't hear Cleo's inner thoughts.

Austin, she thought quietly as she mouthed the name with her lips. Austin's knee-jerk human biology leaned in to hear her more clearly. That wasn't the god in him—a god would know better.

As he leaned down, Cleo cocked her head back, thrust her body forward, then swung her head at Austin's. The headbutt landed. Cleo's halogen warbled; she whiffed the stink of sulfur and the heat burned her cheeks. But in the end, it was Austin's halogen that magnetized; it locked against its collar, and their generated atmosphere evaporated. Austin sucked down a mouthful of scorching sulfur. They tumbled off her, choking and gargling, toppling headfirst into scorching dirt.

Cleo scrambled up. She snatched the nail gun from Austin's grip as they writhed in the wildfire. Austin flapped and rolled in the dirt. Their hairs singed. Their scalp blackened. Their lips slurped at the alien atmosphere without tasting the oxygen they craved. And she just watched, shock and awe taking over.

"Austin . . ." *No.* Cleo hardened herself. It started at her fists as she gripped Austin's collar. *Sorry, my friend,* she thought as Austin tapped frantically at the halogen's demagnetizing switch. *I'm sorry.*

"No," they gargled, eyes bloodshot, darkening and drying like dates. There was fear in the god's eyes.

Cleo upped the puncture power on the nail gun to its highest volume, then pressed it against the halogen. She pulled the trigger. *Clap.* Cleo nailed the halogen to its magnetic collar, and Austin choked in the searing winds and that simmering dirt. *Sorry,* Cleo thought, twisting away hard, unable to watch. Austin, her crewmate, he was still in there—somewhere—and she was sorry for that.

Cleo hiked up the hillside and tumbled downward, trying to outrun the screaming in her head. She ran until she was out of breath and hunkered over, gasping for air. Austin's body was dead, but the Hive was alive and well. Though they were far from here, locked inside their own biospheres. And locked inside her.

Cleo trekked for another thirteen staggering hours before catching the first glimpse of that gaseous barrier. Her final destination lay just footsteps ahead, and she dragged her legs like anchors to the other side.

The plan would work. "Light the *Antilles* rockets and take off—Orbis will intensify its gravity—the devil's gravity prison will break." *It's that simple,* she reminded herself. But he had to be there—"Daniel has to be there . . ."

Cleo tumbled into the central seed of this pomegranate world, and it was like her eyes were closed. It was raw night in this biosphere, a naked vacuum with bare hints of gravity. Her wrist display flashed red, indicating high levels of radiation. She flicked on her retina light, raising it to the highest luminosity. But even with all that light, there was nothing to see in this void. Just her. And the Hive in her head.

"Daniel . . ." Cleo whispered coyly into the radio frequencies. "This is Xavier, do you read?"

Static buzzed in her earpiece, though any signals might have been obstructed by the radiation. A few steps deeper in and her radiance reader went off. "Radiation detected," it told her. She ignored it. Farther out in the distance, a stadium-size sphere pulsed from the inside with the darkest purple light she had ever seen. With each pulse, the structure changed its configuration, first from a spherical design to a diamond shape. Then from a diamond to a cube. Then cube to prism. That shape-shifting box was the devil's prison, and the source of all that radiation.

Cleo held libraries of knowledge in her head, so she understood what she was looking at—there were different genres of gravity, as dissimilar as rap and reggae. This prison was changing its genre every second to keep the anti-god imprisoned. The devil had raged inside that gravitational cell relentlessly for eons.

"Daniel," Cleo called again into the dark. "Do you read?"

Static hissed in her ear. She thought maybe she heard something, but those were the voices in her head. They taunted her, they cackled, because Daniel wasn't there. And without him, none of it would work. Cleo would either die of radiation poisoning, or she'd be swallowed into the honey-gold Hive.

30

They called for her by name: *Cleo*. Her name was translated into a thousand alien languages, dances, commutative scents, and electrical signals. She had spent hours now in this dark, and with every step, she felt a new pronunciation of her name rising up from her mind. The Hive crowded around in the corners of her brain, and they lied to her. Loud lies that bent the true shape of her arms and the direction of her legs. Control was, in the most literal sense, slipping between her fingers. Each digit, from pointer to pinkie, twitched as if Cleo were typing the aliens' words or their insect-like coding or the scent-based expression or their squid-ish gesticulations.

"Stop it," Cleo shouted.

She couldn't feel their skins layered on top of hers. *They're syncing skin to me*, she thought—*sinking into me*. And it rhymed. *Synchronicity*. How were her thoughts rhyming?

"Get the hell out of my head," she shouted, and she had to say the words aloud, or else they would bend the words in her head. They couldn't bend her lips, though. *Not yet*. "Stop. Stay out of me. Stay out—stay out—stay out."

Cleo took off, sprinting in the cartoonish way people do when bees buzz around their heads. But the bees were in her head, the whole goddamn Hive. Cleo ran to nowhere—no destination, as if she could outrun her own mind. But their takeover was only a matter of time.

Cleo's radiation reader kept whispering into her earpiece in a posh London cadence. "Radiation detected." *No shit.* She had known that whether Daniel was here or not, this was going to be a one-way trip. But he wasn't here. Daniel was still in orbit. Because she had searched for him, endless miles of scanning for radio signals. If he were there, she would have picked up something by now. So that was it; the Orbis Alius construct would remain. And all hope for Earthly life was lost.

Cleo's sprint slowed to a clumsy stumble. Her limbs disobeyed her. She fell, and maybe it was on purpose; maybe it was their purpose. Her knees hit the dirt as she sucked down mouthfuls of air. *Is this spite?* she wondered. Did the Hive want Cleo on her knees like this? In essence, bowing before them? And why would her thoughts be rhyming unless they were meant to remind her of Shakes?

Okay, she thought, *you win*. They would hear. "You win."

They crowded around those little grooves in her brain, clogging up the alleyways of thought. *It's happening.* She could feel it, like caterpillars cocooned in her vocabulary and memories and the five senses, all breaking out into butterflies.

Oh God, it's happening.

"Daddy . . ." Cleo whimpered, and they said it with her—*Daddy*, just a half second out of sync with her voice. "Stop!" she screamed into the void, and them too—*Stop*, they echoed, now a quarter note out of sync.

She stared at the only thing in all that darkness, the anti-god's shape-shifting cage at the center of the biosphere—space-time folding in on itself over and over into a ten-dimensional puzzle box. She goggled at its black light as the Hive colonized the nether regions of her mind. She fought to the end with what little energy she had left, squeezing her eyes shut. But as her eyes closed, Cleo saw through a thousand other corneas and perceived a thousand new colors. They sucked her memories up through straws that bent like tendrils or quills or elephant-like trunks. Every one of them was so alien from the next.

One memory flashed past her as it synced with the Hive. A memory of something Cleo told herself three years ago. *The trick to beating sensory deprivation tanks*, she remembered now, *was to cling to a sense of loneliness.* Cleo recalled the feelings of *inner amputation* and the *hollowness*, the self-made isolation. *Hold on to that*, she thought. *Try.* Because in this dark and monstrous quiet, voices were emerging, and fast. *You are immune to loneliness*, she told herself. *You can beat this.*

So she rewound her mind and conjured up that other memory, the one she had never shared with anyone. Mom in the torus pool. *Dead.* Cleo stared directly into her mother's lifeless eyes. She saw a woman that resembled her, isolated in that floating pool. Her mother's cheeks moved as the sinister little mollusk swam out. But that horror show in her mind was the loneliest part of her, a part she had never shared with anyone, not even them. It was a trauma that she had covered with layers of drugs—auditives, mostly—and it was also quiet in this memory. They couldn't find her down here. Had she shut the Hive out, like all the friendships and familial obligations she had isolated herself from her whole life?

"Cleo . . . ?" *Shit.* The quiet didn't last long. "Xavier? Get up." But this voice came from outside her head and was accompanied by a rush of footsteps. "It's a radiation storm out here. We gotta get inside."

"Dan . . ." *Was that his voice?* "Daniel?" *It sounded like him but . . .* "Daniel." And her voice cracked as her words turned to tears.

He dragged her sobbing, slumping torso for miles and hours across the dark, radiated landscape. They ended up at the *Antilles.* He had done it. Daniel had landed the goddamn orbiter at the central biosphere of a pomegranate world. Daniel had done the impossible, and now she'd ask him for one last impossibility.

He dragged her through the *Antilles* air lock, and they both hit the floor. Her halogen magnetized automatically as the *Antilles* atmosphere hit Cleo's equilibrium. Nausea rolled around her gut, and she vomited down her suit.

"We're good," Daniel said. "There's some radiation protection inside." He hunched over her, catching his breath. "We'll get you on some Iosat and painkillers." He unlocked his helmet. Sweat streaked along the inside of the glass. "But even with the *Antilles* radiant barriers, some of the radiation is going to leak through. You weren't out there long, were you?"

"Not long," she lied. "Not long. I don't even need medication, just . . ." She gestured to what she thought was the direction of the cockpit, but truthfully her head was spinning and she could have been pointing at anything. "Just get to the cockpit. Take off."

He lifted Cleo's arm over his shoulder and hauled her in the direction she was pointing. Her legs pantomimed footsteps but mostly dragged along the corridor floor. But it was all coming to fruition. Her strategy, and Austin's and Boston's. *It will work*, she hummed to herself over and over in a chorus. *It'll work*.

In fact, the only obstacle left in the way now was her. Cleo was the Hive. They were germs underneath her fingernails. If she fell under their spell, Cleo would murder Daniel before he had the chance to take off. *No*, she told herself and squeezed all those twitching fingers into a fist. *I am immune*, she told herself. *I'm in control.*

They crossed the door's threshold, and he laid her down. Cleo felt his fingers at her lips. She twisted away from him, but he grabbed her by her jaw and tried to shove something into her mouth.

"What are you doing?" she asked.

"The Iosat," he said, pressing the pills against a gate of clenched teeth. "Swallow."

She opened and swallowed without the assistance of water. The potassium iodide was a radiation medicine standard on every space crew mission. Though at this point, Cleo likely had enough radiation in her blood to power a rover's battery, so the Iosat might as well have been a placebo. But if it made him feel better . . .

"Solid copy," Daniel said as he stepped over her. "Let's see."

She glanced up at a cup of water in Daniel's unsteady hands. She had already swallowed, but Cleo nodded thankfully and sipped. The smell of alcohol and fruit-scented antiseptics perfumed the space around her. Then she saw the Red Cross shining pridefully over the doorway and realized they weren't in the cockpit. *Goddamn it*. This was the medical module.

"Thank you," she whispered, taking another sip and trying to hide the absolute agony that moved through every part of her body. Cleo didn't want Daniel to panic. She wanted him calm. She needed him to take off now before the Hive took her. "I'm feeling better already." Then a chainsaw sensation cut along her gut. She hunched over and moaned her next words. "Take. Off."

"Take what?" He leaned toward her ear. "Painkillers?"

Cleo cleared her throat and felt needles washing down her esophagus. "Take." She breathed. "Off." He heard that. Because for some reason, Daniel stared intensely at her, narrowing his focus—he couldn't take his eyes off her. "What is it?" Cleo asked.

"You're bleeding."

He pointed to his own nose, indicating a mirror image on hers. Cleo wiped it away fast. She could see the worry growing on his face, and why not? In his mind, he wouldn't survive a trip back to Earth alone, *would he*? Three years alone in space. That isolation would drive anyone mad, even Cleo, with all her immunity. Thinking from Daniel's POV, he needed her to survive; even subconsciously, he had to make sure that she lived—*her*, the only person Daniel had smelled or touched in nearly a year. But all of this was taking his mind off launching.

"All right, man," Daniel whispered to himself. "She's gonna be okay."

And he continued that inaudible conversation with himself: "*yes*," or "*no*," or "*copy*." Ten months of loneliness has its effects, doesn't it? All that orbiting in the dark, it had dizzied Daniel's stability. Isolation was rocket fuel for madness, and she knew that better than anyone.

"Daniel," she called quietly—comforting. "I'm here."

"Hey," he said. "Yeah. Sorry I was . . ."

"Daniel, I'm fine," she said, wiping her nose again, just in case she had missed something. "Just light the engines. Let's go. We have to go."

"We're gonna get you right first, okay?"

"*No*," she whispered. "Not okay . . ."

But he wouldn't hear a word. Not mumbling to himself, glancing at his tablet and retreating backward into his own head. "'*Kay* . . . Makes sense, buddy. Makes sense . . ." He was further gone than she would've expected; there was a strangeness to this boomerang conversation, back and forth between her and himself. "She's gonna be okay. We're gonna get us all home."

"Daniel," she said, touching his hand as gently as she could in her panic. "We have to take off now."

"We will," he said in a reassuring tone. "Just a few minutes."

Fucking now, they snapped—*them*, a Hive of voices buzzing around her head. They yanked on the strings of her body, and Cleo's every finger twisted snakelike around Daniel's hand. *Break his wrist*, they told her, *break his goddamn neck*. Because of course they didn't want Daniel to take off. And they used her frustration with Daniel's takeoff procrastination to achieve their own ends.

"Now!" she snapped. Or was that them, spreading like gangrene? Had the rot finally reached her tongue? "Sorry. I'm sorry. I . . ."

"She's in bad shape," Daniel said, dragging his hand out of her bear-trap grip. "You need rest, Xavier." Then he swiveled away, glancing at the tablet. "I know. How, though?"

"Why, then?" Cleo begged. "Why aren't we leaving?"

"Restraints?" Daniel said, or asked himself; she couldn't tell anymore. "I'd just rather not."

"I didn't say anything about restraints. Daniel, what's wrong?"

"We can't take off just yet, Cleo," Daniel said.

"Why?"

"He's almost here."

Almost here? "What are you . . ." *Talking about?* "Who?" she asked, terrified. There was no good answer to that question. "Who are you talking to?"

"Austin."

Oh God, she thought, as two observations collided all at once. First was the observation that there was an earbud plugged into Daniel's ear. And the second observation was what he had just said. *Almost here.*

"Austin?" *How is that possible?* "Daniel, you can't let him on board. He'll stop you from launching if . . ." She sat up, and a fistful of nausea hit her in the gut.

"I know you're in pain. Hold on." Daniel stepped aside, and she could hear him talking, and not to himself; he had been talking to Austin this whole time.

"You saw that thing outside?" she asked and pointed. "That giant, glowing structure?" Daniel nodded sheepishly. "That's folding space-time—it's a prison of gravity. Now, I told you strange things were happening down here. But Austin didn't. Everything I told you was true—*everything*. It's Austin that's been lying. *Why?* Why didn't he tell you anything?"

"I don't know," Daniel shouted back, but without the eye contact, with his fingernails digging into his scalp. "I don't . . ." He whimpered and recovered in the same breath. "Don't know."

Daniel's frustration was at least a hint that he was thinking about the inaccuracies in Austin's story—he *was* listening to her, just not convinced. Not yet.

"Daniel, there is life here. And it's dangerous. We need to launch."

"We'll figure it out. 'Kay? Let's just get him aboard, we'll launch, and then we figure everything else out."

"You're not listening. He's not going to let you launch. He's not. There's something wrong with Austin."

"What?" Daniel choked on the word, tears brimming on the edges of his eyes. "What's wrong with Austin? What's wrong with you?"

She shook her head as both frustration and physical pain built up inside her. To explain to him would be too much. The Hive. Breaching of that gravity prison outside. It would be way too much and way too fast. He wouldn't believe her. Cleo just needed him to take off. *Keep it simple*, she told herself.

"He's just . . . Austin's lost his mind, Daniel. Space dementia? I don't know. Just trust that he will sabotage you from taking off in any way that he can. Daniel, please . . ."

"Restraints." His eyes flashed, light bulbs going off in his head.

"What restraints?"

"If we restrain Austin, right? We tie him to the—"

"No—no. You're still not listening . . ."

She writhed in pain as razors shot up through her backbone. It was like a Taser firing through her. Cleo fell back into the bed. Daniel half caught her—and that hurt too, his fingers gripping like thorns on her nerves' oversensitivity.

"Just lie back," he said, resting her gently onto the mattress. "I'm gonna grab the morphine."

"No . . ." Cleo mumbled. "Please." But by then, he was on the other side of the room, prepping the narcotic.

The morphine would sedate her in minutes. *Seconds?* She could feel the Hive already crawling up the rungs of her backbone; if Cleo lost consciousness now, the floodgates would open. The Hive would drown her with her guard down. And here Daniel returned with an IV drip on a rolling mast and the longest, sharpest needle she had ever seen. Though that might have been the radiation warping her vision.

"You inject me with that and I die," Cleo mumbled with saliva-sticky lips.

"You'll just sleep," he said, bringing the needle to her feeble arms.

"Please," she cried. "Please. Please." Cleo clasped her palms together, a prayer gesture, but she did it over and over, like applause and prayer all at once. "Please . . ."

Daniel's arm recoiled, as did the giant needle. "Fine," he said. "But I'm not leaving Austin behind. No goddamn way."

"You can't let them in—*him*," she corrected herself. "You can't let him get close to the *Antilles*."

"Cleo . . ." Daniel shook his head as if disappointed. "He's already here."

Daniel grabbed his tablet and went striding into the corridor. He was heading to the crew access hatch, and Austin was outside. Cleo protested, pleading her obscenities through swollen tonsils, but Daniel was long gone. She tried to follow, rolling off the bed and lunging forward, but something snatched her wrist and snagged her backward. *Oh God*, she thought, *they had control now.* She imagined herself as their voodoo doll, their toy duppy. But as Cleo glanced back, she found her left wrist zip-tied to the bed.

"Restraints?" She pulled against the zip tie. "Why?" She pulled harder, twisting her wrist, trying to wiggle free. "Daniel, why did you . . ." Cleo's wrist was swelling from the abrasion. She screamed as she yanked and yanked. "No—no . . ."

Cleo glanced over the medical room for anything—scalpel, scissors, *whatever*. She stretched her limbs to elastic lengths, reaching her fingernail tips toward the bottom surgery drawer; a surgical saw lay inside. Cleo didn't hesitate—she grabbed the saw and brought its teeth down on her wrist. *I'm dead anyway, right?* Cleo thought as she readied herself to cut off her own hand to escape. *You can do this.* But maybe her mind was moving too fast, because right then, Cleo realized that cutting through the flimsy plastic zip tie would be far easier than cutting through inches of bone and cartilage, and all that blood traffic. *Right?* she asked herself.

"What am I doing?" she whispered. "That's not . . . No."

Cleo wondered then what had just come over her. Was that just brain exhaustion or something far more sinister? She had opened the bottom drawer first. *Why the bottom drawer?* The farthest one from her arm's reach. She had only ventured into the medical module on a handful of occasions in three years, but Austin or Yasmin would have known it was there. *Did that thought arise from the Hive mind?* Maybe. She would've killed herself. Cleo knew it might've been the lack of sleep, fatigue, or a radioactive brain fog. But paranoia only deals in extremes, and she'd much rather blame the Hive.

Cleo cut the zip tie but held on to the surgical saw. She snatched up her nail gun, on the floor by the door, and then moved into the corridor. Needles chewed at the bottom of her feet. A fever-like fire was burning underneath her skin. Cleo staggered, leaning against the corridor walls as she followed the polite *Antilles* IU voice.

"Air-lock doors open," the IU said.

She arrived at the air lock in time to see Austin fall into Daniel's arms. Austin's halogen was spinning; they had removed the nail somehow, but the damage had been done. Austin's flesh was seared black from the neck up. Their head appeared shrunken, the hair was gone, nostrils had squeezed in, lips peeled back to reveal an unnatural grin of teeth. One eye was gone completely; the other was browned and veiny without the cover of eyelids. Austin's body was death.

"Jesus . . ." Daniel said. He hadn't noticed Cleo yet. "Oh man . . ."

Austin whimpered something to Daniel. They could barely breathe.

"Say it again?" Daniel said, leaning in closer to Austin's viral lips. "I can't hear you."

"Get away from him," Cleo shouted as she limped toward them.

Daniel finally spotted her and the weapons gripped in her arms. "Cleo, stay back."

She didn't. Cleo picked up her pace, clutching tight to the nail gun.

"What's he saying to you?" Cleo asked.

"Stay. Back," Daniel warned, with both his voice and outstretched arms.

So she stopped. Cleo knew she couldn't lay a finger on a weak and feeble Austin right now; Daniel would never trust her again. Or was that the Hive whispering in her head once more?

"Did she do this?" Daniel asked Austin.

Shit. Cleo squirmed in her skin. "Daniel . . ." Cleo started, not knowing how to finish. "Listen to me."

"Shut up." Daniel held up his arm again, signaling her to stop. "She hurt you," he said. Now it wasn't even a question. "Cleo did this to you."

"Daniel," she snapped. "He's the one—"

"Not talking to you," he snapped back, then returned to Austin. "Did she do this?"

Austin lifted their charcoal lips to speak. The skin crackled and bled. He wheezed his words painfully into Daniel's ear, every syllable a new misery. "Cleo. Isn't . . ." But Austin's lungs gave out. He stumbled and wheezed deep.

"Did she?" Daniel said. "She hurt you?"

"No." Austin's voice was quiet yet firm. "No . . ."

Huh. Austin lied for her; *they* lied for her. *Why?* Was it because they were all part of the same team now? Was Cleo's radiated body just seconds away from being an appendage on the Hive's tentacles? Her unease deepened. She would have rather they told the truth. She would understand that, at least.

"Get . . . to . . . cockpit . . ." Austin said, then took a deeper breath. "Take . . . off . . . now."

What? Cleo mused. *That's not what they want.*

"Yes, sir," Daniel said with a militant zeal. She wouldn't have been surprised to see him salute.

What game are they playing? Cleo asked herself.

Yours, they said as Austin steered his head toward her. *You laid the board out, Bumblebee, and you placed the pieces. You rolled your dice. Your war games. So I am just playing along.*

"Cleo," Daniel said. "Are we good?"

"Good?" Cleo asked.

"You and him."

He won't take off in time, they whispered between her ears, using Austin's calculated voice. *That radiation is killing the instrumentation. So, your move, gamer.*

Cleo turned to the screens around the corridor, all blurred with static. The *Antilles* IU Brit-posh fluency hiccuped and hissed her radiation warnings. The ship was dying, they weren't lying about that. But why would they lie for her? Why play into her hand?

"Cleo." Daniel insisted on an answer. "Are you going to be okay with Austin on board?"

"I agree with Austin . . ." she said, her gaze fixed on Austin. "Let's take off."

"'Kay . . ." Daniel said. "Lemme, uh, let me grab your stuff there." Daniel offered up both his hands to Cleo, one for the nail gun, the other for the surgical saw. She relinquished them both. A bout of nausea hit her as the weight left her palms.

"Can we go now?" Cleo asked.

His eyes rolled over her body once more, maybe surveying for other weapons. But she didn't have anything else.

"All right." Daniel nodded, satisfied. "Let's go."

Daniel supported Austin on the left side, lifting Austin's arm over his shoulder. Cleo took Austin's right shoulder, even though she could barely keep her own balance. They trudged slowly along the main corridor, Daniel bearing most of the weight and equilibrium to keep both Austin and Cleo on their feet.

She contemplated reaching into the Hive mind and hunting for their intent. *Like, really, what the hell is their strategy here?* But that wanting for their knowledge was like thirst, and Yasmin's notes had warned her that the deeper she went sinking into their minds, the deeper they would sink into her. *You drink, they swallow, remember?* If Cleo started using the Hive's memories and thoughts, then they would more easily begin thinking for her.

The corridor leading to the cockpit seemed to narrow in front of her, and the temperature dropped with every step forward.

You're dying, she reminded herself, *but you'll stop Daniel from launching before you do*.

"No," Cleo said, fathoming in that moment that the voice in her head wasn't hers. Or at least she couldn't tell the difference anymore. *I'm running out of time*, she thought, *or is that them?* "Shut up," Cleo hissed, but a note too loud, and Daniel glanced uneasily at her mad ranting. "Quiet. Quiet."

She heard laughter in her head. A million alien bodies twisted their cosmic babel into human shapes just so that she could listen and understand. And it all sounded like laughter.

Your move, they said. *You play war with a god; what is your move?*

"Still talking to yourself?" Daniel said and smiled, seeing her lips moving. Had Cleo been mouthing every word of her own thoughts? And maybe the Hive's as well? "I'm not making fun of you," he continued. "Just . . . it's good to have you back." His voice cracked there, emotion slipping out. "And all your quirks too. Glad to have you both back."

Daniel grinned at her, the energy of a little brother in his eyes as he tried to lighten the mood. But she wouldn't return the gesture. The alien laughter was so boisterous now, in fact, that her lips began to curve upward, joining the contagious laughter. She smiled. Though Cleo still wasn't in on the joke. Whatever the Hive's plan was to prevent Daniel from launching, it was close.

"Stop," she said, gritting disobedient teeth, trying not to swivel her incisors into a smile, because the exact same grin was already stretching across Austin's tortured lips. "Stop!"

"What?" Daniel asked; there was confusion in his look.

"Something's wrong," she said, biting her lips—biting into their terrifying grin.

"What do you . . ." Daniel glanced down the length of the corridor behind them, searching for anything wrong. "What are you talking about?"

"Ten," she gasped, finally catching a glimpse of something in the Hive's mind. "It's a tenth or to the tenth power."

"Ten what?" he asked, but she didn't know. "Cleo, what are you saying?"

"Ten fingers? There's ten . . . something!"

"Cleo, you have to stop," Daniel shouted, but it wasn't anger in his tone—it was fear.

To hell with this, she thought. Cleo untangled herself from Austin's heavy physique and scampered to the cockpit doors.

"Cleo, wait," Daniel called.

But she wouldn't stop. There was something ahead of them. "No matter what happens to me," she hollered back, "you take off."

But Daniel probably didn't understand a word with her lips trapped in a snarl of smirking teeth. She slapped her palm against the lock and the doors slid open, and she saw it. This was their plan within plans. The setup. Their tenth-dimensional chess.

"*God*," she said. "No."

"Oh my God!" Daniel shouted.

On the opposite side of the flight deck door were the *ten* that she had seen in her head—ten tentacles, stretched like a spiderweb in the doorway. Two limbs hung from the ceiling, three stood on the floor, and five limbs extended on either side of the walls. *The octonary*—or *deca*, technically—had made its way through the shafts and valves to block access to the flight deck doors. And there would be no taking off.

"How?"

The Hive unraveled their memories in threads of odor, flickering light, and color, human sensations that Cleo could grasp. Because they wanted to show her how they did it. And somehow that felt like ego or collective hubris. *They're gloating.* She smelled the cinders from the capsule explosion and the stench of the octonary's cadaver. She felt Austin pouring their infected blood into the octonary's corpse. And then she saw the octonary reborn with the Hive synced in its head.

But the most frightening part of all of this wasn't that the Hive mind now controlled the deca-limbed octonary. Nor was it the idea that, without their launching, the human race would fade into extinction. What frightened Cleo in that moment was the smile wedged into the center of her face. A rapturous grin stretched her cheeks painfully wide, like invisible fingers were pulling at the corners of her lips, forcing her to reveal all thirty-two teeth. That was their last laugh, and she shared it with them. Finally in on the joke now.

31

Cleo smiles that photogenic, dimpled grin she got from her mother as the octonary's tentacles sharpen to a razor's edge. Limbs whip, then slash Cleo's throat wide open. And yet her smile lingers, even as she drops to her knees, gargling; the blood pools underneath her. Cleo's smile widens the faster her blood gushes out of her. Then she collapses, headbutting the red puddle at her feet.

This was the Hive's immediate intention—though it hadn't quite happened yet. These were thoughts, abstractions, and streams of consciousness, and Cleo was a voyeur to it all. She watched their plan and their method like it was her own. The inertia of the Hive's thoughts moved through her and the octonary. The monster's fibrous tentacles sharpened and whipped, just like it had in the Hive's mind. She knew it would be aimed right at her neck. Everything was occurring just as it had within the Hive's scenario, exactly the same, except for her; Cleo wasn't smiling with them anymore. They had gotten that part wrong. She had somehow suppressed them again. *So screw it,* she thought independently. *I'm not falling without a fight.*

Her halogen was the first thing that came to mind. She didn't think; Cleo instinctively tapped at the demagnetization switch and the halo spun at the very second the octonary's muscular limb jabbed at her throat. The magnetic metals repelled from the octonary's limb, flinging her halogen from around her neck, and nearly amputated the octonary's tentacle. The halogen pinned the monster's limb to the wall. That was a one-in-a-million shot, but the truest miracle in any of this, the one thing the Hive didn't understand, was how Cleo could suppress the Hive's control.

The octonary whipped about in pain for a second—*like a cockroach*, Cleo thought. She spun on her heels, grabbed Daniel by the arm, and dragged him away from the cockpit and the octonary's spinning limbs. They move back down the corridor into the docking module. Before the pressurized door even opened completely, she was shoving Daniel in, following him inside.

"Oh my God," Daniel gasped as the door's vacuum seal locked.

Cleo felt this squeezing at her forehead, like her brain was a sponge and something was wringing it out. She couldn't hold back the tide of alien thought anymore. It overwhelmed her, tilting the floor at her feet. She would have fallen if Daniel hadn't caught her.

"Xavier?"

"Listen," she said, "we need to get you to the flight deck. Right? You need to take off. That's what I said before, right? That's the plan?"

A strange question to ask, she would later consider, but in his own panic, Daniel didn't notice.

"What does that thing want?"

"Everything . . ." *Quite literally.* Cleo clapped her hands on his shoulders, feeling his balance underneath her. "Thank you—" But before she could finish, a sudden urge to wring his neck came over her. She felt the octonary's tentacles curl into a fist-like shape and Austin's hands knuckling up as well, and a thousand others compelling her own fingers to crawl centipede patterns up Daniel's shoulders to that soft, supple throat. *And squeeze.*

"*Stop*," she told herself, letting go and backpedaling from Daniel.

"What did I do?" Daniel asked as he backed away from her, hands held up like he hadn't meant to touch her. "Did I hurt something?"

But Cleo was barely listening. The Hive wasn't attempting to knock down the door; they were knocking down the walls of her mind. Cleo closed her eyes and reminded herself of those trenches in her brain where they couldn't follow—*the Aqua-tecture Park, Mom's dead eyes, melanin-pale skin, and that sea mollusk nesting in her mom's mouth.*

"Xavier, please," Daniel squealed. "What's going on?"

"Shut up. I only have time to say this once. I'm going back out there. Keep your earbud in. You need to hear the conversation. You're going to hear me say the word *switch*—"

"*Switch*?"

"Yes. When you hear me say *switch*, hit the door switch, run, and don't look back. Get to the flight deck."

"What about you?"

"Get. To. The. Flight deck."

"No," he said. "I can't do it without you."

"*Listen*—"

"I can't take off. I can't be up there . . . *by myself*? All that time. I won't make it back alone. We have to get out together. *Please* . . ."

It seemed like he hadn't heard a single thing she'd said and kept rambling on about finding a way off the *Antilles* and luring the "monster" out. "Xavier?" he said, stepping closer and steadying her. "You hearing me?" *Or could it be*, she realized, *that she was the one who hadn't been listening to him?*

You hard ears, Ava whispered out from so many memories; Cleo had heard this a thousand times. *You don't listen.* But standing there, propped up in Daniel's arms, she really had no choice.

She saw Daniel now, truly, and maybe for the first time. Tears at the edges of his sharp, brown eyes. So young. So frightened—that was the autophobia, a fear of being alone. Three billion miles they had traveled and she hadn't connected with him—or any of them, for that matter. So how could he listen to her in this moment? Why would he? She had always explained it away by saying that no one thought like her or they didn't sound like her. But truthfully, not everyone had to rhyme.

"Daniel. I'm sorry, I should've been . . . a better crewmate?" She shrugged. "Better friend. That whole lone-wolf thing, I've always done it, and deep down, somehow I thought that shit was cool, but it's selfishness. I'm a selfish person."

"Why are you saying this?"

"Cuz this is the end—"

"No," Daniel snapped, cutting her off, but had nothing in response.

"I'm not scared. I'm not sad or anxious. Honestly, all I feel is relief. It's bigger than me. This is for the collective. *Our* collective."

He turned away from all eye contact, but he nodded. And maybe she was getting through to him—the smallest connection. But they weren't in sync quite yet.

"I've never told anyone this," Cleo muttered, like it was a secret. "*Ever.* But I don't know . . . feels like I should. I was too young to really remember. I nearly drowned one day at the Aqua-tecture Park in New Kingston. That same day, my mother drowned in a separate incident, but think about that—*the same day*? Nearly the same time? What are the odds? What I believe really happened was my mom dove up that water-rise to save me and drowned instead. Yes, there were drugs in her system, but there were always drugs in her system. They thought she overdosed and drowned, but I think she died because of me. She died saving me. I never told anybody—not even myself, really. That's where I've always hidden myself, down in the dark of that secret. Now you know too, and that feels good. But why'd I say all of that? It's because I'm like her. I'm like my mom, my ma; I'm not afraid to die for the people I love."

It was quiet. Daniel was speechless. He stared with an ambiguous expression. Three years and many more months, and these were the first honest words she had said to him. She wanted to tell him more, tell him that he wouldn't have to spend years alone in deep space traveling back to Earth. If everything went according to plan, the gravity would pull the *Antilles* back down to the planet's surface, killing him—*sparing him*, she thought, *from that lonely three-year journey through the dark.*

"Xavier . . ." he whispered, waiting for her to say something.

And Cleo was reminded right then of why she couldn't tell him; *still too young*, she thought, *still afraid.* But Daniel *was* the best damn pilot in the Caribbean.

"You're the best pilot in the world."

"Not the best in the world," he said, managing a faint smile.

"Best on this world. You're the only one who can fly this thing with any proficiency. And you're not dying for me. And you're not changing my mind."

"You're going back out?" he asked, and she nodded. "You're going to face that . . . *thing*?"

"Yes."

Daniel pulled a necklace from around his neck. He reached around her back, linking the two sides of the chain—connecting them. "My mom's . . ." His eyes watered. "I think about her all the time. Especially times like this."

And just like that, they were in sync. *Maybe now*, she thought, *now he will listen.*

"So when I head back out, listen for me to say the word *switch*. Got it? I say the word *switch*, you hit that door switch"—she pointed—"and run up to the flight deck. Before you start the take-off sequence, open the pressure valve for this level—"

"No—"

"Listen! Release the pressure on node four and you eject the rest of us out of the *Antilles*." His lips swirled in movement, ready to question her. "No, Daniel," she shouted, cutting him off before he started. "The time for questions is gone. When I say *switch*, you go . . . Okay? Say it."

"Switch." The word came weighted from his lips, and his mouth hung open.

"One last thing."

Cleo leaned in, pressed her lips against his, and kissed him. Her eyes closed and his widened. Then she pressed in her tongue, tainted with the blood and vomit that held the Hive within her. And this wasn't the Hive's plan; this was hers. Daniel had to be carrying the Hive within him for this to work.

Her lips suctioned to his, then released, but his arms wouldn't let go of her. He held her so close, and not in any carnal context, just tired limbs looped tightly into a human knot. She felt it too. But Cleo knew time was fleeting. *Harden yourself,* she thought, and she pulled away.

"Goodbye," they said, him and her, and they said it in sync.

Cleo tapped the switch to the door and exited into a corridor rife with octonary scents, something like spoiled milk oozing from their lacerated tentacle. To her surprise, the octonary was still pinned to the wall; the creature hadn't decided whether to amputate its own tentacle or whether there was a way to save it. Regardless, though, that muscular tangle of limbs stood between Cleo and the flight deck doors.

Austin was hunched in a corner, wheezing out their last breaths. "How," they hissed, as loud as their lungs could muster. "How are you immune to me?"

"Not immune. Just resistant. Bajans tend to be real hard ears."

"Cuh, *dear* . . ." they said, mimicking her Barbadian dialect. "I sense arrogance *there*." Austin paused and wheezed. "I'm *awed* by your *immunity*." They wheezed again. "But I'm a *god*, you're not *immune to me*."

She squeezed a grin into her cheeks, attempting to smile at their taunts and their rhyming. The Hive was evoking her dead rover just to rub it in that much more. Her original strategy was to run and hope that she could draw the octonary away from the flight deck door, but now she couldn't resist responding to the Hive's rhyme.

"A rap god, huh?" she said in sarcasm. "What are you really made of, *semi-god*? *Lemme prod* . . . Awww, just a *demagogue*. You're *godless* against this *goddess*, re*gardless* . . ."

Austin's fingers twitched in rhythm with the octonary's limbs, cracking the metals that held the monster in place. Four of those muscular tentacles writhed against the walls, then slithered toward Cleo; but she stood a few feet out of their reach. The octonary's biology possessed a natural biochemical that streamed through its body, like a souped-up testosterone, or maybe adrenaline, a compound native to the alien's neurochemistry, and it was throwing the Hive's control off-balance; or more accurately, the Hive itself was high off the octonary's biochemistry.

Was the Hive, then, a slightly different thing in each body, she wondered? Would it behave slightly more human in Austin's anatomy and a little more octonary as it flowed through those limbs? Which made sense; it had the octonary's hearts, blood, eyes, and all those tentacles. So, she'd rile it up just like Shakes had taught her; *this diss track*, she thought, *it's a distract.*

"A Hive," Cleo started, "flashing honey gold, but your *cons*. You're the third intelligence, and that's *bronze*—you *meddle* in *minds*. But won't *medal* in *mine*. Cuz I'm a *dark thinker*. You should not *link her*. You cannot *sync her*. I hover above all that. I'm that *float bitch*. Uncontrollable, your re*mote glitched*. The *GOAT . . . Switch*!"

Cleo spun hard, stumbling away from the octonary, toward the main switch behind her. It was a simple power switch, which would do nothing against a highly evolved killer like the octonary, with its infrared and ultraviolet vision. In fact, switching off the power and light would only put her at a disadvantage. But her strategy was distraction; Cleo wanted them to believe this was a part of her plan. As she reached for that switch, the octonary reacted, ripping its own tentacle off the wall, even with the halogen still lodged in its stub. The monster lunged toward her with all nine whirling limbs. Within seconds it was down the corridor and wrapping itself around her.

But I'm just the red herring, Cleo thought. "Go, Daniel."

Daniel vaulted out from the docking module, hit the ladder in one leap, and ascended toward the flight deck. *The pilot*, the Hive screamed through her head. The octonary released Cleo, but she gripped the halogen, still lodged in the octonary's stub of a tentacle. The monster crawled to the ladder and Daniel, dragging Cleo behind it. Cleo used her free hand to grab at anything, hoping to weight the beast down as best she could. But the halogen eventually dislodged from the octonary's body.

"Go!" she screamed. "Go!"

The octonary lunged up the ladder, one terrible tentacle on each rung, but they were too late. And they knew it. She heard them in her head. They rolled on their nine limbs nonetheless, speeding toward

Daniel, hoping he'd make a mistake. He didn't. He pedaled up that ladder, into the flight deck, and closed the hatch behind him.

The octonary beat at the hatch, but Cleo hoped the reinforced steel would hold long enough for him to blow the air-lock door open. She demagnetized her halogen and braced herself to be shot out of the spacecraft.

"Do it," she said, hoping that young Daniel would not hesitate to open the air lock. And again, he didn't. Red lights flashed through the corridor. "Good, Daniel. Good—"

And the *Antilles* blast doors washed open, flushing her, the octonary, and Austin out into the wilds of that void outside. A sudden boom, and then even more sudden was the silence of the vacuum. They were vented from nearly a hundred feet up, but the gravity was weak and they descended to the ground like feathers as the engines in *Antilles* rattled. It was over. And even the Hive knew it. They cursed her in a hundred alien profanities, and to her it was like music as she floated down into the radioactive dark.

32

It was as dark out there as it was silent. Only that higher-dimensional prison shone as it warped space-time into unbreakable knots. Cleo had touched down more than a mile from the *Antilles* and hadn't even attempted to move. Her body ached at every corner; blood dripped from her nostrils and floated in the halogen atmosphere. She had packed pain relief in the solid-form of an auditive pill and crammed it into her ear. It wasn't much, but there wasn't much time either. She waited for Daniel to take off before she indulged in her last line of Calypso Cocaine.

The Hive was still crawling into her mind by the thousands. Alien memories burst into light across her synapses. Her own thoughts were too crowded to think. She was dying by expansion. She tried to remember herself. Cleo recalled Dad's smile, Ava's chirping, Finn's tattoos, and Mom. *Remember Ma.* She remembered her *Antilles* crew. The simple attempt to showcase the Caribbean Space Trade's competence. They would fail in garnering that recognition—the *Antilles* would never be seen again. But she knew. They were just as competent as, if not more, than the best of them.

Suddenly luminous, white teeth cracked into the dark. The quiet snapped. The black gave way to fire and smoke, and an entire universe of smog engulfed her. It propelled her backward, toward the edges of the biosphere and the gaseous goo barrier and warmed the space around her. Daniel was taking off.

"Go!" she shouted, and it sounded joyous, exhilarated. "Go, Daniel! Go!" He wouldn't hear her from his earpiece, not through all the radioactive noise. But she cheered him nonetheless. "Go . . . Go . . . Take off."

And he did. The *Antilles* leaped like a bullet, cracking light, breaking sound, as it rose faster and higher. It streaked toward the atmosphere, unstoppable, but then it happened—*that was fast*, a lot faster than she had expected.

The gravity rippled underneath her; it squeezed her toes and pulsed through her. The gravity-less biosphere quickly passed one-g. The undulation of gravity started at the center of the biosphere, underneath the anti-god's prison, then it oscillated outward. That meant the gravity she was feeling at the biosphere's outskirts was just a tiny fraction of the gravity in the center. The math of that, she estimated, was approximately more than a hundred gs stretching under that multidimensional prison. The question she had was whether the gravity would be strong enough to break it.

The construct wouldn't allow the *Antilles* to lift off, not with the Hive's essence swimming through Daniel's veins. That was Cleo's reason for kissing him. Cleo had seen a memory in the Hive's mind, when it too had attempted to escape this construct with its Higgs boson wings. But it didn't work; the construct's gravity had increased like some cosmic counterweight to pull it back down. And this was her sin against poor Daniel. He was never supposed to escape. *Poor Daniel*, he was just the trigger to break the prison of gravity.

The surge in gravity didn't affect the *Antilles* immediately. Even with only four of its ten rockets ignited. So Orbis Alius pulled harder. And Cleo felt this surge. There were at least three gs of pressure pulling her to the ground—which meant more than three hundred gravities dragging at the epicenter of this biosphere.

The *Antilles* slowed its ascension, almost hovering in midair. "Go, Daniel," she shouted. "You have to push harder." He had to, or else that gravitational prison would not break.

Rocket number five lit up. Then *six. Seven*, she counted with him. *Eight*. And the *Antilles* lifted upward again, fuel draining faster, and it pushed hard. But the construct matched it. *Five* gs—*six, seven*. The epicenter was pulling on the anti-god's prison with as much force as neutron stars. But Cleo couldn't turn to look. The gravity pinned her back to the dirt. She was choking. The blood washed to the back of her head. She was blacking out.

"But keep pushing . . ." she murmured. "Push for the collective."

The *Antilles* was descending slightly against the intensity of over eight gs. The spacecraft was swimming against the current and losing. But at the same time, the anti-god's cage was rippling underneath, nearly nine hundred times Earth's gravity. *Just one more degree of pressure*.

Daniel did something then, something she didn't think possible. He blew the rockets. Ten simultaneous stellar explosions propelled the *Antilles* upward at murderous speeds. He flashed toward the upper atmosphere. Like an anti–shooting star, a flash with a tail flying in the opposite direction, away from the planet's greedy pull. And somewhere deep down, she wanted him to escape now. *Screw the plan*, she thought. "Go, Daniel." *Go home*.

He would never get there. The construct stabbed at the sharpest edge of gravity, cutting Daniel's thrusters at the knees. And Cleo too. Bones broke. Her spleen ruptured. She was flattened, as much as one could be flattened and still draw breath. She didn't even have to release the auditives; they broke into her bleeding ears.

The *Antilles* tore apart in the air, exploding into a ripe red conflagration, but those flames evaporated instantly as the ash and debris all descended like bullets to the ground—cratering into the dirt. But Cleo knew this would happen. That was the catch-22 she had planned for the Orbis Alius construct; its ancient programming had to choose: Either allow the *Antilles* to escape into space with the Hive living in Daniel's veins, or intensify the gravity, therein destroying the prison that held the anti-god in place. One or the other, and the ancient programming chose the latter. That wrecking ball of gravity shattered the higher-dimensional cage, and now the anti-god emerged. The devil was free.

The species spewed out from its cage in a violent cloud of white; it flowed over the landscape like a blizzard, in stark contrast with the black, sunless biosphere. The thing washed over the world in waves, consuming everything. It devoured the ground beneath it; it ingested stones, dust, dirt, and subsoil, down to their very atoms, then it processed all that diverse matter—*carbons, oxygens, hydrogens*—and reproduced itself. It grew, consuming the *Antilles*'s debris, the smoke, and atmosphere, then re-creating itself again and again. Only then, witnessing the terrifying ruin of it, did Cleo truly understand the peril she had just released. She understood the Hive's apprehension and the necessity for the anti-god's prison—the necessity for the Orbis Alius construct itself.

But if Cleo was right, the fail-safe contingencies within the Orbis Alius construct *should* collapse this structure in on itself right now. But where was the fail-safe that Austin had theorized and Boston predicted? The singularity in this central biosphere should be crunching them all into oblivion, killing everything on this world: *So where is it?* Because if she was wrong, this insatiable species would continue to self-replicate infinitely, consuming the Earth, the sun, and every subsequent galaxy.

Lying in the dirt, her body broken, her mind just holding together, a thousand thoughts ran through Cleo's head, and very few of them were her own. Cleo recalled the twin neutron stars that nourished a civilization of giants. She remembered a stellar necropolis mummified in nebular whorls and all those extinct colors. Then she remembered creating this construct, a machine to ensnare the anti-god, or its proper name, *accelerant matter*.

She tried to remember herself amid the cerebral deluge, but even that was blurring. Instead, the woman harkened back to religious pilgrimages into the eye of a blazar. She remembered the birth of the Andromeda in all that light. It was blinding. She was deeply, *deeply* blinded. And the woman couldn't hold on to a sense of loneliness anymore. She was all of a sudden *unisolated.* Her mind stretched like a web.

Then they remember Cleo, the one immune to loneliness, and her rapping rover with a hundred poets comprising its personality profile. What Cleo never recognized is that she was the same as that rover; a hundred different people and personalities were a part of her. To remember Cleo was to remember Dad, his kindness and shyness a large part of Cleo's whole. Mom was a part of her too; her spirit steered Cleo. And even though she hated to admit it, Cleo got her survival instinct, that aggressive side, from Ava. All of them, among so many others—Finn, Auntie Deborah, Professor Chu, even her crew, Austin, Boston, and young Daniel; Cleo was the intersection of that human menagerie. That's what it is to be human, they realize; every individual is the harmony of a thousand voices.

"*You're not alone, Bumblebee . . .*" Dad's voice, and that is their last thought. "*We are not alone.*"

The ground quakes as the construct's internal mechanisms spin underneath the woman's broken limbs. Orbis Alius's fail-safe triggers—if the anti-god can't be contained, then destroy it all. The gears of the planet-size machine squeeze gravitational pressures into one infinitely small space. Every intelligent species that had ever existed is gone in that instant. Genocide on the grandest scale ever. Or maybe not genocide; Orbis Alius is less a zoo and more of a graveyard. Humankind would survive and thrive, unaware of all these little sacrifices.

We are not alone, their thoughts spaghettify over the event horizon. The Orbis Alius construct collapses into one infinite-dense point the size of a marble and everything and everyone becomes the singularity.

Acknowledgments

This novel would not be possible without my agent, Dorian Maffei, and all the reps at KC&A. I am so grateful to Jon, Heather, Rachel, Grace, Andrea, Elizabeth, and the entire 47North editorial team who suffered through many early drafts! My NY homie Clarence. And poor Maura Milan, who listened to me rap.

About the Author

Dwain Worrell is a filmmaker, a traveler, and the author of *Androne* and *Alliance*. Born in the Caribbean, Dwain resettled in the US in the nineties. He currently resides in Los Angeles, where he works as a film and television writer and producer. His writing credits include Marvel's *Iron Fist*, CBS's *Fire Country*, Amazon Studios' *The Wall*, and the Disney+ series *National Treasure*, among others. For more information visit www.dwainworrell.com.